Lady in Waiting

Lady in Waiting

A NOVEL BY

ROSEMARY SUTCLIFF

Coward-McCann, Inc.   New York

Library of Congress Catalog
Card Number: 57-6689

MANUFACTURED IN THE UNITED STATES OF AMERICA

CONTENTS

ELIZABETH

JAMES

CONTENTS

PART
I
ELIZABETH

CHAPTER I

THE QUARTZ MASK

The boy at the end of the Ralegh pew leaned far forward, his hands on his knees, his eager face lifted to the old stout figure of the Rector, who had a short while before mounted into the pulpit. The intent and vivid stare of his very blue eyes was a little disconcerting to the Rector, but certainly it was gratifying. It was always gratifying to feel that one had touched the shining spirits of the young. There came to the old man in that moment a warm sense of encouragement, and he leaned forward to thunder in a tone even louder than was usual to him at sermon time, against the sin of Sabbath-breaking. He spent so much of his time thundering against the manifold sins of his parishioners, so much of his strength in fighting the Devil and striving to plant the good seed in decidedly stony ground; and it was not often that he saw the good seed quickening into life, as in the wrapt face of this child.

In actual fact, the boy at the end of the Ralegh pew was not conscious of the Rector at all. He was watching the dancing golden dust-motes in the shaft of evening sunlight that slanted down like a sword blade from the high window beside the pulpit; and he heard the old man's thundering only as a background to his own thoughts, like the wuthering of the high west wind round the ancient walls of the church.

He was lost in a pleasant dream in which those bright, dancing motes turned out to have real gold in them, and he devised some means of catching them and separating the gold from the rest. A large bag of gold-dust would be so very useful to the Ralegh family, even enabling them to live again in the great house at Fardel, as they had done before he was born and they came on hard times. Only that would mean leaving Hayes Barton. No, on consideration, he would not give his family enough of the gold-dust to return to Fardel. Instead, he would give his father an Indian falcon and his mother a ruby bilament, and presents in proportion to the rest of the family, always supposing that they were not being

9

tiresome as they sometimes were. And with the remainder of the gold? There were so many things that one could do with a large bag of gold-dust, even when the price of a ruby bilament and an Indian falcon and all the other things had come out of it. But Walter Ralegh had no hesitation. He would use it to build ships.

A fleet of three, to begin with, he decided; and he would call them the *Garland*, the *Crane* and the *Revenge*. His gaze left the dancing motes in the sunbeam, and came unconsciously to rest on a carved bench end just across the aisle. The carved bench ends of East Budleigh Church had been his solace through many and many a sermon. They were wonderful carvings, each one different; a dragon, a man in a feather headdress, a monster eating someone from the feet upwards, and loveliest of all, this one; this ship. A valiant cockle-shell of a ship, storm-tossed but still jaunty, with a look-out posted in her rigging as though she expected her land-fall at any moment. Walter knew ships; ships at a distance, watched from the cliff tops beating up channel in a rain squall, or outward bound into the unknown. He knew them at close quarters too, for he had good friends along the coast, at Exmouth and Budleigh Salterton, who often took him on board their vessels; salt-stained and redolent of rope and pitch and bilge-water, salt fish and raw hides and wool; less obviously romantic, but more satisfying. Ships and the sea, they were in Walter's blood; for between them, his mother and father claimed kinship with almost every great sea-faring family of the West. Grenvilles, Stucleys, Courtneys, St. Legers, Champernouns; they all had their part in him, and the Gilberts more perhaps than all beside.

Walter was very fond of the Gilberts, his mother's sons by a former marriage. For the large Ralegh half-brothers who now and then returned home on visits, he had little feeling save a vague jealousy when they laid claim to his father. But with the Gilbert half-brothers it was quite otherwise. When they put affectionate arms round his mother's shoulders, he did not begrudge even John and Adrian their share in her; and with Humphrey, he would cheerfully have shared his head—or the bag of gold-dust. There was a strong bond of friendship between Walter and Humphrey, which took no account of the fact that one was twelve and the other twenty-four; a bond of understanding and shared dreams and enthusiasms; for with his share of the gold-dust, Humphrey Gilbert

—soldier though he was—would also have built ships and sailed to discover the glories of the New World.

The Rector's voice boomed on, but Walter no longer heard it, even as a background to his thoughts. He was the man in the rigging of the carved ship, no longer part of a wooden bench end, but live and rejoicing in her liberty, and riding seas mountains high. Humphrey was the crew (Humphrey was always the crew on these secret voyages, given precedence even over Walter's adored cousin, Richard Grenville), and Walter, naturally, was the Master. What the Master was doing in the rigging he did not trouble to consider; one could, presumably, do as one wished and go where one wished, in one's own ship. The wind sang past his ears, strumming through the rigging as through the strings of a lute, the salt taste of the spume was on his lips, and all around him swelled the great sails, and the green seas hissing along the ship's sides far below. The horizon rose and tilted and dipped as the mast-head swung, so that now there was the deck below him, and now only the dark foam-streaked trough of the sea; and he shielded his eyes with his hand, gazing into the fiery distance for the first sight of land.

A violent poke from Carew—thirteen years old, home from his first term at Oxford and taking his position as elder brother heavily—fetched him abruptly out of his dream, to find that the sermon was over and the congregation rising to their feet. He sprang up, causing the bench to rock violently, and creating a disturbance that made people look round. Carew, who found his younger brother something of a responsibility in church, blushed furiously, but Walter was completely unabashed. If others wished to blush for him, they were welcome to do so; he never wasted time or energy in blushing for himself. Never in all his life.

Evensong drew to a close, and presently they were out in the churchyard, where the wind from the sea hummed around the buttresses and laid the long grass over in swathes among the leaning head-stones. There were many little groups in the churchyard, and the Ralegh family's progress to the gate seemed to Walter—no longer dream-bound, and beginning to feel hungry—to be made unbearably slow by their many halts to speak to this one or that. But they reached it at last, and passing through the huddle of cottages below the church, turned into the lane that led home.

The wind blustered overhead, lashing through the storm-twisted oak scrub that crested the banks, and filling the lane with the soft turmoil of the distant surge and the sway and flicker of moving shadows and westering sun that rimmed the shrivelled leaves with gold. And through it all, the Ralegh family walked home sedately as a family should walk home from church; Mr. Ralegh and his wife in front, he holding on to his bonnet, she clutching at her dark cloak as the wind tried to snatch it from her, yet both contriving somehow to keep the dignity proper to the occasion. Then small Margaret, demure but with a dancing step, her blue cloak and her bell-shaped skirt billowing joyously in the wind. Finally the two boys in their Sunday doublets of French-green broadcloth, Carew kicking at stones as he went, Walter with an exaggerated seaman's roll which he had seen and admired the week before in Budleigh Salterton.

The lane rose and dipped, turned and twisted, following the contours of the land, until the oak-crowned bank gave place to tamarisk feathering darkly above a cob wall, and a huddle of reed-thatched roofs beyond, and they were home. "Look!" said Margaret, "Someone is come!" And she pointed into the stable yard, where Tom the groom was rubbing down a chestnut horse with a posting brand on its shoulder. She raised her voice in an enquiring squeal. "Tom! Tom! Who is it?"

But the wind was high and Tom rather deaf, and Mr. Ralegh was already opening the garden door; and so the guest dawned upon them unannounced as they trooped into the courtyard garden and a tall young man with a murrey-coloured Spanish cloak flung back from his shoulders sprang up from the porch bench and came striding down the path, with the dogs of the house cantering around him.

"Humphrey!" cried the family in one breath, and Mrs. Ralegh let go her cloak and hurried to meet him with little chirping cries of welcome; while Mr. Ralegh hung back slightly, as always in the first moment of his stepson's arrival, with a shy man's shrinking from intrusion. The children, having no such scruples, thrust after her like eager puppies to greet the newcomer.

To all the young Raleghs, Humphrey's unheralded arrivals were occasions for rejoicing, both because he *was* Humphrey, whom they delighted to honour, and because of the entrancing presents that generally came with him. But to Walter they were events of

plendour, accompanied by unheard trumpets sounding to
venture; and now, as always, those soundless fanfares were
g down the wind, and the garden with its storm-wrecked
of late summer flowers quickened into magic at the call.

the midst of a clamorous group of children and dogs, Hum-
ey had both his mother's hands in his; and she was saying in
nes of gentle reproach, "Humphrey, have you forgot what day it
s? Could you not have contrived to reach us yesterday?"

"I had meant to, indeed and indeed." Humphrey smiled down at
her apologetically. "But Silver went lame in the off foreleg, and I
must needs spend the night at the inn at Countess Weare, and come
on post this morning. Tell me you are glad to see me, My Lady
Mother."

"You know that I am always rejoiced to see you," said Mrs.
Ralegh, and reached up to kiss him.

He gave her a quick, warm hug, and turned to shake hands with
his stepfather; touched Margaret's round pink cheek with one
finger, and enquired after Carew's spar-hawk which had been only
a half-made eyas when he was last here. But as the whole family
made their way up between the battered pinks and snapdragons to
the porch, he and Walter were walking together, and his hand was
on the boy's shoulder.

They were the last of the little cavalcade, but at the door, Margaret turned suddenly and darted back to them, slipping a hand into
Humphrey's free one, and gazing up at him confidingly. "Humphrey, *dear* Humphrey, *have* you brought me my golden thimble?"

Walter looked at her with distaste. He had reached the age when
one did not ask, one merely hoped—in his case, for a dagger.

Humphrey cocked a vague eyebrow. "Thimble? Was there some
talk of a thimble? Alas, my poor memory."

Margaret's round pink face was suddenly tragic, and her lower
lip trembled a little. No one, not even herself, knew exactly why
she had set her heart on a golden thimble, but she had. And
Humphrey, seeing that quivering lip, cursed himself for a brute.
He could never resist the temptation to tease Margaret, and always
he was sorry the moment after. He said quickly, "And yet I seem
to have seen a golden thimble somewhere, not long since. . . .
Yes! a golden thimble with a fleur-de-lis fretted on the tip! I
wondered what such a thing might be doing among my gear, for

I do not sew, and it was something small for my finger beside. Do you think that we should go after supper and see if it fits yours?"

And presently, supper being over in the parlour where the great ilex tree made sea-hushings outside the window, they went, the four of them, for Carew and Walter had contrived to attach themselves to the party, crowding upstairs to the boys' room. There was a fine guest-chamber, with a bed hung with curtains of faded sea-green damask and a long mirror of polished steel on the wall; but the boys had laid claim to Humphrey long since, and he always shared their room, sleeping on the truckle-bed which normally lived under their own. Now it had been pulled out, and made up with one of the best linen head sheets, and the gay but shabby coverlet worked with knots and small fantastic birds, which Mrs. Ralegh kept for the best beloved but not particularly honoured among her guests. Humphrey's saddle-bags lay on the big clothes chest, among hawk leashes, pots of glue and odd shaped lumps of unknown substances, all the property of Carew and Walter. His tasselled riding gloves had been tossed down on the window seat, and his velvet-sheathed rapier hung from the foot of the boys' uncurtained bed. It had been growing dusk on the stairs, but here the last windy sunshine of the August evening slipping sideways through the star-shaped panes of the window which was the room's one beauty, filled the embrasure with an amber radiance.

Blinking in the sudden light, the three followed Humphrey to the clothes chest, and stood watching with bated breath, while he delved into the contents of a saddle-bag. Several objects spilled out, among them a small packet wrapped in crimson silk, which chimed faintly, as it fell. Humphrey gathered it up, folding back the brilliant stuff. "Finger please." Margaret put out an eager right hand, with thimble-finger extended, and with ceremony proper to the occasion, he slipped a minute golden thimble on to it. "A trifle large," he said, critically regarding the result. "You will have to grow to it, baby."

Margaret spread her hand like a plump pink starfish, and gazed at the golden thimble, speechless with happiness; then raised her eyes to the young man's face and heaved a deep sigh.

"So; that is well then, small sister Meg," said Humphrey, smiling down at her as he freed something else from the folds of crimson silk. "Carew, I hope you have not belled your hawk yet?" He tossed the boy a pair of silver hawk bells.

Carew caught them with a whoop of delight. "I say! Oh I say!" He tossed one in the palm of each hand, listening to the chime, one bell a semi-tone higher than the other. "Milanise!" he proclaimed blissfully. "Humphrey, I'd do *anything* for you!"

He began to hover from foot to foot as he spoke, torn between his desire to rush straight down to his beloved hawk with the new Milanise bells, and a feeling that it was rude to rush away the moment somebody had given you a present. Humphrey saw his predicament and laughed. "Do you go and bell your hawk; the sooner 'tis done, the more time will she have to grow used to them before we fly her."

Before the words were out of his mouth, Carew was off and away; and hard on his heels, Margaret had flown to show her golden thimble to her mother; and Humphrey and Walter were alone together. As by common consent, they moved into the window.

"And now, having provided for housewife and country gentle-man," began Humphrey, and was struck for the first time by the significance of the gifts that he had brought for his three young kinsfolk. He took something from the breast of his doublet; something much too small to be a dagger. "For you—this."

For an instant Walter was conscious of acute disappointment, then he was gazing in bewilderment at the thing Humphrey had put into his hand. A piece of pink quartz, not much larger than a bean. It lay on his brown palm, translucent in the last reflection of the sunset, with a glow of deeper warmth at its heart. "What is it?" he asked at last.

"Only rose-quartz, but it comes from the New World. Turn it over."

With excitement stirring in him, Walter did as he was bid, and found himself looking down at a face—no, a mask, for there was nothing of humanity in it—carved from the rose-quartz. A laughing mask with a certain haunting beauty that in some indefinable way was part of its grotesqueness and not in contradiction to it. For a long moment he remained staring at the thing, silent; then without looking up, he demanded: "What is this thing? How did you get it?"

"An amulet—a talisman of some sort. Maybe it is the face of some god or hero. I bought it in Dartmouth from a seaman who was light in the pockets, and he told me he had come by it in the New World. He did not say how."

"The New World," said the boy, with an odd lingering in his voice; and an instant later looked up with a flashing smile. "I wanted a dagger—but I'd a hundred times sooner have this."

"It was in my mind that you would," said Humphrey, and seated himself on the broad window-sill. Walter remained standing, cherishing the tiny quartz mask in his hand, his face turned to the last slantwise gold of the West. The wind hurried by, bringing with it the wet thunder of the distant surge. It would be a wild night presently, and the sunset was a tumbled glory that spread southward behind the dark mass of Hayes Barton woods; a chaos of dun and purple clouds rimmed with incandescent gold, from the midst of which a great sunburst leapt upward to burst fountainwise against the very floor of heaven. But Walter, his wide eyes full of the brightness, did not see it, for he was looking beyond it, a long, long way beyond. The dream that he was to follow all his life was not born in that moment, for it had been within him always, but it had suddenly gained purpose and vitality; it was no longer a child's dream, and the symbol of it was the tiny and terrible mask in the palm of his hand.

Humphrey, looking up at him as he stood there, wondered, not for the first time, under what strange conjunction of planets that quiet pair his stepfather and his mother had begotten and conceived this shining, tempestuous creature. Strength they both possessed, of the kind which is steadfastness, in light of which both had at different times risked death for the Protestant faith; but not this strength of Walter's that was a two-edged sword of the Spirit, albeit not without surprising flaws. Certainly neither of them had given him the flaming pride which already showed in his eyes and the carriage of his head. They had not given him his ruthlessness, nor his power of dreaming, nor, most assuredly, his personal beauty.

Neither of them spoke for a while, for both had a gift for silence. Then Walter sighed, and stirred a little on his heels, as though coming back from the distant place that he had been to. And Humphrey produced the piece of news that he had been keeping for his young half-brother. "There was an old shipmaster at the inn where I lodged last night, and we got talking, he and I. He had been something of a navigator in his time—serving with the Portuguese—and he was convinced that there is in truth a passage round the North of America to Cathay!"

Walter's swift gaze came down to him in a flash. "Why was he?" He subsided on to the broad sill, drawing one leg under him. "Tell, Humphrey."

And Humphrey told. It was a familiar and beloved subject for discussion between them, and instantly they were enthralled in it, as he produced stylo and ivory tablets and began rapidly to draw coastlines and ocean currents. "See now, according to this fellow the current here below India and Africa, running thus—westerly— is so strong that the Portuguese in voyaging to Calicut have trouble at certain seasons of the year in making headway against it. The same current, still running its appointed course, comes up—here, against South America, and since the Fret of Magellan cannot carry it, turns northward along the coast, right up here to beyond Labrador. Well now, if there be no outlet for the water round the North of America, the current must strike over eastward on to the coasts of Iceland and Northern Europe——"

"And it doesn't." Walter said quickly, his eyes fixed on the tip of the other's moving stylo.

"No, it doesn't!"

"Humphrey—the open waterway that Sebastian Cabot found— the waterway he could not follow up because his men mutinied!"

"Yes, my shipmaster was of the same opinion. About here: Latitude 67½ degrees under the Pole, and bearing in this direction— you see?"

Walter saw. "Is he going to search it out?"

"No. A man must needs have letters patent from the Queen for such a search; also it is years ago that he worked out those currents, and he is an old man now; too old to go exploring again."

Silence fell between them for a few moments. Both were looking with sombre eyes into that appalling wilderness of time when one was too old to follow the dream; not knowing that, one by drowning and one by the headsman's axe, they were to be delivered from that time.

"He said," Humphrey added at last, "that it was for younger men to carry on the search."

"Men like you," Walter said slowly. "And me, when I am grown." He looked up, his eyes blazing with eagerness, the chill of the past moment quite forgotten. "Humphrey! Let you and I go to find that passage one day! I shall have left Oxford in five years' time; we will go then!"

"We must needs get those letters patent from the Queen, first," Humphrey said. He looked at Walter, half smiling, yet with his own eagerness kindling to match that of the boy. "I wonder if we could do it."

"Do it?—Oh, the letters patent you mean." (To doubt that they could find the North West passage never entered his head.) "Of course we could! You shall make drawings like these ones—only clean—and copy out all the evidence you have collected, into a book, and call it 'A Discourse for a Discovery of a New Passage to Cathay,' and I shall help you. And when it is writ, we will take it to the Queen's Grace, and she will give you your letters patent, and maybe a ship as well! We can explore for new territories as we go —places where we can found colonies and set up ports of call for shipping going through to Cathay! We could——"

Steps came scurrying up the stairs, and Carew's voice reached them, upraised in triumph. "Humphrey! Humphrey, are you there?" The door burst open, and Carew appeared, his face flushed with pleasure, carrying a slightly ruffled spar-hawk on his gloved fist. "I've belled Cloe, and I've brought her to show you."

Walter uncoiled himself and leapt from the window-sill to the foot of the bed, where he sat cross-legged like a tailor on his counter, squinting horribly at Cloe. There was no particular point in such a proceeding, but he had needed sudden action to shake something that had been uppermost in him back into the secret place where he normally kept it. The rose quartz mask was inside the breast of his doublet, where he had thrust it at the first sound of Carew's approach. Presently of course, Carew would want to know what Humphrey had given him, and he would have to show his treasure; but not yet. He did not want to show it to anyone, just yet.

CHAPTER 2

THE ISLAND OF WHITE BIRDS

The high west wind of April was blowing over Westminster, and on the trailing skirts of the wind came rain-squalls to damp down the smells of the open kennels and lay the dust along the narrow streets, and ragged bursts of sunshine that lit the steep wet roofs and swimming cobbles to silver-gilt.

In the gallery of the Sidney's house, the windows had been shut against the April rain—shining rain that spattered on the panes of the oriel, blurring the view of the gardens and the River; but no closed window could keep out the flying bursts of sunshine that seemed to small Bess Throckmorton like a fanfare of trumpets such as one heard faintly echoing from the Queen's tilt-yard on tournament days.

Lady Sidney sat in the curve of the oriel, retelling the story of St. Branden and his search for the Land of Heart's Desire, to an attentive audience of three. That story had been a favourite with all the Sidney children, largely because of the incident in which the Saint and his followers, with regrettable lack of observation, landed on a whale under the impression that it was an island, and lit a fire on its back before discovering their mistake; and Lady Sidney had told it so often that she knew it by heart, and could follow the thread of her own thoughts at the same time, letting them move with her eyes over the three sitting side by side on a long stool before her. Tom, her own last-born, Robin Devereux with his crest of guinea-gold hair, and between them, Bess Throckmorton, her hands folded demurely in her orange-tawny lap, her eyes, bright as those of a harvest mouse, raised to the rain-streaked window that she was evidently not seeing.

But these three were not the only people in the gallery; a little beyond them, clearly conscious of being too old to listen to stories, yet well within earshot all the same, sat Mary Sidney, with Pipin, the little Italian greyhound cuddled on her feet: Mary in the green and silver of the Queen's Maids of Honour, her pointed face under the cloud of fair hair downbent over the mass of carnation damask in her lap. In three days Mary was to be married, and for weeks the

house had been overrun by sewing women, engulfed in a billowing
tide of tiffany and cambric, watchet satin sleeves, and undergowns
of citron lutestring, point lace ruffs and curled feather fans and
tinsel shoe roses; while Mary herself, normally a serious child,
seemed to have few thoughts to spare from the two pairs of silk
stockings in her dower chest. How would it go with her, her
mother wondered—fifteen years old, and married to a man three
times her age? But Henry Herbert, Earl of Pembroke, was a kindly
and intelligent man; he would be good to his small Countess; above
all, he would allow her the freedom of her mind. The marriage
promised more of happiness, surely, than many of the made
matches of the Court.

Still further down the gallery, two boys were playing chess. Of
her own Robert, all that Lady Sidney could see was an angular
back and a bent barley-coloured head; but the other Robert—
Robert Cecil—was clear to her view in the tall light of a nearby
window. He too was fair, but with a redder glint in the bent head,
and his face cupped in one thin hand as he gazed down at the
board, was sallow with the dull tinge of ill-health. A strange face,
old beyond its years, brilliant, subtle; not, in Lady Sidney's judgment, altogether trustworthy. Young Cecil would likely grow to be
a fine statesman like his father, but she doubted his ever being the
good man his father was. Well, he would have need of all the
tortuous subtlety of brain that he possessed, poor lad, since his
crooked body could never be other than a brake on him.

Sheer physical sympathy twinged in Lady Sidney, marred flesh
feeling for marred flesh; and she was suddenly aware of the light
pressure of the velvet half-mask that had become almost a part of
herself in the years that she had worn it to cover the ravages of
small-pox. For Lady Sidney, brave enough to nurse the Queen
through the dread disease, catching it from her, had never been
brave enough to show her scars to the world.

Somewhere near at hand, a door opened, releasing into the quiet
gallery the notes of a carelessly strummed lute, and a burst of
laughter from the chamber where Philip, the eldest son of the
house, was entertaining a couple of friends of his Oxford days.
Listening, a shadow of anxiety touched his mother, for she could
not find it in her heart to approve one of the guests. Walter Ralegh
was a wild, and, she greatly feared, Godless young man, who

seemed to have brought home with him from his late service in
Flanders more long-drawn foreign oaths and fantastic foreign garments than she could think seemly, and no reverence for anything
under Heaven. She made excuses for him; the boy's apprenticeship
to life, served with the Huguenot army and culminating in the
bloody horrors of Paris on St. Bartholomew's Eve, was likely to set
its mark on the man; but she could not consider him a suitable
friend for Philip, and had had more than once to remind herself
that Philip was a man now, and his choice of friends no longer any
concern of hers. "Walter, a'God's name drop it! We are all tired
of the North West Passage!" cried a laughing voice. The strumming
lute had strayed into the popular air of Greensleeves; then the door
closed again, and the gay young voices were cut off.

The story was drawing to a close. Lady Sidney always ended it
with St. Branden's homecoming, and did not continue, as did the
written version in the Golden Legend, to his death in an over-
powering odour of sanctity; for it seemed to her that that was the
true end of the story. One found the way to the Far Country, and
came home, with the scent of its flowers clinging to one's garments
for an earnest that the way was there. There was no more that
needed to be told.

So the story ended; and Bess Throckmorton coming slowly back
to her surroundings, found that the rain was ended too, and the sun
turning the wet window-panes to a dazzle that almost blinded her
with its too much glory. She blinked as though just roused from
sleep, and saw that Lady Sidney was looking at her with a half
smile curving her mouth under the pale velvet mask. Bess smiled
back, with a small, cosy wriggling of her whole body. All children
loved Lady Sidney, and Bess was no exception.

"That," said Lady Sidney, "is the end of the story. And see, the
sun is shining again! Run away, all three of you—run and play in
the garden."

The three slid obediently to the ground, and made the small bow
or bobbing curtsey which custom demanded, after which the two
boys departed at full speed, followed by Pipin, to call on a friend
in the stable yard. Watching the little upright figure of Bess trotting
away after them down the gallery, Lady Sidney saw her linger a
moment in passing the chess players, and Robert Cecil look up
quickly, his hand poised for a move, to smile at her. It was quite a

different smile from the one he kept for normal use, lighting his sallow face with an unexpected sweetness; and the watching woman found herself wondering if that was where little Bess's future lay. There was an old friendship between the two families. To be sure, the Throckmorton family was not one that any man ambitious of Court favour would be likely to marry into; and Lord Burleigh's son, hunchback or no, would be able to choose a wife from among the most powerful families in the land. And yet she had an instinct that Robin Cecil, because he *was* a hunchback and Lord Burleigh's son, might cut across Court custom, when the time came, and choose a wife for love, where a hale and hearty man, or one whose own family were less powerful, might choose for convenience or advancement of worldly position. Assuredly they were fond of each other, in the way of fourteen and ten, but who should say what might happen in the four or five years before Bess was old enough for marriage.   Meanwhile there were a thousand things still to be done in preparation for Mary's wedding. She should not have taken time off to tell stories to the children. And with a small sigh, for she was very tired, Lady Sidney rose to go and do them.

Bess returned young Cecil's smile joyously, but did not stop to speak, for she knew that one did not force conversation on chess players; also she was a child of few words. She reached the end of the gallery and made her way down the circular stair to a small side door, and thence out into a paved courtyard with a well in one corner. This she crossed on flying feet that skidded a little on the rain-wet cobbles to another door, of ancient silvery timbers, and opened it, slipped through almost secretly, dropping the latch into place behind her.

Instantly a sense of sanctuary enfolded her as with wings. The Sidney garden was not really a very secret place, for there was another door in the lower wall, and the household and their friends were constantly coming and going through it as the quickest way down to the Strand; but the sense of sanctuary clung to it, none the less. And young as she was, there were enough complications and perplexities in the life of small Bess Throckmorton to make her glad of sanctuary. She came of a great house long out of favour and split between the old faith and the new. She could just remember her father, who had been one of Elizabeth's diplomats, a sad man, eating his heart out in the seclusion that followed his own unmerited fall from grace, before he died at My Lord of Leicester's supper table, reputedly of poison. Her mother she could not remember at all; and she and Nicholas had been brought up by a stepmother who, though far from being the stepmother of tradition, was inclined to be heavy-handed. Arthur and her two elder sisters were more fortunate, having been already brought up. They were married now, and Arthur had entered into his heritage, the old house in Northamptonshire; and only she and Nicholas were left. Bess was happy enough at home, but always conscious of the shadow lying over her and her people; and she had grown more conscious of it since coming on this long visit to the household of her father's old friend Lord Burleigh. She did need sanctuary, and it was only here, in Lady Sidney's garden, that she found it.

She gave the door a final push, to make sure that it was shut, and started down the path between formal beds edged with box and rosemary, unpausing until she reached the foot of the garden, and the more wayward loveliness of ancient, leaning fruit trees, where the white pheasant-eye starred the long grass. This was the heart of the garden, the inner sanctuary, and in it there lived a toad. A fat and freckled toad, to which she had been introduced by Tom Sidney the last time she was here. Presently she would look for the toad, but not yet. Bess was not a child to snatch her pleasures in handfuls; she took them delicately, a little at a time, careful to bruise nothing in the taking. Presently the toad; for the present moment there was joy enough without. High against the rain-washed blue, white cloud galleons sailed towards London; and around her feet the rain-wet stars of the narcissus swaying in the wind, and the first-fallen petals of the fruit blossom drifting down before every gust, like a snow-storm out of elfland. Overhead in a damson tree, a Jenny-whitethroat was singing—not the rather strident full song, but the little rippling under-song, very light and sweet—and Bess, standing close beneath and looking up through the blossoming boughs, could not see the singer, only the wind-swayed white blossom with the sun behind it, translucent, edged with pale flame, so that it seemed as though the blossom itself were singing . . . surely the trees of St. Branden's Isle had been like this; those trees on which the little white birds gathered so thick that the boughs seemed clothed in blossom; and every bird singing. . . .

The spell of the story she had just heard was still upon her; and suddenly as she stood with the windblown petals drifting all around her, and the shining drops spattering into her upturned face, she was filled with the urgent longing to find something, some place, beloved and long since lost, to which all this—the damson tree, the wind-stirred shadows, the singing bird—were for an outer threshold. It was the oldest longing in the world, old as the Fall, the longing of man for the lost Eden; but Bess knew nothing of that; she knew only that she wanted to kilt up her skirts and run and run until she found it, whatever it was, and that if only she could find it, there would be nothing to be unhappy or afraid for, ever again.

The rippling song fell silent, and with a sudden flutter of wings the Jenny-whitethroat was gone to her half-built nest in the honey-suckle by the door. Only a little bird singing in the damson tree, after all. But the spell of the shining moment was still just a little with Bess, as she turned and went, trailing her dreams behind her like her skirts through the long grass, to find the toad.

She found him in the ditch that ran close under the wall, sitting under a dock leaf, very portly, like an alderman taking the air at his front door. Bess sat down on her heels before him, and they surveyed each other gravely. The toad was clearly of a friendly disposition, for he made not the least attempt to move, but sat there, his warty sides panting in and out like a tiny pair of bellows, and his bulging eyes jewel-bright in the shadow of the dock leaf. It was very damp along the ditch, but neither of them cared; they were in perfect sympathy with their surroundings and each other, and they were still improving each other's acquaintance some while later, when the garden door opened and closed again, and one of Philip's guests came down between the box and rosemary hedges.

He had almost reached the lower door that would let him out into the Strand, when his eye was caught by something incongruous to this springtime garden; a patch of orange-tawny that seemed to belong rather to the last warmth of St. Martin's summer, glinting behind a mass of tall growing water plants and drooping apple branches. He halted in his tracks, and being of an enquiring mind, went to investigate.

The patch of orange-tawny proved to be the back folds of a small girl's gown, and the wearer, sitting on her heels on the edge of the ditch, was apparently engaged in staring out of countenance a large and peculiarly repulsive toad who sat under a dock leaf and stared back. An autumn-coloured child, sitting very still, her thin attentive little body arched forward, her small brown hands folded in her lap, so intent upon the toad that she was quite unconscious of any presence beside her. For a few moments young Ralegh stood as still as she, holding aside the apple spray that had all but hidden her from view, and looking down at her. The little absorbed figure appealed to him oddly, and the vague springtime discontent of his mood crystallised into the desire to make her notice him. It was the merest whim of the April moment, but he was a man who acted on his whims. The question was how to catch her attention without startling her or the toad and so spoiling a pretty idyll. The tune which Fulke Greville had played on the lute a while back still lingered in his mind, and he puckered his lips into a low liquid whistling, not unlike the whitethroat's in its quality.

The first few bars of Greensleeves whistled close above her made Bess sit back on her heels and glance up quickly. She was looking at a tall young man in a wonderful doublet of golden green, the colour of spring itself, who stood holding aside a blossoming apple spray from which a few crushed petals fell under his heedless hand, and looking down at her with the bluest eyes she had ever seen. A man like a drawn sword, like a dark flame in the sunlight. After her first startled gasp, she sat quite still, gazing up at him; and as she gazed, something in her small flat breast found wings and flew from her to the young man, that never in all her life returned to her again. If she had been a little dog she would have lain at his feet inviting him to trample on her; being a small girl, she sat and dimpled at him, her whole face shimmering with delight.

After they had surveyed each other in silence a few moments, the young man doffed his hat with the utmost gravity, sweeping it so low that the peacock's feather in it whispered silkenly across her hand, and replacing it very much on the back of his head, sat down beside her, still without a word. Bess accepted his coming with a tiny movement of welcome, then turned her attention back to the toad. But either the toad had after all been disturbed by the new arrival, or the combined stares of Bess and the young man were too much for him, and he no longer seemed completely at his ease. Little tremors began to run through his body; he stirred uneasily in the shadow of the dock leaf, and then—was no longer there. His dive had been so swift that no eye could follow it; only the widening ripples in the ditch bottom told where he had disappeared.

"Oh!" Bess spoke for the first time. "He is gone!"

"Do you mind?" enquired the young man, turning to look at her. "Is he a friend of yours?"

"Not really. Tom Sidney showed him to me last week, and this is but the second time I have seen him. Tom said maybe he was an alderman who somebody magicked into a toad for a grudge they bore him."

"We haven't missed but one alderman lately, and he was eaten by the Lioness at the Tower," said the young man regretfully. Then, seeming struck by an idea, he added: "He might of course be a foreign princeling; no one keeps count of those, and princes are much more susceptible to enchantment than aldermen. You did not chance to notice if he was wearing a crown?"

Bess shook her head positively. "No, he was not."

"It is a grey world.   Ah well, there are other possibilities. He may be the Queen's head cook who has met with reverses, or an enchanter who mingled the wrong spell in a moment of absent-mindedness—or a poor devil of a soldier of fortune under a cloud, in which case he has my heartfelt sympathy as one sufferer to another."

"Are you a soldier of fortune under a cloud?"

For the first time he smiled, a swift and flashing smile, but rueful. "You could call me so, small mistress."

Bess gazed at him pitifully. She knew something about being under clouds, and her faith in her new friend was unshaken and unshakeable. "Whatever it is," she said with the utmost firmness, "I do not believe you did it!"

"Thank you. It—is not that sort of cloud."

She said nothing, but her whole thin body and little eager face were one sympathetic question-mark that could not be denied.

"Oh—lack of funds and lack of influence, and banging my head against circumstances until it sings like a beehive on St. Benedict's Eve, trying to make the Queen's Grace listen to me, and——" The young man broke off with a laugh. "Nay, what am I talking about? You would not understand."

Bess's eyes were fixed on his face, gravely beseeching. "Indeed, I understand a great deal! I am all but eleven, and very sensible for my age. My Lord Burleigh says so."

The young man surveyed her consideringly. "Does he so? Well then, give me proof of it. Have you ever heard of the possibility of a North-West passage to Cathay?"

"Oh yes! Sir Martin Frobisher is going to discover it, and when he *has* discovered it, all the spices and silks of the East will be able to come by a shorter way, and so they will be cheaper in the London shops, and that will annoy Spain."

"You have it in a hazel husk," agreed the young man gloomily.

Bess noticed the gloom. "Do you not *want* to annoy Spain?"

"Yes—I do, I do!"

She was puzzled. "But if Sir Martin Frobisher is *going* to discover the passage——"

"God's life! It is not his to discover! It is mine! Mine and my brother Humphrey's!" the young man burst out in swift indignation. He broke off a narcissus flower growing beside him, and beat it lightly on his open palm, glaring. "We always planned to find it, Humphrey and I. Humphrey tried once before to win letters patent from the Queen, but he had no success. I was but just started at Oxford, then, and the poor old lad's not one to carry things through on his own, so 'twas not surprising. But this time 'twas another matter; this time he had me to load for him, and we put all the evidence together in a book and called it 'A Discourse for a Discovery of a New Passage to Cathay', and took it to the Queen's Grace together."

"She did not like it?"

"Oh, she liked it well enough." His young voice was suddenly weary. "She was greatly impressed with it—we knew she must be; it was bound to carry conviction. That was why she gave the search to Sir Martin Frobisher; because she said Humphrey had not the name for being either a leader or a navigator—the which is damnably true."

"But you?" suggested Bess softly, after a pause.

"Me? I am only Walter Ralegh, a creature of no account. I still have to prove my sword before the Queen will entrust me with such a venture."

Bess hesitated, then laid a small consoling hand for an instant on his knee. "But one day she will," she said. Surely, oh surely, one day the scales would fall from the Queen's eyes, and she would see that this was the best of all her knights. "One day she is bound to;

and then you will go to find it—and take Humphrey with you."

"Frobisher will have gained the Passage by then."

"You could always search for something else," said Bess, who knew as well as he that it is the search, more than the finding, that matters.

Her words acted like a charm, dissolving the barrier between man's world and child's. He turned and sat forward, arms laid across knees, vivid blue eyes fixed on her face, and burst into a spate of eager words, with as little thought of the dozen years dividing them as there had been between himself and Humphrey. "Aye, and I will, one day! It is full time and running over, that some soul followed John Cabot's lead, to make good our claim in the New World! Every day the Dons strike deeper into the West Indies and the Orinoco country, carving an empire for themselves in the South; and every day France does the same in the North, and what do we? We sit on our haunches and twiddle our thumbs and belch! Save for a merry handful of fishermen and pirates we might not know that there is any world under bright Heaven but the old one! If the Queen's England is to keep place and power among the nations, the Queen must have a greater Indies than Philip of Spain, and somebody must venture to win it for her. And God's sweet life, what a venturing! A whole new world for the seeking through!" With a swift movement, he thrust a hand into the breast of his doublet, and brought forth something which he held out to her on his palm, like an eager boy. "See, this came from the New World. My brother Humphrey gave it to me, years ago."

In the brown palm, as Bess leaned forward, lay a tiny face—no, a mask, for there was nothing of humanity in it—carved from rose-quartz. Such a small thing to hold so much of awe and beauty, to speak so clearly of the unknown, the far country. "May I touch?" she asked, her glance fleeting upward, then down again.

"You can hold it, if you like."

Bess advanced her hand, then hesitated, hovering it a moment over the tiny, terrible mask, then drew it back and glancing up again, shook her head. It was as though the thing itself had denied her. It was not for touching; not for Bess's touching at all events.

A spate of words was pouring from the young man beside her; for Ralegh was now fairly launched on the subject of his heart. He was of the true minstrelsy, to whom the power is given to kindle

the listener from their own fire; and sitting in the ditch, he declared
to the child sitting beside him, his dream of colonisation, of explor-
ation and empire building. The dream of a man of action lit
through with a poet's vision that transmuted its whole fabric into
something infinitely more shining. And to Bess, caught up, dazzled
and entranced, the ditch and the apple trees and the high sailing
clouds dissolved away into the country of her companion's dream.
A country of wide green plains mazed by the tracks of the light-
footed deer, of great rivers whose falls, seven times taller than the
steeple of the tallest church in Christendom, filled their rainbowed
gorges with a thunder of bells in their falling; of forests of flowering
trees among whose branches there sang and fluttered birds of white
and crimson and carnation. . . . A country beyond the sunset, yet
not strange; for in some way that she neither understood nor
questioned, but accepted joyfully, it lay as the Island of White
Birds did, just beyond the wind-swayed shadows and the singing
bird in the damson tree.

How long the enchanted hour lasted, she never knew; it ended
with a sharp pattering among the broad dock leaves, a scent rising
like incense from the earth, and all around them, the shining lances
of the next shower. The glory faded, and her companion was
scrambling to his feet, the rose-quartz mask already restored to the
breast of his doublet.

She sat among her outflung skirts, and blinked at him, not quite
returned from the far place to which his spell-binding had carried
her. "Run!" he said. "Run indoors, or you will be soaked. Lord!
It is later than I thought; I must be shogging or I shall miss supper."

He was turning carelessly away as he spoke, and suddenly half
crying, she did not know why, Bess gathered herself inelegantly
together, and ran. Behind her as she scurried up the path, she heard
the lower door slam, as Ralegh went to seek his waiting supper.
The rain was already slackening as she reached the door into the
courtyard, and she turned with a hand raised to the latch, half
hoping that he might come back. But the moments passed,
and he did not come. Only something of the glory he had conjured up remained behind him, under the apple trees in the shining
rain.

Ralegh went his way, wondering a little at first what had possessed him to pour out his dream to the little maid in Lady Sidney's

garden; and by the time he reached his lodging in the Temple,
forgetting that he had done so at all.

But Bess remembered.

CHAPTER 3

THE TRIUMVIRATE

Bess saw no more of Ralegh during that visit. She did not expect
to; the shared hour among the dock leaves had been a thing complete and perfect, rounded on itself with no loose end to trail out
into the life of every day.

Her visit being ended, she was duly returned to the stepmother
who was inclined to be heavy-handed; and it was nine years before
Westminster knew her again. She grew up very uneventfully, at
first with her stepmother, later with Arthur and his wife at Paulers-
bury; later still, having reached years of discretion, at Beddington
with her Uncle Francis Carew who had adopted Nicholas as his
heir. The Throckmorton family were still, if not actually under a
cloud, certainly not in favour, and the death of her cousin Francis,
hanged at Tyburne for treason and popery in 1584 did nothing to
bring even the Protestant branch of the family into better odour.
Their ways lay far from the Court, and Bess's way lay with theirs.
She grew up very much to pattern, mastering all those arts from
playing the lute to lancing boils, which became a gentlewoman;
and failed to conform in only one thing: that at the unheard of age
of nineteen, she was still unwed and seemed likely to remain so.

It was not for lack of asking, either. Having no particular beauty
of feature, she was possessed of a warm and shadowy charm and
the beauty of motion that made her tall rather thin body seem
always to move to unheard music, as a reed bed when the wind
blows over. Two perfectly respectable matches, Uncle Francis could
have arranged for her; and the young man in each case most
willing; but neither time had Bess been willing at all, and since
Uncle Francis was unmarried and found it pleasant to have her for
the Mistress of his house, he had made no attempt to force her.

But married or single, Bess was not destined for long to be the

Mistress of Beddington. In her nineteenth spring she went for a while to be with Lady Sidney, who was newly widowed and sorely in need of the comfort and companionship which Mary, with the cares of a great house and a young family, could not give her. Lady Sidney was, as she always had been, a close personal friend of the Queen's, and so it was that before the summer was out, Mistress Throckmorton was become one of the Queen's Maids of Honour.

And so, after nine years, she met Walter Ralegh again.

She had heard of him in those years. Who had not? Only a few weeks after her first encounter with him she had heard that he was newly released from Newgate on promise of future good behaviour, after serving there six days for causing a breach of the peace by sealing up a friend's beard and moustache with wax to stop him talking. Rumours followed of wild service in Ireland, from which he returned with his sword proven, a Captain's commission and a reputation for reckless courage combined with ruthlessness that was remarkable, even in his day. Tidings reached her of his embassages to William of Orange and the Duc d'Alençon in the Queen's service; of Royal gifts and Royal favour; Durham Palace to be his town house, green acres in Ireland, a knighthood, the Lord Wardenship of the Stanneries, the Captaincy of the Queen's Guard. Word of expeditions to the New World, fitted out and financed by a man who yet himself remained behind at Court. Word also of his increasing unpopularity among ordinary folk, as a man too rich, too quickly raised to power, too insufferably proud. But she had held him in thought always as the companion who had sat with her in the ditch at the bottom of Lady Sidney's garden, and declared unto her a far country. She had not allowed for changes; and changes there had been, in the years that had raised a young, eager soldier of fortune to be the Queen's favourite and the Captain of her Bodyguard. The ruthlessness had deepened in his face, and some of the laughter had died from it; the flaming pride of his carriage had set into a harder and more considered arrogance. But these things Bess could forgive, together with the fact that he had forgotten the encounter in the ditch and was now as unaware of her existence as it was possible for the Queen's Captain to be of one of the Queen's Maids. What disappointed her, making the real man less than the remembered one, was something she had known all along, but which had not come truly home to her until she saw him again: that, having dreamed a dream, he had sent other men to follow it, instead of going himself.

At first he seemed almost unreal to her, a shining and remote figure in a silver breastplate, a great pearl drop in his left ear; unreal with the flashing unreality of a figure seen in sunshine from a place of shadows. For there was a shadow over the Court, those first few weeks of Bess's service, and it made Ralegh's dragon-fly brilliance appear brittle and heartless; the shadow of Philip Sidney's death in action against Spain.

The whole court mourned for young Sidney, with a personal sense of loss, from the Queen herself to her newest Maid of Honour. To the Queen he had been something very like a son; "My Philip" the gentlest and bravest of all the lighthearted lads she gathered round her. To Bess he was only a memory from that long-ago visit to Westminster: but a happy memory, nonetheless. And his mother, not yet fully recovered from her husband's death, turned herself very quietly to follow him.

An autumn evening came: a golden evening, harking back regretfully to the vanished summer, though the brown leaves lay underfoot. It was fitting that Philip should have a golden day and not a grey one, Bess thought, as she rustled upstairs and down through Whitehall Palace, looking for a gold and coral button which the Queen, always prone to shed small portions of her attire, had lost from her sleeve.

A few hours earlier, Philip Sidney's body had been laid beneath the choir aisle of St. Paul's. The Netherlands, for whose freedom he had died, had wanted the honour of burying him, but that was a thing too dear to his own people for them to yield it up to anyone. So the gallant, broken body had been brought home, and earlier that day, Bess Throckmorton, in company with almost every soul in London and Westminster, had watched his funeral procession pass, with solemn pomp and to the music of black-draped fifes and drums, along the streets through which he had so often ridden with his gay companions. The Sergeants of his infantry in the Netherlands, his standards and colours, his friends and brothers-in-arms, his war charger ridden by a page with reversed battle-axe, his tournament horse by a squire with a broken lance. The heralds, Portcullis, Blue Mantle, Rouge Dragon, carrying his spurs, gauntlets and porcupine-crested helmet. Then the quiet thing under a

black velvet pall, that one could not believe had ever been the
outward seeming of Philip. More mourners, headed by Robert and
Tom; the Lord Mayor and Sheriffs; the City trained bands with
weapons trailing. A long, dark river, winding between silent
crowds; the tossing plumes, the set faces of the men who marched
with Sir Philip Sidney for the last time; the slow, deep rolling of the
muffled drums. . . . The sound was still with Bess as she sped her
search from room to room, a stifling weight over the heart. It
seemed such a heavy requiem for the lad she remembered, laughing,
with a lute across his knees.

It seemed that she was not alone in that, for as she crossed the
threshold of yet another gallery, a familiar voice with a strong
West Country burr was exclaiming vehemently: "A black extin-
guisher to smother out the living flame! What had Philip to do
with that sable panoply?"

"It was the Nation's love dictated it," said another voice.

Two men stood together in the oriel window of the otherwise
deserted gallery. Fulke Greville and the Captain of the Guard. Bess
would have slipped away, but the Queen's button must be found
before she would go to supper, and the Queen, ranging far and wide
through her palace with the restlessness of grief, had spent some
time in the gallery earlier that evening. She moved to the bench
beside the Clavichord, and began to turn over the cushions. The
two men must have known that she was there, but they were unaware of her with the chief part of their minds. She was supremely
unimportant to them. Drawn together by their deep caring for the
dead man, they were antagonistic as they had not been in his lifetime, eyeing each other a little jealously over his memory, like two
dogs across the feet of the same master.

Ralegh said, "Not for me! Dear God! Not for me, when my
time comes!"

"I do not imagine that you need fear it," said Fulke Greville
quickly. "You are not so near to the people's heart that they are
likely to need the easement of trailed weapons and muffled drums
for your loss."

"No." Ralegh gave a short laugh. "I am not such as wins a
people's love. I am the Queen's favourite lap-dog, tied to the
Queen's apron strings. Not for me to serve her as she allowed to
better men—as she allowed Philip."

2

"Mixed metaphors, Queen's lap-dog," said the other. "And from you of all men. But is not the lap comfortable, for a powerful lap-dog? Was not that what you wanted?"

"Power? Aye, I wanted it. Wanted, and worked for it, and paid for it too. God knows I have paid for it!—I wanted it for a sword, and now I have it—my most fine sword. Jewels on the hilt, it has—only that I may not draw it from the sheath!" The bitterness in his voice sparked into sudden angry mirth. "There is another metaphor for you, friend Fulke. It seems to me tonight that I am fit for nothing better than the coining of such."

"Why this so unusual mood of spiritual abasement?"

"Philip is dead," Ralegh said simply.

"I did not know you for such boon companions."

("Why cannot they leave each other alone?" wondered Bess, on her knees and searching under the little gilded organ. "Aren't they unhappy enough, that they must needs do this because they both loved Philip and he is dead?")

Ralegh had been resting one arm along the transom of the window, looking out into the golden evening. He lowered his arm and swung round to face the other man. "No, we were never boon companions," he agreed, "never as you and he were. I am not seeking to rob you, Fulke. But I feel as though some better part of myself was gone with him. He was all that I wish to God I could be. I shall be a worse man for his death."

The gold and coral button came to light at that moment, among the strewing rushes. Bess caught it up and fled. She did not want to hear more; it was not hers to hear. But as she sped back to the Queen's apartments, the companion of the shining hour in Lady Sidney's garden was become real to her again.

Her understanding was increased a few weeks later, when Mary Herbert showed her an elegy for Philip scrawled on a blank leaf of his Arcadia. It was her first experience of Ralegh the poet. She had seen his verse once or twice before, but that had been the charming, polished verse that could as well have been written by most of his peers. This was a very different thing.

> What hath he lost that such great grace has won?
> Young years for endless years, and hope unsure
> Of fortune's gifts, for wealth that still shall dure.
> Oh happy race, with so great praises run!

England doth hold thy limbs, that bred the same;
Flanders thy valour, where it last was tried;
The camp thy sorrow, where thy body died;
Thy friends thy want; the world thy virtue's fame!

As time went by, the life of the Court, which had at first been unfamiliar and vaguely terrifying to Bess Throckmorton, became the natural order of things. The Queen's day was her day. The Queen rose early, prayed, broke her fast, and turned to affairs of state with her ministers. Then she walked in the gardens or the long galleries, attended sometimes by a single favourite, sometimes by a group of learned grey-beards or a cluster of boys scarce out of their teens. At eleven she dined, and thereafter rode hunting or hawking, returning to hear evening prayer, and to sup with a few chosen friends. The evening might be spent quietly reading, or playing chess or cards; or at other times, especially if foreign ambassadors or such were present, given over to music and dancing. There were variations, of course: Christmas festivities, masques and mayings, and great doings in the tilt-yard on tournament days. But save for these, whether the Court was at Greenwich or Hampton Court, Richmond or Whitehall, the pattern of the Queen's day remained the same, and the days of her Ladies followed it of necessity.

The pattern continued much as usual into the spring and summer of 1588, a delicate arabesque of custom laid upon the fiercening background of an England making ready for war. Ships being hastily armed and victualled, militia trained, the gun-foundries of Kent working overtime, the drums of war beating from end to end of the Kingdom. A great Armada massing on the Spanish coast, and beacons ready built on English hilltops, ceaselessly watched, waiting to send the message of its coming in red flame across the land. Drake and his squadrons at Plymouth, Ralegh training militia-men in Devon and Cornwall; little valiant ships waiting like hounds in leash, in ports all round the coast. The Queen, as she so often did, turning niggardly, and Lord Howard of Effingham pulling at his spade beard and swearing, at his wits' end for supplies.

The Queen had moved to Greenwich to be near her troops massing at Tilbury; there were longer sessions—frequently stormy—with her Ministers and Admirals, less hawking and dancing.

Otherwise the pattern continued as before, continued even
more meticulously than before, as though in direct defiance of
Spain.

"It is a statement of faith," Bess thought, sitting one evening in
the Queen's privy chamber, industriously stitching at a crown
imperial in her tapestry. "We ride, we distil toilet waters, we laugh
—rather quietly—we practise on the lute, and Lady Scrope con-
tinues her translations from the Greek; with the threat of Spain and
all that Spain stands for hanging over us. And the darker grows the
threat, the more important it seems that I should shade this petal to
perfection." She chose another strand of silk with infinite care from
the gay tangle beside her.

It was a hot, still evening of early summer, and in the Queen's
privy chamber the doors and windows stood open, but scarce a
breath of wind stirred the tapestries, and the unmoving air was
heavy with the scent of bruised meadowsweet among the strewing-
herbs on the floor. The Queen had returned from evensong, and
in a little while she would go to supper, with her ladies attending
her. There were several of them gathered here in the lower end of
the room, heads bent, hands industriously moving over embroidery
frames. Bess glanced round at them, Lady Warwick, Lady Howard
and the rest; not one of them but had son or husband, father,
brother or lover with the Fleet or the Militia. Not hard to guess
where their minds were, while their hands attended so carefully to
the setting of their stitches.

At the upper end of the room, the Queen sat beside an open
window, bending down to watch the movements of the young
man who knelt at her feet among the very folds of her silken skirt,
playing with the little merlin on his gloved fist.

"A pretty toy," she said, half mockingly. "A toy for a lady's
hand, Robin, surely unworthy of the Earl of Essex!"

"I have a big German goshawk for use," said the young man
quickly. "But he is not well enough mannered for the Queen's
privy chamber. Clyté can be a fierce small devil when she chooses.
See. . . " He began to tease the merlin, roused her temper more
swiftly than he had expected, and not quite swift enough to snatch
back his ungloved hand from the lightning stroke, got a gashed
thumb for his pains. "Ah!—Damnation!" He sucked the thumb and
glared. The goaded merlin bated from his fist with a loud clapping

of wings in the quietness, and the Queen laughed on a clear, shrill note.

"A bad falconer, my Robin! Never tease your falcon, nor ever lose your temper with her. Captain Ralegh will tell you that, an you ask him!"

The Earl of Essex pouted like a spoiled child. "Ralegh! Everything is Ralegh! Well, I shall not ask him. Anyway, it is easy to see why he is so skilled with the brutes. He has had to be. *My* father kept an Austringer."

"Never fall into the error of looking down your handsome nose at the man who has trained his own hawks, for he is apt to have learned certain useful lessons that you have not," said the Queen. "Robin, you are jealous! I do believe you are jealous! Is that why you have been so ill-tempered these last three days since Sir Walter returned to Court? He will be away to his press-gangs in three more."

The boy knelt up suddenly, his face turned up to hers, beautiful, arrogant, pleading; the face, half of a petulant child, half of an ardent lover. "What do you want *him* for, when you have me? Why do you turn to him when I would die to serve you?"

"You are already the Master of my Horse; would you be the Captain of my Guard, also?"

"Yes!" He was half in jest, half in deadly earnest. "Send him back to his Devonshire mud, Belphoebe, and when he's gone, I'll be the truest knight to you that ever Queen had for the Captain of her Guard!"

"A naughty—jealous—brat," said the Queen, nodding between each word.

"I only ask to serve you."

"Robin, Robin, the smallest powder-monkey with the Fleet tonight serves me well."

He flushed. "That was not my meaning. You know it."

"I know it; indeed I do! You want a little service with much power, do you not, my Bonnie Sweet Robin?" She bent nearer, drawing him to her without touch or word, as she still knew how to do. "Gin you want power, earn it. Gin you want Sir Walter's place, prove yourself the better man—if you can."

The gilt and lacquer clock between the windows struck the hour of six, and the Queen's Ladies laid aside their embroidery frames and rose, like a flock of pale birds, shaking out satin skirts over wide farthingales. It was the hour to make ready the Queen's supper. Leave being asked and given—rather sharply—they withdrew, rustling through the open doorway into the next room, the Queen's dining parlour. Several Gentlemen of the Guard were on duty there, and their Captain stood before the Queen's door, a very brilliant figure in silver breastplate over the orange-tawny taffetas of his uniform. He leaned on his tasselled halberd, smiling a little, idly and rather contemptuously, the light striking starwise on the diamond on his halberd-hand, which the Queen had given him. He must have heard every word spoken within.

Bess glanced at him in passing, and the smile broadened into a flash of very white teeth in the swarthy face, a swift kindling of laughter in the vividly blue eyes under their rather heavy lids. How could he look like that, Bess wondered, as she followed Lady Scrope through into the great dining hall beyond. How superbly, insufferably sure of himself he must be, to stand there, casually amused, listening to his rival's efforts to bring about his downfall. Yes, and Essex too, who must have known that the man he sought to oust was hearing every word, even as he spoke it. What strange manner of duel was going on between them?

That evening after supper, they danced in the Long Gallery, where seven years before, Elizabeth had plighted her troth to Anjou, her "Poor Frog", kissing him on the mouth before her whole Court, and dancing with him till dawn. But tonight, when the dancing was fairly started, she withdrew to her private apartments. Tonight she had other business to attend to.

The breathless day was turning to a breathless night beyond the long uncurtained windows; a blue velvet night, by contrast with the yellow damask radiance of tapers in many branched candle sconces along the tapestried walls. The first stately pavane, danced by the older and most noble of the Court, was over; and now the young men laid aside their cloaks and rapiers, donned their jewelled and feathered bonnets, and asked the girls to dance.

Bess found young Killigrew bowing before her, his bonnet feather sweeping the polished floor. The viols and lutes had struck up again, a blithe tune this time, that lilted with a heart-catching gaiety. She gave him her hand and moved forward to take her place in the galliard. She loved dancing; her body felt light as she moved to the music, light as a blown petal, tracing the mazy patterns of the dance. There were fewer dancers than usual; so many of the young men were away already; most of the lads now bowing and pacing with their partners would change their silken doublets for buff and steel tomorrow, or the next day, or the next. . . . Suddenly, piercingly, Bess wondered which of them would ever come back to dance in the Long Gallery again; and the flutes rose into a wailing sweetness, and the galliard was become a thing to break the heart.

Midway through the dance, turning once again from her partner, she caught sight of a man standing in one of the doorways. A young man, darkly clad, a hunchback, watching someone among the dancers with an oddly shuttered look. For some weeks Robert Cecil had been abroad with Lord Derby's mission to the Spanish Netherlands, helping to play England's part in that unreal meeting with Spain, in which the diplomats of both countries had exchanged flowery platitudes and polite vows of friendship, while along one coast the attack gathered, and along the other defence was hastily made ready. The mask was down now; the mission had been recalled, but this was the first time that Bess had seen him since his return, and her pleasure was naked in her face, for he was one of the very few people at Court she counted truly as a friend. As she drifted by, he turned his head, and seeing her, gave her the quick, unexpectedly sweet smile that he always had for her.

When the galliard was over, he came to join her, threading his way through the drifting couples, his bare head with its cap of smooth chestnut hair shining coppery in the candle-light, the short Spanish cloak flung back from his painfully hunched shoulders to reveal the lining of waspish gold.

"God den to you, Bess," he said.

She gave him both hands. "Robin! I heard that you were returned. Oh, I am so happy to see you again."

"It is worth a journey to have so pretty a welcome home," he said, smiling. "You would have seen me ere this, had I been less fully engaged with the dregs of this insane mission." His young voice was suddenly weary. "It is as hot as an oven in here. There is no air; not so much as will serve to stir a candle flame. Do you want to dance again, or shall we find some corner where there is a little air to breathe, and we can talk in peace?"

Side by side they slipped out from the over-bright gallery, and
down to a postern on to the terrace. Other couples had come out
in search for air, but turning aside from them Bess and her companion mounted a few shallow steps and came to a small secret
corner, half screened by pleached vines from the main terrace
below. A bar of light lay across it from a window, showing it
empty, and Bess moved across to the balustrade and leaned there,
drawing back her pale skirts to make room for him beside her. A
thin thunder haze had blotted out the stars, but all along the river
the riding lights of the shipping formed new constellations, and in
the faint light of the window behind them, the scented white stars
of the jessamine arching over the balustrade seemed to shine of
themselves.

Leaning side by side on the cool stone, they watched the gay girls
and their escorts on the terrace below, drifting into the light of the
many windows and out of it again; and talked quietly, with long
pauses between. Presently, in the midst of a delicately malicious
word-portrait of some member of the Spanish Mission, Cecil
checked abruptly, as a group passed across the lit terrace, the spun-
glass figure of a girl in their midst, laughing over her shoulder to
someone in the shadows.

"That is Elizabeth Brooke, My Lord Cobham's sister," Bess said.
"Is she not a pretty thing? She has but just come to Court, since
you have been away."

"I know it. I met her last night at supper, at my brother's house,"
Cecil said, and something in his voice made her turn her head
swiftly to look at him. The light from the window fell full across
his face, and the shield that had been drawn over it in the gallery
was no longer there.

"Go down and join her," she said impulsively.

"No." He turned to her slowly; his mouth twisted in wry amusement. "I did not know my face was so transparent."

There was a moment's silence between them, and then Bess said,
"I am wondering something."

"What are you wondering?"

"I am wondering why you came to me in the Long Gallery, a
while since—instead of going to her."

"The answer is very simple. I was sure of your welcome."

"And are you not sure of hers?"

"I—do not dare to so much as hope for it," he said, almost under his breath.

She put a hand on his arm. "Try your fortune, Robin."

"Oh, I shall, rest assured of that. It can do no harm." But his voice told her how hopeless he was of it doing any good.

She said defensively: "I do not see why you should have so little hope of the issue."

"Do you not?" He gave a short unhappy laugh. "Kind Bess—or very blind Bess. I am scarcely formed for a successful lover." He turned back to the balustrade, and folding his arms along it, spoke to her over his shoulder. "Sufficient unto the day. . . . First there is this little matter of a Spanish Fleet to be dealt with. Brother Thomas is with his ship even now; and tomorrow I join him."

"You too," Bess said. "When the bells ring for our victory, I shall have a threefold pride in their pealing."

He laughed again, with a faint mockery "Nay, my sweet Bess, you must keep your pride for your brothers, and be content to have it twofold. As for me, I go because at this time the sword is mightier than the pen, or at least—a swifter way to advancement in the Queen's favour. That disappoints you, doesn't it?"

"A little," she said, chilled and startled by the sudden turn to cold calculation.

He seemed to feel her recoil, and instantly to draw away from her in return. "I could have let you believe what you wanted to believe; remember that."

"You are very ambitious, are you not, Robin?" she said after a moment.

"Very. But of power, not mere position. I want my father's power when the time comes for him to lay it down. I want to do things with it that he has never done. I want to guide the delicate threads of destiny, braiding them at my will. I want men a little afraid of me—tall men, with straight backs."

She protested sharply. "Robin—don't!"

He looked round again, the light from the window shining on his coppery head. "I crave your pardon. You must make allowances for the Queen's Pigmy—it is a hunchback's privilege to have a warped nature, you know." And before she could speak, he had pushed off from the balustrade, and half turned towards the steps, then back to her again with a small, oddly expressive gesture as though slipping something, a dark cloak, a dark mood, from his deformed shoulders. "Bess, Bess, I am sorry. It is that I am tired, and—something heartsick with reaching for the moon; but I had no right to vent my ill humours upon you for no better reason than that I was assured of your friendship. Forgive me."

Bess said in her warm, quiet voice: "If there were anything to forgive, I would forgive you, Robin."

He moved aside for her to go before him down the shallow steps, and as she gathered her skirts and passed him by, she heard his light, curiously prowling step turn in behind her. She was acutely aware of him, and anxious for him, as she made her way back to the postern door; and yet suddenly two other men were joined with him in her thoughts: the Master of the Queen's Horse, the Captain of her Guard. All three linked by their questing after power. Power; Walter Ralegh seeking in it the tool, the weapon with which to serve his dream; Robin Devereux wanting it for a new plaything, a gerfalcon, a golden cup, a jewel for his bonnet; Robin Cecil desiring it because his brilliant brain was sheathed in a lame body. They came together in her mind with a queer significance. It was as though in that moment a wind out of the future touched her; a little chill wind, in which she shivered.

CHAPTER 4

THE OPEN RIVER

The beacon fires carried their message across the land, and the little ships put out from ports and harbours all along the coast, and flung themselves against the might of Spain, and by good seamanship and the Grace of God, prevailed. The shadow passed, and the bells rang to the summer sky, and the young men—most of the young men—laid aside their buff and steel, and came back to dance in the Queen's Long Gallery again.

Three times the roses bloomed in the gardens of Ely House; three times the hot chestnut sellers appeared in the London streets; three times the proud white swans on the Thames trailed their grey streamers of cygnets behind them; and it was June 1591.

That June the Court moved to Richmond, to Bess's great contentment. She was always glad to be back in Richmond. The Palace was smaller and more intimate than the other Royal residences, and the row of pleasant small houses that were the quarters of the Maids of Honour gave her a sense of home that she missed when the Court was at Greenwich or Windsor or Westminster. She loved the upper reaches of the Thames, too. The open river with its salt smells and crowding shipping, its restless gulls, its ceaseless change and turmoil and out-flowing into the unknown always frightened her a little. But these quiet silver reaches with their weirs and willows and drifting swans satisfied her longing for quietness and security.

It was this same longing for security, legacy from her uncertain childhood, that drew Bess back at the earliest moment, whenever the Court returned to Richmond, to a certain forgotten corner of the garden which offered sanctuary a little as Lady Sidney's garden had once done. It was only a half-moon of turf, sloping down to a quiet backwater, and shut away from the rest of the pleasance by a little wood. Somebody must originally have meant to include it in the formal plan of the gardens; they had made a turf seat and an arbour, and then grown tired of it, or found it unsuitable for their purpose. Nothing was left of the arbour now, save the blue convolvulus that had been meant to grow over it, and which, left to its own devices, had grown up the trunk of the nearest alder tree. But the green half-moon of turf between the wood and the river was enchanted ground.

Would the blue convolvulus be in flower yet? Bess wondered on this particular morning, as she made her way down towards the river, forsaking the formal pleasances for the joys of the wilderness, just as she had done on that long ago day, in Lady Sidney's garden. It had been spring then, and Bess had been very young. It was summer now, and Bess was six and twenty, and judged by the standards of her day, no longer young—really young—at all. But this morning, speeding down through the pleached ways and nut alleys, her green skirts gathered in either hand, she was a child, running to her secret sanctuary. And as the springtime Bess would have done, she checked her running among the trees of the little wood that guarded it, and came at last, quietly and delicately, through the willows and alders on to the half-moon of turf sloping to the river. One did not snatch at sanctuary. As with all lovely things, one came to it humbly, gathering its joys a little at a time, careful to bruise nothing in the gathering. The blue convolvulus was not yet in flower; but time would bring the flowering, and for to-day, there was delight enough in the secret garden. A fitful wind blowing from the south; a soft, warm wind, full of the liquid song of a Jenny-whitethroat in the wood behind, that might have been the song of that other time, rippling from the heart of a damson tree as though the blossom itself were singing. And as Bess moved across to the crumbling turf seat, a remembered magic touched her, and fled away, leaving a small unexplained heartache behind it. She sat very still, her hands folded in her green lap, watching the river under the silver turmoil of the willows and letting the peace of the sanctuary flow into her. But the passing touch of the old magic had brought very vividly into her mind the man who had conjured it up for her; and with him, those others who were always linked with him in her thoughts.

In the three years since they had become so linked, Robin Cecil had prospered most in his quest for power, she thought. Walsingham's death had given him his chance, and he had been quick to seize it by bringing himself before the Queen as a suitable successor. He was Sir Robert now; he was acting Secretary of State, with the fine threads of destiny running through his hands as he had wanted them. He had prospered in other ways too. For almost two out of those three years he had been married—most happily married—to the spun-glass girl, despite all his fears.

The Earl of Essex also had prospered at the first, for Leicester's death had served to raise him still further in the Queen's fondness. He was only Leicester's stepson, but in many ways very like him, so that it seemed sometimes to the Court that she looked on him as the son she might, in happier circumstances, have borne to the man she loved. And with the loss of the old love, the companion of her distant girlhood, she had turned more and more to his young counterpart to fill the place left desolate. But it had not been altogether as a son that the Queen loved her Robin; and when, becoming so much the Queen's Robin that he felt safe to do as he pleased, he had married Philip Sidney's widow, he had found himself mistaken in the strength of his position. He had hastily returned her to her mother as he might have returned a horse or a doublet that did not meet with the Queen's approval, and since even that had not been quite enough, he was now abroad, in command of the force sent to aid Henry of Navarre, striving by a display of courage and generalship, to win back the full favour of Belphoebe.

And the third of the Triumvirate? She could not be sure. She knew so little of him. Robin Cecil was a close friend, Robin Devereux a casual one; but Ralegh, although she had shared with him for six years the life of the inner circle who attended on the Queen, was a stranger. Yet her face grew troubled as she remembered the sight that she had had of him that morning outside the Queen's apartments; the brilliant figure in the flower-broidered doublet; the weary, seeking, embittered face under the arrogant crest of the Queen's Captain. The years had brought him increase of power and riches, but the increase had been paid for, and stranger though he was, Bess's heart whimpered over him as his mother's might have done, because that morning his eyes had looked hot in his head. Less than a month ago he had returned from his Irish Estate to become Second-in-Command under Lord Thomas Howard of the expedition that was forming to intercept the Spanish Plate Fleet; and only yesterday, at the very last moment, it had become known through the Court that the Queen could not after all bring herself to part with her Captain and that his cousin, Sir Richard Grenville, was to take his place, in his—Ralegh's—own ship, the *Revenge*. That was why he had been outside the Queen's door this morning instead of posting down to Plymouth. That was why his dark face had worn that restless, seeking look, and his eyes had been hot. No, the past three years had not been kind to the Queen's Captain.

Bess had the sudden thought that if she could have given him those three years out of her own life for a second chance, she would have done it very willingly. She could have spared them well enough, for they had brought her neither gain nor loss, no change save that she was three years older. She remembered something that Penelope Devereux had said once, pitifully, of an aged aunt who had just died. "It must be so sad to have nothing to look back on, not even sorrow." Was it to be so with her, she wondered, with a sudden poignant sense of the fleetingness of youth, of life slipping by without using her. Such a little while since, she had sat in the ditch with the damson petals drifting round her. . . .

She gave herself a shake. Best go and find some work to do, and do it, said her more practical self. And with a sigh, she got up, shaking out her wide skirts over the Spanish farthingale, and turned to go. But in the act of turning she saw that the blue convolvulus was in flower after all, and instantly her more practical self was forgotten.

Just one blue trumpet, wind-swayed high among the sprays of the alder tree. She reached up with quick pleasure to touch the flower. It swayed into her hand, the silken fragility cool against her finger tips; then before she could avert the disaster, the wind caught her light oversleeve and tossed it upward into the alder tree, and the sharp twig-tangle snatched at the filmy stuff and held it, so that she was a prisoner. With an exclamation of annoyance she released the flower and turned her attention to her tangled sleeve. But the place where it was caught was just out of easy reach, and she could not free the gauzy stuff from the twigs which held it. She could drag it free easily enough, but that might spoil her gown, and it was a new gown and she could not afford to spoil it. Mistress Throckmorton was a woman of independent means, with an estate of her own at Mitcham, but the estate and consequently the means were very small ones on which to keep up an appearance at Court, and for her a ruined gown was a minor tragedy. Realising that she was only making matters worse with her fumbling, she ceased it, and stood with her arm raised so as not to drag on the sleeve, considering the situation. If she called for help, somebody would hear her eventually, though not many people came down to this corner of the gardens. But she did not want to call. She was a gentle and self-effacing woman, and the idea of raising a tumult actually frightened her. Above all she did not want to raise a tumult here, and bring scurrying gardeners into her sanctuary.

If only someone would come uncalled!

And then she thought that she heard whistling. She listened anxiously, her head turned in the direction from which the sound came. It died away, then rose again quite near at hand. Somebody in the little wood was whistling Greensleeves.

Bess gathered her courage in both hands, and called, "Oh please —will you help me!"

The whistling broke off between note and note. There was an instant's silence, and then she heard someone brushing through the undergrowth, and called again, half laughing, half apologetic. "My sleeve is caught in the twigs, and I——"

There was a flicker of pale colour among the wild fruit trees, and out on to the half-moon of turf stepped the Queen's Captain.

Ralegh had come out from the Queen's privy apartments that morning in something very like a passion, a passion against her, himself, and all things under Heaven. The day was his, but he could make no use of it. He would have liked to ride, far and fast, but his favourite mount had gone lame, and he was in a mood to refuse any other with loathing. He was reduced to wandering drearily up and down, in and out through the palace gardens and cursing fate, his very soul uncomfortably hot within him. He had flung himself heart and soul into this expedition against the Spanish Plate Fleet, for the adventure and the hope of gain, but chiefly for the striking of a blow at Spain's stranglehold on the New World. Now here he was, recalled at the last moment, his command given to Richard, while he remained to dance attendance on the Queen. He was the Queen's very loyal servant; he would have died for her without question if the need arose, but his loyalty was becoming perilously strained by her constant refusal to allow him his freedom.

It was the same with his efforts at colonisation. He might have letters patent to send out colonies to his heart's content, so long as he did not go with them; small wonder that, lacking his leadership, his Virginia colony had failed like the rest. He would have broken free of it all, he thought, riches and power, and the delicate, dangerous game of wits, and followed his dream without her leave. He had the *Garland* and the *Crane* for his own, even with the *Revenge* otherwise engaged. But without letters patent for himself, he was helpless.

Little by little, as he wandered the slow hours away, his rage died down, and dying, left behind it a fever of unrest, a sick longing after his dream, a most bitter contempt for himself and his way of life, a divine discontent. It was a young man's mood, such as the soldier of fortune might have known, but which was less familiar to the Captain of the Queen's Guard. A dangerous mood that was dry tinder ready for the spark.

In this mood he found himself presently in the wild fringe of garden running to the river, where something that had been planted as a classical grove had developed with neglect into a most enchanting English spinney. The oak trees were in their first warmth of summer leaf, the young fern uncurling its dragon-head fronds, and somewhere among the branches a Jenny-whitethroat was singing. And suddenly for a flashing moment, the Queen's Captain was a boy again in Hayes Barton woods. He began to whistle a tune that had been new to him then: and "Greensleeves, Greensleeves," fluted the whitethroat, "Greensleeves was my heart of gold, and who but my Lady Greensleeves."

As though in answer to the whistling, a voice called through the trees, a woman's voice, with a little breathless catch in it. "Oh please—will you help me." He hesitated an instant, wondering if she were calling to some companion, for the call had been pitched as though to carry only a few yards. Then as no other voice answered, he turned his steps in the direction from which it had come.

"My sleeve is caught in the twigs, and I——" began the voice, as he reached the woodshore. He stepped out on to the half-moon of turf, and saw a woman in a green gown, standing among the branches of an alder tree, one arm raised, held captive by her filmy sleeve that had blown upward and tangled in the twigs. A tall woman, with a sensitive troubled face turned eagerly toward him.

He doffed his feathered hat without a word, and strode quickly to her side. Her eyes, raised to his, were the deeply muted blue of wild columbine, giving her face a gravity which her wide warm mouth belied. Warm mouth and shadowed eyes; a quality of quiet in her that it seemed to him he had not met before in any woman. And God knew how he longed for quiet.

"I would curtsey if I might," Bess said, "but I shall tear my poor sleeve if I do."

"Hold your arm higher," he commanded. "So—like that." He tossed his hat aside, and set to work, Bess standing like a docile child, her arm held high, watching the small pucker of concentration between his brows, while his skilled falconer's fingers made short work of the tangle that had defeated her.

In a few moments the thing was done, and he turned to her, letting the soft stuff slip through his hand. "The bird is loosed from the fowler's net. See, it is not hurt—your wing."

"The bird is most grateful to be loosed."

"How did you come to be caught?"

"I saw the blue woodbine," Bess began: but before she could get further he had reached up and broken off the flower, and was holding it out to her. She took it from him wordlessly; she had not wanted it picked, but she would not have told him so for anything the world could give her. The calyx was brilliantly, vibrantly blue, the very colour of joy, as she bent her head to fasten it into the low square cut breast of her gown. It took her a little while to accomplish this, for the stiffened bone-lace flutings of her ruff made it hard to see what she was doing; but when she looked up again, Ralegh had not moved.

He was standing very still, watching her, his face puzzled and almost indignant. He demanded with the air of one whose rightful inheritance has been kept from him, "Why have I not seen you before?"

She was puzzled in her turn. "But you have, almost daily when you have been in attendance on the Queen. You have even danced with me, often and often."

"Oh that——" He made an impatient gesture. "I have danced with all the Queen's Ladies. Why have I not seen you—as I see you now?"

There was a little silence, and an odd hush seemed to have fallen on Bess. "You did, once," she said after a moment. "Just once before. But it was sixteen years ago, and you have forgotten."

"Make me remember."

"The ditch at the bottom of Lady Sidney's garden," she prompted. "You were but lately come home from Flanders, and I was ten years old. It had been raining, and it rained again at the end, and you went away to your supper."

Light sprang up in his face. "There was a toad with a gold crown on his head."

"No, it was because he had no crown, and therefore could not be a prince under a spell, that you said he was maybe a poor devil of a soldier of fortune under a cloud."

"And you remembered," with a note of wonder in his voice. "All these years you have remembered, while I forgot. Forgive me."

But it was typical of him that even now it was a command, not an appeal, just as the hands he held out to her were a command. They were broad hands, strong and sensitive, and a little ruthless, and she knew more surely than she had ever known anything before, that if she put hers into them, life would take her henceforth, for making or breaking. There would be no return to the backwater, and she had always been afraid of the open river. She did hesitate, but for the merest breath of time; then she put her hands into his.

Something leapt between them through their linked palms; something as positive, as irrevocable as the firing of a charge. They parted touch, a little shaken, and stood looking at each other.

"I must go," Bess said. "The Queen will be going to her supper in half an hour."

"Last time it was my supper, and now it is the Queen's. You are an Elizabeth, too, are you not?"

"For the most part, I am called Bess."

"Bess," he said; and the name became a caress; but he did not touch her again, and she was grateful to him for the forbearance. "Do not you go leaving me for fifteen years, Bess."

"It will scarcely take so long to set the Queen's table," Bess said softly. And she swept up her skirts and went hurrying back through the wood without a glance behind her. The blue convolvulus in the breast of her gown was already fading, but it would revive in water, and the colour would deepen again to the blue that was the very colour of joy.

.   .   .   .

In after years Bess remembered that summer as wearing a bloom of light. A kingfisher summer, all the more shining because it might have no aftertime. Love between those nearest to the Queen so often had no aftertime. There were snatched moments in the Palace gardens; brief meetings under the scented lime trees; the lingering of hand in hand when the galliard brought them together. For Bess, that summer, the scent of lime blossom on the evening air, the notes of a lute, the praying hands of a candle flame, became things of exquisite and painful joy, and the whole world was transmuted. But for Ralegh, though the joy was there for him too, there was also a growing discontent. It was not so, in secret snatches, as though it were a shameful thing, that he wanted his love.

Matters would have come to a head before long, but at summer's end, word reached England of the fate of the *Revenge* and the death of Sir Richard Grenville.

"And so, because the Queen cannot spare her Captain, Richard dies," Ralegh said to Bess, bitterly, on the day he received the full details. And within a few days he was spending every free moment, every thought on writing "A Report of the Truth of the Fight about the Azores," to silence the critics who were already calling Grenville's conduct in question.

Before this blazing defence of his beloved cousin was published, the Queen, perhaps wishing to recompense herself for the failure of the first venture, had given him leave to fit out another expedition, even promising to hazard a small sum herself. Ralegh brought to the second project an even fiercer eagerness than he had brought to the first, for now, added to hopes that he had had before, there was the need to avenge Richard. He pledged almost everything he possessed to raise money; he rode to and fro between London and Plymouth like a man bedevilled, all winter long; even when the Queen gave him the Manor of Sherborne for a New Year gift, he scarcely spared the time to look at it, though he had loved it in his passing to and fro, since he was a boy.

So while winter came, and turned to spring, between the trips to Plymouth and the business of the Fleet, the stolen meetings with Bess continued.

And then on a May evening, she came in haste along the upper gallery of Whitehall Palace, while below her the great hall swam in an amber haze under the torches and the candle sconces that hung like crowns of light from the rafters, and the shifting throng came and went, jewelled and peacockwise to the thrumming of many lutes; and in the deep shadows at the foot of a private stair, found Ralegh waiting for her.

"Bess!" he whispered, as she checked in the narrow arched entrance, and held out his arms; and she went straight into them. He was in his uniform as Captain of the Guard, for there had been a state revel that night in honour of a stout Venetian Ambassador; and the unyielding cold of his breastplate bit through the thin stuff of her gown; but his arms round her were warm and vital, and she sniffed the fragrance of tobacco smoke that seemed always in his hair and beard, and which, because it was part of him, had grown familiar and dear. But after an instant she freed herself.

"Walter, we should not be here. It is madness."

"Then how sweet is madness! I have not seen you alone since I returned from Plymouth; and in a few days I ride again to join my Fleet in good earnest." Then with a sudden burst of exasperation,

"Bess, Bess, how long is it to be like this? How long am I to have you only in stolen moments like a kitchen wench stealing to be tumbled under a hedge by her backgate lover?"

There was an angry, almost disgusted note in his voice; and Bess was conscious of a chill. She had had no sense of guilt in her stolen meetings with him; but for him, evidently it was otherwise, and suddenly she was afraid. "Walter, I cannot help it!—What can I do?" she protested, as though he had accused her of something.

"You can marry me before I join the Fleet," Ralegh said.

She caught her breath, her heart suddenly racing. "The Queen would never allow it. She cannot bear her maids to marry, and you are—the Queen's Captain."

Ralegh said very deliberately. "She need not know, until afterwards."

"You mean?—Walter, no! I daren't!"

"Do you love me, Bess?"

"God knows I do! It is because I love you so much that I am afraid. . . ." Her voice trailed into silence.

"Afraid? Of the Queen's anger?"

"I am afraid that her anger might do to your love what it did to Robin Devereux's."

Ralegh did not answer at once, and when he did, he was stuttering with indignation. "Are you d-daring to suggest that I would send you b-back to your mother, to pleasure the Queen?"

"I haven't *got* a mother!" Bess almost wailed.

Instantly his indignation died, and he was holding her close, rubbing his bearded cheek against hers. "Dear Bess, we belong to one another, you and I, like the two halves of a hazelnut, making one whole and perfect. Even the Queen cannot undo that. . . . Marry me before I ride for Plymouth."

"I daren't! I daren't!" She drew her breath in a sob, clinging to him. "After you come back—let us wait until then. Please Walter —please!"

"What shall waiting avail us? Bess, cannot you see? I am no better proofed against Spanish shot than was my kinsman Richard; I want my wife now, while my arms are warm to hold her, lest maybe I hold her not at all."

In the long pause that followed, Bess heard the music in the hall below very clearly. That fear had been with her for months, sleeping with her at night, waking with her in the morning. How many, many women, since the world began, had carried the same fear, refusing to acknowledge it lest by doing so they gave it substance. How many had listened to the urgent pleading, "Now, come now, lest there be no other time."

"I will come," she said.

"Thank you, Bess," Ralegh said very simply. He was silent a moment; then, having gained his point, plunged into rapid plans. "Now listen, for we may have no other opportunity to speak together before the time comes. You are pledged to go down to Beddington on Tuesday, are you not? Who rides with you?"

"My uncle always sends one of his grooms." Bess readjusted herself to the swift change of mood.

"The same one?"

"No, not always."

"Good. Then write to your uncle, bidding him not to send the man. You cannot come at present—the Queen cannot spare you— you will know the best tale to tell. Let me have the letter tomorrow, and I will arrange for its dispatch; then forget that you ever wrote it. On Tuesday at noon, a groom will come for you, but he will be no man of your uncle's. Go with him, and he will bring you to my house at Islington." He checked abruptly. "What of your maid?"

"Joan? I would trust my life to her; she has been with me since I was a little girl."

"Bring her with you, then. I shall leave Court that morning as though for Plymouth, ride to Islington and have everything in readiness for our marriage. Your maid and the man I send for you will serve to witness our declaration, and——"

"Walter," Bess interrupted. "I would like a Minister of the Church."

"Sweet, what difference can the few mumbled words of a parson make? Our declaration before witnesses will join us in the eyes of the world; we are already joined in the eyes of God."

She hesitated. "I wish that you were less contemptuous of all religion."

"If you had seen, as I have, the evil that men can do to each other in the name of religion—aye, Protestant as well as Papist— maybe you would feel as I do."

Bess knew the evil that he meant. She knew that he had seen the
smoking out of Catholics in the caves where they had taken refuge,
in the year of the Bartholomew Massacre. She knew that he had
seen that Massacre, and what it had done to him, a boy of sixteen.
Still, "I would like a Minister of the Church," she persisted.

Ralegh laughed softly. "You shall have the Archbishop himself,
if 'twill make for your happiness."

"The Vicar of Islington will serve."

"You shall find him waiting you on Tuesday, and be married
as you wish."

"And after?"

"After, we shall have three shining days and nights to bend into
an eternity. Then, I go to join the Fleet, and you, back to Court,
as from your Uncle's house."

"And the Queen?"

"When I come back with the riches of the Indies and King
Philip's beard for a peace offering, we will go hand in hand, and
tell the Queen."

"God help us!" Bess said quietly. "I will write to my Uncle
before I sleep. Walter, let me go now; every moment that we are
here together adds to the danger of our being seen."

"I will let you go until Tuesday." He kissed her and dropped his
arms; and stood looking after her as she gathered her pale skirts and
sped away down the gallery. Then he turned back to the private
stair.

They had parted none too soon, for someone was coming along
the gallery, and Bess checked her frightened speed at sight of him.
But it was only Robin Cecil with some papers in his hand.

CHAPTER 5

THE STARS AND THE SEA

It was under weeping skies, and accompanied by a grimly disapproving henchwoman perched up behind the unknown groom,
that Mistress Throckmorton set out for her wedding. Joan, in the
few days since the news of the intended marriage was broken to

her, had been anything but a cheery companion. "A man like that's
no good to any woman, for his life be already full without one,"
had been her constant theme. "Why else should a'be still unwed,
I'd like to know, and forty if he's a day?" And her henchwoman's
constant prophesies of doom, together with her own misgivings
had given poor Bess a very heavy heart, which the rain blowing
down the chill spring wind did nothing to lighten.

She was possessed, too, of a forlorn sense of loneliness. She would
have so dearly liked to have someone of her own with her; Arthur
or Nicholas—even Robin Cecil. She would have liked them at least
to know that this was her wedding day, and wish her well. Then
she put the thought away from her. Better for them that they
should know nothing; it would be unfair to risk embroiling them
in the Queen's displeasure.

They passed Charing Village, and swung into the Strand. The
Carillon of the Fleet Bridge Conduit was chiming as they rode by,
the high sweet bell notes caught and tossed to and fro by the wind
as though it were juggling with them, so that it almost seemed to
Bess that she could see them like silver balls dancing above the
fretted gables of the Conduit. It was surely a happy thing, she
thought, that the bells should ring for her as she rode by; and
unreasoningly, her heart lightened a little, from that moment.

When they turned northward soon after the Fleet Bridge, leaving
the busy Strand for the quiet of a lane through market gardens, she
reined back a little, to allow her escort, who had been riding half
a length behind, to draw abreast of her, which after a perceptible
hesitation, he did.

He was a stockily built man, some ten years younger than
Ralegh, she judged, with a bullet head covered by crisp, dark curls,
and a pleasant face lit by far-sighted grey eyes; seaman's eyes, Bess
would have said. She had been puzzled by him from the first, and
as he ranged alongside, she turned to look at him again. "Now that
we have leisure for such things," she said, "may I know who rides
with me?"

"For today, I am Sir Walter's groom," he replied gravely.

"But on other days?"

He smiled. "On other days, I am Lawrence Kemys, one of Sir
Walter's Captains. Do I make so poor a showing as a groom?"

She surveyed him carefully; the flat cap and homespun jerkin, the leather leggings, the broad pillion-belt round his waist, to which the dour Joan was clinging, were all in keeping with the part; but the eyes were undeniably those of a seaman. "As to your clothes, a most perfect groom," she assured him, smiling in return. "Yet I think I should have known you for a seaman, had I met you in the habiliments of an Archbishop."

"And yet I was not always a seaman—save in my inclination. I was Notary and Bursar of Balliol when Sir Walter took me for his man."

He was a friendly soul, and responded to her encouragement with a half-shy eagerness that made him seem younger than he was. And as the market gardens gave place to fields, and they followed the narrow lane onward between hedges of rain-wet hawthorn, he told her a little of his old home—he was a Somerset man—and his days at Oxford, and a great deal about his service with Ralegh, who was clearly his God.

They clattered through the cluster of cottages and small merchants' houses that was Islington, and turning down beside the Church, reined in before an open gate in a wall of ancient rose-red brick. A genuine groom had appeared from a huddle of stable buildings and gone to the horses' heads, and then Ralegh himself was there; Ralegh in a pearl-coloured doublet, far more bridal than Bess in her tawny velvet riding dress; standing bareheaded in the rain to lift her down. "Kemys, you are an accomplice without peer! Bess, Sweeting, I have captured the Vicar." She slid from the saddle into his arms, and was set down lightly, while Lawrence Kemys swung a leg over his horse's neck, and dropping from his own saddle, turned to dismount the still rigidly disapproving Joan.

As in a breathless dream, Bess was swept up a flagged path and into the house. Someone was taking her wet cloak from her. "You should have sunlight," Ralegh was saying. "Sunlight, and all the bells of London ringing for your wedding!"

"The Fleet Bridge Carillon was chiming as we rode by," she said.

There were stairs then, Joan thumping up behind her with the saddle-bags, and a low-ceiled bed-chamber where she was to make ready for her wedding. It was an impersonal room, having the air of one used only rarely in passing. Very clearly, it was a man's room, but some attempt had been made to prepare it for a woman. A hand mirror of fine Venetian glass lay before the plain steel mirror on the dressing chest, and beside it, someone had set an inexpert posy of pinks and early roses in a silver cup. Her room, and Walter's.

But she must not keep him waiting.

While her tirewoman, in grim silence that developed gradually into a doleful sniffing, began to unpack the saddle-bags and set out the few possessions she had been able to bring with her, Bess herself took off her small beaver hat, tenderly smoothing the drooping white paradise plume that had suffered from the weather, and set herself to do what she could about her dress and her damp hair. There was little enough to be done. She had dared to bring no change of dress with her, since she kept two or three gowns at Beddington, and so never carried more than a change of linen with her on her visits there. She gathered the damp masses of her hair into a caul of gold mesh, shook out and brushed her skirts, twitched and pulled at her close ruff, which being too small to need starch, had suffered less from the weather than might have been expected. On a sudden impulse, she took a musk rose from the silver cup, a white rose, but with buds faintly yellow and delicately pointed as candle flames, smelled the warm sweetness of it, and stuck it into her pomander girdle.

Then she stood to survey the result, a little wistfully. The face that looked back at her out of Ralegh's great steel mirror was paler than usual, and the hair which she considered her best point had been darkened by the unkind rain, so that the gold was gone from it, and it was merely brown, and the short ends clung damply in wisps about her temples. It seemed to her that she had never looked so old, or so plain. Yet even as she looked, the reflected mouth lifted in rather tremulous joy, and her face had its own beauty as she turned away, holding out both hands to her tirewoman. "Joan, dear Joan, cease your sniffing, and kiss me and wish me happy."

Joan promptly burst into tears and caught her to her rather meagre bosom. "Ah, my lamb, what will become of us! I do wish you happy, as happy as a Queen! There now, do you go down to the man, for your heart is away before you and 'tis too late to mend that now, though the Lord knows I've done all I can to bring you to your senses. Run along now, and I'll be close behind you to see you wed."

Beside the empty hearth in the hall, Ralegh was waiting for her, and for an instant, as Bess checked at the stairhead, panic set her heart drumming. What had she to do with this man who carried his head as the Prince of the Morning? Then he turned, and his eyes met hers, and the panic died. He stood unmoving, watching her as she came slowly down the stairs. "I have been waiting for that all my life," he said.

"For what, Walter?"

A couple of strides brought him to the stairfoot, his head tipped far back on the strong neck, his eyes caressing her across the space between. "To see you come downstairs with a rose in your girdle."

Her hand was in his, as she walked beside him across the hall and up three worn steps to a little chamber that, from the shape of its one window, seemed to have originally been a private chapel, and from the faint sweet smell that hung about it, to have lately been used for storing apples. It had returned to its old use now; a chest under the window spread with a fine white damask cloth, and two crimson cushions ranged before it; a yellow glow of candle-light triumphant over the grey of the wet spring afternoon and the shadows of an ilex tree outside. Lawrence Kemys was already there, and with him an ancient cleric of gentle, cobwebbed aspect, nursing a great Church Prayer Book as though it were a baby.

The old man turned a troubled face to her as she entered, and reverently laying down the great book, took her hand between both of his old dry ones. "Mistress Throckmorton, my mind mis-gives me in this matter; but if you will tell me that you have considered well this step that you are taking, and that you are resolved upon it and content to abide by it, I shall perform my part with a quieter mind."

Bess smiled reassuringly at the anxious old man, who was clearly afraid that she had been swept into this marriage by the same high-handed methods as had doubtless been used on himself—as in a way, she had. "I have considered, and whatever the outcome, I am con-tent," she told him.

A renewed sniffing behind her told her that Joan was of the company, and Job's comforter though she had been of late, the presence of her dour little henchwoman gave her a sense of having someone of her own with her after all. And she was very glad of it, as she turned beside Ralegh to the makeshift Lord's Table, and the Vicar once again took up the great Prayer Book.

It was soon done; the final words spoken; and Bess and Ralegh rose from their knees, still hand in hand.

"May I be the first to wish you happy unto your life's end, Lady Ralegh," said the gentle old cleric. "It may be that you will have more of tribulation—more of testing also—than is the common lot in marriage, but I think also that you will have much joy. . . ." His old quiet eyes drifted from her face to Ralegh's and back again; and his voice began to drift too. "Many waters cannot quench love, neither can the floods drown it. . . ."

Afterwards they supped in a panelled upper parlour where bowls of late spring flowers had been set to bring scent and colour into dark corners; Bess and Ralegh, Lawrence Kemys and the ancient Vicar, served for the most part by a square man who seemed to stand in much the same relationship to Ralegh as Joan did to herself. A strange wedding feast, and would have been rather a muted one, but for the bridegroom. The Vicar was clearly still unhappy about the ceremony that he had just performed, both for Bess's sake, and for his own, and even got so far as murmuring to himself distressfully, "I hope I have done right, I do trust that I have done right; I do trust the Queen's Grace never comes to hear of my hand in this!"

To which Ralegh replied with an odd blend of laughter with a very real gentleness for the old man's fears. "If she does, I will swear I forced you to it at the rapier point, and Captain Kemys will bear witness to the same. No man shall suffer for my joy."

But Ralegh himself seemed in dancing spirits, and by little and little his mood irradiated the other three, until even the Vicar forgot his scruples and his fears, and sat smiling quietly on his companions, presently even blossoming into three classical jests and a long and somewhat rambling story concerning the poet Simonides. The meal became an intimate and joyous occasion; and they pledged each other in thin Greek wine that tasted of the grape, eye smiling into eye above the rim of the fragile calyx of Venetian glass.

When the guests were gone, one to his vicarage, the other to his ship refitting at Deptford, Bess and Ralegh, alone in the panelled parlour, turned to look at each other as though for the first time. "I have been wanting to do this all through supper," Ralegh said, and began deliberately to loosen the points of her close ruff. "I want to see your neck—you have a beautiful neck. I want the warm

white hollow at the base of it.   ." He opened the throat of the
mannish doublet, and laid a caressing forefinger on her skin. "Soft,
warm hollow. I can feel the life beating in it—like a small bird."

"A very happy small bird."

"Bess—oh Bess, my heart! my most dear!" He flung his arms
round her, straining her close. "You're mine! Mine to me! And
not even the Queen's Grace can come between us now!"

Not even the Queen's Grace. The words could scarcely have
been more unfortunate. A blight seemed to fall on Bess as she heard
them, and she pressed back from him to look up into his face.
"The Queen—Oh Walter, what have we done?"

He pulled her into his arms once more. "What have we done?
We have noosed three shining days and nights out of Eternity to
be our own! A day for every petal of the flower-de-luce, a night
for every star in Orion's Belt!" He kissed her again and again, as
though to drive the sudden chill out of her with his own flame;
gradually succeeding; kindling her response until for a while she
forgot the world and the Queen's Grace, and her whole being
leapt to him as a lark into the sunlight.

At last she drew away from him, laughing at her own fears, and
gathering up a strand of hair that he had dragged loose, moved
across to the deep window-seat, and sat down, drawing her skirts
close to make room for him beside her.

The window was a little open, letting in the scents of the rain-wet
garden, and the thin hushing of the wind through the leaves of the
ilex tree.

She put up her hand with a child's joy in little things, to trace
the pattern of the leaded panes. "Stars in your window," she said,
and paused, head cocked to listen. "How like to the sea the wind
sounds in the ilex branches."

Ralegh looked at her quickly. "You hear it, too? It was for the
stars in the window and the sea in the ilex branches that I bought
this place, when first I needed quarters of my own within reach of
Westminster, long before Durham House was added unto me." He
turned a little, resting one hand over hers, to look out into the quiet
garden. "There were just such stars in the window of my own
chamber, in my old home, and just such an ilex tree outside the
parlour window. But the Channel was only a mile away, and save
in a flat calm the calling of it was always mingled with the sea-sound

in the ilex leaves. The place went to strangers when my father died. I tried to buy it back when first I was possessed of sufficient fortune, but the new owner would not sell. You would have loved Hayes Barton."

She smiled at him fondly. "I am very sure I should. Tell me of it."

And Ralegh told; sitting in the deep window-place with her hand in his, while the twilight stole up through the garden, and the sea-hushing of the wind in the ilex leaves sounded softly behind his words. A peaceful and reflective mood seemed to have fallen on him; and he was no longer the Queen's Captain, the will behind great enterprises; no longer even the poet or the lover; only a quiet man talking quietly of places and people that were dear to him, to the companion with whom he was content.

And Bess, listening to him, saw before her inner eye, the old farmhouse among the Devon hills, the walled garden, and the woods across the lane; dogs, much loved and long since dead; gatherings round the fire on winter evenings with some seaman from half the world away, the centre of an eager audience. She heard of Richard Grenville, the splendid cousin of Ralegh's boyhood; of Lewis Stucley: "He was always inclined to be odd man out, and of late years, since his father lost money by one of my Virginian ventures, we have had little enough to say to each other; but as a boy, he had the finest way with grass-snakes that ever I knew." She heard of the small sister Meg, long since married and living near Exeter. But one figure came again and again upon the scene; the figure of a young soldier who had dreamed Ralegh's dream with him; his half-brother Humphrey.

"The first time that ever you and I met," Bess said presently, "at the bottom of Lady Sidney's garden, you told me about Humphrey. About——" She hesitated, searching back across the years for the exact words. "About his 'Discourse for a discovery of a New Passage to Cathay' that he had written with your aid. You were very angry, because the Queen had given the search to Sir Martin Frobisher, after all. But he never found it."

"No," Ralegh said. "It is still for the finding. . . . Two years we had to wait, before Humphrey won his letters patent from the Queen; not for the search, even then, but to colonise. But we both intended that the colony should make a base for the search when 'twas founded! I should have gone with him, but the Queen denied me. Well, he planted his colony in the New Found Land—and was drowned off the Azores on his homeward voyage, as you know."

"I am so sorry," Bess said after a moment. "You were very fond of him, were you not?"

"Very. He was a man easy to love, also he was one of the best and truest souls that ever I have known. He set down his statement of faith, in that Discourse that we concocted together, and he abode by it to the end." Ralegh's voice dropped, the words falling slowly as he quoted: "Therefore give me leave to live and die in this mind —that he is not worthy to live at all, that for fear, or danger of death, shunneth his country's service or his own honour. Seeing death is inevitable and the fame of virtue immortal."

Silence hung between them for a space, only the sea-song of the wind in the ilex leaves seemed to comment on the low-spoken words. The rain had ceased. A pale-winged night moth fluttered in through the window, and behind the dark mass of the ilex tree the sky was flushed with a hint of afterglow from the sun that had not shone all day. Into the hush stole a faint sound, dying away and strengthening again as the wind caught it; the drumming of hooves upon the road, casting a triple braid of sound across the waiting quiet.

"Some soul rides in haste," Ralegh said.

Nearer it came, and nearer yet—and stopped before the house. And as the rhythmic beat fell silent, Bess's heart took it up, racing with sudden apprehension.

Ralegh neither moved nor spoke, but his quietness had become that of a coiled spring. A little later there came a knocking on the parlour door, and Talbot the manservant entered. "This has just come for you, Sir Walter," he said; then as his master sprang up swearing, "Very urgent, the messenger said, or I'd not have troubled you, Sir."

It was almost dark in the room, but Bess saw the pale oblong of the packet as Ralegh took it from him, and knew past all doubt that she might bid goodbye to her three shining days and nights.

"Light a candle, you fool," Ralegh said, his fingers busy with the seal as the man stooped to kindle a spill at the sinking fire. Light sprang up from the tapers on the mantel, one—two—three long tongues of flame leaping a little raggedly in the draught, and the room started out of its obscurity. Ralegh crossed to the hearth, unfolding the crackling sheet as he did so. "Give the messenger some beer," he ordered; but he spoke automatically, his whole attention on the paper in his hand.

For a moment after the man had gone out, Bess sat rigid, staring at him, while the scent of musk and rosemary stole into the room from the melting candle wax. Then she started up and went to him. "Is it—Walter, what is it?"

"Now I wonder how a'devil he knew," Ralegh said, half to himself. Then he looked up, and she saw his eyes full of a dancing blue light at variance with the grim set of his mouth. He gave her the letter. "Look and see."

She had no need of the signature to tell her who was the sender. It was obviously written in haste, but even so, Robert Cecil's graceful Italian hand was unmistakable. "If this find you at Islington, as I pray God it may, return at once to Court," she read, "bringing with you your companion, whether she be Lady Ralegh or yet Mistress Throckmorton. A short while ago, the lady's brother, being up from Beddington, came to visit her, *since that she was detained by the Queen's pleasure from her three days' visit to that place;* whereas all knew that she had indeed set out for Beddington full three hours before he came, there having been no let or hindrance from the Queen to her visit. There have been no lack of wagging tongues, you may believe, to bring this to the ear of the Queen's Grace, nor was there lacking one to swear to having seen her ride away with a man (being come as a groom from her kinsman) who he had seen beforetime in your company. Make all speed back; an hour's delay will harden the Queen's anger by just so much. R.C."

She was still reading when Ralegh strode to the door and plucked it open, shouting "John! John Talbot, my boots and riding-cloak! Bid Peter bring round my horse, and the sorrel mare for Lady Ralegh as quickly as may be, and bid him be ready to ride with My Lady himself." The door crashed shut, and he swung back to Bess where she stood frozen before the hearth. "Sweet, you must rouse out your woman and make ready to ride. My old Peter goes with you; he is not known about the Court, and you may trust him to keep his mouth shut——"

She cut in breathlessly. "Walter, I do not understand—do you not ride with me?"

"I? If I return to the Queen now, it is farewell to my command of this venture against Spain! I am away to overtake this morning on the Plymouth road." He was kicking the fire into a last blaze as he spoke; he plucked the letter from her numb fingers, and stooping, thrust it into the flames. They burned with no red or yellow of the steadfast earth, those flames, but with the cold blue and green of shifting seas. Driftwood, Bess thought dully, watching; old ships' timbers, maybe, burning with the blue and green of distant seas.

"I am to go to the Queen—alone?"

"Yes." He was quite clear about it. "Hold the Queen in play, Bess—your woman's wit shall furnish you some tale to tell—any tale but the truth—ere you reach Westminster." He had his arms round her, crushing her against him, seemingly unaware of her lack of response. "Lie to the Queen, Bess, at least until I am beyond the reach of her recall."

Beyond the reach of the Queen's recall. And after that, she was free to face the Queen's wrath—alone. But he was not thinking at all of her, now; she knew that; even with his arms around her, he was reaching out to something beyond.

Suddenly it was as though she were looking down the long vista of years, through the many times that she would lose him to his dream, to the last time of all, on a grey autumn morning when the clocks were striking eight, and a headsman's axe flashed down in Old Palace Yard.

CHAPTER 6

ORLANDO FURIOSO

Bess lied to the Queen, lied and was not believed, and still refused to admit that she had been with the Captain of the Guard, let alone that she was married to him. She faced the towering fury of the Queen with a desperate courage that astonished her fellow Maids of Honour, and lied and lied, to gain Ralegh the time he needed;

while at the other side of England, Ralegh, on the point of sailing, was indignantly denying that he had ever had any dealings with Mistress Throckmorton, marital or otherwise.

It was all in vain. Ralegh was recalled by pinnace when the Fleet was already at sea, and once again Sir Martin Frobisher was given the command in his stead. There was one last horrific interview in which they faced together the lightnings of the Queen's rage, and then the Tower for both of them.

The Queen was nothing if not Old Harry's daughter.

For all that summer, they remained pent within the grim walls, despite all Ralegh's frantic efforts to get out. From the Tower, in the early days, he wrote to Cecil a most piteous appeal. "I leave to trouble you at this time, being become like a fish cast on dry land, gasping for breath with lame legs and lamer lungs," in the hope that it would be shown to the Queen, and that being shown, it would soften her heart. But Robin Cecil proved a less staunch friend than he had expected, since at the moment friendship with Ralegh was no way to the Queen's good graces; and the hot lag-end of August found them still prisoners, with no prospect of enlargement.

Ralegh spent his time in railing against his fate; in sending frantic messages to the Queen, protesting that the light of his world was gone out since Belphoebe turned her face from him; in raging up and down his prison like a wild thing caged, and reviling his friends when they came to console with him.

He sent no word to Bess, waiting while the weary days went by, in her own lodging in the house of the Head Gaoler. At first she was tortured by the fear that his silence was because he thought she had failed him; but in a little, she rid herself of that fear. He had failed her, yes; faced with the choice between them, he had chosen unhesitatingly to break faith with her that he might keep faith with his dream; but she was possessed of a broad enough charity to accept that without bitterness, though not without hurt; and she acquitted him of the injustice of holding her guilty for what happened. No, he sent no word simply because for the present, he had forgotten her. She realised that whatever the outcome of the present coil, he would spend much of his life forgetting her, and she would spend much of hers waiting until he remembered her again.

She got through the days somehow; she was allowed to exercise in the garden, pacing up and down the walks where the grey towers frowned down on roses and pinks that gave way presently to goodbye-summer. She had books and her embroidery; she was allowed to see Nicholas who was lodging in the City so as to be at hand. Nicholas who had come to her on her first day as a prisoner, half like a sack-clothed penitent, half like a very wrathful brother, saying, "Oh Bess, I would not have done such a thing for the world! I could tear myself to shreds when I think that it is all my fault: but how was I to know? Why did you not tell me, you *silly* wench? God's life, Bess, I think you might have told me what was in the wind!"

And Bess had said: "I longed to tell you—you do not know how much; but I feared to embroil you in the Queen's displeasure. Oh, that was coming sure enough; you did but hasten it, my dear."

Nicholas came almost every day, and since he had often been with Ralegh before he came to her, it was from him that she gained all her news of her husband. News of his wing-beating, his passionate loverlike letters to the Queen. "A veritable Orlando Furioso," said Nicholas. There was something faintly ridiculous about it all; but Bess knew that to Ralegh there was nothing ridiculous; and her heart ached for him—and a little, for herself.

On a day early in September, Nicholas burst upon her at an unusually early hour, obviously big with news which he could scarcely hold back until he had greeted her. "Bess, Oh Bess! Ralegh's ships have come in! They've taken two East India carracks, and brought them into Dartmouth! Ralegh is bating like a haggard hawk because he's mewed up here and cannot get to them!"

It was not the full and overwhelming vengeance for Sir Richard Grenville that his cousin had hoped for, but it was not to be sneezed at all the same. Already Sir John Borough, the Vice-Admiral of the Fleet had written exultantly to the Queen, that they had taken such a prize as never had been seen before. And now they rode at anchor under the guns of Dartmouth Castle, the *Santa Cruz* and the *Madre de Dios*, cut out from the Plate Fleet as sheep are cut out from a flock by the shepherd's dog, and towering many-decked like floating castles among the smaller, lighter craft of an English harbour.

The Queen was pleased. Royal commissioners were appointed to secure to her the lion's share of the prize, which she took to be her due; but quick as she was to act, the men of the West Country were quicker. Before the commissioners could lay a finger on the rich cargoes, a large part had disappeared, and more followed every hour, carried off by seamen and merchants, gentle and simple. The whole West Country gathered to the spoil like a flock of joyful ravens to a kill, and the Queen's commissioners were powerless to stop the looting.

Robert Cecil, sent down post-haste by the Privy Council, wrote to his father that every traveller he met on the road carried a bag that smelled of musk or amber. He descended on Dartmouth like a whirlwind, and the Queen's commissioners were only too thankful to shift the burden of responsibility on to his thin, crooked shoulders. He demanded to know where the missing treasure chests were hidden, and finding the people stubborn, remitted two innkeepers to gaol. That had some effect, but not much. He ransacked Dartmouth and Plymouth, bringing to light a good deal of booty under beds and up chimneys, including a large pot of musk and a bag of seed pearls. He intercepted letters from public-spirited citizens to their friends in London, bidding them come down without delay and promising to do what they could for them. But all this was of little real avail. "Fouler weather, more desperate ways, more obstinate people did I never meet with," he wrote home.

Word of all this trickled through to Ralegh in the Tower, and sent him into a fever of rage and frustration. To hear of the richest cargo that the world had ever seen, running through the hands of incompetent zanies, while he, who alone could have dealt with the situation, was mewed within stone walls at the other side of England, was enough to drive a man mad. He changed his tactics with the Queen; he ceased to write her the letters of a spurned lover, and instead, concentrated on convincing her that he and he alone could save her share of the *Madre de Dios* for her.

He was not alone in this belief, for unknown to him, Sir John Hawkins was even then writing to Burghley to the effect that no one but Ralegh could deal with the Devon and Cornish men looting the treasure carracks.

Early on the morning of September 16th, the Lieutenant of the Tower himself brought Bess the news that she was free. Ralegh's letters to the Queen, or Hawkins' to Burghley, or a combination of both, had borne fruit, and her husband was to be released immediately and sent down to Dartmouth, albeit with a Keeper. The Lieutenant was a courteous soul; he offered his felicitations, bowed over Bess's hand, and departed, twiddling a clove carnation.

When he had gone, Bess turned to the Head Gaoler's wife, who was with her, smiling a little uncertainly. "It is so long since I had my liberty, that I have forgot how to use it. What shall I do now?"

"If it were me, I'd wait," said her companion judicially. "I'd wait quietly here until my man came for me," and she bustled away to attend to her napery.

Left to herself, Bess did not summon her henchwoman, but herself gathered her few possessions together, and tied them in a cloak, that she might not keep Ralegh waiting when he came. That done, she went to the window, and stood looking out. She could glimpse trees above a grey rampart, trees turning dun and golden against a harebell sky, and a blue waft of bonfire smoke drifting across the morning.

Someone pushed open the door behind her, and she whirled about. "Walter!"—she began, and broke off. Nicholas stood in the doorway. She looked beyond him, but he was alone.

He came in, leaving the door wide. "Bess! I've but now heard the news!" He slid an arm round her and kissed her loudly. "You have your bundle ready? Good girl. We'll have you out of here in ten minutes."

Bess hesitated, uncertain. "Is Walter coming to me here, or am I to go to him?"

Nicholas, looking suddenly uncomfortable, said with false heartiness; "Ralegh bade me take you home to Beddington, and keep you there until he comes for you."

"But—am I not to see him before he goes?"

She was searching his face with eyes grown more shadowy than usual. He shook his head. "He is already gone. He was leaving as I arrived."

       .

So Bess rode down to Beddington with her brother, and was greeted with worried kindness by her Uncle Francis Carew. She slipped into her usual place there; she rode hawking with Nicholas and their Uncle, helped the housekeeper in the still-room, sat over her embroidery or played the virginals in the evening. Save for Joan's ceaseless scolding, it was as though the ride to Islington had never been; as though Ralegh had never stood at his stairfoot, looking up and telling her "I have been waiting for that all my life —to see you come downstairs with a rose in your girdle."

She was waiting now.

It was well into the next month before any further word of Ralegh came to her; and then, being told by a servant that there was a gentleman wanting speech with her, who had come a long way seemingly, she hurried to the gallery, where the stranger had been left, and found a thick-set man standing by the table, lightly fingering over a posy of autumn violets in a crystal cup which she had set there earlier in the day.

He wore a plain, dark doublet and hose, old, but well cut, and a case of rapiers at his hip; and it was not until he heard her step and looked up, that she recognised Lawrence Kemys; and the sick disappointment that had swept over her as she realised that it was not Ralegh ebbed a little.

"These are pretty," he said, with a final touch to the dark petals, and came to bow over her hand. "Lady Ralegh."

"They smell less sweet than in the spring," Bess said. "You bring me a letter from my husband, Captain Kemys?"

He flushed, suddenly ill at ease, as Nicholas had been. "I—Not exactly. He had no time to write one."

"Oh," said Bess; and another small bud of hope died in her. "He sent me some message by you instead?"

"A message—yes." Lawrence Kemys recovered himself at once, but for one instant he had looked completely blank; and the blankness told Bess all too plainly that Ralegh had sent no message, had probably not even known that his Captain intended coming here. The man had come in the kindness of his heart, to bring her word of her husband, not word from him.

She smiled into his troubled face consolingly. "He has been so very busy.   You have been down to Dartmouth, then? How did that come about?"

He returned her smile, obviously thankful for the change of subject. "Sir Walter sent me word that he needed a man to his back, one who was not of the venture, to act as his Lieutenant, as 'twere. So I left the *Crane* to herself awhile, and posted down to the West after him, and now I am on my way back."

They were seated by this time, she in a high-backed chair, he in the window-seat, and she looked up at him, seeing his pleasant, guileless face dark against the sunlight of the autumn afternoon. "This is well off your direct road to Deptford; have you turned so far out of your way, to bring me news?"

"I thought you would be glad of news."

"That was very kind of you," Bess said. "How is he?"

"Working like a man possessed of the devil. You will know what like he is, when he has a venture on his hands, or an idea in his head. And just now the idea in his head is to save every seed pearl and drop of musk that is humanly or inhumanly possible, out of the West Indies cargo—above all, to save the Queen's share for her."

"The Queen's share, yes, that before all," Bess said. "And how does the work go?"

"Well enough," Kemys told her. "He has every seaman in the West eating out of his hand. I did not see his first coming among them, but those who did, told me that the men who had been acting like bloody Barbary corsairs came tossing up their bonnets and shouting round him as they had been little lads out of school." He sat silent a moment, and then added thoughtfully: "That is a passing strange thing about Sir Walter; he is not what you could call popular—not the people's darling, as My Lord of Essex——" Bess appreciated the understatement, knowing well that she had married one of the best hated men in England. "But where West Country folk—West Country seamen above all—are concerned, he has but to whistle, and they are his, body and soul!"

"He is a West Countryman and a seaman himself," Bess suggested.

The other shook his head. "So was Sir Richard Grenville, so are Drake and Hawkins, but none of them could count the whole West as his demesne, and every man who goes down to the sea from Seaton round to Minehead for his liegeman."

Bess said nothing, but warmed to her husband's Captain still further.

Kemys gave a reflective chuckle. "Sir Robert Cecil would have had him keep his gaoler in the background, thinking it might harm his prestige if it were seen that he was not yet wholly free. But Sir Walter knew better than that. He kept the man well to the fore, all the while, and when any congratulated him on his liberty, he shook his head and said that he was still the Queen of England's poor prisoner. He—I think he enjoyed that very much."

Their eyes met in complete understanding. Both of them knew and loved Ralegh. "I am very sure he did," Bess said, with the sudden laughter twitching at the corners of her mouth. "But you speak of all this as in the past. Has he finished that which he went to do?"

"Very near. It is so, that I am on my way back."

"And will he be coming back soon, too?"

"Any day. I should think any day; but one can never count one's chickens with Sir Walter."

They sat talking for a while, until Lawrence Kemys got up, saying that he must be on his road. Remembrance of her duties as a hostess woke belatedly in Bess, and she prayed him to stay to supper; at least to drink a cup of wine before he went. He accepted the stirrup cup, but refused supper, saying that he wished to be in Deptford before dark. Heaven alone knew what those fools at the Dockyard had done to the *Crane* in his absence. He drank to her happiness, took a grave and courteous leave of her, and departed.

Three days later, Bess came down the great staircase to find Ralegh shedding a wet riding-cloak in the hall.

She had been at the back of the house, and had heard no bustle of arrival to warn her of his coming, and at sight of him her heart lurched into her throat, and began to race, wildly, frantically, like something caged and battering for freedom in her breast. She checked an instant, and he looked up and saw her, flung his cloak to the old steward who stood by, and came striding to the foot of the stairs.

"Bess!" he cried. "Bess, my heart!" and held up his arms to her.

She had thought so much about the manner of their next meeting. She had resolved to be so careful, to wait to be claimed, making no claim herself; but at sight of him, all that was forgotten, and she gathered her wide skirts, and ran down the last flight to him like a child running home.

Ralegh caught and kissed her, loudly and possessively, sublimely indifferent to the presence of the steward and several other members of the household who were by this time appearing on the scene. She clung to him, half crying with the blessed sense of sanctuary which his nearness brought her, repeating his name over and over again. "Walter! Oh Walter!"

Suddenly he held her off a little, looking with quick concern into her face. "Bess, you have grown thinner than ever! I feel as though my hands would meet through you, and you are all eyes. What have you done to yourself?"

"It has been so long—so long—and no word from you all the while," Bess said.

He was puzzled. "Did you want me to send you word? I was busy, and really there was little enough to tell—save that I love you."

"You might even have told me that."

His voice shot up in ludicrous indignation. "God's life, woman, you *know* I love you! .   And now what are you laughing at?"

"You," said Bess, dissolving into soft, helpless mirth.

He stared with puckered brows at this beloved, incomprehensible woman who appeared to find him funny. "But I do," he said.

CHAPTER 7

THE CROCK OF GOLD

In the end, the treasure carracks yielded £80,000 to the Queen, lesser profits to the other shareholders, and to Ralegh himself a clear loss. The Queen's share gained him his freedom, but not his return to grace. And while Robin Devereux, having rid himself as far as might be, of his own wife, had been recalled from Navarre's train and restored to the full favour of Belphoebe, Ralegh retired with Bess, to Sherborne.

It was a soft, blustery autumn afternoon when Bess first saw Sherborne; a day of drifting skies, and distances deeply blue as bittersweet flowers. But even on that grey day, warmth seemed to linger in the golden stones of the castle, built to be his fortress palace by Bishop Roger, five hundred years before; and all around it, the gently rolling parkland stretched away down the quiet Blackmore Vale. The peace of the place seemed to hold out its arms to her. "This is a happy place," she thought, and did not wonder that Ralegh loved it.

Ralegh was like a boy on the first day of the holidays, bright-eyed and eager, full of questions and greetings for every member of the assembled household; and when the evening meal was scarcely over, he swept Bess off to explore her realm, upstairs and down through the old castle, from the Keep-turret to the little Norman Chapel that seemed made for defence, rather than worship, and back at last to the lower chamber of the Keep, which was now the living room, where wide windows—jewelled Tudor windows —gave to the place something of the air of a grim old Norman knight decked out in the silks and damascening of the seventh Henry.

"Do you wonder at the love I have for it?" Ralegh asked her, laying a hand against one of the squat columns that upheld the groined roof, as though it were a sentient thing. "Ever since I saw it from the road yonder, as I rode up to London for the first time, it has been the home of my heart, and since that day I have never passed it by, but it pulled at my heartstrings. I have loved every curve of the encircling hills, every shadow of a tree on the grass for so long a time that I can scarce believe it is but nine months since it came to me."

"Since the Queen gave it to you," Bess said. "Walter, will you ever regret all that you have lost by me? Will you ever find the price you paid for me too high?"

"By God's grace, I shall win all back, one day," Ralegh said. "But whether I do or no, you are beyond all price to me, Bess."

And she was content.

But the old castle was not, after all, to be her home and Ralegh's very long. Save for the Tudor windows, Sherborne was much as Bishop Roger had left it, but in considerably worse repair; and even in good repair, a Norman castle scarcely reached the standard of comfort of Ralegh's and Bess's day. There was no privacy, and the domestic arrangements were deplorable. There was nowhere to house a guest, certainly nowhere to put the children that might presently need house room. So not many weeks after that first home-coming, a site on the far side of the deer park had been chosen, and workmen were digging the foundations of a new house.

"A new house for you, and for me," Ralegh said. "New to us as the first morning of God's creation! A light, shining house, with wide windows to catch the sun. And you shall have your bower painted in the new fashion, with vines and foxgloves and passion-flowers on its walls, so that it will be always summer for you, even when the snow comes blowing down the wind."

So Sherborne Lodge began to rise from its foundations, and while it was a-building, life ran gently for Ralegh and Bess. They watched the progress of the house, and planned the garden; here was to be the herber and the orchard, here a nut alley, here smooth lawns in the curve of the old lime avenue. Ralegh ran the estate with the help of John Meeres, his steward; and from time to time departed to visit his other estates, or on his yearly tour of the Stannery Courts or some business of the West Country Militia.

Occasionally Ralegh's affairs took them up to Westminster, where they lodged themselves in Durham House, a cloud-cuckoo-land castle of many turrets, inadequate drains and defective chimneys, in which poor Bess found it almost impossible to housekeep at all. They were cut off from the Court, but not from their old friends, and the house was seldom quite empty of company; Ralegh's kinsman Sir George Carew; the Pembroke family; rather surprisingly, Robin Cecil and his wife—for Cecil's failure to stand by Ralegh over his marriage had slipped into the background, forgotten by both men with what at first seemed to Bess surprising ease. But in a little while she found that she herself was forgetting also, returning to the old friendship as though the chilling interlude had never been. She liked to see Robin Cecil with his Bess, (always it was "Your Bess" and "My Bess" when the two men spoke to each other of their wives), for with her, he was a different man from the faintly sinister Secretary of State whom the English called "Robert the Hunchback" and the French "Monsieur le Bossu"; a man with a gift for laughter, and quiet eyes.

At Durham House, Ralegh was happiest in his study, a turret room high among the stars and the winds of heaven, with the Thames flowing far below its windows. There he wrote a few winged and lovely verses—not the gracefully artificial verse that had flowed so easily from his pen in his early years, for his muse came upon him ever more rarely, these days, and his poetry was a harsher, a brighter and an infinitely better thing that cost him something in the making—there he talked with his oddly assorted friends. Spenser had come there in the old days before Ireland became his home; and Kit Marlowe, dead this year and more in a tavern brawl at Deptford; and Philip Sidney and many more. Richard Hakluyt came now, always full of the latest voyage of discovery; and young poets and playwrights such as Ben Jonson, picked up over the Canary

wine at the Mermaid Tavern, to argue the night away, puffing at
their pipes until the room dissolved in a dun fog of tobacco smoke.
Or again, it might be the wizard Earl of Northumberland, or Dr.
Hariot the Mathematician, or John Dee the Astrologer and Alchemist. And when John Dee was there, Bess knew that Ralegh would
most likely not come to bed at all, for the two of them would sit
pondering Rosicrucian Mysteries, or discussing perspective glasses
or his great map of Atlantis until dawn.

Most of these odd friends of Ralegh's were often at Sherborne
also, and the School of Night sat in the old chapel there almost as
often as at Durham House, debating amid the wreathing tobacco
smoke such questions as the exact nature of the human soul.

At Sherborne, Bess had made a still-room out of one of the
groined store chambers and gradually her shelves were filling; a
hound bitch had puppies, and the new flamed and feathered tulips
came into flower, and these were the things that contented her. On
Sundays she walked to the Abbey with Ralegh, carrying her posy
of bee-balm and bergomot, while he carried the family Prayer
Book. She loved those Sunday mornings, kneeling beside Ralegh
in the little chapel of St. Catherine. She loved the glimpse of the
choir, with its columns springing fountain-wise from floor to arched
and jewelled roof, like prayers caught in golden stone as they leapt
heavenward. People said that Ralegh had no God, but that was not
true; he was an explorer, not an atheist, Bess knew that. But she
knew also that because he was so much an explorer, the services in
the Abbey had little meaning for him, and she was grateful for the
willingness with which he came with her, Sunday after Sunday.

It was all very peaceful.

But under the peaceful surface of life there were harsher currents
setting; for as the months went by, Ralegh became filled with a
growing fret, and poor Bess, knowing it, was powerless to help
him, and so lost her own contentment. From the first, he was constantly striving to win back the Queen's favour, less for its own sake
than because it might yet—though it had never done so before—
enable him to follow his dream. There were always seamen and
explorers at Sherborne or Durham House, wherever Ralegh was.
His study table was for ever littered with maps and charts, and for
ever the centre of report and discussion of foreign lands and un-
explored seaways, and as time went by the tide of these discussions set

ever more strongly Westward. Ralegh's mind was becoming increasingly full of Guiana. To him, as to the rest of his day and kind,
the land between the headwaters of the Orinoco and the Amazon
was a Promised Land. Many before him had set out to find it, and
failing, had generally paid for the failure with their lives; but where
many had failed, one more might yet succeed. Ralegh had been
only a few months married when he sent out Jacob Whiddon, one
of his Captains, to reconnoitre the Orinoco, and in due course the
reconnaissance party returned with glowing accounts of the country
and its richness, and reports of Manoa, that the Spaniards called El
Dorado, the Place of Gold; a city of which even the streets were
paved like the City of God. The search for El Dorado appealed to
Ralegh at many levels, for a colourful exploit that might recapture
the Queen's favour, for the fascination of exploring new lands and
seeing new and curious things, for the riches that it would yield to
its discoverer. (Yet his desire for the gold of El Dorado had in it
some almost mystical quality, which Bess guessed at but could not
understand; it was poet's gold, alchemist's gold, the Flower of the
Sun, not the mere stuff of buying and selling.) Above all, convinced
of the dire necessity that England should have possessions in the
New World, to combat the growing strength of Spain; new
Englands linked to the old one, where men for whom there was no
opening at home could make a new life; new Englands to stand
shoulder to shoulder with her in time of danger, and be a market
for her woollen goods and a source of raw materials, he hoped that
the bright goal of El Dorado, if he could uncover it, might draw
men Westward in good earnest. The impetus was desperately
needed; so little had been accomplished, so tragically little, since he
sat with Bess in the ditch at the bottom of Lady Sidney's garden.

So as the second winter of her marriage went by, Bess grew more
and more unhappy. It was not that she wanted to keep him tied to
her; let him go down to the sea and seek out fresh lands for his
empire, only not this obsession with the West, with El Dorado that
had been the death of so many men. The thing became a nightmare,
growing in her mind to be a tangible enemy striving to draw her
love from her. She would wake in the mornings and find Ralegh
sleeping quietly beside her, the vital warmth of his body against
hers, and wonder where his spirit was; if it had gone Westward to
his land of golden cities and great rivers and singing trees, and be

almost sick with a mingling of fear and jealousy. By that time she was carrying Ralegh's child, which perhaps had more than she guessed to do with the hideous fears and fancies that crowded upon her that winter.

In February, Ralegh went up to Westminster again; a mere flying business visit, and Bess did not accompany him, being four months gone with the baby. He returned to her unheralded, on an evening when the gutters spouted and the courtyard cobbles were a-swim; but for Bess, it was as though the sun came through. She was a naturally happy person, and the happiness in her, however low it sank, was always there, ready at a slight incident to leap up and fill her whole being. This evening, when supper had been cleared, and she and Ralegh were alone in the living-place, save for a couple of setters asleep before the fire, she was happier than she had been for months. Outside, the rain swished by, spattering against the glass, but in here there was firelight and taper-light, warmth and safety; and Ralegh, safely returned to her from the dark world outside, seated on the other side of the hearth, puffing contentedly at his pipe. For a little while she was free of her fear.

But presently Ralegh sprang up, reached a candle from the smoke-hood, and crossing to the chest which stood beside his great writing table, opened it and began to take out papers, scanning each briefly, and laying it on the table beside him. For a few minutes Bess continued to stitch at the baby's cap she was making; then she looked up, her needle poised. "Is it the Militia papers? Leave them until the morning, Walter."

Ralegh answered her without raising his eyes from the paper he held. "No. These are some papers for Robert Cecil—Jacob Whiddon's reports and suchlike." He added the paper to those on the table, his face suddenly kindling in the way she knew so well. "He thinks at last that he may possibly be able to help me to my letters patent!"

Bess jabbed her needle into her sewing, and through it into her finger, and a bright speck of crimson stained the cambric. She gave a little cry.

Ralegh looked up with a bright abstracted eye. "Hmm?"

"I—have pricked my finger," Bess said. She felt sick, and her hands were shaking so that she laid down the scrap of sewing, and gripped them together in her lap.

"Poor sweeting," said Ralegh with perfunctory sympathy, and returned to the task in hand. He did not even notice her lack of response to his news.

After a few moments, her voice once more under control, Bess said: "Walter, if you will be sending someone with those papers, will you add a packet for me? I promised Elizabeth Cecil some recipes for rose water and green ginger conserve, and I forgot to send them up with you."

So next day when a groom set out for Westminster, he carried, beside the Guiana papers, a packet addressed in Bess's hand to Lady Cecil. But inside it, between the recipes for rose water and green ginger conserve, lay a letter to Cecil, begging him for old friendship's sake, to dissuade Ralegh from his wild project, and employ him, if, as it seemed, he must go to sea, "In sure waters toward the East, rather than help him forward toward the Sunset."

A wild March day came, a day when rain and sunshine were sharp as a stiletto, and the crocuses in the new garden were blowing like gold and purple flame in the wind. For Ralegh, determined that the house should not stand naked in its first years, as so many new houses did, had planted the further parts of the garden already. They had been looking over the house which was nearing completion, and now, leaving the busy workmen, and the harassed master builder who Ralegh had been reducing to apologetic pulp over some question of the staircase, they had wandered out to see how the garden did.

"Presently," Ralegh said, "we will have some yellow wallflowers seedlings over from Ireland. I brought the first plants home from the Azores and planted them at Youghal, but they are wasted in that lost land; and they have the sweetest scent of all, in the springtime." He bent to free a rush-daffodil that had failed to burst the brown membrane over its head, with deft and gentle fingers.

"This is going to be a most lovely garden," Bess said softly, watching him.

"As fair as we, with God's help, can make it," Ralegh said. "When Cecil gains me my letters patent, I shall bring back flowers from the New World for it—flowers and trees and all manner of curious growing things; and herbs for your herb garden, Bess."

The New World! Always the New World, as though the old world here at Sherborne on such a morning, was not fair enough to break any heart. She said quickly, a little too quickly: "You are very sure of Robin Cecil's success in the matter."

"Yes," Ralegh said. "Cecil is very near to the Queen in these days." He turned to look at her, for there had been something unusual in her voice. It must have been in her face also, for after a moment he asked abruptly, "Why? Bess, why did you say that?"

She did not answer, and he reached out and caught her by the shoulders. His hands were not gentle now; they bit into her flesh through the stuff of her cloak, and his face was as hard as his hands. "Why did you say that, Bess? What did you mean?"

"Please, Walter—you are hurting me."

His hands gentled instantly, but he repeated his question mercilessly. "Tell me what you meant. You know something. You *shall* tell me, Bess."

Bess drew a sobbing breath, and told him, with the desperate defiance of a child confessing some wickedness that it refuses to be sorry for. "Robin Cecil will not get you your letters patent, because I sent him a letter with those recipes for Elizabeth—because I begged him, if you must go to sea, at least not to help you towards the Sunset!"

For an instant she saw such blazing anger in his eyes as seemed to scorch and shrivel her very soul; then it was gone, and the brilliant blue eyes staring into hers were only puzzled. He let his hands slip from her shoulders. "But why, Bess? Is it that you would not have me leave you before your time? If I gained my commission tomorrow, I would not go until after the imp is born, you know that."

Bess gulped and shook her head.

"Then what is it, Bess?"

"If it were another woman," she burst out, "if only it were another woman, I could fight it; but it is not—and I can't, I can't."

There was a long silence, and then Ralegh said very quietly: "No, you can't." He drew her to him, and put back her hood. Her face was wet with rain and tears, and he kissed it, and stood holding her in the curve of his arm. "Sweetheart, I have never loved any woman but you, and I never shall. I love you quite enough to lay down my life for you if the need arose; but you must not try to come between me and my own soul."

She stood silent in the curve of his arm, resting against his shoulder as though she were very tired .She was accepting defeat, absolute and final. It was very peaceful to stop fighting.

Then Ralegh turned her round, saying with a sudden quick pleasure as he did so. "Look, Bess! Have you ever seen so glorious a rainbow as that?"

The rain squall that had been beating about them a few minutes ago had sped on before a burst of acid-yellow sunlight, and against the blue-black storm cloud shone a dazzling arc of colour. One end rested on the high rim of the Vale, and the other, sinking lower even as they watched, came to rest like a benediction among the hanging woods that were called Jerusalem. For a moment it seemed as though the whole world was holding its breath for fear of breaking the circle of perfection; nothing moved; even the wind had dropped away. Then a small figure appeared from behind a clump of bushes, a little square figure in a brown doublet, heading at a purposeful trot towards the foot of the rainbow.

"Oh look, Bess," Ralegh said softly. "It is Meeres' little lad— going to look for a crock of gold!"

"A crock of gold," Bess thought. "El Dorado. But it is the same thing; this dream, this Unattainable, that men search for all their lives."

The little figure was growing smaller and smaller in the distance, and already it seemed to her that the rainbow was less brilliant than it had been. With an instinctive unwillingness to see the brightness fade and the little boy deserted by his dream, she turned from it to Ralegh. "I will write again to Robin Cecil," she said.

His mouth quirked into a smile under the clipped beard. "There is no need for that. Cecil is very fond of you; but he'll not lift a finger to keep me back from my venturing, for all your tears and prayers, my sweet Bess."

.   .   .   .   .   .

The new house was finished, a small, pleasant house, many-windowed and shining. Much loving care had gone into the making of it, from the cooking arrangements to the painted walls of Lady Ralegh's bower, where on a painted trellis, roses and leopard lilies and climbing passion-flowers made a summer that would last, as Ralegh had promised, when snow came blowing down the wind.

It was July now; a wild night that seemed full of flying wings, as the southerly gale came beating up from the Channel. And in his new and shining study, Ralegh was pacing restlessly up and down. There had been a sea-coal fire on the hearth, but he had let it die down; several candles on the mantel guttered wildly, thick rolls of wax running down and filling the cups of the candlesticks, for he had forgotten to snuff them. Still he walked, up and down, up and down; and after a while the old setter who had been sleeping before the fire, rose and walked with him, up and down.

Presently he halted by the writing table, and took up for the dozenth time an official-seeming document that lay there. He snuffed one of the candles now guttering into a pool of molten wax, and held the document to the light, reading it again, as though he did not already know it by heart; feasting his eyes on every word of it, on the fat crimson seal and the flashing signature of Elizabeth with the final flourish that bent itself into a tiny arabesque, noting for the dozenth time, with sardonic humour, the pointed omission of the words "Trusty and Well Beloved". So he was not yet forgiven. Well, Rome was not built in a day.

He refolded the document and slipped it crackling into the breast of his doublet, then returned to his pacing, still accompanied by the mutely protesting dog. Outside, the summer gale hurled itself upon the new walls as though striving to destroy them, and the rain slashed and rattled at the windows, drowning all sound from the rest of the house. Up and down, up and down, the old setter plodding at his heels.

The candles had guttered out one by one, and the first sodden pallor of the gale-rent dawn was stealing in at the windows, when the wind dropped an instant; and in the trough of the quiet between gust and gust, Ralegh heard the thin, outraged wailing of a new-born baby. The setter heard it too, and raised his head, whining softly, as his Master strode to the door and jerked it open.

A short while later, upstairs in the big bedchamber that was still strange to her, Bess was pitting her will against Joan and the fat midwife, who wanted to take from her the tiny, new-washed, curiously living thing that they had put into her arms only a few moments before.

"No. He is mine," she said.

"Of course he is yours, the blessed lamb," said the midwife in motherly tones, "but you must let me take him down to his Daddy. You want his Daddy to see him, now don't you?"

"His Daddy must come and see him here. He must come now," Bess said.

"Presently, presently, my duck. Do you take another sup of your cordial and have a little sleep first."

"You'd a deal better, My Lady. Come along now." Joan added her voice to that of the midwife, with less of cajolery and more of command.

Lying blessedly flat in the great bed, Bess defied them. She would not take another sup of her cordial, she would certainly not go to sleep, until they let her husband in to her. Utterly spent as she was, she still possessed reserves of quiet obstinacy against which stronger wills than Joan and the midwife had broken before now.

Finally an expressive glance passed between the two older women, and Joan, with a parting shot of "Stubborn as a mule you always were, My Lady, for all your pretty soft way with you, and stubborn as a mule you'll be to your dying day!" rustled out of the room. Bess lay with her eyes fixed on the door. Voices sounded beyond it, and it opened again so quickly that she knew her husband had been waiting just outside, and he appeared on the threshold. The midwife sidled past him into the gallery, admonishing him wheezily as she did so, "'Tis but for a minute, mind; and don't you go for to tire the poor blessed dear. You men, you don't know——"

But Ralegh had shut the door on her, and come striding across to the bed. "Bess," he said, "Oh, my Bess."

Bess put back the soft fold of the shawl from the little head in the curve of her arm. The baby was asleep now, its rage at being born all spent. It was red and rumpled, but rather less so than most new-born babies, with a head of black down, and a mouth like a three-cornered poppy. It was altogether enchanting.

"Here's a little son to go adventuring with you, one day," she said.

Ralegh slipped to his knees beside the bed, one arm across her body so that both she and the babe were within the curve of it. His hand stole up to caress with light finger tips, her bare shoulder where the shift had fallen back. "Dear Bess," he said. And she saw in the fading candle-light that his face, bent over the two of them, was almost devout.

A wild gust of wind swooped against the house out of the greying sky, driving smoke and sparks from the fire, hurling the hissing

rain against the windows, making the candles gutter so that all the
room was filled with a dancing turmoil. Ralegh's arm bent more
closely round his wife and son as if to hold them safe; and Bess
turned a little on her goose-down pillow, to smile at him. "He has
chosen a wild night for his coming," she said.

"He is come in a happy time!" Ralegh raised his head to return
her smile, his eyes suddenly blazing blue. "I received my letters
patent from the Queen, a few hours ago!"

CHAPTER 8

"FORTUNE MY FOE"

Ralegh got his Captains together and set about gathering his crews;
and in February of the following year, the little fleet of five vessels
set sail from Dartmouth, and Bess was left to rear her small son and
wait through the lonely months until they came back again—if
they ever did.

They returned at last, beating up channel in a full gale, to drop
anchor in Dartmouth Harbour, and by mid-November, after a brief
and tempestuous descent on Sherborne, Ralegh was in London.

Two or three days later, in the high turret room at Durham
House where he had made his study, he stood facing the Secretary
of State across a shining litter of ore and spar-fragments on the
writing table. "Madre del Oro, the Spaniards call it," Ralegh was
saying. "Mother of Gold. Westwoods of Wood Street have found
it to contain gold at the rate of 1,200 lb. a ton. So much for that
damned half-wit at the Mint who has been bruiting it abroad that
Sir Walter Ralegh has brought back nought but Fool's Gold from
the New World!—Yellow dross that I learned to know at a glance
in my own West Country when I was scarce breeched."

Cecil, seated beside the table, one hand playing with the shining
quartz, raised his eyes to the other's face. "Yet an officer of the Mint
is not much given to the making of groundless statements. Was this
one completely without foundation?"

"No," Ralegh said. "That's the damnable part of it." From the
litter on the table he picked out two or three fragments, thrust them

under Cecil's nose, and cast them back with a little clatter among
the rest. "There is his foundation. . . . While we lay at Trinidad,
certain natives told us of a ruined mine that they believed to be gold.
I sent men to bring in stones from it for trial; but it was Marcasite
after all. I told them that it was so, but some of them mistrusted my
judgment, and kept their shining stuff and showed it to the assayers
in Dartmouth on our return. Hence the mischief."

"So." The slender hand had taken up one of the pieces of Marcasite, and was turning it over and over. "How much does it mean
to you, this mischief?"

"To me, merely that a few thousand fools will count me of their
number; but to England—to the future of England in the New
World, it may be deadly."

He was pacing up and down, flinging his words now over this
shoulder, now over that, to the quiet man who sat toying with a
scrap of Marcasite. "If the gold that we brought from Guiana be
but Fool's Gold, how shall it seem to others that our report is to be
trusted in anything beside? How shall it seem to them worth while
to follow our lead? And I tell you, Cecil, that whatsoever prince
possesses the Empire of Guiana will be the greatest in the world;
and if Spain enjoy it, she will become irresistible thereby."

"Tell the Queen that."

Ralegh made a small helpless gesture. "The Queen will not
receive me, nor pay any heed to my letters."

"If you could but have come to her Presence Chamber dangling
the golden keys of El Dorado . . ." Cecil murmured. Their eyes
met. They had few illusions about the Queen.

Ralegh said defiantly: "I did not find El Dorado. The season was
over late; it lies six hundred miles further from the coast than
Whiddon supposed, and there are pitfalls on the way, of which he
know nothing. *But it is there!* I have seen gold that came from it,
soft red gold with the power of the sun in its substance! Soon the
Dons will find the way—God knows they seek it hard enough—
and then there will be no more gold in El Dorado. But if we can
but find it first——"

Cecil's voice slid silkenly into the harangue. "Then there will be
no more gold in El Dorado."

Ralegh checked an instant, and surveyed the Secretary of State
with brows twitched to meeting point above his nose, then

returned to his pacing. "I was not thinking in terms of piracy. Guiana is rich in more than gold, even throughout those parts that I have seen with my own eyes. For colonising, the open land has no equal. Therefore I have held my hand from easy riches, and the hands of my men also, which was something harder. There is neither tomb nor temple rifled nor woman raped because of us, in all Guiana, though the tombs and temples are as rich in gold and the women full as comely as any in Peru or Darien. I could have had wealth beyond even my wants today, but I took them not, for I would not do that which might jeopardise the Queen's Empire in the New World. So from this venture, for the Queen's sake, I have brought back debts to hang round my neck for years to come, and a palm full of quaintly coloured stones. . . . You are a collector of precious stones, are you not—it might interest you to see them." He thrust a hand into the breast of his doublet, brought out a small wash-leather bag, and spilled half a dozen uncut gems among the quartz. "This, I am told, is a sapphire; but this, I like better—this one, hot hearted like a ruby, I shall have made into an eardrop for my Bess. Well cut, and set around with pearls it will become her as the red spot becomes the cowslip." His manner had gentled for the moment, but as he cast the jewel back on to the table it exploded once more into blazing vehemence. "But how in God's sweet name shall anything be brought to birth if no man follow my lead, and the Queen refuse even to see me?"

Cecil did not answer at once. He had left the gold ore and was fingering the gems. "This is undoubtedly a sapphire, though not of the first water. Why trouble to bring back this piece of rose quartz among gems of so much greater value?"

Ralegh made an impatient gesture. "For the merest whim, because I had already a piece the brother to it but curiously worked." He fished again in his doublet, and brought out a piece of rose quartz not much larger than a bean. "This was given to me when I was a lad, and I have carried it ever since."

Cecil took it from him and turned it over, and so came upon the carved mask on the other side. For a long moment he looked at the thing in silence. "It is not often that one holds in one's hands the seed of a dream," he said at last; and handed it back. "For me, my cut gems are enough. Dreams are uncomfortable travelling companions."

"Cecil," Ralegh said abruptly. "Four years since, when men were blowing upon my kinsman Richard's name, I made and published him a defence, and I think that it served its purpose none so ill. If now I were to make and publish a report of Guiana, think you that it might serve some purpose also?"

The other hesitated. "I—am not sure," he said slowly, after a moment; then he sat forward as though making up his mind. "But I believe that it is worth the trial. . . . Aye, write your report of Guiana, but do not be too long in the writing of it, for there may be other work for you in the spring."

Ralegh's head whipped up. "What work?"

"Another Armada to be dealt with," Cecil said.

. . . .

As it turned out, that work was upon him long before spring. There was a plan afoot to strike Spain at her main port of Cadiz and so prevent the sailing of the new Armada, and by the turn of the year, Ralegh was in it up to his arrogant eyebrows; for though he might be in disgrace at Court, his powers as a leader were too well proved for him to be left out of such a venture. He sat at Council tables with the Earl of Essex, keeping a kind of working truce with the reigning favourite. He delved into armament and store lists, put his own vessels in fighting trim, and gathered others; listened to reports brought in by spies, and rode wildly between London and the West Country all that winter. And whenever he had an hour to himself, he returned to his Discovery of Guiana. "The deer crossing in every path," he wrote, "the birds toward evening singing in every tree with a thousand several tunes, cranes and herons of white and crimson and carnation perching on the river's side, the air fresh with a gentle easterly wind, and every stone that we stooped to pick up promised either gold or silver by its complexion."

He finished it, sitting up into the grey hours of a March morning to do so; and almost before the ink was dry on the last words was with his ships at Mile End.

The squadron was gathering in London River. All down the Limehurst Reach, Bess, who had come to join him, could see them from the window of the waterside inn where she was lodged; great ships riding at anchor, their masts and spars and spiderweb of rigging rising against the spring-flushed woods of the Surrey shore; small craft water-beetling hither and yon among them; and the never ceasing shift and flow and hurry of London River running to the sea.

Sometimes Ralegh took her with him, out to the *Warspite*, his flagship; and then she saw an aspect of her husband that she had not seen before, being tied to Sherborne and Little Watt when the Guiana venture was forming: Ralegh complete and in his own element, among ships and seamen, with a deck beneath his feet.

He showed her his ship with the pride of a boy. He presented to her his officers; it seemed strange to miss from among them Lawrence Kemys, who had been sent off on the old quest earlier in the year, and find in his place as Ralegh's Captain a piratical individual by the name of William King. He sent for the Master Gunner to demonstrate for her the use of the culverin in the waist. Presently he took her to the State Cabin, and bade her wait for him, and then went flying off in a cock-boat about the crowding business of the squadron. And Bess sat quietly, listening to all the strange sounds about her, waiting to be claimed. Once he sent her brother Arthur in his stead. Nicholas was fully occupied just then in getting himself wed to a flirtatious chit of fifteen, but Arthur, whom she had scarcely seen since her marriage, had most unexpectedly come south to put his sword at Ralegh's service. Once, he forgot about her altogether, and Sir Allen Apsley, a young gentleman of the venture, found her long afterwards, still waiting, and ordered away the jolly-boat since the Admiral's barge was gone, and sent her ashore. And climbing the stairs to her chamber, she heard Ralegh's voice from the big room where the Fleet Councils were held. And later, when he came to bed, he did not even remember that he had forgotten her.

. . . .

On the evening of June 1st the citizens of Plymouth gathered to see the greatest fleet that England had ever known lying at anchor in the Sound, and pointed out to each other the *Repulse*, ablaze with lights from stem to stern, where the Earl of Essex was entertaining to dinner the Admirals and Captains of the Fleet. And before dawn they had weighed anchor and slipped out on the morning tide. At the head of the first squadron, the Earl of Essex in *Repulse*, leading his Fleet to sea; Effingham, in *Ark Royal*, Tom Howard in *Mer-honour*; Ralegh in *Warspite*, leading the fourth squadron; and the shore lights of Plymouth fading into the mists astern, and the lilt of a ship's fiddle stealing back down the long line of the Fleet.

And then only silence, where the Cadiz Fleet had been; silence, and the long waiting.

Three weeks went by, and a morning came like any other fine summer morning. And at Sherborne, Bess sat under the lime trees in the early sunshine, and watched Little Watt scuttling among the pinks of the border with a setter pup for company, and wondered where his father was and what he was doing.

His father was standing with Captain King on the poop deck of the *Warspite*; and the *Warspite*, with fifes and drums playing "Fortune my Foe", with red sendal battle-pennant at her masthead and the cross of St. George fluttering bravely at her stern, with nets rigged and men at action stations, was sailing straight into Cadiz Harbour, leading *Mary Rose*, *Lion*, *Rainbow*, *Swiftsure*, *Dreadnaught* and *Nonpareil* into the massed fire of the galleys drawn up below the town.

Putting an end to the argument that had broken out at last night's Council of War, as to who should lead the naval attack (for which he himself had made the plans), he had weighed anchor just an hour before the agreed time.

To his Master Gunner, waiting the order to return the galleys' fire, he said, "Nay man, they are but wasps compared to what comes after. We will not waste good powder and shot on them; they shall be answered in another kind." And the *Warspite* swept on, replying to the cannonade with a derisive burst of trumpets.

The day passed, and the evening came. The sun that sank so peacefully behind the rim of the Blackmore Vale, gilding the quiet trees of Sherborne, went down red and swollen behind the rolling murk that was the smoke of half Cadiz burning. The naval battle was over, Essex had led the land assault, and while English troops and seamen were storming through the blazing streets, and while Bess sat in the twilight at the window of her painted bower, putting off the moment for having the candles lit, Ralegh was lying in torment in the cockpit of the *Warspite*, while a rough and ready surgeon probed the wound in his thigh—a jagged wound, laced with splinters from the *Warspite*'s bulwarks, where almost the last round-shot of the action had landed.

The light wind brought out to the ships in the harbour the acid smitch of the burning town; brought also the shouts of the looters who were ransacking the place for jewels and plate, rich hangings and fine weapons, and maybe a dark-eyed woman here and there, and Ralegh, his wound finally dressed, lay in his bunk and raged, cursing outrageous fortune that had laid him there (not for him the fierce joys of the assault, the burning streets and a bishop's golden chalice or the jewelled sword of a hidalgo), while the rest of the Fleet went looting.

.   .   .   .   .   .

Seven weeks later, Bess was jolting along the Dorset lanes in the family coach, to meet Ralegh at Weymouth. The family coach was a square box-like vehicle, upholstered in straw-coloured damask, so heavy that only farm horses could pull it, lacking springs of any kind, and quite phenomenally uncomfortable. But to Bess, trundling and jolting southward that day, it might have been carved from a hazel shell, and the feathery-heeled wain horses that drew it a team out of fairyland.

Ralegh was wounded, and still sick of his wound; his letter from Plymouth had told her that, but she had taken the coach instead of her own horse litter, which would have been infinitely more comfortable for a wounded man on the homeward journey, because she knew that nothing under Heaven would induce Ralegh to ride in a litter, whereas the coach was the pride of his heart because so few people possessed one. She was desperately anxious about his wound, agonising over the fact that he had been ill and in pain, and she not there to comfort him; but so soon now, she would be with him again, and she was as happy and excited in the prospect as a young girl. She was happy too, in the hope—of which she was ashamed, though she could not quite cast it out—that now he was hurt, he would have to stay at home with her, at least for a while.

Three times during that long day they changed horses, and each team seemed to Bess slower than the one before; but at last, towards evening, they came over the final lift of the Downs before the sea, and slithered down by the chalky road into the little town of Weymouth.

As they rumbled and clattered to a stand in the yard of the only inn, a familiar figure stepped forward to open the coach door and help her down. "God den to you, My Lady Sister."

"Arthur!" Bess rose in her place, and put a hand on the arm he held up to her; she was stiff and aching in every inch of her body, as she stepped thankfully down to the cobbles. "Arthur my dear,

I did not think to see you here. Is Walter——" She hesitated, and changed the form of her question. "How is Walter?"

"He is mending. It would take more than a leg full of splinters to keep that one down!" Bess's brother turned to Mine Host, who was hovering near. "I will take Lady Ralegh up."

Mine Host bowed. "Very good, Sir Arthur."

And Bess catching his words, turned to her brother quickly. "Sir Arthur?"

"Yes," he said, non-commitally.

"Oh my dear, I am so——"

He checked her with an eyebrow cocked in rueful amusement. "There is no call for your congratulations, sweet sister; His Grace of Essex dubbed sixty and six knights the morning after Cadiz; and a Cadiz knighthood is become a jest for the gods in consequence."

"Oh," said Bess, damped. Then in swift championship, "But I am very sure that yours was earned, however it was with the other five and sixty!"

He laughed, and swept her indoors and up a winding stairway; and at the head of it, halted before a door carved with roses and dolphins. Bess, who had donned a jonquil damask that morning although it was most unsuitable for travelling in, because it was Ralegh's favourite, and who had been trying to shake out the creases all the way upstairs, gave a final despairing shake to her skirts. Arthur flung open the door. "Here she is," he announced, and thrusting her through with a brotherly hand, shut it again behind her.

Ralegh was standing by the window. He turned quickly but awkwardly as she entered, and took one pace towards her, leaning heavily on a stick. "So you have come to collect the pieces, Bess," he said.

She was across the room before the words were well spoken, and his free arm was round her, holding her close. She put up her hands and drew his head down and kissed him. "My dear, my most dear, how is it with you?"

"I am still damnably lame," he said ruefully. "How is it with you?"

"What need to ask, now that I have you back? But you must sit down or you will tire the wound."

He laughed, half angrily. "I am tired of sitting down." But he obeyed her, all the same, lowering himself into a cushioned chair by the window, and stretching out his right leg with a sigh of relief.

Bess slipped to her knees beside him, among a swirl of out-flung skirts like a huge yellow flower, and looked up into his face, studying it gravely. He was woefully thin, and his eyes, sunk deep into his head by fever, seemed a deeper blue than was their wont, less of the sapphire about them, more of the muted colour that distant hills wear before rain. Very gently she touched his right knee, where the fashionable Venetian breeches were ungartered. "Is it here? Under my hand?"

"Further up—here." He took her hand and moved it midway up his thigh.

"Does it ache?"

"Not with your hand over it."

She smiled at him fondly. "Have you wanted my hand over it?"

"I have wanted all of you," Ralegh said. "I have longed for you as a sick child longs for his mother."

"Oh my dear," she said, in a small, shaken whisper.

He bent down to her. "Will you take me home and look after me, and make me well again, Bess?"

The humility of him, so unlike his normal self, tore at her heart-strings. She perfectly understood its cause; Ralegh had never in his life been really ill, and now he had been very ill indeed; he had wanted her, and had to do without her, which was a new experience. He was very weak, and that too, was a new thing. So came humility. She understood all that, and understood also, with an inner gleam of amusement, that it would not last. But while it did last, it was very real; and she put her arms round him as she might have put them round Little Watt if he had hurt himself, and pressed her cheek against his. "Darling, we will go home tomorrow," she said.

She began to tell him the odds and ends of home news that she knew would please him. Little Watt had lately added a new word to his vocabulary—unfortunately it was a profane word, but that could not be helped. The lime saplings in the lower meadow were doing well. Cherry, the old sorrel mare had dropped a fine foal. . . .

Presently Mine Host and his henchman appeared, the man to spread linen on the table and lay supper, the master to stand watch-ful in the doorway and ask if everything was to My Lady's taste, and the wine sufficiently cool.

Arthur joined them at supper, and with his coming, Ralegh's mood returned to normal. They made a merry meal, pledging each other in the canary wine; and the two men proceeded to re-fight Cadiz for Bess's entertainment, while she sat looking from one to the other, perfectly content to be entertained by them in whatever way they thought fit.

"And Bess——" Ralegh remembered something, and bent eagerly towards her. "What do you think was the first sight that met my eyes when we dropped anchor in Plymouth Sound, last week?"

"Nay, you must tell me. I was never any good at guessing."

"Why, the *Darling*, riding at anchor in the mouth of the Hamoaze, as peacefully as though she had not been to Guiana at all!"

"So soon? How did the voyage prosper?"

"None too well, it seems. The Spaniards have grown busy again in the Orinoco basin. God knows England has only herself to blame that Spain is before her!—Kemys told me he could not reach the mines where we found the gold ore last year, for there is a Spanish trading post with six pieces of ordnance astride the way."

"Could he not have landed lower down, and worked round behind them?" Throckmorton put in.

"With Trinidad a hornet's nest of Spaniards, and Don Berrio's ships between them and the sea, to cut them off at any time? Use your wits, man!"

The other poured himself a glass of wine. "You had neglected to mention those facts," he said. "Are there any further depressing details?"

"When I know that, I will tell you." Ralegh flashed a smile at him. "There was but small time for talking in Plymouth, and I have bidden Kemys come up to me at Sherborne as soon as he is through with paying off. Do you stay and make one of our Council of War!"

"Marry-come-up! I am no adventurer! I am away back to my wife and my acres."

"Council of War!" Bess thought. "Council of War. Oh God, not yet, not again just yet!" Aloud, she said, "How bad is it, that the Spaniards are up the Orinoco? What will it mean?"

"It will mean no more letters patent to explore, with a caution against trespass on the territory of other Christian princes," Ralegh said. "Christian princes; God save the Mark! It will mean that the next attempt must be made, not in peace, but with guns. It will mean sacking this strong-post that they call San Thomé, and sweeping Guiana clean of Dons and burning out the stink of the Inquisition that they leave behind them!" He caught up his glass, holding it aloft, and the light caught and kindled in the heart of it with a ragged scarlet flame. "I drink to our next attempt on El Dorado! Arthur—drink, Bess!"

Bess raised her glass to his, smiling, and drank. She had not noticed until now, how sour the wine was; sour and salty, as though there were tears mingled in it.

CHAPTER 9

"HERE WE GO UP—UP—UP"

Ralegh was an impossible patient. The melting mood of his reunion with Bess wore off even more rapidly than she had expected, and left behind it a restless and furious rebellion. He was a man whose body had never meant very much to him—even his love of luxury was because it ministered to his pride, not because it ministered to his comfort—but always it had been his instrument; the sword to the soldier, the lute to the minstrel, and he had kept it and used it accordingly. Now the wretched thing was out of order; it creaked and ached and was unduly heavy to carry about. The great purplish rent in it which was so slow to heal offended his fastidiousness, and his weakness outraged his pride, and he glowered at poor Bess when she wished to change the dressing, as though the whole thing were her fault.

Bess bore with him patiently, tended his wound and brewed him strengthening draughts, provided such of his favourite meals as she deemed good for a man in his condition, and loved him. He had need of all her love and forbearance, in the months that followed.

Kemys' report, when given in detail, was not good hearing, making it abundantly clear that if nothing was done soon, England's chance in South America would be gone for ever. Essex and Effingham and Tom Howard were at Court. Effingham had been created Earl of Nottingham for his part in the Cadiz victory; Essex had been made Master of the Ordnance—albeit a little grudgingly; but Ralegh was not returned to his old place as Captain of the Guard. He was here at Sherborne, tied by the leg, unable to take his part with the others in their Councils, unable to bring himself to the Queen's notice and lay Kemys' report before her and make her send her ships westward before it was too late.

But the obverse side of that difficult autumn was Little Watt. When his son was born, Ralegh had been astonished and delighted as though such a thing had never happened before; but in the preparations for his Guiana venture, he had soon lost interest. One baby was, after all, very much like another. Now, all that was changed. Little Watt was two years old, and no longer a baby, but a person, and a person after Ralegh's own heart. Outwardly, he resembled Bess, but inwardly, he was, in embryo, all Ralegh's, to understand the same things and dream the same dreams; and already there was growing between them the bond that was to link them so closely all their lives. Little Watt repaid his father's new interest with a swift and complete devotion, and was seldom willingly apart from him. He sat under the table with his father's legs through the interminable conferences with Lawrence Kemys and others, that went on all that autumn, and when Ralegh hobbled about the demesne, Little Watt invariably trotted behind, thrusting among the dogs for pride of place next to the heels of his private god. They began to do things together. "Come along, Imp," Ralegh would say, and they would set forth, generally deep in conversation, to visit the stables or the mews or see how the lime saplings were doing. And Bess, watching their absorbed backs disappearing round some corner, would experience an amused and slightly wistful sense of looking in on something from the outside.

By degrees, Ralegh grew strong again, despite all his rebellious fretting, though he still walked with a stick. Autumn turned to winter, and on a day early in December he came looking for Bess, and found her in her herb garden, gathering sprigs of rosemary for her next boiling of candles. He had an open letter in his hand, and his eyes were at their brightest and bluest. "Word from Effingham, Bess!" he called, the instant he saw her. "I crave his pardon— Nottingham, rather. If I am sufficiently well of my wound, he bids me come up to Westminster. Some question of the Cadiz prizes, seemingly."

Bess added an aromatic sprig to those already in her basket, and went to meet him. "And you are sufficiently well?" she asked, a little anxiously.

"Of course I am! Plague take it! I cannot roost here like a pelican on the housetops for the rest of my days! How soon can we be away, Bess?"

She heaved a little sigh of regret for her quiet home and the boiling of candles, that she would not now have time to attend to. "Tomorrow, I suppose," she said, and then, catching sight of a second packet held between two casual fingers under his letter, "Walter, was there anything for me in the bag?"

He glanced at his hand. "Eh?—Ah yes—here you are."

Bess took the little packet, half laughing, half exasperated. "Walter, you are too bad! You know I am waiting news of Elizabeth Cecil's new baby—and it should be here by now." She was breaking the seal as she spoke; she opened the sheet, her eyes skimming along the lines. Suddenly she gave a little cry, and looked up. "Oh Walter, she is dead!"

"Who is?" Ralegh, who had returned to his own letter, raised his eyes again.

"Elizabeth. This is from Mary Herbert, to tell me so. The baby is well enough, she says; another little daughter—but Elizabeth ——" She let the page flutter to the chill winter ground, and lie unheeded. "Oh poor, poor Robin."

Ralegh said, "Aye, poor Robin," and stooped stiffly for the fallen letter.

And that was all.

But throughout the rest of that day, whenever he had a moment to spare, he came to find Bess, wherever she was busy about her preparations for the journey, just to look at her, and go away again, and presently come back to look once more, as though to make sure that she was still there.

Christmas found them still at Durham House. The Court was at Westminster, and though they had no part in the Court festivities, there was a good deal of coming and going between Durham House and the houses of old friends. But one familiar face was absent from all the festivities, Court or otherwise. Robert Cecil

appeared in public whenever his duties as Secretary of State or
Minister in Attendance demanded; otherwise nobody saw him that
winter, save the men who worked with him. He and Essex and
Ralegh were much together, a queer triumvirate that had no
official existence, but about which men were already beginning to
whisper, looking to the future.

But Bess did not see him at all, until the morning of New Year's
Day, when she had gone down the garden to gather some Christmas roses, and hearing a light step on the water stair, turned to find
him standing behind her.

Something about him was unfamiliar; something more concrete
than the changed look in his eyes. And then as he doffed his cap,
and stood uncovered before her, she realised what it was. His hair
was grey. He was not quite thirty-five.

"Robin!" she exclaimed.

"I am sorry; I have startled you," he said. "I came to wish you
happiness in the New Year."

"And you——" she began, and checked, holding out her hands
to him, forgetful of the Christmas roses. He cupped his hands under
hers, saving the flowers, and greeting her with a touch. A smile
that it was not good to see twisted his long, sensitive lips. "No, you
cannot return it, can you?" he said. "Poor Elizabeth, it is difficult
for you."

"I—was not expecting you," Bess said.

"Because I have been so long in coming? I would have come
before, but I was busy. You will have heard that I have gotten me
the Chancellorship of the Duchy of Lancaster, for a Christmas
fairing?"

"Yes, I heard," Bess said. "Oh Robin, I am so sorry. So—very
sorry."

"Thank you, Elizabeth." His voice was completely unemotional,
almost dry, but a muscle twitched in his sallow cheek. "I came to
see your husband, as well as to bring you my New Year wishes;
is it a propitious time?"

"Walter is from home. He is gone to the Mermaid with Ben
Jonson, to talk with a seaman who is newly returned from the
South Seas," Bess said, turning towards the fantastic turreted mass
of the house. "Do you come in and drink a cup of wine and wait
for him. He cannot be long, at least I hope not, for he has been

gone since early morning already, and his wound still tires so
quickly. But Master Jonson will take good care of him, for he is
really most reliable when he is sober, and he was as sober as a judge
—almost—when they set out this morning. Though what state he
may be in by now is quite another matter, of course——" She was
talking completely at random, unable to stop, and acutely aware of
his light, prowling step behind her as she led the way indoors and
up to the long gallery.

She sent a servant for wine and a bowl for the Christmas roses,
and slipped off her heavy mantle of olive velvet lined with squirrel
fur, and let it fall across a chair. The wine came swiftly, and a silver
bowl; and she poured for Robin Cecil, quite unable, now that her
breathless chatter on the stairs was silent, to speak at all, though
there was so much that she longed to say. And having poured for
him, and put the cup into his hand, she turned her attention to the
Christmas roses. They were chill with melted frost under her
fingers, for the sun had not reached them under the wall; flawless,
coldly pure as the frost itself, yet with a flush of warmth on the
outer sides of the petals.

Behind her, Cecil had moved over to the virginal that stood open
before a window. Still standing, his wine cup in one hand, he ran
the other over the narrow keys, and began to play, idly and caress-
ingly, with a touch that brought out the nostalgia of the slight
song-tune with unbearable poignancy. The last time that Bess had
seen his wife, she had sung that song; it was a favourite of hers.

> Sweet Adon, dare'st not glance thine eye,
> N'oserez vous, mon bel ami?
> Upon thy Venus that must die?
> Je vous en prie, pity me:
> N'oserez vous, mon bel, mon bel,
> N'oserez vous, mon bel ami?

The sappy stem of a Christmas rose broke in Bess's finger, and
she swung round. "Robin, don't!"

He drove a hand along the keyboard with a crashing, deliberate
discord, and turned away from the virginal. "Crave your pardon,
Elizabeth. There was a somewhat oppressive silence that seemed to
require filling."

"But why with that tune?" Bess thought, knowing, even as the question sprang into her mind, that the answer lay in the man's warped instinct for self-flagellation. Aloud, she said: "I am sorry; there are so many things that I would say, but I do not know how to say them."

His old, sweet smile flickered for an instant into his eyes. "Then let us take them as said, since we both know what they are."

"Robin," she said after a moment. "What will you do now?"

"Do? Much as I have always done. My father grows old and tired; soon there will be more work for me to do."

She had joined him at the window. "And the children?"

"I have given Frances and the babe to my sister, at least for the present time."

"But Will?"

"I shall keep the boy with me. He is six—old enough to do with a tutor."

"Poor little boy," Bess said, and she put out a hand to touch his sleeve. "Robin, if you should find at any time that he is not—that he needs mothering—or even another little boy to play with, send him to me. I loved your Bess."

"I know you did," Cecil said. "You make a most kind offer, Elizabeth; I shall not forget it."

It occurred to Bess for the first time, that he had called her Elizabeth throughout their conversation. It seemed as though, with his own Bess dead, he could not use her name for another woman.

Silence fell between them again, but this time it was not one that required filling; and they stood together in quiet companionship, looking out at the world. The window at this end of the gallery looked down slantwise to the Strand and the crowds who came and went along it. There were many gay companies passing, this New Year's Day, most of the people known to the watchers in the high window. Presently one of the passing throng hesitated in his walk, looking up at the house, and moved a step or two towards the gatehouse as though minded to ask admittance, a tallish, thin-nish man with a rapier of exaggerated length at his hip and a hat of exaggerated height on his head.

"There is Sir Lewis Stucley," Bess said. "I do believe he is coming in." Then with relief, as he turned away to continue his walk, "No, he has changed his mind."

As the man disappeared from view, though not without one

uncertain backward glance, she looked at Cecil with puzzled eyes. "Now that is a strange thing."

"That your husband's kinsman should turn away from the door?"

She shook her head. "That he should come and hover before it, clearly half minded to enter. . . . In all the while that I have been Walter's wife, though I have seen the man maybe half a score of times, I have never known any word to pass between them because of some stupid grudge he has borne against Walter these twelve years and more. Yet three nights since, at Mary Herbert's revel, he was one of the company, and showed himself—not friendly, but as though he would lief be on better terms, and yet was nervous for some reason—ready to shy like a startled colt. Now he comes to the gate on New Year's Day, and hovers—and passes on. Why, Robin?"

Cecil's face was sardonic. "Do you need me to read the riddle for you? Before your husband fell under the cloud of the Queen's displeasure, the grudge was still sweet. Thereafter, your husband *was* under the Queen's displeasure. Now he thinks it possible that the cloud may be going to lift: and what, after all, when one has had twelve years to think it over, is a threadbare grudge, compared with a friend in the Queen's favour? So he comes to your gate. He is nervous, and he hovers, and he goes away because he fears lest, after all, he is mistaken."

Bess's eyes had never left his face while he was speaking. They were startled and questioning. "Is the cloud going to lift?" she asked after a moment, "or is Sir Lewis mistaken, as he fears?"

"You could be happy if the recall never came, could you not, Elizabeth?" he said shrewdly.

She considered, then shook her head. "If it were but myself, yes; but Walter could not—and that breaks the circle of contentment for me."

"I think that it will come, and before so very long," Cecil said.

"What makes you say that?"

"Signs and portents. Maybe the same ones that brought our friend here this morning. My Lord of Essex is no longer quite so secure in favour as of yore. He grows over sure on his dunghill; and the Queen—for all that she gave him the Ordnance when he begged her—was not pleased with his Cadiz knighthoods. . . . Also, my influence increases a little with the Queen."

A shadow crossed Bess's face. "I know that it does: I know that you do your best for Walter. But it is hateful, this jostling for places—playing off one against the other in the Queen's favour."

"Here we go up—up—up. Here we go down—down—down," Cecil quoted softly, mockingly, the chant of children on a see-saw. "A good game—played with one standing in the centre of the plank to control the balance."

Bess, still looking at him, had no need to ask who that one was, and was conscious of a little trickling fear. She had always been sure of Robin Cecil's friendship; she was sure of it still. And yet she wondered. . . . He had not been quite a friend over her marriage; and now—his Bess was dead. Part of Robin Cecil had died with his wife, she thought, and it was the happiest part, and the best.

. . . .

A few days later they were once more at Sherborne, and though Ralegh was back and forth all the rest of that winter and the following spring, Bess remained for the most part quietly in her home. But she was with him again in lodgings at Deptford, where he was busy on some matter of the Fleet, when the long-hoped-for recall finally came.

The Court was at Greenwich, and acting on a sudden impulse the Queen came down unheralded among her ships in the Royal Dockyard, as her father had so often used to do. Ralegh was in one of the Mould-lofts when she arrived, so hotly engaged in arguing a point of construction with one of the senior shipwrights, that he was completely unaware of the buzz of excitement running through the yard, until, limping out through the huge entrance without looking where he was going, he all but ran into her.

He had tried so often to bring about a meeting, written her sonnets, humbly implored her forgiveness, and never seen her once, save as a distant glittering figure riding by in some state procession. Now, here she stood, so near that he could have touched her, could have knelt at her feet. He had already started forward with bended knee, but her strange eyes that could be pale as shallow water or black as midnight looked him full in the face, and she moved on without pause. Only as she passed, she spoke to him, casting the words carelessly over her shoulder. And the words, whether of sudden impulse or long deliberation, were: "Come to me before

Evensong, Sir Walter. The Chamberlain shall have orders concerning you."

Then she had passed on, jewelled like a quetzel bird in the sunlight, with Petit, the Master shipwright at her side, and the gentlemen of her train around her.

The Presence Chamber in Greenwich Palace was a long and lovely room, lit by many windows through which the late afternoon sun streamed in upon the shifting throng who waited to see the Queen. Feet moved quietly over the strewing herbs on the floor bruising and bringing out the scent of mint and marjoram and yellow iris leaves, and the buzz of talk sounded sleepy in the hot air as the drone of bees above a bed of sun-warmed snapdragons. They were a fantastically assorted company, almost exclusively male; merchants in flat caps and long gowns, an old scholar with a book for Her Majesty and hope of her acceptance writ large upon his face; young men up from the country and hopeful of making their way at Court; an alderman with a rich chain round his neck; a soldier with a rose in his cable hatband; a lawyer; a shipmaster, a bishop, a lute player; and moving here and there among them, the quiet Court officials.

Ralegh had drawn aside with Bess into one of the window embrasures, aloof from the main throng; and standing there in the full flood of the sunlight, he caught and focussed the whole attention of the room. He had elected to wait upon the Queen in a magpie symphony of frost white doublet and hose under an excessively short and wide pearl-embroidered black velvet cloak; the great pearl in his ear was translucent in the sunlight, and the Queen's diamond burned on the hand which rested on his jewelled sword hilt. But even in sackcloth, he would have stood out in any company, Bess thought, his eyes and the carriage of his head would see to that.

He was holding himself with the coldly perfect arrogance—insolence might be a better word—that had won him the hatred of his peers and the common folk alike. Not so much disdaining the throng in the great room as unaware of their very existence; he seemed as indifferent to their veiled glances as though they had been so many apes behind bars. Not by the twitch of a muscle did he betray the fact that he knew himself pilloried there; knew that the Queen, by ordering him to wait among all these others, had pilloried him and his wife for their curiosity, their whispers and covert glances. Not by the twitch of a muscle did he betray his sickening anxiety as to the meaning of her action. A last flick of the whip before forgiveness?—or no forgiveness after all? But Bess, knowing almost all that anybody could know about him, saw the fears and the hopes and the raw, scarified pride.

"It will come to a happy issue," she murmured, her head half averted from him toward the window. "She is a woman, and she acts in a woman's way, that is all."

"A woman should know a woman," Ralegh returned in the same undertone. "But can even another woman know the Queen?"

He swung round as one of the Queen's Gentlemen, slipping through the crowd, touched him on the arm. "Sir Walter, Her Majesty commands your presence."

So he was not, after all, to be received with the herd. With superb confidence in the very swirl of his cloak, he turned to follow the other man, gathering Bess after him. But for one instant Bess remained as though rooted to the ground. "Walter, the summons is for you—I will wait here."

"No," Ralegh said. "We will go to the Queen together, Bess."

She cast one agonised, questioning glance at the young man who had brought the summons. She had danced with him last Christmas at Baynard's Castle, but his face told her nothing. She was shaking from head to foot as, with her head braced high, she moved beside her husband through the shifting, curious crowd towards those folding doors.

Two of the Guards moved aside to let them pass; two more, at another door hung with gold and crimson; and they were in the familiar chamber where Bess had watched the Earl of Essex teasing his merlin and bargaining for Ralegh's downfall, nine long years ago.

Several of the Queen's Ladies, gathered at the lower end of the chamber, rose and fluttered away, through an inner door, as they entered, and, save for the Guards at the door behind them, they were alone with the Queen. She was fresh from the hands of her tirewomen, and in a few minutes she would pass out into the crowded Presence Chamber on her way to Evensong. She was sitting by the window, the light falling full and mercilessly upon her, faintly gilding the stiff creamy folds of her gown, blazing in

the jewels with which she was hung, kindling her auburn wig to
a harsh metallic red. A very splendid, very lonely figure. She had
been reading; the book lay open on the pedestal table beside her,
but she was not reading now. She sat upright, motionless, her hands
folded in her lap, her jewelled head turned a little on the long,
jewelled neck, to watch them.

"Come here," she said; and that was all.

Bess was not conscious of crossing the rush-strewn floor, but she
found that she was kneeling at the Queen's feet, her head bent in
a passion of wordless supplication; and Ralegh was kneeling beside
her.

There was a long silence; a silence drawn out thin and brittle like
spun glass, and then the Queen's voice above them, forceful, clear,
yet a little dry, as though the sap no longer rose as it used to do.
"So you have brought her with you, Sir Walter."

Ralegh raised his head, his bright blue eyes looking levelly into
her bright dark ones. "My wife always companies with me, Madam,
wherever it is possible for a woman to go." And a thrill of mingled
pride and fear shot through Bess, as she realised that he was calmly
stating his terms to the Queen.

The Queen knew it also, but she said only, with a note of regret:
"So. You are a more stubborn creature than my Robin," and the
regret seemed to be for Essex's lack of stubbornness, rather than for
Ralegh's abundance of it.

"I am your Majesty's most faithful servant," Ralegh said, simply.

She leaned down towards him a little. "A proud, stiff-necked
servant," she said, but there was no censure in her tone.

"But a faithful one," Ralegh insisted.

In the silence that followed, Bess raised her head a little, and the
Queen's hands came into her sight. They were loosely folded, but
Bess knew instinctively that they were only held from convulsive
tightening by the will of their owner. They were still beautiful,
those hands, but suddenly it dawned on Bess that they were the
hands of an old woman, the skin puckered into soft wrinkles, the
blue veins prominent, the joints of the slender fingers a little en-
larged under the sparkling load of rings. Slowly her gaze crept
higher, higher yet, until it reached the Queen's face, down-bent
towards Ralegh's; a shrinking gaze that yet sought to pierce
through the pink and white enamel, the powder and the eye

cosmetic, to the woman beneath. It was five years since she had looked into that face, and it came to her with a sense of shock and pity —yes, and fear—that the Queen, like her hands, was growing old.

People older than Bess had been born into the reign of this Queen; it had been a great reign, a flowering-time for England, the like of which had not been seen before. It was the only reign that Bess's generation knew, and somehow it had seemed that because one had not known a beginning to it, one would not know an end. It was the established order; and now it seemed that the sands were beginning to run low, not only for Elizabeth, but for a whole way of life.

But Ralegh and the Queen were unaware of the cold wind out of the unknown that had touched Bess. Their whole attention was turned on each other; the Queen, perhaps, making her decision, Ralegh certainly waiting for it, and meanwhile, making small bold love to her with his eyes. They were all a little in love with her, Bess thought, young and old, because they were in love with England. That was her power over them.

"Faithful, yes, I believe so," the Queen said at last. "Else I had not sent for you again. Indeed you have proved your faith. You are still lame: does the wound irk you yet?"

"It irks me the less that it was gained in your service, Madam," Ralegh said; and his complete sincerity was in his face.

"From some men, I might take that for a mere pretty speech— one such as men make to their Queen," Elizabeth said, "but from you, though you are nothing lacking in the courtier's art, I am inclined to accept it for very truth." She sat upright, with a quick change of tone. "Well, if my service means so much to you, my Bodyguard lacks its Captain yet. Your old place is empty for you; go and try if it still fits."

With a quick gesture she held out her hand to him. And Ralegh's face, as he took it and bent to kiss the jewelled fingers, was the eager face of a very young man. "Now you must get up or you will strain the wound. And as for your wife——" the Queen's bright gaze flicked from Ralegh to Bess for the first time as she withdrew her hand, and there was a glint of snapping laughter in it. "Since you are graciously pleased to deem my Court a fit place for her, let her come and take her place as your wife in it. . . . What a-devil are you crying for, woman?"

Bess had not known until that moment that she was crying—crying for regret, for relief, for pity; crying for the sands of familiar things that were running low. "I hardly know, Madam." She raised her head, blinking. "But indeed and indeed I am not greatly prone to tears."

"No, I remember that you are not, which is just as well, for I detest weeping women about me." The Queen reached for the little silver bell beside her, but paused without touching it. She was looking up at Bess who had risen to her feet, and the glint of sharp laughter spurted up again. "Five years," she said, speaking as one woman to another and ignoring Ralegh now, as completely as she had ignored Bess before. "Five years since you ran away to him. Tell me, Bess, was it a good bargain?"

Bess returned the laughter, warmed by a sudden sense of fellowship with the other woman. "It was a good bargain, Madam."

CHAPTER 10

THE GAZING-CRYSTAL

The Queen's Captain was back, but with a difference; older than he had been, in more than years, lame, and grey at the temples. His relationship with the Queen was altered, too. Gloriana still carried on the old, delicately artificial play of lovemaking with her Courtiers, but from Ralegh she no longer desired the extravagant gestures of a lover, and from Ralegh she no longer got them. He was not now a favourite in the old romantic sense, but a trusted councillor and a friend. But the world saw what it had always seen, the Queen's Captain carrying his head like the Prince of the Morning.

The Earl of Essex, returning from his ships at Chatham to find his fallen rival risen again, seemed, rather surprisingly, not to care. And for the moment all rivalry was laid aside, as they set to work on the fitting out of yet another English fleet for action against yet another Spanish one—an Armada which Philip, mad to avenge Cadiz, was selling even his gold candelabrum to raise.

A few weeks after Ralegh's reinstatement, the fleet sailed under

Essex's command, with Ralegh seconding him. But when, after
struggling through the most appalling series of summer gales, they
reached the coast of Spain, the new Armada, in an impregnable
position, refused them battle, and there was nothing for the English
to do but return home, looking slightly foolish.

Nothing daunted, the queer triumvirate set to work again, got
rid of many of the soldiers and patched up the storm damage, and
by early autumn, Ralegh and Essex were off once more on a grand
and glorious Spaniard-hunt, officially supposed to be an attack on
Ferrol, where a large part of the Armada was assembling; while
Cecil, who had watched over them throughout with something of
the pleasure in his own skill of a man driving a superb but unruly
team, turned himself once again to the myriad other matters that
beset the Secretary of State.

Left to herself, Bess would have dearly liked to go home to
Sherborne, but when she had spoken of it to Ralegh, he had protested. "Bess, you cannot do that. All that we have won might so
easily be lost again! Stay about the Court, sweetheart, and keep me
in the Queen's mind, if you love me." And Bess did love him. So
she sent for Little Watt and his nurse, and settled down in Durham
House as best she might. The familiar life of the Court drew her
back into herself. She was in occasional attendance on the Queen,
rode with the Court party, danced now and then at Whitehall, sat
embroidering in a vine arbour with Mary Herbert, while the
Queen walked to and fro upon the terrace with her Councillors;
and in between whiles, contrived to live her own life as Mistress of
Durham House and mother of Little Watt.

Meanwhile the Spaniard-hunt had collapsed into farce, with
Essex off and away on one wild goose chase after another, and
Ralegh, grimly obedient to his contradictory orders, following in
his wake. The climax came when, acting on an urgent summons,
Ralegh arrived with his squadron at Fayal, to find that instead of
keeping the rendezvous, Essex was off on the trail of yet another
wild goose. Ralegh waited for him three days, and then determined
to act on his own initiative and take Horta, the chief town, without
further delay.

That afternoon—a fresh autumn afternoon of great drifting
clouds in a clear-washed sky, and the brown leaves showering down
the wind—Bess rode hawking in St. James's Park with the Queen's

party. She was carrying Ralegh's Indian falcon, Jezebel, which was too big and fierce for a woman; but Ralegh had asked her to fly the creature while he was away. Far ahead, the Queen rode among her chosen gallants. The green-clad falconers and huntsmen with the leashed hounds moved among the party, but not of it, with the authority of men doing their own skilled work; while the Court party called to each other, laughing, under the russet trees, as they made for the lake where the heron were to be found.

Ralegh and his band of West-countrymen were rowing in to the assault; they were making their way along the unprotected reef under the guns of High Fort, to rush the defences.

And the falcon on Bess's gloved fist roused, as the excitement of the chase touched her, rattled her barred feathers, and settled again. Twice more, and it would be safe to fly her.

Ralegh had sent back for his Dutch war veterans.

The lake in St. James's Park was a sheet of ruffled silver, the brown-tipped rushes swaying in the autumn wind, and out of the rushes a heron broke cover, and rose, with Sir George Carew's falcon after her. She was circling swiftly higher, climbing the blue spirals of the air, with winged and talloned death mounting hard behind, up and up into the eye of the sun, until the winged death overtopped her victim, and stooped, despite the heron's rapier beak, and struck.

Ralegh was bringing up his troops, limping serenely along at their head, oblivious of the bullets that splattered on the rocks around him, with an ash-plant to help his wounded leg and the faithful Lawrence Kemys at his shoulder. He had elected to go into action that day minus any armour save a steel gorget, and despite his usual preference for pale or muted colours, in a doublet of scarlet tuft-taffetas which was easy for his men to follow, and also made a superb target for the enemy marksmen.

As the hawking party rode home that evening, resistance was crumbling at Horta and High Fort; and for some unaccountable reason, Ralegh was still alive and unscathed. But My Lord of Essex, arriving just too late to find that Ralegh had stolen from him the one successful action of the expedition, was raving like a hysterical woman.

Finally the whole ugly affair blew over, and late that autumn, the Fleet returned home. But meanwhile, the Spaniards, taking advantage of their absence, had sailed from Ferrol, and only been prevented by storms from reaching Falmouth. The Queen could not suffer fools, even fools she loved, and she laughed at her Robin, ridiculing his conduct in minute detail, and with a delicate, rapier malice that set him writhing and did nothing to sweeten his feeling towards Ralegh.

For a while, the life of the Queen's Captain lay through comparatively tranquil waters; and he had leisure to spend in his backwater at Sherborne, which made Bess happy. He did not want it so; he wanted the stress and turmoil of the open seas; his dream was calling to him again. But Ralegh's adventuring days, it seemed, were over. For one thing he was a sick man; he had paid a heavier price at Cadiz than he had realised at the time, and was to carry pain with him for the rest of his days. That alone would not have held him back, but it was coupled with the fact that he was, as usual, short of money, and the Queen and the Government could spare him nothing, either in cash or ships or men. The Irish rising which had broken out in 1595 had become by now a nation-wide revolt; and with Spain on the alert to make the most of the situation by a landing at any time, Ireland was to demand the whole of England's fighting power for years to come. Spain in the New World must wait its turn until the nearer threat was over.

Ralegh must possess his soul in what little patience he could lay claim to.

The brief fellowship between himself and Essex, now that it had gone up in a shower of sparks, had added bitterness to their antagonism that had not been there before, and the steel was out between them. But their ways were to lie divided in the months that followed, for in March 1599, after quarrelling with the Queen and being only half forgiven, Essex departed for Ireland with a small army of horse and foot, to put down the rebellion.

Summer passed, and on Michaelmas Eve, Bess sat beside the fire in Ralegh's study, working a new set of bed-curtains with gay flowering branches and birds between.

The group round the table consisted of Ralegh himself, Lawrence Kemys, old Dr. Dee dragged from his study at Mortlake, young Ben Jonson still slightly under a cloud for killing a fellow actor in a tavern duel last year, and Thomas Hariot the astronomer and mathematician who had done so much survey work for Ralegh in the New World. They were typical of Ralegh's catholic taste in friends; and save for Lawrence Kemys, who was by this time one of the household, Bess could not in her heart of hearts approve of them. Especially she could not approve of John Dee, nor of the interests that bound him and Ralegh together; those interests which set people whispering, naming them atheists and dabblers in forbidden things. Bess, herself of a simple and orthodox faith, had never been able to understand Ralegh's experimental attitude to the hidden side of life. The idea of turning base metal into gold, about which so much of the talk seemed to centre whenever the School of Night gathered, was something she could grasp; but when the gold-making became a symbol, an outer garment for mysteries of the Spirit that had no name, then she was left bewildered, and afraid.

But tonight they were not talking of hidden things, and Ralegh, as he sometimes did, had asked her to give them her company; and so here she sat, in the tall tower chamber that always seemed to her a little too near the stars for comfort, stitching at a stiff honeysuckle head, by the light of a candle behind a globe of water. The men at the table bent together, pouring over some new charts spread there. Their voices murmured on, weaving a background to the tiny sharp pluck, pluck, pluck of her needle in the stiff green damask. From time to time she glanced up, her eyes lingering now on one face, now on another, returning most often, with a kind of shrinking fascination to the face of John Dee that might have been that of a rather cobwebby archangel.

John Dee, who kept Cornelius Agrippa's *Occult Philosophy* open on his study table, who had foreseen the execution of the Queen of Scots in his gazing-crystal. What would he see if he looked into his crystal now? Bess wondered. Changes were in the very wind, everything shifting and changing and flowing on into the unknown, like the Thames below the terrace of Durham House. What *would* he see?

Wise old Burghley who had been Elizabeth's Councillor all her Queenhood, and her sister's before her, had been dead more than a year, and his son was come to his full estate. Out of a long past summer night Bess seemed to hear his voice again. "I want to guide the delicate threads of destiny, braiding them at my will. I want men a little afraid of me—tall men, with straight backs." He had that now; and what next? The old ambition had been warped but

human, but in the past few years it seemed that much that was
human had died in Robin Cecil. The man had given place
to the Secretary of State, an impersonal force who could not care
who was caught and strangled in those delicate webs of his
weaving.

Philip of Spain was dead, too; after lying for weeks cankered and
stinking, with his black confessors about him, and his open coffin
beside his bed. The arch-enemy who had been bound to the Queen
for almost half a century by ties of animosity as strong and constant
as ever ties of love could have been.

And the Queen herself was growing old. . . .

And the Queen's Robin? Strange rumours were filtering back
from Ireland; rumours of a shameful truce with the rebel Tyrone;
rumours that it was more and worse than a truce. Small wonder
that here at home the defence forces had been turned out in case of
need. Bess's resentment rose against the Earl of Essex, not for his
threat to the realm, but because he was making Walter work so
hard when his leg was troubling him. She always knew when
Walter's leg was troubling him, because he had a trick of keeping
his hand over the place where the old wound ached—just as he was
doing now.

Ralegh, Essex, Cecil; still the strange triangle, and over them,
as over the rest of England—but more urgently over them—the
threat of change, the future closing down. If John Dee looked into
his gazing-crystal now, what would he see? Another execution,
maybe? If so—whose? Perhaps he had already looked. She glanced
up again at the old, absorbed face, her gaze lingering there as
though trying to read the answer in it, then with a little shiver, drew
a strand of golden silk from the rainbow tussy-mussy beside her,
and bent to thread her needle. What was the matter with her
tonight, she wondered.

Trying to escape her own thoughts, she gave all her attention to
the careful setting of her stitches, and it was not until hurried footsteps sounded on the winding stair, and the door burst open, that
she realised that yet another visitor was come among them out of
the autumn night. He set the manservant aside, and entered with
the unceremoniousness of an old friend, saying as he did so: "God
den to you, Gentlemen. I wondered if I might find you at home,
Ralegh."

The five men had turned at his entrance, and Ralegh greeted him in surprise. "Cobham! What a-devil's name brings you back to Westminster at this hour? Have you had supper?"

"I supped at the Boar's Head on my way here, but I'd like a drink—several drinks——" Suddenly becoming aware of Bess, he bowed deeply, his doffed bonnet brushing the floor. "Ah, Lady Ralegh, I crave your pardon. I am half blind from the wind and darkness, or I must have seen at first glance, the fairest ornament of this assembly."

Bess bent her head in acknowledgment of the greeting. "God den, My Lord. Pray you excuse my rising; you are most welcome, but if once I lose the thread, I shall not find myself again in this flowering wilderness."

Ralegh was bidding the servant who still hovered in the doorway to bring wine, much wine, for the whole company; and the new-comer was standing by the table, talking excitedly with the others. Lord Cobham was a tall man, with an impetuous boyish charm, that frequently got him what he wanted, even from the Queen. He had evidently been riding hard, and his soft fair hair, the only feature he had in common with the gay, gentle little spun-glass sister who had been Lady Cecil, was in wild disorder.

Ralegh swung back to him again, demanding "Well?—You have not yet told us what brings you here in such a smother."

The newcomer laughed, looking from one impatient face to another with obvious pleasure in having news to impart that would burst among them like a fireball. "'Tis a mere matter of family business that brings me up," he began, prolonging the pleasure. "But being up, I called in here on the chance of finding you, Ralegh, for I bethought me you might be interested to know that My Lord of Essex is once more with us!"

He gained his effect, all right; he had several of the party on their feet, startled and exclaiming, though Ralegh himself remained seated and completely still, his brows twitched together above his arrogant nose, as he stared at the latecomer with an odd look of suspended judgment.

Then as the burst of exclamation fell away, Dr. Dee asked in his beautiful voice: "But are you indeed sure, My Lord?"

Cobham swung round on him impatiently. "Marry-come-up! Of course I am sure! Am I not this instant from Nonsuch? This morning he arrived, mud to the eyebrows, the veriest slubber-cullion; and forced his way into the Queen's bed-chamber, still foul from the journey."

"And what becomes of his Command?" It was Lawrence Kemys, also a man under authority, who spoke.

Cobham shrugged. "His Command may go to the devil and take Ireland with it, for all My Lord of Essex cares."

Ralegh spoke for the first time, crashing an open hand on the table. "But in God's name *why*? What can the young fool have hoped to gain by such insane conduct?"

"Why, I suppose having made his truce—if indeed it be no worse than a truce—with the rebels, he is come home post-haste to fling himself at Belphoebe's feet and make his peace with her as swiftly as may be."

"He would seem to have chosen a strange way of doing that," Ralegh said dryly.

"But then, Belphoebe is a strange soul; unaccountably strange. She was not ungracious towards her Robin this morning, as I hear."

"The Queen," Ralegh said, "is never one to be storm-swept into a decision before she is ready to make it."

"Have a care that when she makes it, it does no harm to your cause!" Cobham said with an excited laugh: "Men who know the Queen as well as you were buzzing round her Robin like bees round a lime flower, ere I rode away!"

Ralegh was silent a moment. Then he said "But then I, who know the Queen as well as they, believe her to be too little a woman and too much a prince to countenance revolt, even in her Robin. . . . Well, God knoweth the right of it; or maybe—Sir Robert Cecil."

The manservant entered, carrying a silver platter on which were tall Venetian glasses and a flask of pale golden wine, which he set down on the table, and withdrew.

Ralegh had risen to his feet. He looked at Bess with a brow cocked in enquiry, but she shook her head. "No? Well—pour for yourselves, gentlemen." He laughed on a note of sudden reckless-ness. "The wine of hypocrites, odorous with the flowers of Mount Hymatos; a wine to put to noble purposes. . . . Gentlemen, I drink to the Queen's mind, being made up."

John Dee took his glass, but instead of drinking, sat gazing into it, as though trying to see some picture in the pale topaz depth of the wine; as though it had been his gazing-crystal.

Suddenly Bess wanted to scream and scream and scream, and beat away with her naked hands the on-pressing future.

CHAPTER II

"OUR JEWEL IS FROM US GONE"

The cold light of a February afternoon fell bleakly into Lady Ralegh's privy parlour. Several months ago, the main part of Durham House had been destroyed by a fire starting in the stables; but this wing had been left intact, and it was a large enough lodgment for the Ralegh household when they were in Westminster. It was a little depressing to live with the gaunt and blackened ruin to which the wing was joined like one living branch on a dead tree, but from the privy parlour which had once been the steward's office, one could not see the stark shell of the dead house, only the river, and the snowdrops on the terrace, and the distant crowding spires and gables of the Southwark Shore.

Bess was sitting beside the fire, telling a story to an audience of two little boys and a setter bitch, who lay on their stomachs at her feet. Will Cecil was often at the house, these days, for he and Watt had struck up a friendship, in which Watt, though he was but six and a half to the other's ten, was definitely the leader. The reason for that was to be read in their faces, turned up to Bess from their cupped hands as they waited in delighted suspense for the moment when the island on which St. Branden and his followers had landed and lit a fire, woke up and wagged its tail. Will's face was stolid and innocent, the face of a nice little boy who was nothing more. Watt's was vividly bold beneath the overlay of his mother's gentler features, with Ralegh's sapphire blue eyes and Ralegh's devil; a nice little boy who was a great deal more, and all of it wicked.

But at the moment, Watt was being good—as good as Will— because he dearly loved a story. Bess had not quite realised the association of ideas that had led her to tell them about St. Branden and his search for the Happy Isles; but now that she was embarked on it she wished that she had not chosen that particular story for to-day, when half a mile away in Westminster Hall, Robin Devereux who had listened to it with her the first time she had heard it, was fighting for his life against a charge of treason.

Knowing St. Branden almost by heart, she found, as Lady Sidney had done, that part of her thoughts were free to wander while she told it; and they wandered persistently back over the eighteen months since Essex had forced his way into the Queen's bed-chamber at Nonsuch.

The account of his conduct in Ireland, which he gave presently to the Council had not satisfied them. Nor had it satisfied the Queen. She had given him in charge of Egerton the Lord Keeper, and he had spent that winter in the Tower. But in June, despite a letter from Ralegh to the Secretary of State, bidding him to forget mercy, since Essex at liberty would be "ever the canker of the Queen's estate and safety," he was released once more, though still forbidden the Court.

After that, it had seemed to most people that his fortunes were on the mend. He had only to wait, and all would be well with him again. But my Lord of Essex was physically incapable of waiting, and presently it began to be rumoured about the Court that failing to gain his way with the Queen, he had turned to James of Scotland, her likely heir, and was intriguing with him to make sure of the succession.

Matters had come to a bitter flowering just ten days ago. Bess's personal memory of that Sunday was only of scared faces and distant shouting; and Ralegh bidding her to keep Little Watt with her and Lawrence Kemys to stand guard over them both, before he went clattering away to guard the Queen. But she knew now that Essex had ridden into London with a following of two hundred hot-heads and malcontents at his back, intending to rouse the citizens to join him, and in the resulting turmoil it was said, to gain posses-sion of the key points of the Palace, force his way into the Queen's presence and dictate to her his terms, which included Ralegh's death and the naming of Scottish James as heir to the throne. But though he was the people's darling, their love stopped short of open rebellion. There was no help forthcoming to him from the crowded streets, and the weaker spirits in his train began to melt away, and when he turned back, Ludgate was defended against him by the trained bands, so that he only reached his house at last by river, and almost alone.

Late that night he had yielded himself up to Lord Nottingham, and his few remaining followers with him.

Surely the trial must be near its end by now?

What the end would be, Bess had small doubt; and she grieved for the beauty and the courage and the shine of Robin Devereux gone down to dust. But if Essex lived, he would be the death of Ralegh one day, she knew that; and she prayed with the ruthlessness of a woman protecting her own, that he might not live. Yet deep within her, far below the level of conscious thought, was the faint fore-knowledge that the web in which destiny had meshed them together was not to be so simply severed; that by his death, as surely as by his life, Essex would be in some sort the death of Ralegh.

She paused in the story to put another log on the fire and smile at the two small boys, who smiled back, Watt disclosing the gap where he had lately lost a milk-tooth.

A little later, she heard Ralegh's step outside, and broke off between word and word, as the door opened, and he appeared on the threshold. He was still clad in the orange-tawny taffetas of the Queen's Guard, just as he had come from Westminster Hall, and the grey February light touched on his silvered breastplate. Bess's eyes flew to his face, trying to read the verdict in it, but it told her nothing. For an instant he paused in the doorway, then advanced into the room; and she turned to the two small boys. "There, that must be all for today."

"But you've not finished the story," Watt protested in righteous indignation.

"I will finish it another day—tomorrow. Run to Joan, sweetheart, and take Will with you, and tell her I said that you might each have three ginger suckets."

The two scrambled to their feet and set off, ducking their heads to Ralegh, who returned a friendly nod to Will, but set a hand for an instant on Watt's shoulder as the small boy passed him. Little Watt checked and looked up, wagging his narrow stern in adoration. "One day I shall be the Queen's Captain," he said.

"Will you so, my valiant Imp? And what of myself? Am I to turn my helmet into a hive for bees?"

"The Queen must needs have two Captains," said Watt, after a moment's consideration. "She would be a deal safer with two of us."

Ralegh laughed, and sped him on his way with a friendly slap on his behind. "Shut the door after you." Then he turned to Bess, who had risen and stood waiting for him before the fire.

She looked up at him, her eyes questioning and very dark, her hands gripped together. "What news, Walter?"

"Death," Ralegh said.

. . . .

The Earl of Essex had been Leicester over again to Elizabeth; lover and son in one; but she signed the death warrant with a steady hand, and five days later he went to the block on Tower Green.

But though Essex's body lay headless in its narrow grave, the life of the Court must go on. If anything it was gayer than usual that spring. The long table was laid every evening in the Presence Chamber, and the Court supped as it was used to do, though the Queen in her Privy Chamber, with none but her nearest Ladies to see, could eat nothing but succory pottage and a little manchet bread. And after dark the lights shone from every window of the Palace, and there would be dancing in the Long Gallery, though the gayest dancer of all was no longer there to call the tune.

On an evening in late spring the light shone as usual from the windows of Whitehall Palace, and music lilted from the Long Gallery, stealing down the terraces to the misty river, and the Court made merry in honour of a Polish Envoy.

Bess, who was of the company that night, had a headache; a small, nagging thunder headache that grew worse as the hour latened. Presently, when the Queen had withdrawn, she began to feel as though a bright worm of pain was boring into her brain through her right eyebrow. There seemed no air in the Long Gallery, and the lights dazzled her and made her feel sick. Sir Lewis Stucley appeared, hovering in her neighbourhood as though he might be going to ask her to dance—he had never quite given up his fainthearted attempts at friendliness, though Ralegh had never appeared aware of them. He was moving towards her, and all at once she was desperate for escape. She could not dance again; above all, she could not dance with Sir Lewis whose nearness always made her vaguely uneasy.

In a near panic, she turned to a door close by, and slipped out thankfully into an ante-room. It was cooler here, but almost as bright as in the Gallery, and there were people standing about or passing through. She turned unobtrusively to another door, then checked, drawing back her wide skirts to give passage to Lord Henry Howard, who appeared suddenly in her path. The old man passed her with a gesture of cold courtesy, and going on her way with a suddenly quickened heart-beat, Bess carried with her the vision of eyes like dark jewels in an ivory mask, a beautiful wicked hand, ivory too, against dark velvet. Lord Henry Howard, a fanatical Romanist, and an ancient enemy of Ralegh's. Not for the first time she wondered how the man, long since exiled from Court for intriguing with the Queen of Scots, and closely bound to the Essex faction, had shaken free and climbed back into the Court circle just as Essex went down into the dark. The nearness of him in his passing made her afraid, but then so many things made her afraid these days, things and the shadows of things, even the sight of Sir Lewis Stucley. And oh! her head did ache!

She turned a corner, and another, mounted a shallow flight of steps into a little used gallery, and found the quiet she longed for. Only a few tapers shed a soft light on the painted escutcheons on the walls, and the hangings at an oriel window stirred in the breath of air from an open casement. She crossed to it, and sank down on the cushioned sill, leaning her aching temple against the cool stone of the mullion.

Far off, like the echo of the sea in a shell, she heard the music in the Long Gallery, and once or twice, distant voices or footsteps; but no one disturbed her. It was quiet here, quiet, and cool.

Gradually she began to feel better; and she was on the point of rising to go back to the dancers, when a light prowling step sounded behind her, and she looked round to see the Secretary of State.

"Robin!" she exclaimed. "What brings you this way?"

"Much the same as I imagine brings you, Elizabeth; the search for a little air to breathe. I have been with the Queen and the Polish Envoy. His Excellency is greatly averse to fresh air."

He moved forward into the deep embrasure beside her, and something in the way he stood there, leaning with one hand on the stonework, made Bess say, "You are tired."

"I am always tired, these days." There was no self-pity in his tone. He was merely stating a fact.

"You work too hard," Bess said, impulsively.

"There is so much work to be done. Beside, what else is there for me to do? I cannot be for ever collecting jewels or watching my new house built, or even playing cards."

There was nothing one could say to that, nothing to be said. Into the silence that hung between them stole the sound of someone singing below in the darkness. The tune was Greensleeves, ever a favourite on which to graft words of the moment; and as the singer drew nearer, the words became plain.

> All you who cry O hone! O hone!
> Come now and sing O Lord! With me:
> For why? Our Jewel is from us gone,
> The valiant knight of Chivalry.

"Even under the Palace windows, they sing that song," Bess whispered, as the singer passed on about his business, and first words and then tune faded.

"Three whole months and more, they have kept faith," Cecil said sardonically. "Never have I known the Mob true for so long to a dead man."

"He was what the song says—their Jewel to them. He was beautiful and full of fire, and they never understood nor believed the rest." She turned to Cecil in the dim light which, shining through the wine-coloured hangings, made a red glow behind his head. "You know they say that Walter lured him to his ruin, and stood by, puffing at his pipe and—gloating over his handiwork, to see the axe fall?"

"They say as much of me, for the first part." Cecil sounded faintly amused. "The second charge, they cannot level at my head, since I do not smoke."

"They can say that your kindness to him in the Tower was but to throw dust in the Queen's eyes!"

"But then," Cecil said gently, "that which were another man's paternoster were ever accounted in me a charm."

Bess rounded on him in sudden exasperation born of fear. "You are as bad as Walter! You seem, both of you, positively to pleasure in the hatred and mistrust of stupid people!"

"Your husband must answer that charge for himself. For myself —I do not pleasure in it. I have merely learned indifference. When

I was young and extremely foolish, it even gave me hurt." He laughed, very softly. "By what right are you so scornful of the Mob's stupidity? Do you not also mistrust me in your heart of hearts?"

"No!" Bess protested. She drew a quick breath. "Not for a moment, if you will tell me that you had no hand in his downfall."

"You see?—Does it matter to you?"

"Yes! Oh, not for his sake; for yours."

"Thank you, Elizabeth. Shall we say merely, as your husband once wrote to me, that the Earl of Essex was a canker to the Queen's safety and estate?—a constant menace to the realm, while he lived?"

Bess's throat felt suddenly dry. "So you took measures to ensure that he should not live?"

"With so rash and headstrong a plotter, there could be no need to take anything so positive or so clumsy as 'measures'," he said deliberately.

Bess shrank from him a little. It seemed to her that the red glow behind his head was an unholy oriel. "Sometimes I think you really *are* a devil!" she whispered.

They had been speaking at half breath ever since he joined her in the window, and now his voice, low pitched as the purring of a cat, barely reached her. "So you have heard my new name? Personally I find it an improvement on the old one. It never amused me to hear myself called Robert the Hunchback. Robert the Devil is infinitely better."

"Infinitely better! You even took Communion with him, the night before he died!"

"Why not? Are you not confusing political expediency with personal animus? We were political foes—all the world knoweth it—not personal enemies. I had already saved most of his confederates; there was small harm in them without his flame to kindle them; and he was grateful. There was no blasphemy in that we took Communion side by side."

The sudden horror had ebbed away from Bess, leaving her chilled and shaking; and utterly baffled by the complexities of men which she would never understand as long as she lived. "How do you dare to speak of these things in the very Palace?" she asked at last.

"There is no arras to hide an eavesdropping page."

"There is—myself."

"You, Elizabeth? What have I told you, other than the whole world and the Council knows already?"

She found herself thinking back over the past few minutes, as though trying to lay hold of the dissolving end of a dream. "Nothing, almost nothing—in words. Nevertheless, you have—allowed me to know. Why did you do that?"

"Because you asked me."

"Would you put your neck in the hands of anyone who asked you?"

He sounded amused, and a little surprised at her lack of wit. "My neck could never be unsafe in your hands, Elizabeth, while I hold a certain letter of your husband's."

It was not a threat, Bess knew that. She had asked him a question, and he had answered it scrupulously; he who had so few scruples in his dealings with the world. All at once her heart ached for him. She asked another question, with a woman's quick change of position. "Do you never trust anyone?"

"Not of late years." He sighed, and turned half away, as a group of strayed revellers entered the gallery. "It was a fine jewel, but with a hidden flaw. God den to you, Lady Ralegh."

CHAPTER 12

FAITH IN ISRAEL

"It appeareth now, by one's example, more bound than all or any others, how little faith there was in Israel," the Queen said to Lord Willoughby when Essex's death was still a raw wound, speaking not only of her Robin, but of all those others who had turned from her to follow him—so many of them, so little faith in Israel.

She had aged ten years in the weeks following the execution, all that was young slipped away from her unawares, so that she was, as Ralegh said of her with a pity that was rare in him, "A Lady whom time had surprised."

But by the autumn of 1602 she seemed to have mastered her own sick heart. She rode and hunted as of old; early in December she was carried in her gleaming litter through the first snow of the winter, to dine at Sir Robert Cecil's great new house in the Strand, and that Christmas was the gayest that the Court had known for years. There was a sudden craze for country dancing, which the Queen had always loved; pavanes and galliards were laid aside, and the long galleries lilted to such tunes as Dargazon and Jenny-pluck-pears.

At the end of January, the Court moved to Richmond; a bitter journey only just accomplished in time, for the wind had gone round to the north-east, bringing in black winter weather that made travelling all but impossible. Frozen mire clogged the ways, and icy sleet blotted out the world for days at a time, and draughts that cut like a whetted knife cried up and down the galleries of Richmond Palace. The Queen refused to dress more warmly; she had never worn furs save for show, and did not intend to begin now. She rustled to and fro in silks and taffetas as she had always done, and laughed at her shivering ladies. It seemed as though the cold could not touch her through the armour of her indomitable will.

And then in mid-February the old Countess of Nottingham died.

The loss of one of her Ladies was not so great a matter, it would seem, as many of the losses she had suffered, the stresses and the agonies she had known, the dangers she had outfaced in the years that were behind her. But Lady Nottingham was an old and very dear friend, almost the last of those who had shared her youth, the very last, seemingly, of those who linked her to the living world. Quite suddenly she became frail, shrivelling before the eyes of her Court like a dead poplar leaf in the icy wind; until a night came, towards the end of March, when they knew that her long reign was within a few hours of its end.

No one retired to their quarters that night. They hung about the Presence Chambers and ante-rooms, speaking to each other in hushed voices. The galleries were full of silent comings and goings, quietly passing feet, uneasy shadows on candle-lit walls. The whole Palace was awake and waiting; waiting for the Queen to die.

Less than a week since, her legs failing her, she had taken to a pile of cushions on the floor of her bed chamber. There she had sat, refusing with all the indomitable strength that was still in her, to go to bed. Her physician, her Chaplain, her Ladies, the Members

of her Council, she had defied them all. Finally the Earl of Nottingham, the Lord High Admiral, who had withdrawn from Court
following his wife's death, had come stalking into her chamber,
and neither pleaded nor persuaded, but ordered the Queen to bed.
And to bed she had gone at last, like a docile child. That had been
three days ago; and this morning, said the whisperers, she had sent
for her Council, and signified to them by signs—she was beyond
speech—that James VI of Scotland was to take her throne after
her.

So the long-debated, long-intrigued question of the Successor
was settled. It was the last thing she had to do in this world.

And now the Queen lay dying, with the Ladies of her bed
chamber about her, and the Captain of her Guard standing before
the door. Bess could catch a glimpse of the Queen's Captain, from
the place where she stood with Mary Herbert, far down the
shadowed privy gallery—a mere streak of silver and orange-tawny,
through the open ante-room doorway—but she glanced that way
repeatedly, as one touching a talisman in a dark place.

In another part of the gallery, the Maids of Honour had drifted
into a cluster, looking in their gowns of white and green like a
huddle of startled birds gathered close for company. Most of them
were crying in a subdued way, for the Queen had been kind to her
Maids after her fashion; and they were frightened by something
infinitely more final than her death.

All along the gallery, people were waiting; the Queen's Ladies,
the Queen's Courtiers, standing and sitting in little groups. They
could do no good by it. The Queen had no further need of them;
and only the Ladies of her bed chamber were held in the privy
apartments by duty; but they lingered about her none the less,
unable to bring themselves to go to their own lodgings, though the
hour grew late, and later yet. Doors opened and closed softly; the
physician's low voice sounded, and was still; gentlemen of the
household congregated near doors that were kept open. The black
and gold lacquered clock on the wall ticked more loudly, Bess
thought, than she had ever heard it before, ticking away the last
hours of the Queen's life, telling them off with a whirr and a cascade
of bell notes that were sparks of clear sound in the murmurous hush
of the waiting Palace.

There had been a breath of spring in the world for the first time, that day, a softer feel in the air, a sense of quickening. Bess remembered suddenly a clump of golden crocuses, like candle flames, like a fanfare of trumpets, rising from the sleet-puddled earth in an angle of the lower terrace. "The Resurrection and the Life," she thought. "The Resurrection and the Life." The thought superimposed itself on the image of the golden crocuses and becoming one with it. But tonight the winter had swooped back, and sleet spattered against the windows, and a little moaning wind ran to and fro along the galleries, swaying the arras and worrying the candle flames

Two men came out through the ante-room; Archbishop Whitgift, the Queen's "Black Husband", and following him the stocky figure of Matthew Sutcliffe, the Dean of Exeter and her Chaplain. They had been with her many hours, but now her need of them was over, too. Faces were turned to them, low-pitched questions asked. They shook their heads. Her Majesty was asleep, very peacefully asleep. It was unlikely that she would wake again in this world.

The black and gold clock chimed one o'clock, two o'clock. Once a shadow that might be the physician's passed across the fretted screen-work that shielded the Queen's door. The Queen's Captain shifted to ease the ache of an old wound.

Still the shadowy people came and went, quietly, very quietly: Lord Cobham appeared in a doorway, and when Bess looked again, had become Nottingham; and when she looked a third time, the doorway was empty. So might figures drift through the dark mazes of a dream. And as a black shadow thrown up out of nowhere by a dream, having for Bess the quality of incipient nightmare, suddenly Lord Henry Howard was there.

He came up the gallery slowly but purposefully; he was not merely lingering about the Queen, as all those other shadows. He had come for a definite purpose; to do something, or speak with someone. A very stately figure, in sombre magnificence of dark velvet, he passed close to Bess; so close that she caught the faint smell of the dried orange he carried in his hand, and it seemed to her that the candle flames burned bluish at his passing.

She shivered uncontrollably, and felt Mary Herbert's small warm hand over hers, and heard the other woman's voice in her ear, asking what ailed her.

"I feel as though death himself had just walked by," she said.

"It was only My Lord Henry Howard." The other soothed her. "I know. I am a fool. It is this long waiting." She strained her eyes after the dark receding figure, and it seemed to her that as it melted into the gloom of the stairhead, it was joined by another shadow, which there was no mistaking, that of the Secretary of State.

She could not know, save by that intuitive sense of death as he passed, that scarcely an hour before, Henry Howard had been writing the latest of many poisonous letters to James of Scotland, in a peculiarly ingenious cypher of his own.

He had devised that cypher some years previously, when he and Cecil had begun their correspondence with James; for they had things to write which were better not read by other eyes than those for which they were intended. That had been when men's minds first began to be occupied with the question of the Queen's successor, and it had seemed to these particular two men advisable that they should forge a close link with the most likely heir. They were an odd partnership, having nothing of their aims in common save a determination to be the new King's Chief Councillor when the time came. Cecil desired above all to effect the change of ruler smoothly, to set James firmly on his throne before rival claimants could make trouble, and himself to be to the new ruler what he had been to the old one. His goal was clear before him, and he paved the way towards it, for the country's good as well as his own, with a cold un-caring for broken lives and personal tragedies by the way. Howard on the other hand, had forged his link with James in order to gain his favour for Catholicism, and, hating Ralegh as the arch-enemy of Spain and the Romish church, his letters were full of subtle attacks on the Queen's Captain. For years he had been preparing, by sneers and insinuations, lies and twisted half-truths, for Ralegh's downfall in the day when James and not Elizabeth should rule England.

And now the day was here. Between three and four in the morning a door banged somewhere, and a gust of wind bellied out the arras in the Privy Gallery: and in the bed chamber before whose door her Captain stood guard, the Queen died.

A few minutes later, in a lull of the moaning wind, Bess caught the sound of horses' hooves trippling into the distance, and guessed that a messenger was riding North already, with news for the

Scottish King. She was right. He had been standing by, his horse ready saddled, for several hours. Cecil had had the letter written in advance.

The Queen lay dead, the Coronation ring cut from her swollen finger; but a ring that Essex had given her was still on her hand.

PART
II
JAMES

CHAPTER 13

A MESH OF MANY STRANDS

James had come to the English throne. Not his kinswoman Arabella Stuart; not Lord Hartford; not the Infanta of Spain. All that, it seemed, was over and done with, the plotting and whispering and intriguing that had darkened the last years of Elizabeth's reign swept away like cobwebs, and the house made clean and shining for its new Master. James rode south in the first flush of spring, and many of the younger folk watched for his coming eagerly, saying to each other that they had been ruled by a woman long enough; looking to good days ahead.

But to Ralegh, the good days were already behind. Almost the first thing James had done on reaching London was to relieve him of his Captaincy of the Guard, and forbid him the Court. Sherborne received him into exile again. And then, most unexpectedly, at the end of May, word came that he was free to attend at Court once more, and he went instantly with Cecil's letter in his hand to look for Bess, just as he had gone to her with the Lord Admiral's letter, six years ago. This time he found her in her painted parlour, copying the receipt for a sure remedy against the colic into the book in which she kept such things; and taking her by surprise, plucked the quill from her hand, spattering ink on the careful page.

"Oh Walter, see what you have done!"

He laughed, completely unrepentant. "Never mind for that. Listen to me, Bess. I am free to attend at Whitehall again!"

Bess got up slowly, the tragedy of the marred page forgotten. "But you will not go, Walter? Surely you will not go?" she said.

"Of course I shall go. Why should I not?"

She answered his question with another. "Does the King return to you the Captaincy of the Guard?"

A shadow seemed to darken the blazing blue of her husband's eyes. "No, not that."

"Or Durham House?"

The shadow was gone. "Madam unreason! Have you not always

5   129

hated Durham House? The Bishop is welcome to what is left of it!"

Bess put out a hand and touched his slashed sleeve. "Walter, the King hates you—he made that clear enough when he found you among those who met him at Burghley House. He hates you because he has been taught to; he has been taught that you are his enemy, that you wrought Essex's downfall, who was his ally."

"Sweet, who should teach him these things?"

"I—do not know," Bess said slowly. "But Henry Howard has small love for you, and he has the King's ear. You know that all men say he and Cecil are the two wheels of James' triumphal chariot."

"Howard, possibly." He sounded a little impatient, for he was disappointed at the way she had taken his news. "A venomous creature. But you are not bidding me to distrust Cecil, are you?"

"I am not sure. He has changed since his Bess died—God forbid that we should mistrust a friend. But Walter, please, please do not go back to Court."

"God's sweet life, Bess!" He was more than impatient now, he was exasperated, and he refused the hand she held out to him. "Cannot you see that those same reasons you have been putting forward against my return are the very reasons why I *must* go back to Court? If anyone is indeed poisoning the King's mind against me, am I to sit here with my hands folden across my paunch, and let them do as they will with my name? You should be ashamed to counsel it."

"And you?" she flashed out at him. "Should you not be ashamed to go crawling back to lick the hand of a fat King who has had you whipped? A King who dribbles in his beard and ends his dinner too drunk to stand; whose Court is already a byword from which many people prefer to stay away? You, who have been the Queen's Captain?"

"I who have been the Queen's Captain," he said harshly. "There is no need that you should remind me. May I in turn remind you that James is the King, named as her successor by Elizabeth herself —and without his favour I am hamstrung as I was without hers. Bess, cannot you understand?"

Impatience and exasperation were gone as swiftly as they had come, and the last words were an appeal.

Against her will, Bess did understand. It was for his dream, the old, all-demanding dream, that he needed the King's favour. He had his own integrity, but for him, integrity lay in keeping faith with his dream. She sighed. "When do we start?"

"I shall start early in the morning, but you must stay here with the boy. You said yourself that the Court was a byword, and I will not have you smeared by it, nor snubbed again by the silly lint-haired Queen, as you were at Burghley House!"

So the next morning he set out for Westminster, and Bess stood with Little Watt beside her, in the house doorway, to see him ride away. It was a golden morning, fresh with the youth of spring, warming to the fulfilment of summer; from the distant woods Jerusalem way, a cuckoo was calling, and Little Watt flung up his head and called back joyously "Cuckoo! Cuckoo!" Ralegh reined in at the turn of the bridle path, under the lime trees in young leaf, and looked back. Always, when he rode out alone, he turned there for a last sight of Bess standing in the doorway of the home he loved. He doffed his hat in farewell, and Bess put up her hand as she had done so often before, and waved to him. But today he seemed to linger a little over his leave-taking, looking back again, as though he had in that moment some instinct that it was for the last time.

But if he had had any such foreboding, it passed as quickly as the shadow of a flying bird. He was free to attend on the new King, and from that, who knew what glorious fortune might follow? If he could gain the King's ear, maybe he would yet see an English Empire of his building, in the New World.

. . . .

A few days after the Coronation, Ralegh was waiting on the North Terrace at Windsor, to accompany the King out hunting. The King was late—the King was generally late; so many things always went amiss to delay him. At thirty-nine he was already a messy old man. He shambled both in speech and gait, he could not eat without spilling his food, he could not sleep without snoring and dribbling in his beard, nor drink without becoming humiliatingly drunk. It was his misfortune. Ralegh, leaning against the balustrade and puffing at his silver-bowled pipe, wondered with casual contempt, what it was this time.

All along the Terrace, gay groups drifted and mingled; the Court waiting for the King. Ralegh's eye sauntered over them, singling out here one, there another. Francis Bacon of the bright hazel eye that always reminded him of a viper's; Tom Howard; Penelope Rich, who had once been Penelope Devereux, like a leopard lily in the sunlight, making pretty play with her gloves for the benefit of Mary Herbert's younger son. Anything that was breeched, it seemed, was old enough for Lady Rich to flirt with. She flirted as a flower gives out scent. Ralegh's gaze lingered on the boy beside her; no trace of his Uncle and namesake in him, indeed the high favour in which he was held by the slobbering King was a measure of the difference between him and Philip Sidney; yet when he turned his head—so, it was odd how the other Philip came back.

A few more familiar figures met his wandering gaze; for the rest, a swarm of hungry Scottish Courtiers who had followed the King south. That ruddy and impudent page of his, for instance, Robert Carr, kicking his heels yonder. . . .

Ralegh's eye fell on a small boy with a guinea-gold head, squatting on his haunches close by to play with a Spaniel pup; and his face momentarily lost its look of bleak distaste. There was one good thing come south with Daft Jamey, anyway; little Prince Henry; nine years old—the same age as Watt. The boy looked up and caught his eye, and the eager pointed face quirked into a faun's smile. He held the puppy up, its pink stomach exposed, its hind legs trailing, as though to share his delight in it with the dark man with the pearl in his ear. Then a group of girls came between them, and Ralegh turned from the crowded terrace to watch the horses and leashed hounds being walked to and fro below; to look out over twenty miles of softly rolling woods and water meadows. Summer was fulfilled and falling like a ripe peach into the hand; shining gossamer on the early morning grass, flecks of gold and lemon here and there among the weary green of elms and poplars, and the broken-voiced cuckoo at point of departure. The distances were very blue, deeply blue as the flowers of the bittersweet. It would be good at Sherborne now.

Standing in bleak isolation among the shifting, chattering, many-coloured throng, he heard a light, curiously prowling footfall behind him, and turned to find Robert Cecil at his elbow. The subtle face of the Secretary of State was shuttered, nothing visible for good or ill, of the thoughts, the emotions behind it. "Sir Walter, I come as from His Majesty the King," he said. "I grieve to spoil your hunting; but your presence is required in the Council

Chamber, to answer certain questions of the Lords of the Council."

And a few days later, after answering many questions of the Lords of the Council, Ralegh was in the Tower, awaiting trial on a charge of treason.

.   .   .   .   .   .

To poor Bess, hurrying through the grim ways of the Tower where she had spent her solitary honeymoon, knowing nothing save the bald statement of the message that had brought her post-haste from Sherborne, it seemed that she had stumbled into a nightmare and could not find the way out. To get to Ralegh was the only clear thought in the utter chaos of her mind, and she clung to it. It was thanks to Robert Cecil that she was to be allowed that. Robin had been a true friend in gaining her the King's leave to be with her husband; he was their friend still; he would help them; he must. And yet at thought of him she was gripped by the formless fear that is the essence of nightmare—the face of a friend changing into evil, the potential horror behind familiar things.

She followed blindly, where the warder led, not conscious of steps and doors and crooked ways, until she came down a last flight, and found that she was in a dark and narrow place, and beside her a door was opening. As she turned to it, someone came out past the turnkey who stood there. A short, burly man. In that dim place it was an instant before she recognised him as Dr. Peter Turner, who had often attended the family when they had need of greater skill than she herself possessed, and an instant longer before the implication of his presence struck home to her.

"Dr. Turner, is my husband ill?"

Gesturing to the turnkey to close the door, the Doctor turned to her with the gruff gentleness that his patients knew. "Lady Ralegh, it is by God's mercy that you come so soon. It is best that you know the truth before you go in to him. Sir Walter has tried to kill himself."

She gave a little gasp, and all the blood in her body seemed to leap back to her heart. "Oh no!" she whispered. "Oh no! Oh no!" as though by the repetition she could make what he said untrue. But it was true, she could read it in the physician's face. "Is he——" she began, and could not finish the sentence.

"No no, he will do well enough with you beside him." Dr.

Turner was giving her arm little clumsy reassuring pats. "It is but a flesh wound—here under the breast—and will soon mend. He has suffered very greatly."

Bess had no need that he should tell her that. Knowing Ralegh as she did, she knew all too well how bitter, how absolute and unbearable must have been the despair in which he made such an admission of defeat. "Let me in to him now, Dr. Turner," she said.

"Aye, poor lass," said the Doctor, returning unconsciously to the broad North country speech of his boyhood. He stepped aside, and the turnkey reopened the door.

As it closed again behind her, Bess walked forward into a small room walled with undressed stone, into an airless and faintly animal atmosphere tangible as smoke. The light from a tiny window— hardly more than a chink—high under the groined roof showed her the Queen's Captain stretched on a narrow plank bed against the oozing wall. He was lying flat, his head turned from her; the dirty covering was pushed down, and where his shirt lay open at the breast, showed the white gleam of bandages. Part of her mind registered the fact that there was no stain on his shirt; somebody must have brought him clean linen. She was across the dim place, and kneeling beside him.

"Walter—I am here."

For a long time he remained rigidly unresponsive, with averted face. Then he turned his head and looked at her, with a frown between eyes that were at once bitter and bright. "So you see, I have botched it," he said, with a jibing note in his voice that hurt her as though it had been a blow. "All my life I have botched all that I set my hand to, but I had supposed I might at least have handled so simple a matter as this without bungling."

"Thank God you did bungle!" Bess said. "Oh, thank God you did, my dear."

He moved his head restlessly. "It would have been better for you and the boy—better for my own name on men's lips, that I died uncondemned."

"They will acquit you!" she protested, with the terror jumping in her voice. "They must! You have touched no treason!"

"Nevertheless, they will not acquit me. Do you not see? My trial will be a form, a mummer's play to satisfy the Mob that their new

King deals in justice, even by their enemy and his. I am finished, Bess."

"No!"

He put up a fumbling hand to caress her shoulder, the bitterness falling from him. "Poor Bess; my poor little Bess. Do not you hope; the outcome will but strike the sharper. . . ." He lay for a silent moment, his eyes on her face. Then, seeming to come to a decision, he began to speak, quickly and urgently. "Listen now, for there is no saying how short a time we may have, nor when we may speak together again, and it is best that you understand the whole. Soon after I returned to Court, Cobham dropped something in my ear concerning a crazy plot with Arenburg for tipping James off the throne and setting Arabella Stuart in his place, with Spanish gold to keep her there, and Spanish gold for Cobham and Spanish gold for me if I would lend them my aid. Knowing Cobham, I thought it merest vapouring—fool that I was—and paid no heed. But a plot there was, Bess, and just before the Coronation, Cecil gathered it in, and with it another in which that idiot brother of Cobham's, George Brooke, was embroiled, which seems to have been for keeping James on the throne but making him dance to the Pope's tune. When Brooke was examined, it seems he stated that he and his fellows had thought me a fit man to be of the action—though God in his Heaven knows why, for I am scarce a lover of the Romish Church. That, and the long association there has been between myself and Cobham, has been enough to drag me into the meshes."

Bess's brain seemed racing round like a frantic caged squirrel. "But Lord Cobham must be linked to a score of innocent men as closely as to you; and it is no crime of yours, that George Brooke has had a thought concerning you! Walter, they cannot bring you to trial on such grounds!"

He laughed mirthlessly. "No. It was enough to gather me in and hold me while they found better, no more. They have better grounds now, and in part, of my own providing. Did I not say I botched all that I set my hand to?"

"What—do you mean?"

"Like a fool, I denied all knowledge of the plots at my first examination. I was bewildered, taken by storm, I had had no time to think. Then later, having thought a little, I saw the danger of that, since every soul about the Court knew Cobham to be hatching something with Arenburg, and I wrote to Cecil and told him that I had heard something, but had given no heed to it, thinking it— as I told you—mere vapouring; also that I had from time to time known Cobham to visit a man called La Renzi, an agent of Aren- burg's. That told him nothing he did not know already, but I hoped that it might serve to cover my blunder." His voice strained hoarsely for a moment. "Cecil took my letter to Cobham. He managed the affair most cleverly—so that my Lord Cobham, conceiving that I sought to save my skin at the cost of his, lost all head he ever had, and denounced me as having been not only aware of every detail, but the ringleader of the whole affair."

"Cecil," Bess said dully, and her mouth felt dry.

"Aye, Cecil. You were right, you see, Bess," Ralegh said. He turned his face into her shoulder. "Mine own familiar friend."

Presently he began to talk again, quietly and intently. Having failed in his attempt to kill himself, he seemed to have put away all thought of a quick way out; his courage had returned to him, and he began giving Bess her directions for the things that she must do, the people who she must apply to for help, to save what could be saved out of the wreck for herself and the child. And Bess listened and tried to remember, since that was the only thing she could do for him now.

He was very collected, with a kind of brittle calm, planning for the future in which he would have no part. "Bess, when all this is over, you must not hide over long from the world. You are too warm and sweet for the dark. One day you must marry again." Then at her passionate gesture of denial. "Ah, but indeed you must, for the Imp's sake and your own. Marry for security, when that time comes, Bess. Marry for comfort and position—for companion- ship if you will. Only do not love him." Suddenly his calm was swept away, and his arms were round her, straining her to him until she was terrified that he would re-open the wound; and his words came hot with an aching urgency. "Don't love him, My Heart, not as you love me—and I will not lie torn with jealousy in my grave."

CHAPTER 14

THE VERDICT

King's Bench kept their next term at Winchester, for the plague was raging in London. And so it was in the Great Hall of Wolvesey Castle, that on November 17th, Elizabeth's Accession Day, the last of her Round Table stood his trial for treason.

The solemn medieval hall was already packed like a popular bear-garden, and enterprising onlookers had climbed on to the stone seats of the windows and the bases of the pillars for a better view of the proceedings on and below the dais at the Western end. And a woman in a dark cloak had come out from the private doorway into the gallery that spanned the East end of the hall, and stood unnoticed in the shadows, gazing, like all those others, down the crowded length of the hall towards the dais.

There, under a brocade canopy, sat the mountainous Lord Chief Justice, Sir John Popham; and with him the Special Commissioners, and the three judges. There too, was Sir Edward Coke the Attorney General, who was to conduct the trial.

The woman in the dark cloak turned her eyes with an aching intensity from one face to another, as though in search of some shred of hope. Popham, who had begun his career as a cut-purse; Henry Howard; Waad, who was Cecil's creature—but they were nearly all Cecil's creatures; Cecil himself. No, there was no hope to be had from such a Court. Her strained gaze turned from them to the figure of the prisoner, who had just been brought in.

He seemed as unaware of all the greedy and curious eyes fixed upon him now, as he had lately been of the crowds that had milled around him and his guards in the streets of London and Winchester, clearly considering it a suitable moment to avenge their lost darling by the murder of the man they still held responsible for his death. A hostile crowd in the streets, a hostile crowd in the Court; whispering, pointing, come to see the best hated man in England condemned to a traitor's death. Their hostility seemed powerless to touch him, but the woman standing in the shadowed gallery felt it beating up to her in dark engulfing waves.

Ralegh did not know that she was in the hall; it was better that way. She should not have been there, she knew; but nothing that anyone could say had had power to hold her back. So here she stood, with Mary Herbert's young William—now the Earl of Pembroke—close behind her for escort. Lawrence Kemys would have been with her, but he was in the Tower himself. Dear, dependable Lawrence Kemys, who had dared the rack to get messages from Ralegh to Cobham, bidding him, since two prosecution witnesses were needful in a treason case, to deny his whole confession and abide by the denial, if he would save himself as well as the man he had falsely accused. Cobham had pulled himself together and retracted his confession, she knew; but could that have any value in such a Court?

She realised that the proclamation for silence was being made; and struggled to focus her swerving and distraught mind as the trial began.

"Sir Walter Ralegh, hold up your right hand."

She saw Ralegh's hand go up, and she tried feverishly to understand, as the Clerk of the Court rose to read the indictment. "Conspiracy to deprive the King of his government," she heard. "To raise up sedition within the realm, to bring in the Romish Superstition, to aid Foreign enemies to invade the Kingdom." The words ran round senselessly in her head, and she could force no sense from them. Walter had done none of these things; Walter, of all men; they must know that, these men with their scarlet robes and raptor faces. The Clerk was still reading: how that on July 9th Ralegh and Cobham had met and laid plans to bring Arabella Stuart to the throne, and for Cobham to apply to Arenburg for a hundred and fifty thousand pounds to finance the treason. How, when it occurred to them that Arenburg's Master could not even pay his own troops in the Netherlands, they had determined to apply to King Philip III. The end of the indictment was reached at last, and the Clerk looked up. "Sir Walter Ralegh, do you plead guilty, or not guilty, to the charges?"

"Not guilty," Ralegh said.

The Clerk sat down, and in his place Sergeant Heale rose to open the case for the Crown. And then somehow it was not Sergeant Heale but Sir Edward Coke; hard and handsome and horribly formidable, fingering his furred gown. And instantly the trial, which until that moment had been a mere inanimate form of word and movement, leapt to life and became a duel. The Attorney General was renowned for the brutality of his methods, and the onlookers, who had been growing restive, drew their breaths in pleasurable expectancy, feasting their eyes and their lust for sensation on the two men who stood before them more like equally matched antagonists than accuser and accused. But there was to be no equality in this duel, for Ralegh was to fight for his life virtually weaponless, without legal advice, without the power to call and question witnesses. The mob had not yet realised that.

Coke, following his usual method, plunged straightway into a vitriolic attack upon the monstrous wickedness of one who could plot treason against so good a King as he who now sat upon the throne of England. Ralegh cut into the flow of words presently, on a quick note of challenge. "Mr. Attorney, your words cannot condemn me, my innocence is my defence. Prove *one* of these things wherewith you have charged me, and I will confess the whole indictment."

Interrupted in his harangue, Coke seemed to swell, his handsome face mottling with the rage into which he was deliberately lashing himself. "Nay, but I shall prove them all! Before this trial is brought to an end, we shall prove you, Sir Walter Ralegh, to have set yourself at the head of this most infamous plot, with Lord Cobham's aid, to deliver this country into the hands of Spain. You monster with an English face but a Spanish heart!"

"I have neither set myself at the head of such a plot, nor had any part in it." Usually Ralegh had some difficulty in making himself heard at a distance, but today, although he did not raise his voice, every word had a chiselled clarity that reached to the farthest end of the hall, even to the gallery, where his wife stood listening. "If, as you say—though for myself I know nothing of it—My Lord Cobham is a traitor, what is that to me?"

Coke's head was low between his shoulders, thrust forward and menacing in the way that had cowed so many in his time. He looked as though he could barely keep his hands off the quiet figure at the bar. "All that he did was by thy instigation, thou viper! And so we shall shortly prove!" He sat down and leaned back, breathing quickly, and beginning again to finger the fur of his gown. And the Judges and Commissioners glanced at each other, nodding.

The Clerk rose again, to read Cobham's first statement before the Commission, in which he swore that he would never have entered the action save at Ralegh's instigation. And that, it appeared, was all the Crown's direct evidence.

"God knoweth how they may convict him on such a case!" the young Earl of Pembroke whispered to Bess. She shook her head, but no hope came to her.

And now it was Ralegh's turn to defend himself against the charges.

There was a long, expectant hush, while he glanced unhurriedly through the notes that he had taken. (He had been allowed pen and paper to aid his memory.) Then he began to speak. Words were to be his only weapon in this fight; he had always been a master of words, and he used his mastery now, to the full. He admitted freely that his first denial of all knowledge of the Arenburg plot had not been true; bidding his hearers remember that it had been made by a man fetched in from the sunlit threshold of a day's hunting, to face without warning what even then amounted to a treason charge. When he had had time to think more clearly, and to realise the gravity of his error, he had at once written to Sir Robert Cecil, admitting that he had heard somewhat of it from Lord Cobham, but had been too little interested to give the matter further thought. He would remind them that he had himself warned Sir Robert Cecil of the man La Renzi. Working up to his final argument, he drew a careful and detailed picture of the present fortunes of Spain and the Spanish King. "My Lords, and Gentlemen of the Jury, I pray you tell me this: why should I have intrigued with my Lord Cobham, a man of no repute, to the advantage of Spain, a sinking power? What had I to gain by such a course? . . . Of twenty-five hundred thousand pounds come from the Indies, the King of Spain has now scarce one hundred thousand left; how then, think you, should this money, of which there has been so much talk, be paid?"

There was a quickly suppressed buzz in the Court, and men looked eagerly to see how the prosecution would answer that argument. But the prosecution was not there to answer the unanswerable, but to secure a conviction; and so, hastily, the Clerk rose to read Cobham's second examination, and thereafter the proceedings tangled themselves into legal chaos which lasted until Cecil brought a lucid interval by rising to speak quietly and most movingly of the affection between himself and Ralegh, and the esteem in which he had held the other man before he fell into evil ways.

"My Lords." It was Ralegh again now, quick and impatient. "All this, surely, can but confuse the issue. It seems that all your accusation against me rests on the uncorroborated word, spoken in haste and fear, and afterwards repented, of my Lord Cobham, whereas, in conformity with the 1st Statute of Edward VI, no man may be condemned for treason unless he be accused by two lawful witnesses; and they must be brought in person before him at his arraignment, if they be living."

"That Statute was found to be inconvenient, and was repealed by one and two of Philip and Mary," Coke cut in, up again, and returning to the attack.

"If that be so, then has justice suffered thereby." Ralegh turned on him in cold accusation. "If you condemn me by bare inference, without an oath, without a subscription, without witnesses, upon a paper accusation, you try me by the Spanish Inquisition!"

"That is a treasonable speech!"

"It was not meant to be so," Ralegh said. He made a small gesture of the open hands. "Since I may not have two accusers, Mr. Attorney, at least let the one I have be brought to face with me."

"So that you, by your devilish influence, may bring him to forswear himself on your behalf?"

Ralegh said gently, "If Christ requireth it, as it appeareth in the eighteenth chapter of Matthew, if by the Common Law, Civil Law, and God's Word, it be required that there must be two witnesses at the least, brought before the accused, bear with me if I desire my one."

For a moment the Judges and Commissioners seemed to waver, and Bess, straining every sense to catch the gist of their murmured conference, felt a flicker of bewildered hope as she realised that Cecil was supporting her husband's claim. But the thing was hopeless, after all. The Judges, clearly afraid of Ralegh's devilish influence, ruled that his demand was dangerous and unreasonable, refused it, and hurried on to the next stage of the trial with almost indecent haste.

The prosecution had begun calling witnesses (there were to be none for the defence), but the supply was so poor that at last they were reduced to using a seaman whose testimony was that in Lisbon a man had asked him if the King was yet crowned, and when told that he was shortly to be so, had replied: "Nay, he shall never be crowned, for Don Ralegh and Don Cobham will cut his throat ere that day comes."

The man before the Court turned his intent gaze from the last witness back to the Attorney General, and asked curiously, "What is it that you infer upon this?"

"That your treason hath wings!"

Ralegh leaned forward, his hands on the table, his gaze travelling unhurriedly from face to face of the men who sat in judgment on him. "My Lords, I find your whole case against me rests still, as it did at first, on the word of one man, *who has since retracted it*. Consider you, Gentlemen of the Jury: I that have always condemned the Spanish faction; methinks it is strange that I should now affect it. . . . If you would be contented on presumption to be delivered up to be slaughtered, to have your wives and children turned into the street to beg their bread; if you would be contented to be so judged, judge so of me."

A murmuring arose in the body of the hall, a rising unrest among the close-packed throng who had come to hear their old enemy condemned to die. A strange thing was happening; the crowd's hostility was changing its direction.

The rising fret was cut short by the Attorney General, who, with palpable triumph, produced from among his papers, a letter from Cobham which he proceeded to read aloud. It was a statement in which the wretched writer withdrew his recantation, and reverted to his original accusations against Ralegh.

The only man who seemed untouched by the sensation which followed was Ralegh himself. He listened to the Attorney General's reading with quiet attention, and as soon as it was done, drew a paper from the breast of his doublet. "Sir Robert Cecil, will you be so good as to take and read this letter, since of all those here present, you will be the best able to identify your brother-in-law's writing."

Bess leaned forward, her hands gripped together until the knuckles shone white as bare bone, as the paper was handed up to the Secretary of State. Cecil took and unfolded it; and after glancing at the contents, read aloud, with no change of expression on his subtle face. "For the discharge of my own conscience, and freeing

myself of your blood, which else will cry vengeance against me, I
protest upon any salvation I never practised with Spain by your
procurement. God so comfort me in this my affliction as you are a
true subject for anything I know. So God have mercy on my soul,
as I know no treason by you. Cobham." And the date was several
days later than that of the statement which the Attorney General
had just read.

Almost before the last word was out of Cecil's mouth, Coke was
on his feet with the furious protest. "Extorted! Extorted!" He was
shouting, his voice thick with rage. Everybody was shouting, it
seemed to Bess. This was a mad trial—unless she herself were mad.

Sergeant Heale was hammering the table and calling for order,
and as the sudden uproar began to subside, an anonymous voice
broke free of the turmoil. "Was the other not extorted?" it cried.
"Tell us that, Mr. Attorney!"

The cry brought some response, for when silence was restored,
the dry voice of the Lord Chief Justice made itself heard almost for
the first time. "Lest there be a doubt in any man's mind, as to
whether Lord Cobham's statement in which he withdrew his re-
traction, was freely written, or was drawn from him by promise of
mercy or fear of the reverse, I would have the Gentlemen of the
Jury assured of that fact."

The Earl of Devon rose with a little bow. "I can give the Gentlemen of the Jury the positive assurance that the statement in question
was written by Lord Cobham of his own wish, and was not in any
way extorted."

The Lord Chief Justice bowed his head. "Thank you. There is
then, no more that need be said." He turned to the Jury, to dismiss
them to consider their verdict.

Lawrence Kemys had risked the rack to no purpose.

And now the Jury were filing out, and with their going, the pitch
of tension in the Court sank like the note of a slackened lute-string.
The Judges and Commissioners stretched and relaxed; Coke lounged
out to a door which gave on to the Castle garden, and stood there,
bland as a cat in the autumn sunshine. But the crowd in the body
of the hall shifted and swayed, whispering among themselves, the
change still working in them like a ferment. Only the unseen
woman in the gallery remained utterly still, her gaze fixed on the
prisoner, who yet stood in his place, for they had not troubled to

remove him. His head was raised, his own gaze turned to the great three-light window above the dais, where a late peacock butterfly that had wandered in from the garden was beating jewelled wings against the glass in frantic and futile effort at escape.

A quarter of an hour crawled by, and then a shrill breath ran through the crowd as the Jury filed in once more. The Attorney General was back in his place. The old white face of the Lord Chief Justice bent forward, hovering as a hawk hovers, under the silken canopy. "Gentlemen of the Jury, do you find the prisoner guilty, or not guilty?"

"Guilty, My Lord."

Bess had known that it would be so, but the word fell upon her like a blow over the heart, none the less. Ralegh seemed as untouched by it as he was by the changing mood of the crowd. In the face of such a travesty of justice, he had been beaten, and known it, from the first, before ever he started his rearguard fight for life and honour; but nothing of that had appeared in his bearing then, and nothing of it appeared in his bearing now. Only, above him, the peacock butterfly still beat and beat with frantic wings against the glass.

Sergeant Heale had risen to demand judgment against the prisoner.

The hovering white face was turned upon him. "Sir Walter, you have put yourself upon your country for judgment, and these your Country, find you guilty of the horrible crimes of which you have been accused. Have you anything to say why judgment of death should not be passed upon you?"

Ralegh said: "My Lords, the Jury have found me guilty; they must do as directed. You see whereof Cobham hath accused me; you remember his protestation that I was never guilty. I desire the King should know of the wrongs done unto me since I came hither."

"Sir Walter, Sir Walter, you have had justice, and no wrong done unto you in this place." The Lord Chief Justice shook his head regretfully. "I thought I should never have seen this day to have stood in this place to give sentence of death against you; for I had thought it impossible that one of so great parts should so grievously have fallen." He made a slow gesture of Finis, with bowed head and spread hands. "Now it resteth to pronounce the judgment which I wish you had not this day to receive of me. For if the fear of God in you had been equal to your other great parts, you might have lived to be a singular good subject. But since you have been found guilty of these horrible treasons, the judgment of the Court is that you shall be had from hence to the place whence you came, there to remain until the day of execution; and from thence you shall be drawn on a hurdle through the streets to the place of execution, there to be hanged and cut down alive, and your body shall be opened, and your heart and bowels plucked out, and your privy members cut off and thrown into the fire before your eyes; then your head to be stricken from your body, and your body divided into four quarters to be disposed of at the King's pleasure; and may God have mercy on your soul."

Cecil bowed his face into his hands.

The butterfly was still battering its wings against the sunlit glass.

For an instant the silence in the hall was so intense that the tiny frantic beating sounded clearly, like the beat of a racing heart. Then it was swallowed up in a rising murmur, an angry confusion of sound with a hornet note in it. The change in the mood of the onlookers was complete.

But Bess knew nothing of that. With the last words of the appalling sentence roaring in her ears, "May God have mercy on your soul—God have mercy——" she had crumpled quietly to the floor in the first and only dead faint of her life.

.

The other trials followed a few days later. Brooke was executed on December 6th, the executions of Cobham and his fellow conspirators were fixed for the 10th, and Ralegh's for the 13th, all the sentences having been commuted to beheading.

In the days between, Ralegh sank to humiliating depths. Suffering the most appalling reaction from the strain of his trial, he lost his courage and laid down his pride, and sued for his life to the King and the Council, promising anything, *anything*, if only he might live.

And then at seemingly the last moment, he found his courage again, and took up his pride, and set himself to make a cleanly and shining finish.

On the morning of December 10th, Bess, who was lodging close to the Castle, but had not been allowed to see him, received a letter

from him. When the messenger who brought it was gone, she took
it to the window, for though it was ten o'clock, it was raining and
the light was bad. She opened it with a steady hand, for fear and
hope alike seemed to have died in her, days ago.

"You shall receive, dear wife, my last words in these my last
lines." His bold writing flashed up at her. "I would not, with my
last will, present you with sorrows, dear Bess. Let them go to the
grave with me and lie buried in the dust. And seeing it is not the
will of God that ever I shall see you in this life, bear my distruction
gently, and with a heart like yourself. Baily oweth me two hundred
pounds, and Adrien six hundred in Jersey, and I have much owing
me beside. The arrearages of the wines will pay your debits; and
howsoever you do, for my soul's sake, pay all poor men. I send you
all the thanks my heart can conceive or my pen express, for your
many troubles and cares taken for me, which—though they have
not taken effect as you wished—yet my debt is to you nevertheless;
but pay it I never shall, in this world. . . . Get those letters, if it be
possible, which I wrote to the Lords of the Council, wherein I sued
for my life. God knoweth it was for you and yours that I desired it,
but it is true that I disdain myself for begging for it. . . . I cannot
write much. God knoweth how hardly I stole this time when all
sleep; and it is time to separate my thoughts from the world. Beg
my dead body, which living was denied you, and either lay it at
Sherborne if the land continue, or in Exeter Church, by my father
and mother. I can write no more. Time and death do call me away.
. . . My love I send you, that you may keep it when I am dead,
and my council that you may remember it when I am no more.
My true wife, farewell. Bless my poor boy for his father's sake that
chose you and loved you in his happiest hour. Pray for me. May the
true God hold you both in his arms."

There was another sheet enclosed, and opening it, she read:
"Take charge of this, dear Bess, since I have no means of doing so."
And under, a few lines of poetry.

> Give me my Scallop shell of quiet,
> My Staff of Faith to walk upon,
> My Scrip of Joy, immortal diet,
> My bottle of Salvation.
> My gown of glory, hope's true gage,
> And thus I'll take my pilgrimage.

Blood must be my body's balmer,
No other balm will there be given.
Whilst my soul, like quiet palmer,
Journeys toward the land of Heaven.
Over the silver mountains
Where spring the nectar fountains.

There will I kiss
The bowl of bliss
And drink mine everlasting fill
Upon every milken hill.
My soul will be a-dry before
But after, it will thirst no more.

A great quiet seemed to reach out to Bess through the written words. Strange that that quiet should be so vital a part of such a restless man. "It is the quiet at the heart of all things," she thought. "The still place at the centre of the whirlwind."—My scallop-shell of quiet. It was out of that quiet that his dream came, the dream that was near to him as his own soul, nearer than she could ever be. "It was for you and yours that I desired it," he had written; but she knew that it was no more for her sake, that he had sued for his life, than it was because he was afraid to die. It was for his dream. He wanted time, time at all costs, out of which one day might flower the opportunity to follow his dream again.

She folded both sheets very gently and put them into her hanging pocket, thinking how she might get those letters back for him. There would be time enough for tears later, all the time in all the empty years ahead.

At that moment, in his cell at the old Royal castle, Ralegh was looking down from his window, on the scene being played out just below him on and around the scaffold that had been set up on Castle Green; Guards, clergy, populace, headsman in black velvet, all the trappings of an execution. Cobham and his fellows had been brought out to die. They had mounted the steps to the straw-spread scaffold and spoken their last words; the scaffold had been cleared, and Sir Griffin Markham was kneeling before the block. Ralegh could see the wide-eyed intensity of his face turned up for one last look at the sky. "It is so that it will be with me, in three days time," he thought. One of the steps to the scaffold dipped in the middle; in the hollow a puddle had collected, and the rain made rings in it.

There came a sudden clatter of horse's hooves. Below on the green, heads turned, fingers pointed. The Chaplain touched the headsman's arm as though to bid him wait. The three men on the scaffold were staring towards the archway with a terrible hope. Nearer and nearer yet. A horse and rider swung in from the street, sweeping close under Ralegh's window, the horseman, bent low in the saddle, calling: "Wait! In the King's name!" He reined back in full gallop, and dropping from his plunging mount, made towards the Sheriff, holding out a paper that shone very white in the sodden winter's day.

A reprieve in the nick of time; so dramatic, and so very well timed. A little smile twisted Ralegh's mouth as he watched. But the horse should have been ridden further; it spoiled the effect a little, that the brute should be so perfectly fresh. "How like His Majesty," he said softly. "How very like His Majesty King James."

A few minutes later, the Governor came to tell him that the King's mercy had extended even to himself. His Most Gracious Majesty had been pleased to lend all four of them back their lives. They were to be consigned to the Tower.

Six days later, in a dun-coloured river fog, Ralegh rode through the streets of London to the Tower. Again, there were crowds to throng his route and see him pass. They were the same crowds that had milled around him, shouting for his blood, when he rode Westward some three weeks before; but their mood was not the same. They were angry crowds still, but their anger was no longer directed against Ralegh. The most extraordinary revulsion of feeling had swept through the country since the trial. Those who were present in Wolvesey Castle hall had spread the report of Ralegh's superb fight against hopeless odds; and the English, loving a bonny fighter, loving fair play, and always on principle loving the underdog, had found in him, rather ironically, a successor to their lost Jewel. Ralegh the wealthy favourite had been the best hated man in the Kingdom, Ralegh ruined and a prisoner was its hero, and in the eyes of all England, the verdict against him had become a verdict against the King.

CHAPTER 15

"EVERY SEASON HIS CONTENTMENT"

At a table drawn close under the window of his prison to catch what little light fell through the narrow aperture, Ralegh was writing a letter to his old friend Robert Cecil, lately become Lord Cecil of Essingdon and soon to become Earl of Salisbury. "Whatsoever your Lordship hath conceived," he wrote, "I cannot think myself to have been either an enemy or such a viper but that this great downfall of mine, this shame, loss and sorrow, may seem to your Lordship's heart and soul a sufficient punishment and revenge. And if there be nothing of so many years love and familiarity to lay in the other scale, O my God! How have my thoughts betrayed me in your Lordship's nature, compassion and pity. For to die in perpetual prison I did not think your Lordship could have wished to your strongest and most malicious enemy."

It was the first of many letters, many agonised appeals for freedom, to the King, to the Council, to the man who had been his friend and who he could still not bring himself to look on as an enemy. With all his faults, he had never himself betrayed a friendship, and he could not understand that it might be possible for the other man to do so. And indeed he was not altogether at fault. The Secretary of State had wanted his downfall lest he menace the smooth working of the new régime, and the rise of the house of Cecil; but he had not wanted his death. It had not been for effect, that he bent his face into his hands when he heard the judgment given, and it had been largely owing to his efforts that it had been commuted to imprisonment. And since then, he had done all he could for Bess and Little Watt, obtaining for them leave to share Ralegh's prison, and for Ralegh himself leave to have his faithful John Talbot to attend him, and to receive visits from his friends.

But to those agonised appeals, he returned no answer.

So the first year wore away, and Ralegh wrote his letters and paced his cell, and stood below his slit window that was too high to see the world out of, staring up at the free sky, or sat hour after hour with his head in his hands, only to spring up and return to his pacing, to and fro, to and fro, until the old wound pulled him down again. Bess watched him helplessly, reminded of some great bird, caged and beating its wings against the bars until the brilliant feathers were bruised and tarnished and the free heart broken. She could not come near him to help him in those first days. Outwardly he behaved to her much as he had always done, but she knew that for all that, he was worlds away from her, battering at his prison to be out and free and following his dream; and the knowledge came very near to breaking her.

Little Watt might perhaps have reached his father, even then, but the boy was too young to understand, too overset by the collapse of his whole sunny world into this dark and narrow ruin, to have anything over from himself and his own bewilderments.

There was plague in the Tower in the summer; and in winter the river mists and all-pervading chill played havoc with Ralegh's old wound, increasingly so as the second winter of his captivity dragged by. But at the end of that winter there came a brief gleam of hope. It was brought into the dark cell by Lawrence Kemys, who, though he had been set at liberty long since, had remained at Ralegh's side, paying his own board and lodging.

"Sir Walter, as I hear, the new Venetian Ambassador comes before the month is out, and the King is to entertain him for several days, here in the Tower!"

The three of them looked at each other; one thought that they were careful not to speak, leaping between them. The Grace and Favour freeing of state prisoners was always a feature of such state visits.

Bess tried not to hope. So long as one did not hope, one was armoured, but the smallest spark of hope made one vulnerable again. But despite herself, she did hope, not realising how much, until almost on the eve of the visit, Sir George Harvey, the Lieutenant of the Tower himself brought them word that since Ralegh had objected to the Tower's lack of sanitation and to his son's being forced to sleep in a cell next door to a woman with a plague sore, he was to be shifted to the Fleet Prison immediately, for a change of air.

"So. His Majesty thinks of everything," Ralegh said quietly. Only his mouth twisted a little under the small clipped beard.

"Sir Walter, believe me, I am most heartily sorry for this," said Sir George with sudden warmth.

Ralegh smiled. "Nay, it is none of your fault, Sir George."

When they were alone again, he stood for a long time looking
down at the scattered papers on his table, with which he had been
occupied before the Lieutenant's coming, while Bess, sick and
shaking, pretended great industry over the shirt she was making by
candlelight. A convulsive movement from him made her look up,
and what she saw in his face brought her to her feet, spilling her
sewing unheeded on the floor. It was as though the whole horror
of his fate had swept over him in one moment of blinding and unbearable revelation. He said quite quietly, "It is for life, Bess," and
then cried it wildly, despairingly: "My God! My God! It is for
life!"

But even then she could not reach him; for in the same instant,
as she moved towards him, he regained the control that had slipped
so perilously, and sat down again to his papers.

During the time that Ralegh was in the Fleet, Bess was not
allowed to be with him. Mary Herbert would have had her come
to Baynard's Castle; Nicholas, with a brand new knighthood from
King James, came to take her back to Beddington; but Bess would
have none of these plans; and with Joan to look after them, took
Watt to a little house in Broad Street that was part of her own small
property. There she waited until, in due course, the Venetian Ambassador had gone back to his own place and Ralegh was returned
to the Tower.

He had been ill in the Fleet, a sudden collapse. All word of it
had been kept from her by his own command, and when she reproached him, he would only lean weakly against the wall of his
cell and laugh at her, without quite enough breath for the laughter.
And she was terrified.

It was at that point that Sir George Harvey took a hand, with the
result that, within a few days of his return, Ralegh had been shifted
out of his old quarters into new ones on the upper floor of the
Garden Tower, which were to be his home for eleven years. These
quarters consisted of a good-sized room opening off the portcullis
chamber, and various small cubby-holes which he could have the
use of for Watt, John Talbot and Lawrence Kemys. Bess was
allowed to have a bed brought in, and a few other pieces of furni-
ture, even to cover the bare sandstone of one wall, in which so
many prisoners had carved their names, with a square of tapestry
depicting the parting of Hector and Andromache in a field of stiff

heartsease and wild irises. Here, there would at least be room to move, daylight, and better air to breathe; and from the corner of the room a circular stair led up to a room above, and thence out to the rampart walk that made the circuit of the whole Inner Ward, on which Ralegh was to be free to walk at certain times daily.

"We are so very grateful to you, Sir George," Bess said to the Lieutenant, standing outside Ralegh's room, by the winding-gear of the great portcullis that guarded the only entrance to the Inner Ward. "When my husband grows strong again, and can make use of your leave to walk on the ramparts—oh, I cannot tell you what the enlargement will mean to him!"

Sir George Harvey took the hand she held out. "When first your husband was delivered into my care, before ever he was tried, I confess I found him guilty and condemned him; from the time that the law condemned him, I began to find him innocent. Believe me, Lady Ralegh, I would give him wider liberty, if to do so were in my power." He hesitated. "One thing more, I can do. You will have noticed that there is a second entrance to this tower in the side toward the Lieutenant's Lodging. That door shall be kept unlocked, and your husband is free of my garden, and most welcome to come and go in it as he chooses, as though it were his own. That is for yourself also, naturally."

"If nothing but my prayers and my gratitude stood between you and damnation," Bess said softly, "I think that you would be safe, Sir George."

In the better air of the Garden Tower—the Bloody Tower, people were beginning to call it, remembering the two little princes who had choked out their lives in the upper room, and been dragged down that winding stair—Ralegh's intense vitality reasserted itself, and he began to mend. He was quieter since his illness; as though his utter collapse had allowed something that endangered his very reason to escape. It was not merely the enlargement of his surroundings, Bess knew that. His longing for freedom was far too great to be assuaged by a rampart walk and the use of a walled garden; that was but the exchange of a small cage for a larger one, to a bird used to the whole sky. And yet in some way, Ralegh had begun to come to terms with himself and with fate. The longing for freedom was as urgent within him as ever, but it no longer rode him as it had done in those first dreadful months.

He had turned once more to his books, and now that he was allowed more frequent visitors, began to gather the old circle round him again; Ben Jonson, Hariot and the rest. Only John Dee, now gone to explore more mysteries in his alchemist's Heaven, was lacking. Bess was accustomed to leave him alone with these gatherings. She could always find plenty to do; housekeeping in the Tower was only different in degree from housekeeping in Durham House, and, save in the coldest weather, there was always the Lieutenant's garden.

She drifted down there one evening, when two strangers had come to see Ralegh on business. The time of hesitant snowdrops was gone by, and there were jonquils and early wallflowers in the long borders now, the leaves breaking on every spray, and somewhere in the garden a blackbird singing. There was an atmosphere about this small green plot within the great fortress that was oddly moving. The heads of the crowding towers frowned above the trellised coping and everywhere was the consciousness—tangible as threatening thunder—of prison walls. Fortress, Palace, Prison; the very stones black with long-spilled blood, scarlet with blood that was as new as tomorrow's sunrise. How many men and women had died in this place, of the rack and the headsman's axe; of long-drawn heartbreak, the eating out of the years? Yet here in the Lieutenant's garden, a blackbird sang, and carefully tended vegetables grew in rows, and the first hyacinths were in flower. To Bess, it seemed a statement of faith; it was life in the midst of death, love in the midst of hate, the Grace of God in the midst of dreadful things.

No one else was in the garden this evening, and so, feeling that her presence was no intrusion upon its rightful owners, she lingered there, sitting on a bench under a pleached honeysuckle beside the disused hen-house—Sir George's predecessor had kept poultry—until the twilight came up through the three apple trees. The chill green twilight of spring, that of all times and lights and seasons, tears the heart out of the breast with longing for forgotten things. And when at last she turned back to the narrow doorway of the Garden Tower, the yellow glow of candle-light squaring the dark wall above it stabbed her with a sudden aching homesickness for other candlelight in other windows. She was so tired; so very tired. If only she could go home to Sherborne and lay down her weariness in the peace of the Blackmore Vale, and rest! All at once she could scarcely drag herself up the winding stair.

Ralegh was alone in the room when she reached it, after looking in on Little Watt, who was in the throes of going to bed under John Talbot's supervision. He was sitting at his table, with the usual litter of papers before him, in a blaze of candle-light. But one look at his face told her that if John Talbot had not lit the candles, he would have sat on in the dark.

"Walter, what is it?" she asked in quick anxiety. "What did they want, those men?"

Ralegh pushed back his stool, and got up. "They want Sherborne," he said levelly.

Sherborne, their home. The home which—since Ralegh had had it conveyed to his son some years before, and therefore the Attainder had been unable to touch it—was the one thing left to them out of the wreck. "*Sherborne?*"

"Yes. It appears that Robert Carr has seen the place with the same eyes as once I saw it; and Daft Jamey can deny his Robin nothing—even though it be not his to give."

She stared at him across the candles. "But Walter, they cannot touch it, for it is not yours either; it is Watt's. You have the deed of conveyance—Lawrence Kemys witnessed it." She was speaking quickly, as much to reassure herself as anything else.

"There is a flaw in the deed of conveyance, it seems," Ralegh said, in the same level tone.

"A flaw? Walter, in Heaven's name, what are you saying?"

"I am saying that the copying clerk left out the words 'Shall and will from henceforth stand and be thereof seized'."

"And because of that, they will take Sherborne from us?"

"I think so. Yes."

She stared at him for a long moment, her eyes dilating. She had begun to shiver, and the cold nausea rose against her breast-bone. Suddenly she flared out at him in a fury that seemed to tear and rend her as she was rending him. "Oh my God, I might have known it! I have been your wife long enough to know what I might expect from you! You fool, you *fool*! Could you not even see that the copying clerk did his work properly? Can you never be trusted to carry anything through in proper manner? Have you no care for the child, let alone for me, that you could not take so small a pain to come between us and destitution? . . ." She heard her own voice going on and on, high-pitched and ugly, but she could not stop. Never before had she reproached Ralegh for anything, and she was never to do so again; but standing there in the candlelight by the littered table, she rent him; rent him with a passion born of her own tortured nerves, and without one shred of pity; while he stood before her, his eyes slowly widening, and a look on his face as though she had struck him.

At last he turned from her towards the window, and seemed to be looking out into the darkening garden.

"Always it is the same!" she flung at him. "Always! Always! You mar everything you touch! I think that you were born under failing stars!"

And then suddenly the bitter stream of accusation was spent to the last drop, and she was emptied. She stood silent, looking at his back, waiting for him to justify himself, and then slowly realising that he was not going to attempt to justify himself. He was still staring out into the garden, where there could be nothing now to see. His shoulders sagged. He looked beaten—beaten as she had never seen him before; certainly not in the great hall at Winchester.

"Walter," she said.

No answer.

"Walter, I—meant none of it."

He raised his head as though it were very heavy, and turned slowly towards her. "But it is true," he said. "It is true, Bess. I have never in all my life handled anything, that I did not in some sort fail in it. Even the knife, I bungled."

She gave a little choking cry. "Walter, don't."

He looked at her in silence a moment. Then his voice came a little hoarsely. "I am so sorry, Bess—for everything."

"Oh my dear." She went to him. "I am sorry too. It is that I am tired; no more than that. I have been so afraid for you—for all of us. I am not a very brave woman."

"Then God give me a like cowardice," Ralegh said.

"Surely even the King will not dare to rob us on so small a legal quibble? But if he does, there is still my money, my little estate at Mitcham; we can do well enough on that."

She had slipped down on to the stool from which he had risen at her coming in; and he was kneeling at her side, his arms round her. She held his head against her breast, rocking a little, as though it were a child she held there. After a long silence, she asked: "Walter, whose was the idea of looking for a flaw in the deed of conveyance?"

"I think it was Robert Cecil. To get Sherborne for the King's Robin would raise him yet further in the King's favour, you see, Bess."

"How very terrible it must be, to be Robert Cecil. It is better to be us—to be you and me."

His arm tightened convulsively round her. "God forgive me, Bess, for the little happiness and much sorrow that I have brought you. Better for you that I had never come to free your sleeve from the alder tree."

Bess said softly, "I am remembering something Penelope once said to me. It was when an old kinswoman of hers died. She said: 'It must be so sad to have nothing to look back upon, not even sorrow'. It was so with me, before you came."

"Yes, at the least I have saved you from that," Ralegh said bitterly. "Sorrow in plenty you will have to look back upon, because of me. And I love you so dearly, I that have brought you into this hideous darkness."

Still holding his head against her breast, Bess said very softly: "Every month has its flower, and every season his contentment. So that it be with you, I am content."

She held him until, by little and little, she felt him relax from his rigid misery. All the many months that she had been unable to reach him, fell away, and he was near to her as he had never been before; so near that she seemed to feel his life beating in her own breast. The flames of the candles were soft and swollen on her sight, like stars before rain.

CHAPTER 16

"THY PITY UPON ALL PRISONERS"

A few weeks later, Bess knew that she was carrying another child. It was eleven years since Little Watt was born, and it had seemed that he was to be the only one. And now, out of that night when she had first known that they were going to lose Sherborne, a new life was begun. In a way she had known, even while she lay quiet in Ralegh's arms, after he had fallen asleep, that something must be begun. It was as though for that one time his whole spirit had turned back from its seeking to meet hers as it had never done before, as it would most probably never do again; and out of that one perfect and complete meeting, more than by any act of their bodies, the new life was quickened.

When she told Ralegh, the result was somewhat as though she had dropped a spark into a powder keg. He strode up and down his room raging—against her, against himself, against fortune that had seen fit to perpetrate this jest for the gods. Finally, crashing both fists on the table, he delivered his ultimatum. "Back you go to Broad Street, my Lady. It may be a prisoner's brat, but by God's wounds, it shall not be born in prison!"

But Broad Street was on the other side of London, and Bess refused with all the gentle mulishness which she could put forth when occasion arose, to go so far from him. So a compromise was reached at last, and she moved into lodgings in a house on Tower Hill; and there, at the dark end of the year, Carew was born.

But long before that, they had lost Sherborne.

James did not, after all, quite dare to seize the Manor on the strength of a few missing words in the deed of conveyance; but his adored Robert Carr continued to beg for the place, and eventually he bought it compulsorily for five thousand pounds—a small sum down and the rest in yearly instalments, when Bess could wring them out of the Treasury, which was to be seldom.

Little Watt did not go with his mother to the lodging on Tower Hill, stating with the utmost firmness when the matter was broached to him, that he was staying with his father. A change had come over their relationship since those first bewildered months the boy had spent in the Tower. With the crumbling of his secure and happy world, his worship of the father who had not been able to prevent it had crumbled too; but in its place was growing up something— stormy enough at times, for Watt was as wild as an unmade hawk —that would one day be friendship in its deepest and strongest form.

So Bess left her menfolk to themselves on the inside of the fortress walls, and went to have her baby by herself in the outer world.

She did not return to her place beside Ralegh after Carew was born, for the Tower was no place in which to rear a baby; but from the time that she could crawl out of bed, she spent much of every day with him.

April came again, and again the blackbirds sang in the Lieutenant's garden, and Bess with a half-made shirt in her lap sat under his favourite singing tree, and watched Ralegh and Watt and Lawrence Kemys, doublets laid aside and sleeves rolled high, all hard at work on the disused hen-house which Sir George Harvey had bestowed on his prisoner for conversion into a laboratory.

It would be good for Ralegh to have a laboratory again, his chemical experiments being of the kind best not made in the room where one has to eat and sleep; so many of them ended in repulsive smells, if in nothing worse. And watching him now, Bess was thankful from the bottom of her heart for the return to his old interests that had made a laboratory necessary.

Presently, from somewhere beyond the high garden wall, they heard the arrival of a carriage and a mounted party, faint sounds of bustle, then a woman's laugh, very clear, sweet and gay. But the things that happened beyond the wall had nothing to do with them.

The three heads were bent close together over some tricky piece of fitting, when some while later, the door at the far end of the garden opened, and Sir George Harvey appeared, ushering in a lady. A lady in a satin gown of ginger-line—the very latest colour —over a preposterous catherine-wheel farthingale, a mannish feathered hat perched on the lint-pale masses of her hair, who came through the doorway with a lilting step, then turned, laughing, to dismiss the flutter of silks and swords that showed for an instant behind her. "Ah—Shoo!—Shoo! You shall walk round by the pr-roper way, all of you; it is for me only, the short cut."

"Good God!" Bess heard Ralegh say softly. "It is the Queen."

She rose to draw back, aware as she did so, that Ralegh was standing his ground. She knew what was happening in his mind; Sir George had evidently not realised his presence in the garden, but that was no fault of his. He would not put himself forward, but neither would he give back one inch. If it made for awkwardness that the Queen should be thus brought face to face with her husband's wrongful prisoner, he could not help it. So he stood his ground beside the converted hen-house, and the others with him.

The Queen was coming along the path, smiling radiantly up at her escort. She had put aside the black velvet mask which almost all women wore in public, nowadays, and it lay on the whiteness of her shoulder. Bess saw Sir George become suddenly aware of their presence in the garden, saw his momentary hesitation, as the poor man tried to make up his mind how to act; saw him come to his decision, and turn towards the little uncompromising group by the hen-house, with a small quick gesture to Ralegh to advance.

"Your Majesty, grant that I bring to your remembrance——"

But the Queen was before him, swirling round with a warm, impetuous gesture of spread hands. "But I remember him already; very well! It is the old Queen's Captain! They said that he had done—Oh, I know not what!—And me, for a little I believed them, but not now!"

Ralegh bowed over her hand, and it came to Bess, looking on, that another man, even another innocent man, might have seemed slightly at a disadvantage. But this tall man with the insolent shoulders and heavy-lidded sapphire blue eyes, was completely master of the situation. Only his mouth was faintly sardonic. "You are very kind, Madam."

She looked at him with a kind of laughing dismay. "I think that I am only tactless; I speak what is in my heart and I do not think. Pray you forgive me, and present to me Lady Ralegh. This is Lady Ralegh? Ah yes, her also I remember—but last time it was not—not happy. So you shall present her to me again, and we will make the fresh start."

Bess, drawn into the group, sank into a deep curtsey, and rising again, found herself looking into the flushed and laughing face of the Queen who she had last seen on that disastrous day when Ralegh had presented to the peace-loving King his plans for another attack on Spain, and been instantly dismissed his Captaincy of the Guard. A vivid, eager face, whose over-large features were turned to beauty by the warmth of colour and expression. The last time Bess had seen it, the chill mask of royal disapproval had shuttered its natural warmth; now it seemed to glow, and she was reminded suddenly of Penelope Rich.

"All these so sad things that have happened," the Queen was saying, her voice warm and impetuous as the rest of her, the fact that she was Danish apparent in a slightly foreign arrangement of

the words rather than in any definite accent. "We should have
known each other so much better. You should have come to Court."
Her large eyes went from Bess to Ralegh and back again; and Bess
knew that this was not mere foolish and insensitive chattering; the
Queen was trying to tell them, as clearly as she dared, that she was
their friend. "So gay! We have such masques! Master Ben Jonson
—he is a friend of yours I think, yes?—he writes them for us, and
we all act in them, and it is of the most joyous and amusing. He is
writing a new one for us now; it is to be called 'News from the New
World!' That would be a thing to interest you, Sir Walter? . . .
Ah, but tell me, what is it that you do here? Is it that you build a
hen-house?"

Ralegh smiled. "Madam, that was done before my time. Sir
George has most generously put it at my disposal, and I am con-
verting it into a laboratory."

"A laboratory?" The Queen's pretty brows went up. "And what
is it that you will make in a hen-house laboratory?"

"Chemical experiments, Madam."

"And—Alchemical?"

Ralegh shook his head. "Nay, Madam, even if it be so, who will
you ever find to admit that search, save among his fellow seekers?"

"Ah, but how do you know that I am not a fellow seeker? How
if I recite to you the pr-roper sequence of colours on the way to
the Philosopher's Stone, this Flower of the Sun? Listen—'the pale
citron, the green lion, the crow, the peacock's tail, the plumed
swan—and——" She broke off, laughing. "And I have forgot the
rest."

"Ben Jonson furnished you that pretty string, did he not?"
Ralegh said with a flash of amusement. "But I shall confine myself
to more mundane experiments. In my lighter moments I shall make
cordials of strawberry water, and possibly sticks of perfume for my
most honoured friends. More seriously, I have long wished to turn
such skill as I possess to devising some means of obtaining fresh
water from salt."

"So? That would be a gr-reat good thing for seamen, would it
not?"

"It would be a great good thing for seamen," Ralegh agreed.

"It is time that I go." The Queen said after a moment's silence:
"I came today, to see how the new tapestries look in the Royal

apartments—and behold, I have found the old Queen's Captain, building a laboratory from a hen-house. So I shall come again, and next time, I think that I bring my Henry with me. He is but twelve years old, but like you, a so great one for ships and for seamen."

"I remember Prince Henry," Ralegh said. "But—forgive me, Madam—will the King allow it?"

"I—think so. Henry, when I tell him, he will wish very much to come; and when Henry wishes, often his father yields." She cast about her smile which embraced Little Watt and Lawrence Kemys, as well as Bess and Ralegh; then in the act of turning away, she paused. "Sir Walter, pray you tell me, is there anything—but anything, that I can do?"

After a moment Ralegh said: "His Majesty has seen fit to cancel my patent to colonise Virginia, and issued it as a fresh charter to the London and Plymouth companies; and doubtless in due course there will be an expedition sailing to plant a new colony where mine failed. You can intercede for me with the King, Most Gracious Lady, that he allow me to sail with it."

"I will try, my friend," the Queen said, with the sparkle fading from her face. "But you mistake the case. I have no power with the King. I am only his wife."

She gave her hand to him again, then to Bess; then turned and set two fingers on Sir George's arm, and walked on.

The hen-house laboratory was finished, and Ralegh spent a large part of every day there. His days were becoming as full as ever they had been, and if their fulness was in some sort artificial, a drug, at least that was better than the wild revolt of those first empty months. Every day he walked on the ramparts, partly for exercise and the wide views that were to be had from them, partly because it amused him to know that people came from far and wide to stand on Tower Hill and watch him, and that James was powerless to stop it because of the outcry that an end to his public appearances would raise throughout the country. He and Kemys tutored LittleWatt between them, and before long, Prince Henry was added to his circle, for having won his father's leave to come once, he came again and yet again.

"Only my father could keep such a bird in a cage!" Prince Henry had declared indignantly, after their first meeting, laying

6

down a quick devotion at Ralegh's feet. They discussed many things together, Ralegh puffing at his pipe, and the two small boys frequently coming to blows. They had all three of them revolutionary ideas on shipbuilding, and that summer, with much eager advice from his youthful helpers, Ralegh began to work out the specification for a warship of a kind unknown in English shipyards before; a three-decker.

He continued to have more and yet more visitors, and in the evenings, when Bess had gone back to her lodging, there were many gatherings of old friends. The Wizard Earl of Northumberland had joined the company in the Tower, following the Gunpowder Plot; Hariot and Jonson were constant visitors, and the School of Night, or something very like it, was in being again. Many a long evening they spent, seeking, in a cloud of tobacco smoke, the answers to questions which more orthodox souls did not realise existed. But occasionally the purpose of the evening would be purely social.

It was on one such evening that Little Watt made his entrance into the world of men. In October, the Earl of Northumberland asked Ralegh to bring the boy to supper in his lodging, to celebrate the laying down, at Deptford, of the keel of the *Prince Royal*—none other than the three-decker of Ralegh's specification. It was to be a small gathering—of prisoners for the main part, and most of them, like Ralegh, under the indefinite threat of the axe. But at such gatherings the usages of gentle society were kept up with a rather especial care, for they were all men of a type who preferred to go to the block in clean linen. Ralegh spoke seriously to his son beforehand, for the boy had grown suddenly wilder than ever in the past few months; begging him at least to try to behave himself. "I suppose that I must take you, for it would be discourtesy to Northumberland to refuse; but I tell you frankly that I am ashamed to be seen with such a bear in my company!"

Watt went to his supper with a face like a fledgling archangel's. Bess had washed it herself, and done her best to flatten the rebellious tuft of hair that always sprang jauntily erect from the back of his head, and watched him depart with Ralegh and Kemys, before she went back to her own lodging and the baby. Afterwards she heard the story of that supper party from a very worried Ralegh.

Watt, it seemed, had behaved himself almost too well through the first part of the meal, and then, becoming either bored or possessed of a devil, had taken advantage of a lull in the conversation to use loudly and deliberately, the foulest word in his deplorable stock. Ralegh, shamed and furious, had turned and cuffed him across the mouth; whereupon Watt, not quite daring to return the blow, had hit the man who sat on his left, saying "Pass it along, and 'twill come back to my father directly."

All this, Ralegh retailed to his wife, but neither he nor Watt mentioned to her the subsequent reckoning that there had been between them; and Bess, though she saw the weals on Watt's back, was too wise to comment. It was a matter between men, and she knew her place.

Ralegh was certainly very worried.

"I am sure that Northumberland will understand," said Bess.

"To speak truth, I do not care whether he understands or not, though he is one of my oldest friends," Ralegh said. "It is Watt that I am concerned about. Why should he do such a thing? Why, Bess?"

"It is a strange training-ground for a boy, this. He will do better when he goes to Oxford next year and mingles more with his own kind. Also—Walter, have you thought that he may be jealous?"

"Jealous?" Ralegh had been looking out of his window, but he swung round to face her. "Who under Heaven should he be jealous of?"

"Of Prince Henry."

"Why?" Ralegh demanded.

Bess got up from her chair and crossed over to him. "Walter, all these months since Henry came—you sometimes seem so near to him; you are never angry with him—but you are very often angry with Watt."

"Henry behaves himself," Ralegh said tersely. "Would you have me not discipline the cub at all?"

"Yes, yes, of course." Bess was pleading with him to understand. "But Walter, cannot you see?—You call him a bear, and he behaves as one. He thinks that Henry has first place with you, and so he behaves badly to show himself that he does not care. He is only twelve, remember, and he is a very loving child; and you have been to him his God."

"I am deeply fond of Henry," Ralegh said slowly, as though

thinking the thing out as he went along. "He has a better brain than Watt, and his character is more formed, though less—vivid. But given my choice of sons, I would keep my wild young falcon against all comers—even Henry."

"Then let him see that it is so."

"I have never stinted him my praise, when he deserves it."

"Praise when he deserves it has a somewhat bleak sound. Let him see that it is pleasant to you to have him with you, let him feel secure in his place with you, as he did in the old days before all this happened, and he will do better."

Ralegh looked at her for a moment in silence, his eyes gravely considering. "Very well," he said at last. "You understand people better than I do, Bess; I will try to do as you say." Suddenly he smiled. "What a pother it is, this manning of the human eyas—and presently there will be Carew, and all to do again."

Bess shook her head. "Carew will take little breaking, he is no haggard hawk, nor ever will be."

"What is he then?"

She began to laugh. "A barley loaf; a plump, wholesome, dependable, rather dull little barley loaf!"

. . . .

Ralegh had perfected his Balsam of Guiana, warranted to cure any sickness not caused by poison. He was writing a history of the world. He received visits from foreign notables rather as though he were royalty. Almost, he seemed to be content, as though the things he had were all the things he needed. If it was a hard-won serenity, hardly held, nothing but his eyes betrayed the fact.

And then, one grey and bitter afternoon of late December, Bess found him pacing his room as he had paced the cell of his first year's imprisonment, his writing lying scattered on the table, broken off between one word and the next. He checked his restless prowling by an obvious effort of will when she entered, and sat down again to his work, while she took out his best doublet, the sleeve of which was in need of mending, and seated herself by the low fire.

Presently she looked up from threading her needle. "Where is Watt away to, this afternoon?"

Ralegh shook his head a little absently. "Somewhere. The whole Tower is his hunting ground. Maybe he has gone to visit the lioness; I believe she has lately whelped, and he grows as interested in her affairs as My Lord Salisbury himself. Or like as not he is down on the quay, watching the shipping. Kemys is with him."

"Then he is not like to get into serious mischief," said Bess.

Ralegh took up a fresh sheet of paper from the pile beside him. "You were right, concerning Watt," he said. "He begins to come to hand."

"I am glad." Something was the matter, but it was not the boy, as she had at first feared.

Ralegh dipped his quill into the ink-horn, and Bess ran her needle into the dark taffeta. For a while both of them worked in silence. Bess was waiting for him to tell her the trouble.

It was cold in the room, for the draughts blew away the warmth of the fire; cold and very dark. Sleet spattered against the glass.

At last Ralegh laid down his pen, and getting up, limped restlessly to the window. His limp, which used to become noticeable only when he was tired, was increasing on him these days, and often Bess knew that he was in pain. It was the dampness and the chill of his prison, she thought. He stood silent a few moments, one arm resting along the transom, looking out. Then he spoke to her without turning. "The ships of the new Virginia settlement sailed from Tilbury on this morning's tide."

"Yes, Walter." She had stopped sewing.

"If the Queen's good offices for me had taken effect, I should have sailed with them."

"Yes, Walter."

" 'This dear strand of Virginia, Earth's only Paradise'." He quoted the words of the charter with a note of raw and naked longing in his voice. And then, after another long pause, "If they succeed where I failed, Jamestown will be the first English settlement on the mainland of the New World. . Bess, would you have been sad to leave England, and all that you know, and come with me into the unknown?"

"Not very, I think—I am like the Honeysuckle Queen of Scots, who would follow Bothwell to the world's end in her shift—a shameless confession for a woman fifteen years wed, to make to her husband."

"It is a shamelessness not hard to forgive." He was silent a moment, watching the sleet blow down the wind. Then he said, "Well, there's no good purpose served by thinking of it. The Queen failed."

"Maybe one day, when Henry is older, he will succeed where his mother could not."

"One day—one day. . . . 'Hope deferred maketh the heart sick'."

" 'But when the desire cometh it is a tree of life'." She finished the quotation swiftly. But he did not seem to hear her. He bowed his forehead on to his wrist against the splattered window, with a gesture that was unutterably weary.

He said hoarsely: "Dear God, thy pity upon all prisoners. Thy pity upon all prisoners!"

CHAPTER 17

THE WIND GOETH OVER

Summer of 1612: Watt eighteen years old, and coming down from Oxford for good at Christmas. Carew seven, and almost ready for his father's tutoring. Ralegh himself, with many more bids for freedom and as many failures behind him, still caged in the Tower; still eating out his heart under the serene and faintly insolent exterior that the world knew. The world, his world, had had no chance to forget him; his converted hen-house was become one of the most famous spots in Europe, since his Balsam of Guiana had saved the Queen's life, and she dying of a fever; his writings on subjects ranging from political philosophy to ship-building were widely used authorities, and the whole Kingdom knew that his word was law to their beloved Prince of Wales. A thing had happened to him that happens to few men; he was become a legend, in his lifetime.

On a morning in early summer, when the midges danced over the scummy moat, and the smell of the City sewage that drained into it was almost unendurable, Bess passed, as she had passed so many times before, in under the arch of the Byward Tower. It was some days since she had seen her husband, for since his old enemy Sir William Waad had succeeded Sir George Harvey as

Lieutenant, even his little measure of freedom had been curtailed; he must retire to his own room at five each evening to be locked in for the night, and he was allowed few visitors. Sir William had even tried to deprive him of the hen-house, saying that he needed it to keep hens in, but Prince Henry had dealt with that situation with a firm hand, and Ralegh still had his laboratory.

But he was not there today, he was in his own room, John Talbot told her, when she turned in from Water Lane to the familiar stairway beside the entrance to the Inner Ward. And there she found him, hard at work on his great History of the World, books and papers scattered around him on the table, the window-sill, the foot of the bed; and Lawrence Kemys leaning against the table beside him, thumbing through the pages of a small calf-bound volume, in search of some reference. When the History was given to the world, Bess had often thought, much of the credit would belong to Lawrence Kemys, and Dr. Hariot, and Ben Jonson. The creative flame of the book would be Ralegh's—it was a poet's history, rather than a scientist's—but the patient gathering and verifying of facts were theirs.

Lawrence Kemys straightened himself at her entrance, making her the small stiff bow with which he invariably greeted her, his face lighting with the grave smile which had never, in all the years she had known him, ceased to be rather diffident. "God den, Lady Ralegh."

"God den to you, Captain Kemys." She returned his smile warmly but a little absently, and turned to Ralegh who had pushed back his chair. "Walter."

He kissed her. "Sweetheart, five whole days, and my eyes grown sore with looking for you. Waad shall roast in hell."

"Yes, my dear," Bess agreed. But she had something else to think of just then, than the afterlife of Sir William Waad. "Walter, have you heard?"

"A truly feminine question! Have I heard what?"

"Robin Cecil is dead."

There was a long silence. Then Ralegh said, "He has been a dying man this year and more. Did he die at Bath?"

"No. It seems the waters did him more harm than good, and he was on his way back to London. He died on Sunday—at Marl-borough, I believe. Will was with him."

"So it is over. He was ten years younger than I am," Ralegh said reflectively.

"Yes; and I am wondering—Walter, listen. Could it be that his death will make any difference?"

"Difference?"

"To you—to us. He has scarcely been a friend, these late years." Out of the tail of her eye she saw Lawrence Kemys' head go up with a quickened attention, and she turned to him almost pleadingly. "Captain Kemys, you think so too?"

"It seems a possibility, Lady Ralegh."

But Ralegh shook his head. "With Henry Howard still flourishing like a green bay tree, and far more my enemy than ever Cecil was? With Robert Carr leaning more to the Spanish party with every day that passes? No, it will make no difference. My freedom is not yet, good people."

Bess sighed, and let the small hope go, as so many had gone before it. The process scarcely hurt her now.

Ralegh had sat down again, and taken up his pen. He reached out his free hand to brush hers with a bent finger, while she stood beside him, looking down through the open window into the Lieutenant's apple trees. "Robin Cecil is dead," she thought, and for the first time it came home to her. It was so long since she had thought of him other than as Lord Salisbury, an enemy. "Lord Salisbury is dead." That was how the news had come to her this morning, and that was how she had thought of it as she carried it to Walter; and yet when she came to tell it, it was "Robin Cecil is dead." And her mind went piercing back through Lord Salisbury the Secretary of State, seeking Robin Cecil. For a moment she could not find him, and then suddenly he was there, clear in her memory, a young man with a coppery casque of shining hair, his nature already a little twisted, reaching out to laughter and happy things, reaching out to beauty with a sensitive half-shrinking born of his morbid awareness of his own deformity. Poor Robin Cecil, marred, body and soul, from the potter's wheel.

"There must have been something to love in him, even to the last," Ralegh said suddenly, looking up from his writing, and she realised that his thoughts had taken the same road as hers; "for even to the last, there were people—a few—who loved him."

"He had a very light touch," Bess said.

But the people who loved Robert Cecil were not many; and within a few days the prentice lads were chanting in the streets:

> Here lies Robin Crook-back,
> Unjustly reckoned
> A Richard the Third;
> He was Judas the Second.

Ralegh was at work in his hen-house laboratory, assisted by a tall young man with a thin, eager face, and ruffled hair of the Stuart gold, who sat on an upturned tub, plying a pair of bellows. The blue reek of a fire burning leaves in the Lieutenant's garden drifted in to mingle with the smells of herbs and chemicals, the fumes of a charcoal table brazier, and the unpleasant odour of some fluid which Ralegh was tending in a glass alembic over the heat.

The young man seemed to be suffering from suppressed excitement of some sort, under the influence of which he was plying the bellows faster and faster, until Ralegh, becoming aware that the brazier was now glowing red hot all through, checked him. "Gently, gently now; you will not hurry the process by blowing us both up."

The young man apologised, flushing a little, as though caught out in something, and returned to a more gentle rhythm.

Presently the contents of the alembic ran up into a burst of bubbles, and began to syphon a clear violet-coloured fluid drop by drop down the tube into a receiver which was already half full of something that looked like muddy water. The smell grew steadily more vile. Ralegh watched the process intently for a short while; then straightened. "Well enough. Let her cool down now," he said.

He turned away, and seating himself on the one stool which the place boasted, produced his tobacco box and began to fill his pipe. "Anything further blown up concerning this marriage plan of your father's, Harry?"

"No. There is a lull in that quarter for the present time. I laid before him all those arguments that you made clear to me; how that it would be but a one-sided bargain, pledging England to neutrality while leaving Spain free to trample out the Netherlands. I told him that 'twould be a deal better policy, instead of marrying Elizabeth and me to Savoy's son and daughter, to pleasure Spain—

which is a waning power at best—to stick to the old plan, and marry Elizabeth to the Elector Palatine and leave me in reserve against a greater need."

"And was the latter argument used with the country's good in view, or Princess Elizabeth's?—or Prince Henry's?"

The Prince of Wales laughed. "All three. I do not pretend myself eager to be married off willy-nilly to a Princess I have never seen. I'd as lief be left to myself for a while yet. My poor little sister has seen neither of her candidates, but the Elector is at least of her own faith." A hint of steel crept into the young voice. "I'll not have two religions lie in *my* bed, and if I can help it, neither shall she. As for the country, I've no wish to see England become even as Savoy, a Spanish vassal, though my father seems to think it a fate altogether desirable." He shifted abruptly, and his tone lightened. "Ah well, he has let the plan drop for the time being, at least so far as I am concerned; though doubtless 'twill be all to do again in the New Year, when the new Spanish Ambassador arrives. Rumour saith that he is being sent 'to keep the King good', though the need is past my imagining, with the King growing more to the Spanish party every day, and the whole Court rotten with Spanish gold."

"Treasonable talk, my friend," Ralegh said softly. "Also the King is your father."

The boy looked at him levelly, his young face suddenly bitter. "The King is my father," he agreed. "He eats too much and drinks too much, both messily. He is full of learning that he cannot digest into wisdom. He is cruel and sentimental and bigoted—and he means well. There's not a living soul, saving yourself, that I could or would say that to, Sir."

"Hmm," Ralegh said, noncommittally, and puffed in silence for a while, his gaze very kindly as it met his companion's. "Do you know yet, who this new Spanish Ambassador may be?"

"Yes. Count Gondomar—Diago Sarmiento de Acuna, Count of Gondomar."

"Sarmiento de Acuna," Ralegh said, as though testing the name on his tongue. "It has a familiar ring. Now where under Heaven . . ." He plucked his pipe from his mouth. "Yes! One of my ships took a prisoner of that name once, and got a fat ransom for him, too. Now I wonder——"

There was a pause. A faint shadow of anxiety seemed to dim the

eagerness of the Prince's face. "I hope you're wrong," he said.
Then, the shadow passing, "At all events I am glad that he does
not come until after Christmas."

Ralegh cocked an eyebrow at him. "Why so portentous?"

"Did I indeed sound portentous? I had no reason—none in the
world," the Prince of Wales said quickly; rather too quickly.

Ralegh's eyebrow remained cocked. "You are a poor liar, Harry.
You have some especial reason for not wanting Count Gondomar
until after Christmas. Has it any bearing on whatever it is that you
have been hugging to yourself all morning like the key of the
comfit box?"

"Nay, but there is nothing——" Prince Henry began. Then
suddenly he gave a crow of excited laughter and shot to his feet.
"Yes there is! There is! Oh Sir, I had not meant that you should
know until nearer the time, but God's my life, I shall split like an
over-ripe fig if I keep the thing to myself another hour. And—
and——" he began to stutter.

Ralegh had risen also. "And what?" he said, "And what, Harry?"

"And—I can scarce believe it myself as yet—at last I have g-got
my father's promise that you shall go free!—at Christmas! Your
enlargement is to be part of the Christmas festivities, and he intends
making a n-noble gesture of it, but doubtless you can abide
that——"

"Yes, I—can abide that," Ralegh said. He staggered slightly,
dropping his pipe, and sat down, rubbing one hand across his forehead. He smiled into the anxious face bent over him. "A mere
trifling dizziness. The air of the Tower is not over-healthy for a
prolonged stay, and—I begin to grow an old man, Harry. I am sorry
to receive your news in manner so lacking in appreciation, but I
am not ungrateful, and presently, doubtless, I shall even come to
believe it."

"Forgive me. I am a fool. I should not have spewed it out like
that," the Prince said remorsefully. "But it is true, Sir, as I live,
you shall be a free man by the New Year!"

But long before the New Year came, the Prince of Wales was
dead of typhoid fever.

Ralegh grieved for him as for a son whom he had loved less than
Watt but infinitely more than Carew; grieved also for the loss of

all hope of freedom. He had too much and too bitter experience of James to imagine for an instant that he would honour his promise to the dead boy.

A few days before Christmas, Bess sat sewing by the fire in her lodging. Carew, his bedtime drawing near, was sprawling on his stomach in the firelight, playing with Hodge, the spaniel puppy which his Uncle Nicholas had given him, and old Joan sat opposite, with a great basket of hose to be mended.

"Maister Watt's late," grumbled the old woman, drawing a dark green stocking from the basket and surveying it with grim disfavour. "A dinner party, this was meant to be, not a supper party."

"He is not so very late," Bess said, looking up from the shirt that she was making for Carew. "And you know how it is, when young men meet together; they forget the time."

"I've no patience with young men and their wild ways! Beating up the Watch and writing poetry!" sniffed Joan, whom the years had not mellowed, though she had been Watt's adoring slave since the day that he was born. "And what he does with his hosen passes my understanding!"

Carew rolled the puppy on its back. "I wish I had some chestnuts to roast," he said. "The fire is just right for them—clear red all through."

"Aye, 'tis the frost makes it burn so," said Joan. "And by the same token, it needs another log on it." She bent forward, then checked with an old gnarled hand to the pile of logs beside the hearth. "There's Maister Watt now—and the lad's in a hurry."

Flying footsteps were coming up the narrow stairs two at a time, and the unmistakable urgency in them had Bess out of her chair even before the door burst open and Watt appeared on the threshold, his cloak flung back to reveal his primrose satin doublet, his face very white.

"Watt!" she exclaimed. "My dear, what is it?"

"It is father," he said breathlessly. "He collapsed in his laboratory this evening. Talbot found him, and went for Dr. Turner. I met him at the door here, come to call on his way back, and he's gone on ahead. I told him we would follow. Where is your cloak, darling?"

Joan, lamenting shrilly, had already gone scuttling to fetch it, Carew had leapt up and flung himself on his mother, demanding:

"Let me come with you! Let me! Oh *do* let me! I'm all but eight, and——" his voice cracking into a wail, "And I *love* father!"

"Not now, sweetheart. Later—a little later," Bess said. She found she was still holding the shirt, and looking from it to Watt and back again. Then she put it down on the table. Her ears were full of Carew's tearful clamour. Joan was muffling her in her cloak and she tore herself away from Carew, leaving him in the hands of the old woman, hearing his despairing wails grow fainter behind her as she followed her elder son downstairs and out into the street.

The moon was rising, and the ruts were full of thin ice that glittered at the edges and crackled underfoot. The lights of the houses on Tower Hill seemed very far away; below the dark wharves the river ran molten silver, and ahead loomed the black many-headed mass of the Tower. As in a dream, she began to run towards it, turned her foot in a frozen rut, and would have fallen but for Watt's hold on her arm. "Steady—steady, Mother. It is as slippery as glass."

"Watt, do you know anything more?—more than you told us just now?"

"Nothing. Talbot was in too much haste to get back to father."

"He did not leave him alone, did he?"

"Surely not. His faithful watchdog was with him."

"His dog? But he has not——" she began stupidly. "Oh, you mean Lawrence Kemys."

"Yes, darling. Here we are."

The men on guard were clearly prepared for their coming, and they were passed through without trouble, and the black mass engulfed them. It was very dark in Water Lane, but the windows of the Lieutenant's Lodging were full of light, and Bess realised with a sense of shock that it was quite early, not black midnight at all.

Talbot was waiting for them at the foot of the Tower stair. "Oh, thank Gawd you come, My Lady, and you too, Master Watt," he greeted them. "No, I don't know nothing more, My Lady. He was fair knocked out when I found him, breathing queer and heavy like; and Captain Kemys and I got him to bed, and Dr. Turner is with him now—and I always 'ave said as those stinking broths 'e brews weren't 'olesome!" They had reached the stairhead by that time, and Watt checked her as she turned to the familiar doorway.

"Wait here, Mother. I go in first."

She looked at him, realising that this was a new Watt, not the lad she had seen off to his dinner party at the Mermaid. "Very well, my dear," she said docilely, and he pushed open the door and went in. She glimpsed a dark figure stooping in a blur of candlelight, heard a murmur of voices; and then the door shut again. She waited a few agonised moments with John Talbot, and then the door opened and Watt came out.

"Watt?" she could not, she dared not, frame the question.

"He is still unconscious," Watt said quietly. "Dr. Turner would have you wait a short while. He is bleeding father now; and as soon as he is done, you shall go in. Come now."

Bess found herself in the closet looking out into Water Lane that had been Watt's before he went to Oxford. "We will leave the door wide," Watt said, "so we shall hear the instant that Dr. Turner comes out." His voice had deepened lately; it was deeper than his father's, with a caressing quality in it.

Bess turned her face to him, white and pleading. "Watt—is he going to die? He's not—If he were dead already, you would not keep it from me?"

His arms were round her, holding her close against his hard young body. "I would not, darling Mother, on my own life, I would not. 'Twould take much more than this to kill father."

Presently they heard the other door open, and Bess was out on the stairhead on the instant, to face Dr. Turner as he emerged. Her whole body seemed shaken by the drub of her racing heart, but she heard her own voice quite level, and controlled once more, asking for news.

"Your husband has had a seizure, Lady Ralegh," the Doctor said bluntly. "I have let him a pint of blood, and he lies easier, but we shall not know fully how much mischief has been done until he regains consciousness. We can only hope, putting our trust in God."

"Is there any hope?" Bess asked very quietly.

"Surely. Sir Walter is a very strong man." He hesitated. "In some sort it is his strength—his superabundance of life—that has come near to destroying him; and paradoxically, that same superabundance may well, if I read the signs aright, be the means of saving him."

"I understand. May I go in to see him now?"

"Aye; but he is quite unconscious, and you must make no trial at rousing him," the Doctor said. "And you, also, Watt; you may go with your mother." He touched Bess's arm with a blunt, kindly hand as she went past him. "Keep a good heart, My Lady."

Then she was beside the bed. The curtains had been drawn back, and the window stood wide, and the room was full of the cold clean tang of the winter night, and underlying it the faint, frightening smell of the blood they had drawn from Ralegh. He lay high on his pillows, his arms at his sides outside the coverlid. The whiteness of a bandage showed on one of them. That was where they had drawn the blood, she thought. His head was a little turned towards her, his dark face was darker than its normal colour, and he breathed heavily, snoringly, in a way quite unlike the quiet breathing of sleep. She was unaware of the slight movement as Lawrence Kemys, who had been standing at the bed foot, went out, the faithful watchdog yielding up his vigil to those who had a nearer right.

Dr. Turner was setting a chair for her beside the bed. She sat down, and very gently stole a hand over the one of Ralegh's that was nearest to her; his left hand, with the Queen's diamond on it. Watt had taken up his stance in the shadow of the curtains at the bed head. The Doctor settled down at the table, with a candle drawn close to him, and taking a book from his pocket, began to read. Bess knew that book of old; it was a pocket herbal; to the Puritan Doctor it was the companion volume to his Bible.

Slowly the hours trickled by; from time to time Watt would move to set another log on the fire; from time to time the Doctor would turn a page worn so soft by many turnings that it scarcely rustled, or lean forward to snuff the candle. Bess never moved at all, nor did the lax hand under hers. Her gaze seldom left the congested face on the pillow; a gaunt and haggard face, deeply lined round the eyes and mouth; and it came to her with a kind of wondering pity that it was the face of an old man. A worn-out old man, and he was only sixty-one. James had done that; might his dull soul rot for it! Sometimes she prayed to the orthodox God of her own simple philosophy, who had never satisfied Ralegh's questing spirit. "Dear God, don't let him die! You cannot let him die—you cannot be so cruel! Dear God, don't take him away from me! I will be good, I will remember my prayers always, I will never question your mercy again, if only you will not take him from me!"

Sometimes the draught from the open window set the candle flame leaping, and the shadows ran flickering up the walls, so that the figures of Hector and Andromache on the tapestry seemed to move as with a kind of stealthy life. Once the candle, neglected too long, guttered over; and a long winding sheet spilled down its length, crystal clear, clouding to opal, to dull yellow wax. Dr. Turner, the Puritan who should have had no truck with superstition, leaned forward and pinched it off.

At last, in the early hours, Ralegh's wandering spirit came back to his body. He began to grow restless, frowning like a sleeper who is uneasy or in pain. Little by little his breathing changed its rhythm and grew lighter, and his head moved slightly on the pillow.

Dr. Turner, the little herbal back once more in his pocket, was beside him now, and Bess looked up mutely in an agony of hope, then down once more at the man on the bed. Ralegh's restlessness was increasing as the minutes went by; his whole face seemed to contract as though in pain or weary effort; once or twice he caught his breath in a moan. And then with startling suddenness, his eyes opened, the male-sapphire blueness of them clouded in bewilderment, and focussed with a frowning effort on her face. He seemed to be struggling to speak. For an instant the words would not come, then he said thickly, "Bess?"

Bess smiled at him. "You have been ill, Walter, but you are better now, much better. See, here is Dr. Turner."

She drew back a little, making room for the Doctor, but he gestured her to keep her place. "Nay, do not you move, Lady Ralegh. I can manage," and he bent over the sick man. "Ah, Sir Walter, this is famous."

"What—happened?" Ralegh asked, stumbling a little over the words.

"You collapsed in your laboratory last evening. It is near morning now." The Doctor was busy with his examination as he spoke. "You are doing well, my friend," he added after a few moments.

Ralegh's mind and speech were already clearing. It was typical of him that even now there could be no half measures for him, no merciful threshold state between conscious and unconscious. He said, "Turner, what the devil's amiss with my left arm?"

"Like as not you jarred it when you fell," Dr. Turner said easily. There was an instant sharp and absolute silence. Then Ralegh said, "There is no need that you should lie to me, my friend. Thank God it is my left arm, at all events."

"If you lie quiet and obey orders, I see no reason why it should be more than a temporary inconvenience, Sir Walter," the Doctor told him, tranquilly, finishing his examination and drawing back.

Ralegh turned once more to his wife, fumbling his right hand weakly across his body to find hers. "It is no use you holding the other, sweetheart. I cannot feel it."

"You will soon," Bess said, "quite soon. Try to go to sleep now."

"Where is Watt?" Ralegh demanded, ignoring the suggestion.

"I am here, Sir." Watt stooped forward from the shadows by the bed head.

"Is not this—an edifying scene? I regret that at the moment, I am—lacking another hand."

"We must contrive without," Watt said, and perching himself casually against the pillows, set his hand on his father's shoulder. "So—you can feel that?"

"I can feel that."

He lay for a while with his eyes on Bess's face, and then little by little the tired lids drooped, and his hand relaxed and slipped from hers.

"Lady Ralegh, you must come away now," Dr. Turner's voice murmured presently in her ear; then as she shook her head. "You have been sitting in the same position ten hours or more; you will faint."

"I am well enough," Bess returned.

But Watt's hand was under her arm. "Come, darling."

She glanced up at him, read the determination in his eyes, and rose. She was so stiff that she would have fallen but for his arm round her.

"It is unjust—damnably unjust that such a thing should happen to father, after all that he has had to bear already!" Watt whispered in sudden, furious rebellion, as he looked down at the still figure on the bed.

"It is no question of justice or injustice, but a direct outcome of what has gone before," the Doctor said. "If you cage a man of Sir Walter's humour long enough, to beat his wings against the bars, something breaks; spirit or brain or heart; something breaks under the strain in the end. It is as simple as that."

Lawrence Kemys was standing just outside the door. He looked as though he had been standing there all the night, and the face he turned to Bess as she came out, was haggard in the light from the doorway. "How is he, Lady Ralegh?"

"He is asleep now," Bess said. "He is better—I think that he is better. But he cannot move his left arm."

Kemys said nothing, but he looked down an instant at his own left arm, moving it experimentally, as though he found it strange that it still obeyed his will. It was an odd, revealing gesture, telling more of his devotion to the other man than any words could have done.

Behind them in the room they had just left, Ralegh roused a little, muttering restlessly in his sleep. Watt glanced to the Doctor who was bending over the bed. "What did he say?"

"Something about the New World," said Dr. Peter Turner.

CHAPTER 18

THE SWORD AND THE SHEATH

For a few days Ralegh hung delicately poised between life and death, and then came down on the side of life. Indeed the strength of his hold on life was almost terrible. He had been a sick man long before his arraignment, and the strain of his trial for treason and the long captive years that followed it in this prison that was a hot-bed of plague in summer and creeping chill in winter, would have killed many a hale and hearty man; had killed many before now. But neither these things nor the seizure that had resulted from them seemed able to quench the flame of life in Ralegh.

He was not now the appalling patient that he had been after Cadiz, for he had learned many lessons since those days, and by late spring he was well on the road to recovery, with the power beginning to return to his left arm.

Some time previously, it had been arranged that Watt was to go abroad after Christmas, in the charge of Ben Jonson, to finish in Paris the education which he had failed to finish at Oxford. He had not done so well as had been hoped of him at the University, and had signally failed to commend himself to his tutors; he had a good brain when he cared to use it, but the wildness of a hawk, and a taste for practical jokes of the more Rabelaisian kind that they found distressing. Hence the proposed year in Paris. But when the time came, Watt had flatly refused to leave his father while he was so ill.

The relationship between her husband and son never ceased to be a bewilderment to Bess, for it was quite unlike any that she had met between father and son elsewhere. It was a turbulent relationship still, flaring up from time to time in sparks and flame, but seeming to exist for the most part on a plane of rather casual friendship. Yet the bond between them, though unexpressed, went very deep; deeper even than she had guessed until now.

But in the late spring, Watt at last made ready for his postponed journey.

Bess was loth to see him go abroad with such a bear-leader. It was not that she was afraid of his being led into evil ways, for Watt was the type who would take to evil ways for himself if he wished to, but would certainly not be led into them by anyone else; but she could not help feeling that the wild and brilliant Ben, notorious drunkard and quarrel-picker, was likely to be a liability rather than an asset as a travelling companion. But neither of her menfolk listened to her. They never did.

The two travellers departed, and behind them, Ralegh in his prison and Bess in her lodging set themselves to live even more frugally than before, since a son completing his education in Paris was a luxury that must needs be paid for. Ralegh set himself with Lawrence Kemys' help, to tutor his second son, finding him eager to please but maddeningly slow after Watt and Prince Henry. He returned to his writing; he returned to his chemical experiments. Time passed, featureless.

Summer chilled to autumn, to winter; spring came back to the Tower, and again the blackbird sang in the Lieutenant's garden through the harsh light evenings; and rather earlier than they expected, Watt came home; wonderously bearded, curiously clad in the latest French fashions, and full of strange oaths as his father had been when Lady Sidney so disapproved of him.

He made his reappearance alone, for Ben Jonson was celebrating his safe return with a three-day drinking bout; but when the three days had elapsed, that worthy also appeared, somewhat the worse for wear, to make formal, and thankful, relinquishment of his charge. And then the whole disgraceful explanation of their early return came out. It appeared that Ben had been invited to take part in an evening debate with—among others—Daniel Featly, a Protestant Minister and old tutor of Ralegh's, on "The Real Presence," and had taken Watt with him, thinking that he might benefit thereby. But the debate had been long, and the wine good and plentiful, and by the small hours, Ben had been peacefully insensible, and the combination of wine and an overdose of theological discussion had had an effect on Watt that was positively frightful. He had coveted a large hand-barrow from somewhere, arranged his tutor in it with feet together and arms extended, and wheeled him home to their lodging through the early morning streets, exhibiting him at street corners by the way, as the best representation of the Crucifixion in all Paris.

Watt was undoubtedly still a little wild.

There was, of course, a superb and thundering scene between him and Ralegh, and apologies to Ben Jonson from Ralegh, but none from Watt.

Through the rest of that year, Watt hung about in London, spending a good deal of time with his father, sharpening his wits against the wits of the Mermaid Tavern, and inevitably, before very long, getting into mischief. In the spring of 1615 he fought a duel with a young gentleman of the Lord Treasurer's Household; and being discovered, departed hastily for foreign parts, not to escape punishment, oh no, but taking his adversary with him, that they might finish the quarrel in peace.

That done, he returned, smiling and unrepentent, to his father.

Bess was present at the encounter, and so was Carew, who, with his tongue stuck out of one side of his mouth to assist concentration, was labouring at a Greek translation under his father's eye, when the door opened and Watt strolled in upon them, twiddling a nosegay of jonquil heads in a silver holder, and announced that he was back.

"So I perceive," said Ralegh, coldly; and ignoring the hand that was held out to him, returned to the business of Carew's education. Watt, not in the least abashed, rapped his small brother lightly on the head, and came to kiss his mother.

"For you," he said, dropping the posy into her lap. "Sweet, it would be pleasant to see you with a lute in your hands, instead of a needle, just by way of a change."

"If I had not three menfolk in constant need of shirts, I might have leisure for a lute," Bess said, returning the kiss.

Ralegh laid down his pen. "Watt."

His son turned to him instantly, with a wicked grin. "Sir, you propose to tell me exactly what you think of me, and I am all attention."

"I rejoice to hear it," Ralegh said with the steel sounding in his voice, "because that is exactly what I do propose to do." He leaned forward a little, his arms folded on the table, and in no uncertain terms, proceeded to do it.

"God alone knows," he ended, after a long interval filled by his quietly scarifying remarks, "what I have done of evil, that I should find myself to have begotten a mere swashbuckling bravo for a son."

At that point Watt, who had listened gravely throughout, remarked in his caressing voice "Mother would seem to be finding cause for amusement in this distressing scene. Share the jest with us, darling."

"I was remembering someone I knew once—oh, long ago," Bess said, "who sealed up another young man's beard and moustache with wax to stop him talking—and spent a week in prison for brawling. Nothing more."

Ralegh choked slightly. Carew squealed, and finding his father's eye upon him, turned himself hastily back to his Greek translation.

"Never trust a woman," said Watt, reflectively. "What did *your* father say, Sir?"

"What my father may or may not have said, has no bearing on the present occasion," Ralegh said, with his lip twitching.

"No?" Watt quirked an eyebrow at him; then went on more earnestly. "But what has a good deal of bearing, is the question of my future movements. I think with your leave, Sir, I should take myself out of England for a while."

Bess looked up quickly from her sewing. "Oh Watt, is it as bad as that?"

He gave her a quick, laughing glance. "I have not killed my man, only laid him by the heels a while to repent his sins and mend his manners. No Sir, it is not to avoid trouble, it is simply that I find London not quite large enough for me—a too close fit altogether, and pinches damnably across the shoulders."

"And what do you suggest doing about it?" Ralegh had clearly set aside the matter of the duel.

"Why, the *Flying Joan* sails for Guiana in a few days time, does she not? I've a mind to sail with Captain King. To speak you the truth, Sir, I think it was the knowing that your two-yearly Guiana venture was due to sail in the spring that has kept me kicking my heels about town all these months."

"Have you spoken to Captain King?"

"I have. With your leave, he will take me."

Ralegh regarded his son thoughtfully for a few moments, while Bess sat looking from one to the other, her hands laid empty in her lap. "Sets the wind from that quarter?" he said musingly.

Watt was seated on the table by that time, swinging a mud-sparked riding boot. "What else would you expect, Sir?" he said. "Almost my first memory is of sitting with the dogs under the study table at Sherborne, listening to you and Lawrence Kemys and some seaman you had brought home, discussing the pilotage of the Orinoco Delta. I was bred on the possibilities of a North-West passage to Cathay, and learned my letters from your *Discovery of Guiana*. I cut my teeth on the wonders of the New World that you declared into me when I was too small to make of them anything but a singing-rhyme. I was breeched with your plans for an English Empire beyond the sunset. . . . If I go now with Captain King, it may be that I shall find some new bearing that shall bring us to El Dorado yet, before the Spaniards. At the least, I shall see the fringes of Guiana."

His voice, as he spoke, had grown very deep, and his face taken on the look that Bess had seen so often in his father's. She had always known that he understood his father's dream, but until now, she had blinded herself to the knowledge that inevitably, one day, he would follow it. The old dream, the old devouring dream, taking Watt as it had taken his father. She found that she was crushing Watt's posy, and relaxed her fingers by a conscious effort, feeling suddenly a little sick. The warm, bruised scent of the jonquils was unbearably sweet.

The discussion had moved on while for a moment she was deaf

to it. "   The quartz mask," she heard Watt saying. "You used to show it to me sometimes, when you had been telling me about Guiana. What became of it?"

"I have it still," Ralegh said. He rose stiffly, and turned to the battered ebony travelling box in which he kept the few valuables that were left to him. He unlocked it with a fretted key which he took from his pocket, and after a brief search inside, turned back to the table, holding something in the hollow of his hand. "Here it is."

He dropped it into Watt's palm.

Bess saw the faint, lovely colour of the thing as he turned a little to catch the light on it. Carew, his Greek translation completely forgotten, was half across the table in his eagerness to see the treasure; and Watt lowered his hand, to show him.

"What is it? I've not seen it before."

Nobody answered him, and Bess, looking at his interested and puzzled face, realised that to her younger son, as to herself, that tiny, exquisite, terrifying mask was a closed book, a sealed mystery. In that, she found a tattered comfort.

But to the other two it was a mystery declared, an Ark of the Covenant.

Watt looked up at last, and made to hand it back.

"No," Ralegh said. "It is fitting that you should have it, now that you go whence it came."

.   .   .

Watt went with the *Flying Joan*, and in due course, returned, far more manned by his eight months at sea than he had been by his year in Paris. And for days after his return, charts and maps were spread on Ralegh's table, and conference followed conference between Ralegh and Watt, Kemys and King and Hariot.

Bess·kept away through that time, knowing that Sir William Waad, though milder in his rule than he had once been, was apt to make trouble if too many of Ralegh's circle were with him at a time; knowing also that her menfolk had no need of her just now.

But at last there came a winter afternoon when she was alone with Ralegh in the gloomy tower room that had grown familiar through the years. The five o'clock bell would not ring for a little while yet, but already it was dark—it had not been light all day, with a swirling dun-coloured river fog that blotted out the world—

and Talbot had brought candles. They burned smokily golden, surrounded by faint haloes, for even indoors the fog seeped through. By their light, such as it was, Bess had been at her interminable sewing; but she had folded it away now, and sat motionless by the low fire, her hands idle in her lap, looking up at Ralegh who stood leaning a shoulder against the smoke-hood, reading over something that he had just written.

He was so near to Bess, had grown so familiar with the years, that she seldom saw him objectively; but now as she looked, sudden awareness of him came upon her, and she was seeing him clearly and consciously as she would have seen a stranger. He looked old, and he looked ill. His badger-grey hair was retreating at the temples, though his finely trimmed beard was still dark and full. His always swarthy skin was sallow and patchy with long confinement, scored with deep lines of pain and frustration, his eyes sunk back into discoloured pits in his head; and the pearl in his left ear seemed to gain a dramatic lustre by contrast with the gaunt cheek against which it hung. Save for the Queen's ring, it was the only ornament he still possessed, and Bess realised that save when he slept, she had scarcely ever seen him without it. She could not imagine him without it; it was part of himself, just as his poetry was part of himself; that poet's vision of his that spilled over not only into his occasional winged verse, but into the fabric of his daily life, and illumined everything he wrote—his political treatise, his great History—with unexpected colours.

He reached the end of the closely-written sheet, and laid it on the table a little clumsily, for his left hand did not even now answer to him quite as it should; then turned back to the hearth.

"Walter," Bess said, "when are you going on with your History?"

He withdrew his gaze from the red heart of the fire, and shook his head slightly. "It was begun for Harry, and when the lad died, the life went out of it also."

"But it seems sad to leave it at the Punic Wars, and the volumes that you published last year were so well received—despite the King's efforts to suppress them."

Ralegh smiled. "No Bess, not even to annoy the King. The fires are out and the hearth is cold. Besides, it is in my mind that the time is ripe for me to lay down my pen for a while, and make one more bid for my freedom."

There had been so many bids for freedom, so very many, through the unforgiving years. Bess stifled a small sigh. "What lever do you plan to use this time, Walter?"

"The old lever," he said. He was staring into the fire again. "Oh I know that I can no longer hold out the promise of El Dorado, since Sir Thomas Roe opened up the Amazon and Orinoco valleys and proved it a myth—at least to his own satisfaction. But the Golden City is not the only source of New World gold. You remember the gold-bearing quartz we brought home in the year after Watt was born? That was gathered near the mouth of the Caroni; there must be a mine there somewhere. And when Kemys went out the following year, he learned a great deal from the Indian guides, of another mine close to Mount Aio, twenty miles nearer to the sea. The mines are there, I am convinced of it; and if need be, I believe that I could reach the lower one without so much as exchanging a musket shot with the Spaniards who hold the trading post at San Thome."

"Walter, do you want the gold so much?"

"I? No Bess, not now. But the King does. The King wants gold and always more gold to heap on his train of handsome lads. We have left an age of Statesmen for an age of favourites, and favourites are ever more expensive. Poor Jamie's pockets are to let, as usual."

"As usual," Bess said. "But since it *is* as usual, why should the old lever gain for you your freedom now, when it has failed so many times before?"

"Because though the state of the King's pockets be as usual, other things have changed of late. My ancient enemy Henry Howard is gone the way of Robin Cecil; and Robin Carr—I crave his pardon, My Lord of Somerset—is none so high in the Royal favour since he and his doxy were linked with the Overbury murder; and young Buckingham, who shares the King's bed in his place, is not ill disposed towards me, and might be won to further favour—so I gather —by a bribe to himself and another to Sir William St. John, who holds his ear."

"But what of these new plans for a Spanish marriage for Prince Charles and the little Princess? Will not the King fear to endanger them by letting you go free—and to Guiana of all places, which Spain claims for her own?"

"There is a strong faction at Court who are against the Spanish

marriages," Ralegh said. "And furthermore, even the King must
be well aware that both marriage plans are like to end in smoke
whatever he does, since Spain's terms for them are that England be
returned to the Papacy by Royal Mandate. Even Daft Jamey knows
that is beyond him."

A long silence, and then Bess said almost timidly: "Now that
your old enemies are dead or fallen from grace, could you not buy
a pardon that did not hang on this New World mine? Oh I know
it would mean heavier bribes, but we would contrive to raise the
money somehow. Then we could live quietly at Mitcham—or if
you like, sell Mitcham and go back to the West Country. Maybe
if you tried again, you could even buy back Hayes Barton after all.
Walter, you have earned your rest."

"Rest?" Ralegh said, lingering over the words as though testing
it in his mind and finding it wanting. "No, Bess, we will put the
money to nobler uses."

She tried once more, rising and moving close to him. "Surely
the enterprise is for younger men."

He turned slowly from the fire, to look at her. "It is not like you
to be cruel," he said. "Bess, Bess, don't you see that there could be
no more appalling fate for me than that, to have outlived my
dream—my destiny? I am growing old, and there is so little time;
so little time—all these years in the Tower eating into what I had
left. Now it seems that there may be one more chance for me, one
last throw of the dice, one last venturing. . . ." He smiled at her,
suddenly fond and rueful. "Dear Bess, try to understand."

"I do try, so hard," Bess said. "All these years I have tried, God
knows."

The five o'clock bell was sounding, small and harsh in the fog;
and she reached for her discarded cloak, and turned to go. She
always left the moment the bell sounded, hating to be fetched away
by the warder.

Ralegh put the cloak round her, muffling her close in its folds,
and they went out together into the portcullis chamber. Beyond
the little window the fog swathed by, visible where the light of a
flambeau turned it to thick golden smoke, making her cough as it
wreathed in through the unglazed aperture.

Ralegh was talking still, his voice low and eager, his hand on her
wrist to detain her.

"If I can but bring back the gold—enough gold—who knows, the King may yet be steered into braver courses. With enough gold in his pockets, he may be done with this mad subservience to Spain. The great days may return to us yet, and we may see an English Empire in the New World! And if that should come to pass, Bess, it will be my hand that brought the thing to birth!"

Bess was staring down through the little window. St. Thomas's Tower rose opposite, its crest lost in the night and the rolling murk, but below it, where the flambeau cast its stagnant radiance across Water Lane, she could just make out the archway of the Traitor's Gate; the worn steps descending to the water. How many feet had walked up those steps; the feet of the guilty and the innocent. The tide was in, and the black water flowing high through the iron grills caught fish-scales of light from the flambeau, where it lapped against the steps. She shivered uncontrollably, and turned away. "And if you fail?" she said. "How then, Walter?"

She could not see his face, but the angle of his bent head against the candle-light in the room behind him told her that he was looking at her intently. The pearl drop, hanging forward against the angle of his jaw, was rimmed with milky light. "I think that I shall pay for the failure with my head," he said. And then: "Bess, you would not have me rot gently into my grave—rusting out for lack of use, like an old sword forgotten in the sheath?"

Bess had a sudden, piercing vision of him as she had seen him that first time of all; a young man like a drawn sword, like a dark flame in the sunlight. "No," she said. "No, not that, my very dear." She reached up and took his head between her hands, and drawing it down to her, kissed him as she might have kissed Watt. "We will sell Mitcham and build a ship."

The warder's heavy step sounded below them.

CHAPTER 19

OFF-SHORE WIND

Very early on a blustery blue March morning, in a hired coach laden with books, scientific instruments and all the accumulated

gear of his long imprisonment, Ralegh passed out under the Byward Tower and across the moat causeway into the world he had
left thirteen years ago; and was driven through the narrow,
awakening way of the City, to his wife's house in Broad Street.

Bess was waiting for him at his destination, where she had gone
a few days earlier, that all might be in readiness for his coming;
and the sound of the coach wheels rumbling up the street brought
her from the parlour before the clumsy vehicle lurched to a stop at
the door and John Talbot leapt down from his perch beside the
driver. The door of the coach was flung open at the same instant,
and Ralegh stepped down on to the cobbles, and paused to gaze
around him as though he were a little dazed. The morning sky
above the gables was milky blue; at the far end of the street, the
trees in the churchyard of Allhallows-by-the-Wall were purple-
bloomed with rising sap, tossing in the wind that fretted the garbage
along the kennels yet seemed also to carry with it a whisper of the
country. And for a moment, Bess was aware of it all through his
senses; the dazzled senses of thirteen prison-buried years.

Then she was hurrying out to him, and as she did so, another
figure appeared in the coach doorway. For an instant she thought
that it was Lawrence Kemys, though she knew that he had already
betaken himself to lodgings of his own. But the man who stepped
down was not Kemys; it was a long, lean man, in respectable black
clothes, with a long blue chin and an eye as brightly enquiring as a
jackdaw's. At sight of him she checked, her greeting unspoken.
"Walter, who is this?"

Ralegh glanced round. "This? This is my keeper; my shadow to
go with me all my days until I sail for Guiana. Partridge by name.
You can furnish him with a place to sleep?" He spoke to the man
over his shoulder. "I know not the precise nature of your orders,
Master Partridge, but I presume that you are not required to pass
your nights as well as your days in my company?"

Master Partridge appeared deeply wounded. "Now, Sir Walter,
there's no need to be cantankerous. We all has our duty to perform
and happy them as can perform theirs without unpleasantness all
round. John Partridge is not the man to go making himself unpleasant. You furnish me board and lodging—with beer—and let
me know when you feels like taking your walks abroad; and I asks
no more."

"Joan will see to it," Bess said hurriedly, becoming aware that, early as was the hour, a little crowd of idlers was gathering out of nowhere. Somebody's serving maid in a cherry striped kirtle, a couple of prentice lads sent out on errands, several ragged children, an old man from the Gresham Almshouse, an itinerant chair mender. They called out sympathetic greetings to Ralegh, and commented freely among themselves on his worn appearance. They were joined by a couple of seamen, and a fat woman with a basket of vegetables on her arm, who became involved with one of the piles of books and gear which Talbot and Master Partridge were carrying into the house. Bess would have liked to retreat into the house also, away from the curious stares of these well-meaning people. But Ralegh had always enjoyed an audience, whether he was its villain or its hero. He was enjoying his little sympathetic audience now, she knew that; so for his sake she continued to endure the interest of the public, until the last pile of books had been carried indoors, when he paid the driver, took his leave of the crowd with a gravely courteous gesture, and followed her into the house.

In the narrow parlour, with its one window looking down into the street and the other into the walled city garden, they turned to each other. "Bess, you are the one familiar thing in a damnably strange world," Ralegh said, and held her at arm's length, looking at her. "Sweet, you are crying."

The door opened, and Joan entered with breakfast. She also was crying, her chin trembling and her old nutcracker face creased with smiles. "Ah Sir Walter, I never thought to see this happy day. Not but what, when my bird first married you, I never thought a day would come when I should be glad to see your face again!" proclaimed Joan, thumping down her load on the damask-covered table by the garden window. "But——" she looked from Ralegh to Bess and back again, "There's one thing I beg to know: do I have to have that serpent in my kitchen?"

"If you mean Master Partridge," said Ralegh serenely, "you do. But take comfort, Gossip Joan; I shall be from home much of the time, and where I go, he goes also."

Joan snorted, setting out bread and dried figs and a flask of muscadel with unnecessary clatter. Meanwhile Carew, who she had detained by main force in the kitchen until now, had entered behind her, but was hanging back in the doorway, suddenly shy of the father he had known only as a prisoner. It was the spaniel Hodge who broke the ice by trotting forward and smelling enquiringly at the stranger's shoes. Ralegh stooped, holding a hand to the cold, questioning muzzle. "Ah, Carew!—and this, if I mistake not, is Hodge."

Carew came forward, forgetting his shyness and suddenly eager as a puppy, himself. "Yes father, that's Hodge. He—he likes you."

"Dogs generally do," Ralegh said. "That is a thing that you have had small opportunity of knowing about me. Presently we must learn many things concerning each other, you and I." He laid a hand on Carew's shoulder, and smiled into the flushed and adoring face of the younger son he had never been able to love or understand as he did Watt.

At that moment Watt appeared in the doorway, side-stepped to allow Joan past him on her way out, and in a couple of strides, was across the room to his father, and had both arms round him. "Father! Oh, it is good to see you here!" he said huskily, and Bess saw that his eyes were wet. Then with a convulsive hug he released Ralegh, and stepped back, laughing. "Marry-come-up! What a sodden salutation! There's Joan flooding the kitchen with salt water, and Mother with tears on her lashes, and I must needs add mine to the general inundation! Sir, I vow you can seldom have been damper in the Tower than you are this minute. . . . Mother, can we have breakfast now? I am as empty as a wine-skin after Twelfth Night."

Ever after, Bess remembered that meal of bread and wine and dried fruit, eaten by the open window. She put from her all thought of Master Partridge and the implication of his presence in the house, all thought of the bitter past and menaced future. Her menfolk were here with her, free and safe in the circle of the present moment. The ilex tree in the little garden was tossing in the spring wind, filling the air with faint sea-music; the first wallflowers were opening in the bed below, and the scent of them on the wind was warm as though it were the fragrance of the sunlight that puddled the white damask cloth with gold. There was a twittering of happy sparrows under the eaves. An odd shyness held them all; they would be very merry one moment, then fall unaccountably silent, catch each other's eye and look hastily away, or be unsure how to look away at all.

Ralegh was constantly glancing about him, with that wide, all-embracing intensity that Bess had seen in his gaze when he left the coach. He ate little, and seemed restless, and as soon as the light meal was ended, thrust back his chair and got up saying, "Watt, do you go tell Master Partridge that if convenient to himself, I should like to walk abroad now."

"Would Master Partridge be the blue-jowled individual I glimpsed a while since, swilling beer in the kitchen, under Joan's malevolent glare?"

"It would," said Ralegh.

Watt hesitated an instant, watched by his mother and brother. "You wish to go alone, I take it, Sir?"

"Alone, save for my shadow," Ralegh said.

And alone, save for his shadow, he went; and all that day wandered about London and Westminster, seldom recognised, looking at the world after thirteen years.

First to the Strand. Essex House, Arundel House, Somerset House, Baynard's Castle, each in turn, he lingered by them, and passed on; pausing by the still standing shell of Durham House itself, to glance up at the blind window of his own turret study. He wandered into the great Abbey, and found the tombs of old comrades in arms, and of the Queen whose Captain he had been. He turned his steps back towards the City; sat for a while in the Temple Gardens, watching the busy traffic of the river; wandered on again like an unquiet spirit.

He did not return home until near supper time, when the candles were already lit in the parlour, and Broad Street quenched in shadows. Bess, who had been anxiously listening for him, let him in herself, and saw Master Partridge depart to the kitchen. Watt had gone out with some kindred spirits; Carew was with Joan, who would keep him for supper, and so for a little while she and Ralegh could be alone to themselves.

"Did you go to the Mermaid for dinner?" she asked, when she had drawn him upstairs into the quiet candlelit room.

"I forgot about dinner; my own, and my shadow's." He smiled at her with dark smudges under his eyes, and turning, limped heavily over to the garden window. Behind the topmost branches of the ilex tree the last warmth of the afterglow still lingered like an echo. "I am glad there is an ilex tree," he said.

"Walter, you are so tired; you have walked too far."

"There was so much to see, so many old haunts to be re-visited; and some, when I went to look for them, no longer there. I feel like a ghost returned to my old world and finding everything strange. . . . I saw the Queen's tomb in the Abbey, Bess. Her effigy is not very like her; the features are there, but the fires are out, and she was fire more than feature. That was why we thought her beautiful." He turned from the dusk-dimmed garden, and looked at Bess. "Tomorrow I shall ride down to Deptford, to set matters afoot for the building of my flagship."

"Another *Ark Ralegh*?" Bess asked.

"No; a *Destiny*."

Later that evening he showed her his commission from James to seek out the mine, passing it across the hearth to her as she sat relaxed in the fire glow. She read it through carefully, then refolding the stiff parchment, sat holding it between her hands. "Walter, why are certain of the words scored out?"

"Trusty and well-beloved?—But I am neither trusted nor well-beloved, by the King. It was the same with the commission that I had from Elizabeth for my first Guiana voyage; but she left the words out entirely, having a more delicate touch than James."

"But Walter, I do not understand. Why does he give you the commission if he feels so?"

Ralegh leaned back in his chair, pressing his hand with the old betraying gesture over the place where the Cadiz wound ached. "He wants the gold; but he wants it without committing himself too deeply," he said, turning his head on the leather squab, to stare into the fire. "He has rebelled in this matter against Count Gondomar, but he knows that he cannot keep up the rebellion. If I succeed in the enterprise, he will have gold past even his needs—immediate and certain gold to balance against the possible damage to his alliance with Spain. If I fail, he hopes that my head on a charger will make his peace with Spain for him. That is what James calls diplomacy."

.   .   .   .

Certainly if he was to fail, it would be through no lack of thought and energy on his own part. He set about the preparations for his venture in his old whirlwind fashion, straining heart and soul for its success; and in all things he had the loyal and devoted help of Watt and Captain Kemys. Bess sold her little estate at Mitcham, and the great elm keel of the ship it was to build was laid down in the Deptford shipyard. The Earl of Arundel had become one of Ralegh's sponsors, Nicholas and Arthur, George Carew and many other friends gave him their support, and little by little, the venture began to take shape.

The *Destiny*, finally launched and lying at anchor in the Thames, soon became a fashionable rendezvous, and many people came to see over her and talk with her Admiral; and amongst them came men clad in the sombre fashions that at that time made most foreigners look like crows to English eyes. They came unobtrusively, and did not make loud report of their conferences with Sir Walter Ralegh in the stern gallery of his *Destiny*; but neither did they make any particular attempt at secrecy. The French Resident sought to persuade him to bring his squadron, when completed, under the Bourbon flag; envoys of the Duke of Savoy tried to interest him in a raid on Genoa which was to all intents and purposes Spanish property—for there had been changes since James had planned to marry his son and daughter in that direction, and Savoy was now at war with Spain—and Ralegh listened to both of them, most courteously.

Bess, almost frantic with anxiety, protested to him one night. "Walter, how *can* you? And with Partridge actually on board."

He laughed. "Why not? There is no law to hold a man from selling his sword to any power not actually at war with England. Many of our gay lads are doing that now, with Venice for the purchaser."

"Nevertheless, it is playing with fire!" Bess insisted.

"Fire is very bright, to play with."

"It burns."

"Where else would be the point in playing with it?"

So Ralegh went on listening courteously to the propositions of the foreign gentlemen; and went on fitting out his fleet to follow his dream.

Meanwhile Count Gondomar was protesting furiously again and again to the King. Gondomar, who had been sent "to keep the King good," had long since by threats and intrigue, got James almost exactly where he wanted him; and he felt for Ralegh all a Spanish patriot's loathing for the man who had inherited Drake's position as the scourge of Spain, together with a strong personal animus on behalf of that kinsman of his who had suffered the indignity of capture and ransom at the Englishman's hands.

"Aye mon, are ye no unreasonable?" James protested in his turn, on one such occasion; almost tearfully confronting the furious Spanish Ambassador across his littered study table. "This Ralegh is commissioned juist to seek out the mine, and naething more. He has ma orders that he s'all na' lift a finger against Spain. And gin he disobey me, it s'all cost him his haed; that I promise ye."

But Gondomar was not mollified. "I think Sir, you forget that my Master, His Most Catholic Majesty, claims not a part, but the whole of the Indies for a dominion of Spain. How then shall this Don Ralegh cross Spanish territory and suck the richness of a Spanish mine, without lifting the finger against Spain?" He thrust his dark face forward across the King's writing table. "Is it, you think, that those who hold Guiana for my Master shall stand by to see it done?"

James, having no argument, took refuge in half intelligible mutterings and a close search for something non-existent among his papers. He wanted to be alone. It was very hot and he wanted to go to sleep. "Gin he disobey ma orders, it s'all cost him his haed," he said again after a few moments. "Aye, it s'all cost him his haed," and his flurried face, as he blinked up at the Spaniard, held a queer sliding gleam.

.   .   .   .

June 1617, and in Plymouth Sound a squadron lay at single anchor, waiting for the evening tide.

On the flagship's quarter-deck, the whole ship's company, with the Captain and Senior officers of the squadron were gathered to hear Divine Service before sailing, and in their midst, Bess stood between her husband and her son, between the squadron's Admiral and the *Destiny*'s Captain; trying desperately to keep her wandering attention on the dark-gowned Chaplain and the altar of piled drums against the break of the poop; trying desperately to keep her heart on her prayers. But between her and them came her too-sharp awareness of all the sights and sounds around her, making a barrier that she could not pierce.

Around her lay the rest of the squadron, twelve ships in all, waiting for the tide. Here on the flagship's quarter-deck their

Captains stood with bowed bare heads. Wollaston of the *Thunder*, Whitney of the *Star*, King of the *Flying Joan*, Lawrence Kemys who commanded the *Encounter*; young Cosmer, a kindred spirit of Watt's, from one of the pinnaces. There were young kinsmen of Ralegh's here too, and the sons of old friends. As for the rest, Bess's heart misgave her every time she thought of them. Impressment was no longer open to Ralegh, and owing to the doubtful attitude of the King, and the shadow that lay over the Admiral himself, volunteers had been few and far between; and he had been forced to gather his crews by issuing broadsides signed by himself and Kemys, promising a share in the gain to all who would throw in their lot with him. The result was a rabble of rogues and cut-throats, down-at-heel gentlemen, and ne'er-do-wells whose families had seen in the venture a chance to be cheaply rid of them. Close on a thousand men, and out of them, perhaps a hundred, perhaps less, whose loyalty could be relied on.

But there were the faithful few. Her mind dwelt on them for comfort; those kinsmen and sons of old friends, and hardy seamen who had served with him at Cadiz and Fayal; John Talbot, Kemys and King and Little Watt.   Carew, now in his first term at Wadham had no particular leanings to adventure, but if he had been two or three years older, the number of the faithful few would have been increased by one. Suddenly Bess thanked God that Carew was not three years older, and the moment after, prayed forgiveness for having thanked Him.

The water lay very still, the brightness of it greening as it went shoreward. The roofs and chimneys of Plymouth huddled under the steep protecting shoulder of the Hoe, the tall warehouses clustering along the Cattewater and Sutton Pool, glimpsed through the crowded masts of the shipping were bathed in run-honey evening light. It was all very peaceful.

Last night Plymouth had entertained Ralegh and his venturers to a banquet with long and eulogistic speeches. Earlier today, there had been shouting crowds; all Plymouth, all his own West Country, it seemed, crowding down to the waterside to see him off as he embarked for the last time; to throng round him and cheer him and bid him God speed; they who had been his liegemen in the days when the rest of England loathed him. Boats packed with sightseers had hung round the squadron for days; there were still a few, still little groups watching from the shore; but the shouting and jostling of leave-taking were over. Only the gulls wheeling among the topsail spars, their thin regretful crying sounding behind the Chaplain's words and the deep responses of the men at prayer on the *Destiny*'s quarter-deck; only the light off-shore wind pluck-ing at the dark folds of Bess's cloak.

She realised that Ralegh and Watt were kneeling down, and sank to her knees between them. Suddenly the fine web of distracting thought and sight and sound that had come between her and her prayers, seemed to part and let her through into sanctuary; the quiet at the heart of the storm. Walter's scallop shell of quiet.

"The Peace of God and the Fellowship of the Holy Spirit be with us all, ever more, Amen," said the Chaplain.

"Amen," came the deep echo of the congregation.

"Amen," Bess said.

Then it was over, and the stress of the storm was upon her again.

The Captains were departing to their own ships, boat after boat ordered away, the crew was springing into the ordered activity of a great ship making ready to sail, and already the tide was on the turn.

There were hurried leave-takings, while the boat that was to carry Bess ashore, waited. Watt was kneeling at her feet for her blessing, laughing up at her. "What shall I bring you from the New World, Sweet?" then leaping up and hugging her. "God be with you, Mother Darling, and with us! Pray for us—I do love you!" and his cold young kiss on her face. Then the arms round her were Ralegh's, the vital warmth of him enfolding her. . . . And then she was going down the ladder, taking the impersonal hand of the man standing to steady her into the boat.

She settled herself in the stern, the desolation rising within her as they pushed off from the *Destiny*'s side, and emptiness seeped coldly into the place that had been warm with beloved companionship a few moments ago. Looking up and back as the gap widened, she saw her menfolk still standing uncovered at the head of the ladder. Watt was gazing after her, and as she watched, he began to flourish his buckled hat in wide and joyous circles. She put up her hand and waved in return, smiling, though it was too far now for him to see her face. His father, standing beside him, was already looking out beyond Rame Head, out to sea. The years in the Tower had made

of Ralegh an old man, and a very sick one; but all that was forgotten now, and standing there was the Queen's Captain, leading
his fleet to sea.

His wife's eyes were on him, pleading, as the distance lengthened,
while still she waved and waved to Watt. "Look round once, just
once, Beloved, before it is too late."

But Ralegh did not look round. He had forgotten her, and once
again, Bess accepted without bitterness the knowledge that he was
away after his dream, and she herself left behind, in spirit as surely
as in body.

There were ships between her and the *Destiny* now. The *Encounter*'s cutwater swung across her sight as they passed under the
bowsprit. In the confusion of departure she had somehow missed
saying goodbye to Lawrence Kemys; dear, constant Lawrence
Kemys, who had been a part of her life almost as long as Ralegh
had. She wished she had said goodbye to him.

A little while more; there was open water widening between her
and the last of the squadron now; and she ceased to look back.
Then she was among more shipping. The boat grated gently against
some weed-grown steps, and Mr. Harris, the old friend of Ralegh's
in whose house she was to spend the night, was descending to meet
her. She rose in the rocking boat, and setting her hand on his wrist,
stepped ashore.

CHAPTER 20

THE SCARLET FEATHER

Bess went back to the little house in Broad Street, to make a home
for Carew in his holidays, and wait until the *Destiny* returned. She
made the usual summer conserves; she boiled candles and dried
marigold petals for winter soups; and worked with her needle in
the evenings while once again Joan kept her company. She had
leisure for her lute now, but the music was gone from her fingers
since she had no one to share it with her.

At first there was frequent word of the expedition, in letters from
Ralegh himself, and through friends who brought her the news

from the Court; for the squadron had run into gales almost at once, and been forced to take refuge in Kinsale Harbour. There they had to remain, waiting for favourable winds while the good days of summer were lost, sickness and discontent began to break out among the crew, and provisions to run low.

Then at last the wind blew from the right quarter, and no more news came to the little house in Broad Street, until, towards the end of March, Henry Herbert returned with one of the pinnaces, bringing home letters and dispatches. The first that Bess knew of his coming was the arrival of a thick packet, with a covering note begging leave to wait upon her shortly. The packet contained a letter from Ralegh and one from Watt. Bess took them out to the bench in the little sunny garden. There was a whitethroat singing his small liquid song in the ilex tree; his nest was in the churchyard of Allhallows-by-the-Wall, but he sang in the ilex tree on most fine mornings, now that the spring was here. Bess opened her son's letter first, like a child saving the finest cherry till last, because much as a letter from Watt meant to her, a letter from his father meant more.

Watt's letter was very short, only a few lines, beginning very dutifully "Honoured and most beloved mother," and ending with a burst of affection in which duty was quite forgotten. "Darling, your graceless but most loving Watt." It was badly written, as though in violent haste, and told her practically nothing; but all the warmth and laughter, the vivid eagerness that were Watt's seemed to flash up at her from the scrawled pages, remaining with her even when she had refolded it and turned to the second packet.

Ralegh's letter was of a length to make up for the shortness of his son's, and Bess settled herself with a sigh of contentment to read it. "Sweetheart," he began, "I can yet write unto you but with a weak hand, for I have suffered the most violent calenture, fifteen days." Her contentment went out like a pinched candle, and she hurried on anxiously. But as she read, her anxiety quietened, for he was better, much better, and Little Watt was thriving on the intense heat as though born to it. There followed an account of the voyage, which seemed to have been one long saga of storms and fever—forty-two men in the *Destiny* alone had died of fever, and amongst them, she would grieve to hear, was John Talbot. She did grieve to hear it; grieved for an old and trusted friend; but she could find only limited room, just now, for any feeling save relief that as yet Walter and Little Watt were safe. She returned to her letter. It was written from the mouth of the Caliana, she found, but soon they were sailing for their old anchorage near Punto Gallo in Trinidad, and then the enterprise would go forward in good earnest. There followed details of the bird life along the shores of their present anchorage, details of some new plants that Ralegh had found; very much love, and that was all.

Bess sat with her letter between her hands, and smiled at the whitethroat still singing in the ilex tree.

But many things had happened since Henry Herbert sailed from Caliana to carry home the mails.

Only a few days after the pinnace sailed, Ralegh had a relapse, and for a while seemed very like to die; but at last the sickness spent itself, and he began once more to mend. As soon as he was strong enough to be carried aboard from the branch-woven cabin ashore where he had lain sick, the squadron sailed for Punto Gallo according to plan. But it was obvious that unless they waited several weeks, he would not be fit to lead the expedition himself, and such a delay was out of the question. So the command fell on Lawrence Kemys with Watt under him, an unfortunate combination, since Watt was a fire-eater, and Kemys too long a second-in-command to be a sound commander, too good a follower to be a good leader.

In the Great Cabin of the *Destiny*, Ralegh, still swaying on his feet, gave them their orders. They were to land opposite the Mount Aio mine, and march the fifteen miles or so through the jungle. They were to avoid a fight if that might be; and if they found the mine impossible to hold until a relief force could reach them, they were to bring back a basketful of the gold to prove its existence to the King.

Early in December they set out, and Ralegh was left with a strong force to guard against their surprise by a Spanish fleet; left to wait through the long empty weeks, just as Bess was waiting in the little house in Broad Street, half the world away. He superintended the building of cabins ashore to ease the chronic overcrowding on ship-board; he fished, he made a study of the medicinal herbs of Trinidad; anything to hold off the fever of anxiety that possessed him.

The up-river voyage went ill from the first. All along the Orinoco, the Spaniards had clearly been warned of their coming, and were prepared and hostile; so much so that Kemys in Council with his officers, determined to disobey his orders, and rather than face the long march through jungle swarming with enemies, to a mine whose exact whereabouts had yet to be discovered, to continue up river, land a little below San Thome, and make for the other mine, whose position, much nearer the river, was known to him. This seemed at the time a wise decision. Events proved it to be a fatal one.

The English, making camp below San Thome, were attacked in the night by a strong Spanish force, and, taken by surprise and low in morale as they were, would have been utterly routed but for the courage of Kemys and a few officers who somehow contrived to rally them, to steady them into a semblance of discipline, and even, when the first pressure slackened, to sweep them forward into a counter-attack.

That counter-attack developed beyond all that had been intended, into a full-scale assault on the town. It was Little Watt, with a handful of yelling English gaol-birds behind him, who made the first breach. In the fiery darkness and the tumult nobody saw him fall. They heard him cheering them on "Go on, my Hearts! The Lord have mercy on me—the Lord prosper you—Go on!" but it was another wave of the attack, thrusting after, that found him lying within the breach, his head on his arm as though he slept, and a red hole below his breastbone.

Next day, in the captured town, Lawrence Kemys buried his dead under the floor of the Romish Church, the only means he had of making sure their graves would be safe from desecration. Little Watt he buried before the High Altar, with full Captain's panoply of muffled drums and trailed pikes, and Colours borne before him to his grave.

The taking of San Thome was disastrous in more ways than one, for the Spaniards gathered in the surrounding jungle so that the English were virtually besieged; prospecting parties in search of the up-river mine were ambushed and cut off, and no trace of the Mount Aio mine could be discovered. Provisions began to run low, and the whole force were growing mutinous, finally demanding of their officers an immediate return to Punto Gallo.

For Lawrence Kemys, there was no choice. Almost a month after taking the town, they fired what was left of San Thome, and leaving the church a red pyre over Little Watt's grave, began the journey back.

Ralegh received a letter from his Lieutenant in mid-February, telling him of all that had happened: and for him, the light went out. No one, not even Bess, had ever been as near to him as Watt, and his world was left empty by the boy's going. To that was added the probable ruin of every hope that he had had of the enterprise, for with the King's orders disobeyed and San Thome sacked, he realised that unless the mine proved to be rich indeed, his last chance was gone. His last chance, not only of life—he cared very little for that now—but of realising his dream of an English Empire in the New World.

And then a fortnight later, the expeditionary force, or the ragged remains of it, returned, having failed to find the mine. The last slim chance was gone, and Little Watt had died for nothing.

Ralegh and Kemys met with constrained quiet, and Ralegh took his Lieutenant's full report of the disastrous expedition without any outward sign of disturbance. A little later that evening, they actually supped together in Ralegh's branch-woven cabin. But the consciousness of all that had happened hung between them like the still oppression of approaching thunder. Ralegh was not aware of holding himself in restraint, indeed, what he felt was a kind of suspension of all emotion, an utter weariness, and nothing more. It could not last, this quiet, stretching into electric tension between them. Presently it must snap, but not just yet.

Not until, supper being ended, Lawrence Kemys went to the adjoining cabin, which had been made over to him, and returned with a little bundle folded in a kerchief, which he set down on the table with a marked hesitation. "The boy's gear is still on board," he said heavily. "These were on his—These were on him."

Ralegh, who had been glancing through the papers, turned from them without a word, and taking up the little bundle, tumbled out the contents with a hasty, almost harsh gesture. Little Watt's small personal possessions spilled upon the table; and among them, a small scarlet feather that must have caught his idle fancy by its sheer perfection. "What of the quartz mask?" Ralegh demanded levelly.

"We buried it with him. I thought that you would have it so."

"Aye, I'd have it so," Ralegh said. "You might have buried the rest of this tussy-mussy with him, for all I care."

"I had thought that Lady Ralegh——" Lawrence Kemys began.

Ralegh was staring down at the scatter of objects on the table; so very unremarkable, save for that small scarlet feather, which somehow spoke more clearly and tragically of Watt, the laughter and the courage and the bright unruly flame of Watt, than did all the other familiar objects that his father had seen in his hands a thousand times. That small scarlet feather suddenly pierced the protective vacuum in Ralegh, filling him with the overwhelming realisation that Watt was dead, and had died for nothing.

"You thought! You thought!" he cried out. "It is a most sad pity, Captain Kemys, that you did not think of other matters beside; a pity that you did not think to obey my orders; that you did not think more to find the mine, as you were sent to do."

"Sir?" Kemys said, puzzled, and no more, for the moment; for he had explained his reason for disobeying his orders; he had explained about the mine.

Ralegh swung half round from the table, the control of which he had not been conscious, snapping and swept away before a surge of sickening rage, such as he had never known before. He had never troubled himself to feel, let alone express, such deadly bitterness towards an enemy, certainly never to anyone who meant nothing to him; it was the shared comradeship of thirty years, the bond of an old and deep friendship that added corrosive poison to his anger now, as he turned and rent the faithful Lieutenant who had so tragically failed him.

Lawrence Kemys, standing like a prisoner before his judge, tried once to justify himself, pointing out how little else there was that he could have done in the matter of the mine, asking not for mercy, but for justice. But Ralegh, almost beside himself with pain and grief, conscious only that Watt was dead and had died in vain, would not even hear him. "By your wilful folly you have brought this whole enterprise to ruin. You have sacked a Spanish settlement in direct disobedience to the King's commission, and you have failed to persevere in seeking out the mine whose riches might have redeemed San Thome in the King's eyes. You could scarce have bettered all our undoing had you been Gondomar himself!"

"Sir," Kemys persisted, "I think that later, you will maybe give more weight to the reasons for my failure. They are, in truth, reasons that have weight and substance, as I am assured that the Earl of Arundel and his fellow sponsors of the enterprise will admit, if all be made clear to them, and will set before the King. Will you give me leave to set down in a letter to them, all those things that I have told you, and when it is written, give me your endorsement to it?"

Ralegh's head was in his hands, his rage had grown cold in him, cold as death. He raised a grey and sweat-streaked face with dreadful, red-rimmed eyes. "I will lend no favour nor colour by any endorsement of mine, to the things that you have done, and the things that you have not done, Captain Kemys," he said deliberately. "You have ruined me."

Suddenly very white, Lawrence Kemys asked: "That is your final resolution?"

"That is my final resolution."

"I know then, Sir, what course to take," Kemys said, very quietly. He bowed, and turning, left the Admiral's quarters, putting out a hand to the doorpost in passing, as though he were blind.

Left alone, Ralegh sat a while with his head still in his hands, staring at the small scarlet feather, that lay like a splash of bright heart's blood, on the table before him; then pulled himself together and tried to busy himself with some papers that Kemys had brought out of San Thome.

He was still engaged with the first of them when he heard a shot which seemed to come from the adjoining cabin. He listened a few moments, then rose, and going to the blanket-hung doorway, called to a seaman standing close by. "Pengelly, find out what that shot meant," and went back to his papers.

The man returned at once. "Captain Kemys says he fired off his pistol to clean it, because it had long been charged, Sir."

But half an hour later, fetched there by a scared ship's boy, Ralegh stood in the adjoining cabin, looking down at the body of his friend and Lieutenant, lying outstretched on the narrow cot of planks against the wall. A discharged pistol lay beside him, but the ball seemed to have glanced off a rib, breaking it but doing little other harm; and Lawrence Kemys, more steadfast of purpose than

Ralegh had been, fifteen years ago, had finished the work with his dagger.

.   .   .   .

News of the sack of San Thome reached London, via Madrid, in May; and within an hour of its coming, Count Gondomar burst in upon the King in his Palace of Whitehall, brandishing the dispatch, and shouting "Pirate! Pirate! Pirate!"

But it was not until a day or two later, when Roger North returned with another of the pinnaces, and the matter became public knowledge, that it reached Bess. North brought home Ralegh's report to the Secretary of State, and with it a letter to Bess, the hardest letter that he had ever had to write.

Roger North was one of the many who, by that time, had turned against Ralegh, and was intent on making his peace with the King; but he brought Bess's letter to her himself, and she found him waiting for her when she returned from a morning's marketing, with a young maidservant behind her, carrying the big rush basket. Eggs, she had bought, and beef, and cinnamon; and because it came from the country, a nosegay of early summer flowers. On hearing from Joan that he was in the parlour, she sped upstairs, and without even waiting to shed her light cloak, plucked open the parlour door and was half across the room with her hands held out to greet him where he stood beside the empty hearth, before she saw his face, and checked.

"It is my husband," she said.

He bowed to her. "I left Sir Walter at Nevis in the Leeward Islands; he sent me ahead with dispatches and—a letter for you."

He was holding out the letter as he spoke, but she made no move to take it. She was looking into his face, normally a pleasant face, but just now troubled and at the same time defiant; and it was as though something cold had clenched itself round her heart, making it hard to breathe. "It is Watt, then," she said.

"Will you—will you read your letter, Lady Ralegh."

He was still holding it out, and she took and opened it with oddly clumsy fingers, turning to the light of the garden window.

Roger North, left forgotten, hesitated, glancing at the door and clearly very eager to be gone; glanced at the stricken woman, and finally moved to the far window and became engrossed in the doings of a stray cat in the street below.

"I was loth to write, because I knew not how to comfort you," Ralegh had written, after briefly giving her the facts. "And God knows I never knew what sorrow was until now. Comfort your heart, dearest Bess, and I shall sorrow for us both. . . . My brains are broken, and it is torment for me to write. The Lord bless you and comfort you that you may bear patiently the death of your valiant son." And his bold signature sprawled across the page. And then, changing his mind, he had written her a detailed account of the tragic venture, page after page of it. She read it through to the last word, realising almost nothing of what it told her, save that Little Watt was dead.

Little Watt had been dead four months. It seemed strange that she had not known—not even when she read his letter. Something should have told her; some empty dragging at her womb that had given him birth. "I should have known," she thought dully. "I should have known."

She stood perfectly still, looking out into the narrow sunlit garden. How strange that the sun was still shining. The whitethroat was singing in the ilex tree too; and it was summer; and Little Watt was dead.

CHAPTER 21

THE PASSOVER

In the pleasant, panelled parlour of Mr. Harris's house in Plymouth, Bess was standing by another window, looking out and down. Beyond the garden where the bees were busy among the roses, the crowded roofs dropped away, and the Sound was a sheet of pearl in the evening light. And Bess's gaze went searching to and fro among the ships lying at anchor, searching for the *Destiny*.

Just a week before, two and twenty years to the day since Cadiz, the *Destiny* had returned to Plymouth—alone. It was a great gesture, greater than the trumpets at Cadiz had been; but Bess could feel no pride in it. She was too spent, too weary to the depths of her soul.

News of Ralegh's return had brought her posting across England to join him; and less than an hour since, she had arrived, to be welcomed by the old steward, and greeted with the news that her host and hostess were at their country house a few miles outside Plymouth, and that Mrs. Harris had left a letter for her. She was holding that letter now. "Dear Lady Ralegh," Mrs. Harris had written. "Our house and household are yours for as long as they are of the least use to you. Pray use them as your own. It has seemed to my husband and myself that you may be more glad to be alone than you would be of our company, at this time. If, however, we are wrong in this, do you send me word by Thomas the groom, and I will be with you as swiftly as horses may bring me."

Bess was touched and warmed by the kindness of this woman almost unknown to her, so touched that without warning, she began to cry. She had not cried since she knew that Watt was dead. It had seemed as though all her tears were drained away into the cold numbness that had been like carrying something dead within her. Now, the dead thing was shuddering back to life and intolerable pain.

She began to shiver from head to foot; and the kind note slipped from her fingers and fluttered to the floor.

Leaning against the angle of the window embrazure, she shut her eyes while the waves of returning life and anguish flowed over her. The child! Dear God, the child! Of what avail to bring a child into the world, in blood and agony, only that, with his manhood scarce dry upon him, in blood and agony he might go out of it again?— and all for the serving of a dream; a bright, devouring dream. Standing there in the sunlit window, her despairing question seemed beating against the very knees of God.

Presently the door opened, and Ralegh was standing on the threshold. She looked at him in silence, with straining eyes, seeing the rigid figure and haggard face; seeing that because of Watt, he was afraid to come to her. And for a long moment, because of Watt, because his dream had killed Watt, she could not bring herself to go to him.

And then suddenly she knew quite clearly that all was well with Watt, and he no longer needed her; but the man in the doorway needed her as never before, and she went to him.

It was a long while later that a knock sounded on the door, and a servant brought in candles, a great branch of candles, flaring in the dusk. They had been talking very quietly, of Watt—never of Lawrence Kemys—and Bess had not seen the twilight deepen, but she cried out against the sudden light. And then, as the servant hesitated, Ralegh rose from the window bench where he had been sitting beside Bess, saying: "Set them on the mantel, so—— Now light the others. We will have a fanfare of light to shame the darkness!"

And when the servant was gone, he turned back to her and caught her hands and drew her to her feet. "Not the sad summer twilight for Watt," he said. "He had no kin with the twilight. A galaxy of candles, a whole Milky Way of candles would not be light enough for Watt. I wish that you were wearing the bravest gown you ever had, and rubies in your ears; and you with a lute in your hands, playing Greensleeves!"

"I am not made of the stuff of Spartan mothers," Bess said.

"It was not so that I meant it." He was holding her hands still, looking down at her. "Let him live, Bess; he loved life very greatly, so is he become a part of life. There should be no sable pall of grief to smother out his flame."

Bess said wonderingly: "You said that—almost that—long ago, for Philip Sidney."

"Did I? I felt it, long ago, for Philip Sidney. But not as I do now, Bess."

No, not as he did now. But from that evening thirty years ago, another memory, linked to the first, touched Bess as with a cold finger, flicking her whole mind over from Watt to his father. "Not for me—dear God, not for me when my time comes," the Queen's Captain had said that evening; and now, how near had that time come? "Walter," she said urgently. "Why did you come home? You should not have come home."

"I should not indeed, but that my crews wearied of a doomed Admiral," Ralegh said. "I should have gone to Jamestown to refit, and tried again; but with one ship and one ship's company left to me, I had no course left but to come home."

"You could have gone to France! The French would have received you gladly; you know it!—You can still go—we will find means; and once you are safe overseas, the Queen will mediate for you; only go, my dear, before it is too late!"

He shook his head. "I'll not show my scut to the likes of Daft

Jamey. Beside, if I ran it would blacken my case; it would be as though I admitted to some guilt, and before God, I admit to none."

"What does the King care for your guilt or your innocency? Your head is promised to Spain, like John the Baptist's, on a charger. The King would do anything, *anything* to bring about a marriage between Prince Charles and the Infanta; he is completely under Gondomar's thumb, and you know how dearly Count Gondomar hates you!" She was pouring out the words with frantic urgency, her fingers clutching at his sleeve. "Walter, the King has even promised to send you to be executed at Madrid if Philip so wishes it. Before ever you landed, he had issued a proclamation of his affection for his Dear Brother of Spain and his detestation of what he calls your atrocious acts of violence!"

"Sweet, that is no news to me," Ralegh said. "There is an order out for my arrest. Indeed I have expected Lewis Stucley at every moment since I dropped anchor. I hear he has bought my sloughed Vice-Admiralty of Devon, and so the task will be for him to carry out."

"Walter, will you not listen to me?"

"Neither to you, nor to anyone who counsels me to run for it—not even to my kinsman George Carew who sits in the Privy Council with his nose in the nation's affairs." As he spoke, he brought out a folded paper from the breast of his doublet, and held it out to her. She took and unfolded it, seeing above the signature, only three words, written with slashing vehemence. "*Get you gone.*"

She refolded and handed it back to him. "You will take no heed?"

"No."

"Then in God's name what will you do?"

"In four days time, the work which keeps me here with the *Destiny* will be finished. In four days, if Lewis still tarries by the way, I shall set out for London. If I can but gain audience with the King, and put my case to him, face to face, I may even now win through. He is a man ever swayed by the nearest presence and the last speaker."

"And do you suppose that he does not know that, and will not guard against it by refusing you the opportunity?" Bess cried. "He means your death! Walter, he means your death! and you—oh, it may seem to you that the Block is a fine dramatic exit for the last of Elizabeth's champions—but it is not you alone who will suffer when the axe falls!—And I have already lost Little Watt to this devouring dream of yours!"

There was a long silence, and then Ralegh said softly: "That was a woman's weapon. I had not thought that you would stoop to handle such."

She made a small hopeless gesture. "I think that I am beyond caring for my choice of weapons."

A voice sounded outside, speaking to one of the servants, and Ralegh's head went up. "Ah, here is Captain King. I bade him bring me certain lists this evening." He limped to the door and plucked it open, calling "Come in here, King. My wife is here and waits to bid you welcome." Then as the familiar piratical figure appeared in the doorway, he turned back to Bess, who had not moved. "A faithful few I have left unto me, even now, you see, Bess; and here is one of them."

"Yes," said Bess. "Yes—I see." She acknowledged the man's salute, and watched him as he tramped forward to the table and laid several papers on it.

"That's a poor welcome, Bess," Ralegh said.

"Captain King knows the greeting I would give to anyone who still counts himself your friend." She turned full to the newcomer. "Captain King, I have been trying to make him go away—for a little, just for a little; but I can do nothing. Can you not make him listen to you?"

Captain King looked from her beseeching face to the set and haggard features of the man beside her, and back again. His small round eyes were dark with trouble.

"Captain King, will you not try?"

He shook his head. "Lady Ralegh, I am as powerless as you—and as the agents of France, who have also approached him. Three days since, I sought out a French pilot and engaged him in Sir Walter's name, for the trip across the Narrow Seas. This very night, they would have sailed. He would not go."

.   .   .   .

There had still been no sign of Sir Lewis Stucley when, four days later, the little company set out on their journey; Ralegh and Bess and Captain King, riding light, for such gear as they possessed had been sent on ahead. They were a silent company, Ralegh looking about him as he rode, with a swift intensity that seemed to rest like a leave-taking on the deep coombes set with apple orchards, on every glimpse of the sea and the moor. This was his own country, the hills that had bred him, through which he rode for the last time.

Towards evening the road began to climb steadily, the country on either side grew bleaker, harder, and the skies more wide, as they neared Ashburton on the skirts of the moor. They were to spend the night at the little moorland town, long since grown familiar to Bess from the many times she had come that way at Ralegh's chariot wheels. Always, until today, it had seemed a friendly place, and she had been glad to reach it at the day's end. But now, tired as she was, hot-eyed and thirsty, powdered with the red wayside dust, she found that she was dreading the place, the familiar rooms of the Mermaid Inn, the friendly faces of Mine Host and his wife; dreading the end of the day's journey that would bring them so much the nearer London.

Almost within sight of Ashburton, a shallow coombe led upward from the road towards the moors, and Ralegh, who had been riding half a length in front, reined back his horse to hers, turning in his saddle. "It is too fair an evening to waste within walls," he said. "Sweet, shall we send William King on for supplies, and sup out here under God's sky, with the linnets for company?"

Bess caught thankfully at the delay, and so, while Captain King rode on into Ashburton, Ralegh dismounted, and leading her horse and his own, turned up the coombe, following the thread of white water that came purling down over trout-speckled stones to join the Yeo. A hundred yards upstream they came to a place that seemed made for their purpose; a sheltered hollow opening to the south, with the dark tors rising beyond it, soft with young heather, murmurous with bees. And there Ralegh checked the horses, and stood smiling up at her, his eyes narrowed against the light. "Behold, our banqueting hall! Down with you, Bess."

She slipped into his clasp, and he set her down a little clumsily because of his left arm, and went to hitch the horses' reins over a low alder branch beside the stream. Then he returned to Bess, where she had seated herself on the sloping side of the hollow, and going down full length beside her into the warm heather, reached out and with lazy masterfulness, pulled her down into his arms. Bess, relaxing to him, remembered the time when his arms about her had been hard and hotly compelling when he held her so. With the passing years, love had gentled and grown silvery, become a thing of dear companionship and shared experience and the quiet touching of hands; but none the less potent for that, it seemed. . . . And the potency of it twisted under her heart as she awoke to the discovery that even now, after all the years together, after all that had happened, after Little Watt, his touch could still set her pulses racing like a young girl's.

He kissed her, his mouth quiet on hers as the hold of his arms about her. "You are so sweet," he said. "There are grey feathers in your hair, Bess—do you know it? But you are still as sweet as linden honey in the kissing. That's because you have a big mouth. Big-mouthed women are ever the sweetest in the kissing."

"Have you kissed so many?"

He laughed, with his cheek against hers. "I do but quote Quintilian."

It was very warm in the little hollow, very peaceful; a tiny, enclosed universe. Only the voice of the stream in the wind-hushed emptiness, only the bees among the first flowers of the bell heather, and the pipits calling. Bess lay quiet, smelling the warm summer scents of the moor, gazing up through height beyond height of a heaven whose sparkling blue was already paling a little at the first touch of evening. A spray of bell heather arched into her field of vision, hung with papery pink bells. It almost seemed to her that she could catch their chiming as the little wandering wind brushed by. What kind of carillon would it be, she wondered. Sweeter than the Fleet Bridge carillon. . . . All her senses seemed heightened, and she was exquisitely aware of the shining moment between the dark and the dark. "It may be that this is the last time I shall lie in his arms," she thought, "the very last time of all," and she held the moment to her, that she might be able to hurt herself with the remembrance of it afterwards, to all eternity.

Once, Ralegh shifted as though to come at his pipe and tobacco box; then, changing his mind, relaxed again. "It would be good to lie out here through the night," he said presently. "Better than behind stone walls. The stars will come out presently. We should see the Pole Star, and Arcturus—and over yonder, Cassiopea. And in the morning we should wake with the curlews calling in the first green light, and the day-spring chill on our faces."

A little later they heard the soft trampling of horses' hooves coming up the stream side, and Ralegh released her and got stiffly to his feet, calling, "Up here, King."

When Captain King joined them, leading his horse, he looked hot and disturbed. He said, "Sir Walter, your kinsman is down yonder at the Mermaid in North Street."

And it seemed to Bess that something twisted in her.

"Lewis?" Ralegh said after a moment.

"Aye, Sir Lewis."

"Have you told him that I am on my way?"

The seaman's face was a little pugilistic, as he hitched his horse to the alder branches beside the others. "No," he said, "I didn't," and he looked with deliberate meaning at Ralegh.

The other shook his head. "Oh no, Captain King. You may shake that bee out of your bonnet once and for all."

"Then—do we ride on now?"

"Not until we have supped. You have brought the wherewithal? Ah, that is good. Let my kinsman wait on our pleasure yet awhile, since presently we must wait on his."

King produced from his saddle bag several articles wrapped in a clean napkin. "The Inn-wife let me have these—very privily. Bread and cold pasty; a trug of strawberries for Lady Ralegh, a flask of muscadel."

Ralegh took them from him and brought them to Bess, where she sat, rigid and unmoving. "Sweet, we have a banquet indeed! Nay now, smile, Bess; it had to come today or tomorrow, or a week hence."

She smiled obediently, and taking the things from him, began to set them out on the spread napkin.

So, sitting in the warm heather, the three of them ate together, dividing the strawberries between them with scrupulous fairness, passing the flask of muscadel from hand to hand. To Bess the food was choking sawdust, and clearly Captain King had little pleasure in it. But Ralegh seemed to enjoy his meal, lingering over it pleasantly while the world drained of warmth and the shadows gathered in the little hollow, and the sky took on the quiet pallor of a fading harebell.

When the meal was finished, they remained sitting for a while in silence. "A quiet evening, this," Ralegh said at last. "See, Bess, there is the first star, and it singing like a linnet if our dull ears could but catch the song." He drew himself together, to rise. "God's life! I am stiff.   We have eaten our Passover meal, my friends, and it is time to go."

CHAPTER 22

KING DAVID'S BEARD

It was almost dark when they rode into Ashburton, and the windows of the Mermaid in North Street were full of candlelight shining welcomingly into the summer night. They dismounted in the courtyard and handed the horses over to the care of the head hostler, who was an ancient friend. Mine Host, who came forth to greet them was a friend also. "Ah, Sir Walter, Sir Walter, us be proper grieved to see this day come!"

Ralegh laughed a little harshly. "Nay, man, never pull a long face. Is my kinsman Sir Lewis Stucley within doors?"

"In the guest parlour, Sir."

"Good. Then I will go in to him—no, do not you trouble, I know my way and he must take me unannounced. Since 'tis to meet me that he comes, he can scarce complain of that."

He had turned down the familiar passage-way as he spoke, tossing the words over his shoulder to the landlord. He reached the door of the guest parlour, and opening it, stood aside for Bess to precede him, then limped serenely in with Captain King at his shoulder.

Sir Lewis was lounging at his ease with a long-necked bottle and a slender wineglass on the table beside him, and his exaggeratedly long rapier hanging by its slings from a chair back near by. He sprang up at their entrance, his pleasant, slightly ineffectual face blank with surprise in the candlelight, his eyes going past Bess to Ralegh. "What the Devil!—Walter!"

Ralegh advanced to the table. "Why so startled, my coz? Is it not, after all, the matter of my arrest that brings you into these parts?"

The other regarded him with a troubled face. "It is," he said at last. "I suppose that I was startled because I was thinking of other things, and—I had scarce thought to meet you on the road."

"You were so confounded slow in coming," Ralegh complained.

"I was as slow as I dared be," said his cousin, with so much meaning that Bess looked at him quickly.

But Ralegh appeared to notice nothing; he had turned to gather the other two. "Lewis, my wife you know, at least by sight, but Captain King is, I think, a stranger to you: Captain William King, my Shipmaster and good friend. . . . And now, suppose that we proceed to business; here I stand for your arresting, Cousin Lewis."

There was a long and utter silence; the two men facing each other, one grave and unhappy, the other smiling with faint insolence, as he waited for arrest. "Walter," Stucley said at last, with unexpected warmth, "I beg you to believe that there is nothing of pleasure for me in this." He reached out with a clumsy, unwilling gesture, and brought his hand down on Ralegh's shoulder. "There, we will count it done."

"So. And now that I am your prisoner, do you require that I deliver up to you my sword?"

"No!" the other said quickly, with the same warmth in his voice. "For the Lord's sake, Walter, do not make this worse than need be, for either of us. We have not been good friends in the past; but when we fell out I was younger and of hotter blood—so were you, for that matter—and at least it has been no fault of mine that the breach remained open so many years." He made a small, earnest gesture of appeal. "It is all such ancient history, and I would to God this task had fallen to another man than I."

Ralegh studied him at his leisure, coolly and in silence. At last he nodded. "It is ancient history, as you say. Nay then, let us call a truce, at least for the time that I remain your prisoner."

The door opened, and another man came in, a little round man in a long black gown, with the bright tragic eyes of a marmoset under a bald dome of forehead, who hesitated at sight of the new arrivals, and began to back out again, saying with a strong French accent, "Ah, a million pardons. I had thought that you were alone, Sir Lewis."

Stucley stayed him as he was half outside the room. "No, no; here man, come you and be presented to my kinsman and his lady." He made the introduction hastily, and with the hesitancy of manner that Bess had noticed about him before, while the Frenchman bowed to each in turn, lingering a little over her hand with the gallantry of his race. "Lady Ralegh, I present to you Dr. Manourie, a skilled physician and a friend and travelling companion of mine. Sir Walter—Captain King."

An uncertain pause followed, which was broken by Sir Lewis speaking rapidly to his prisoner. "Walter, you will not object to Dr. Manourie remaining one of our company? He is a Frenchman, and as such, has small sympathy with the aims of the Spanish faction."

This time Ralegh seemed to catch the meaning in his tone, and turned a searching look from him to Manourie. "We shall have much in common," he said.

The little physician raised those tragic marmoset's eyes to his. "The French have little cause to love Spain. A few of us still remember St. Bartholomew's Eve, and have even less to love the Papacy."

Bess found her world swimming. Could it be that in this cousin who had come to arrest him, Ralegh had found a friend? Had she been unjust to Sir Lewis Stucley all these years? It seemed so, and yet—she could not be sure.

Next morning they took the road again. Exeter, Honiton, Sherborne—Sherborne that had passed from Robert Carr now, as it had from Ralegh, with all its lime trees in flower and the cuckoos calling broken-voiced from Jerusalem woods—Shaftesbury, Salisbury.

In the private parlour of the White Hart at Salisbury, Ralegh and Bess, with their three companions, were waiting for supper on the evening of their arrival. The table was already laid, and Mine Host was supervising the bringing up of sundry pies and a pair of roast capon from the kitchen. Mine Host was a friendly soul, and having seen the capons arranged to his satisfaction, he turned an expansive face to his guests. "Fine doings here next week, Gentlemen."

"Fine doings?" Ralegh who was lounging before the hearth, asked, without interest.

"Why, haven't you heard, Sirs? They say the King is due in Salisbury in four days." He grinned. "King James, he do seem to grow a-most as fond of progresses as her late Majesty."

There was a small, startled silence in the room, and then Ralegh began to fiddle with the snuffers on the mantel, leaving the resumed talk to his companions. But as the door closed behind Mine Host

and his minions for the last time, he dropped the snuffers and
swung round from the hearth. "Lewis," he said, "we must wait
four days! No, listen, man: I *must* gain an audience with the King,
here, where his evil genius Gondomar is not at his elbow!"

Lewis Stucley began to bite his nails. Bess watched him with
aching intensity; they all watched him, as the silence lengthened.
He went on biting. "I daren't," he said at last.

"What a-devil do you mean?" Ralegh demanded.

"Simply what I say—I daren't." Stucley lowered his bitten hand.
"I delayed as long as might be—longer—in making this arrest, and
my orders, now that I have made it, are to bring you to London
without delay. One day, we may wait, since tomorrow is the
Sabbath; more, I cannot do without good excuse."

There was a long pause. Ralegh was looking at his kinsman
speculatively. Slowly his eyes brightened with an idea. "No, I see
that you cannot—without good excuse," he said.

Alone with Bess that night he told her abruptly. "I want you to
break the Sabbath and ride on tomorrow."

She looked at him questioningly, her comb in her hand, her hair
falling round her shoulders. "I thought that you wished to stay
here," she said.

"I do. I *am* staying here. Captain King will ride with you. Go
home to Broad Street and wait there till you have word of me."

"But why? Walter, why are you sending me on ahead? I had so
much liefer stay with you."

He set his hands on her shoulders among her hair, gazing down
at her. "I know, but I had liefer that you went on before. Listen,
Bess. I have hit upon a device whereby I can furnish Lewis the
excuse without which he dare not delay four days. But I have a
singular objection to playing the buffoon in your presence."

So next morning, with Captain King for her escort, Bess broke
the Sabbath and rode away.

And on the following morning, Ralegh, who had begun to
vomit in the night, was discovered in a raving delirium, sitting on
the floor of his bed-chamber clad only in his shirt and covered
from head to heel with great purplish blotches.

From his bed, when he had been tenderly put back into it by
Stucley, and the French doctor, he croaked triumphantly. "So—
you have your good excuse for delay, sweet cousin." Then in a fresh

access of sickness, "Oh *God*, I feel like the Day of Judgment! What hell's broth have you given me, Manourie?"

The Frenchman smiled. "A simple decoction of my own, harmless, but effective. There can be no question of your travelling while you continue the draughts and the unguent."

Ralegh lay sick and fevered until Stucley brought him word that James was arrived in Salisbury, from which moment the sickness began to abate and the blotches to fade. By next morning he was clearly mending from his strange disease, and supporting his aching head on one hand, he wrote from his bed of sickness a humble petition to his Most Gracious Majesty, that he might be received in audience and accorded some opportunity to justify himself, before being hurried away to his fate.

After it was signed and sealed, and Sir Lewis had taken charge of it, the time that followed seemed to drag itself along like a wounded thing on its belly. When his cousin had been gone a while, Ralegh got up, swaying on his feet in a swimming world, and donning shirt and breeches, crawled to the window. Here, with the fresh air blowing in his face, he felt less miserably sick and dizzy, and the sight of the people passing in the street was vaguely comforting. And he was still there when, seemingly an interminable time later, his kinsman at last returned.

He swung round at the other's entrance, the world swinging with him, and stood looking across the room with a moment's almost painful hope. But at sight of Stucley's face, the hope died.

Stucley came forward into the room, and tossed the appeal that had meant so much on to the bed. "He will neither see you nor receive your justification. I did what I could, but it was not enough."

Ralegh took up the unopened packet, and tore it across and across, letting the pieces drift to the floor. "Strange and passing strange, the power that we poor mortals have, to blind ourselves to truths we have no wish to see. I do not think I understood until now, the utter hopelessness of my position. Bess understood it, but I would not heed her. Poor Bess, she must be used to that by now." He dropped the last fragment of paper. "Well, I have used a deal of Manourie's vile unguent to no purpose, that is all. We can resume our journey tomorrow. My thanks, that you tried to help me, Lewis."

Late that night, safe from interruption, with Ralegh in his

chamber and one of Stucley's servants on watch before the door, Stucley and the French doctor faced each other across the table in the inn parlour.

"I think, my dear Manourie, that we have turned this unlooked-for visit of the King's to not unsatisfactory account," Stucley was saying, and his face in the candlelight was no longer either pleasant or ineffectual.

The other shrugged. "It seems to me a small matter about which to take so great pains."

"No matter can be too small, when it comes to propping a weak case. The King's case is damnably weak—so weak that we cannot let slip the least opportunity of causing my dear kinsman to discredit himself, however slightly. If he could be persuaded to attempt escape, and then taken in the act, that would be an undoubted point to us in the game."

Manourie set down the glass he had been holding, and leaned forward across the table, gesturing with plump hands. "Ah bah! Why does your King trouble with this—this child's play? He has promised Ralegh's head to Spain as part of the Prince's Marriage portion; ver' well; why does he not send for Monsieur the headsman and make an end?"

"Because he daren't, you fool. There's a wind rising against Gondomar of late, and Spaniards are already unsafe in the streets of London. There's always the risk of a revolt, and Ralegh's death for a Spanish holiday might well touch it off. No no, the King must have some show of justice to please the fools in the gutter."

"Justice, yes; and so you and I enter upon the scene, that we may perhap—at a price—from Ralegh get some damaging admission that shall help this show of justice. But how shall it serve any purpose, this that we have arranged with such care?"

Stucley's face was malicious. "It is hard to make a hero of a man who runs about in his shirt and sprouts purple blotches by the aid of a fair-ground ointment; hard to care greatly what becomes of him. Laughter is a powerful weapon, my friend."

.   .   .   .

Ralegh had expected, on reaching London, to be committed to the Tower, but instead he was allowed to return to the little house in Broad Street. He was not even troubled with Master Partridge or another of his kind.

The story of the affair at Salisbury, ably spread by Dr. Manourie who had left them at Staines, was in London as soon as he was, if not sooner. Stucley appeared almost inarticulate with indignation, and reproached himself bitterly for having brought the Frenchman into their party. But Ralegh was completely unabashed at the publishing of his ruse. He had never blushed for himself in all his life, and saw no reason to begin now, when so little of his life was left to run. Had not King David feigned madness and dribbled in his beard to save himself from his enemies? And should he be ashamed to follow in the footsteps of King David? And somehow the laughter that was to have been such a powerful weapon against him, lessening him in the eyes of all men, never materialised. Sir Lewis had under-estimated his kinsman, for there was about Ralegh a power of personality that could invest even purple blotches with his own distinction.

Day followed day, and still Ralegh was left in the little house in Broad Street. Truth to tell, James did not quite know what to do with him; did not quite know what Philip of Spain wanted doing with him, and was writing muddled letters to his brother monarch to find out. Meanwhile, if left to his own devices, the old Queen's Captain might incriminate himself in some way.

And then, very late one night, Ralegh received a visit from Le Clerk, the French Resident.

Bess would have gone to her bed and left the two men alone, but Ralegh had bidden her remain and bear them company, and so throughout the interview she sat beside the fire—for the summer night had turned chilly—her gaze moving constantly between the two at the table, resting always on the last speaker. They were a dramatic contrast; the tall grey Englishman, ill and haggard, yet with something of the old fire burning in him still; and across the table from him the darkly dapper French Resident, with his mobile, expressive Gallic face and quick-gesturing hands.

"When we approached you before you left Plymouth, you would not accept our offer," Le Clerk was saying. "But now, since this most sorry affair at Salisbury, it has seemed to us that you may well have changed your mind; and behold, I come, Mon Ami, to make the offer again. His Majesty King Louis is anxious—so very anxious—concerning this projected English-Spanish alliance, and it would give him so great pleasure to offer sanctuary to the Scourge of Spain." He made a little complimentary bow to Ralegh.

"I will not take service under a foreign flag," Ralegh said.

The expressive hands were deprecating. "But no! There is no need; all that can be settled later, in leisure—and in safety. For the present it is only that we offer sanctuary until—how you say it?—until the storm is blown out. Listen Mon Ami, the anti-Spanish faction here at Whitehall are as eager to aid you away as the same faction at the Louvre to receive you. You have but to say the word —one so little word, and I will engage to bear you safely to a channel port and across the Narrow Seas."

There was a long pause, in which Bess could hear the whisper of the flames and the soft, heavy breathing of Hodge, asleep before the fire, and the sudden sharp spatter of rain against the window. Ralegh was sitting with his head in his hands.

"When your agents approached me in Plymouth, I believed against all reason that there might still be for me a slim hope of justice at the hands of my own King," he said at last. "Also I was strung to a fine heroic pitch. That is all over now, the one with the other; and I am past caring overmuch for the niceties of my honour. I accept the sanctuary you offer." He dropped his hands and sat up, his eyes suddenly very blue in his grey face. "But I have my own means of escape, and I will come to it under my own sail."

Presently, when Le Clerk had departed as quietly as he came, into the silent City, Ralegh returned to the parlour, and found Bess waiting for him before the dying fire. "What's amiss, Sweet?" he asked.

"Walter, this other means of escape that you spoke of—I am afraid of it."

"Why Bess, it was you and King yourselves who beat up that old boatswain of his, and arranged him to stand ready to ferry me across the Narrow Seas; and you have been urging me to make use of him ever since. You do not mistrust Hart, surely?"

"No no, not Hart. I—wish that you had not spoken of it to Sir Lewis."

"Lewis? But if I am to go forward with this plan, as now seems to be the case, I shall need Lewis's help; someone who can come and go freely and unsuspect, about our own arrangements, as you and King cannot do."

"I know, but.   "

"But what?"

"I am not sure. His eyes are narrow-pupilled, like a goat's."

He laughed. "Is that all? Bess, you will be mistrusting your own shadow next."

"It is maybe only that I am tired—and afraid—afraid of everything and everyone." She shivered a little. "I wish to God that you were relying instead on Monsieur Le Clerk for your escape. Lewis has been so long your enemy."

"No, never quite that. There has been bad blood between us in the past, but no friend could have stood by me more truly, in this tangle."

"Despite Dr. Manourie?"

"Despite Dr. Manourie. Lewis was gulled by that gentleman, and so was I."

So Bess tried to believe that she was merely overwrought, and Sir Lewis Stucley, having borrowed from Ralegh the needful money to oil the wheels of the escape mechanism, continued to be a friend indeed.

The evening came; and in the parlour of the house in Broad Street, Ralegh stood ready to go. Carew, newly home from Oxford, was waiting in the hall with Captain King. Carew seemed much older, these days; he had taken his brother's death, as he had taken all else, very quietly; but at thirteen, he was suddenly no longer a boy.

Ralegh was clasping his black cloak. Outside the windows, the heat-drained August day still hung colourless behind the dark masses of the ilex tree, but in the parlour the shadows were gathering thick and fast; and to Bess it seemed that the tall, cloaked figure was merging into them, sinking away from her, further—further. . . . She cried out in sudden panic, reaching out as though to catch and hold him back. Her terrified hands were caught in his hard, vital ones. "Bess," Ralegh said; and then, "Sweetheart, there is no call for that! It is but for a little while."

"Yes, only for a little while," she said breathlessly. "The Queen will intercede for you with the King. I will go to her as soon as I know that you are safely away. And if that fails, then I am to join you in France, and bring Carew with me. Monsieur Le Clerk will arrange it." It had all been settled in advance, to the last detail. She was repeating it now as one repeating a charm in a dark place.

Ralegh held her close; but even now, there seemed no substance in him, and his mouth on hers was remote, as though some vital part of him was already elsewhere. They had put off their leave-taking until now there was no time for leave-taking at all. "God keep you, dear Bess," Ralegh said, "until we meet again. No, do not you come down with me. Wait here."

He released her abruptly. And then he was gone, shutting the door behind him, and she heard his retreating footsteps on the stair; heard his voice below, and Carew's; another leave-taking, quickly over. Then the house door shut.

The rattle of the falling latch sounded unnaturally loud in the silent house; sounded with an appalling finality. And to Bess, it brought suddenly the hideous presagement of something else falling, flashing down with death in its sweep. Once before, on her wedding night, she had glimpsed that horror, but then it had been far off, down a long corridor of future years; now the years were in the past, and the horror was almost here, leaping on her out of a bleak autumn morning with all the clocks of London striking eight, and the headsman's axe crashing down in Old Palace Yard.

CHAPTER 23

TRAITOR'S GATE

With the sound of the falling latch in his ears, Ralegh walked forward into the twilight. Captain King, feeling instinctively that the man wished to be alone, dropped back a little, walking into exile with his old Admiral, but leaving his solitude inviolate. So, threading their way through the maze of mean streets and alleyways, they went, one behind the other, wrapped in the anonymity of their dark cloaks, of the deepening dusk and the teeming city.

The streets and alleyways grew more squalid as they went, the houses jostled each other more closely, the lanterns before doorways grew fewer and fewer, and presently the smells of the river began to creep chill into the reek of running kennels and crowded humanity. Soon the river smells began to overpower those of the land, and they were in a strange hinterland where bowsprits peered in at

windows and masts mingled with crazy chimneys, and ships seemed
to have run aground and houses to have launched themselves, and
everywhere was the dark glint of water.

And so they came at last to the agreed rendezvous, not far from
the Tower. There was a faint and ragged mist down here, hanging
low over the water and veiling with mystery the lower stories of
the pile-propped waterside buildings. A wherry rocked gently at
the foot of the short flight of weed-slippery river stairs, and a figure
loomed out of the shadows as Ralegh and King appeared.

"Thank God you are come," said Stucley.

"Why so vehement?" Ralegh asked quickly. "Is there anything
amiss?"

"No no, what should be amiss? But I have been imagining all
manner of horrors and mischances, waiting here for you." The
other sounded nervy, a little fretful.

Ralegh turned to the stairs. "You should not have arrived before
your time, my coz; indeed there is no need that you come at all.
You have already done all, and more than all, that I had a right to
expect from you."

"I'll see you safely to Gravesend," Stucley said, less fretfully. "I
like not to leave a task half accomplished. Mind how you go. The
steps are slippery."

"Thank you, Lewis," Ralegh said with asperity. "A wreck I may
be, but I can still negotiate a few river steps and come aboard a boat
unaided." He cast one glance up at the sky, which was beginning
to glimmer with the rising moon. "We shall have a fine night; a
fine white night for leaving by the back door, my friends." Then
he went steadily down the river steps, one hand against the slimy
wall of the jetty.

The coxswain of the wherry rose to meet him, and he set his
hand on the man's wrist, and stepped aboard. "God den to you,
Hart."

"Sir," said Hart, and as Ralegh made his way aft, turned to
Captain King as he also came aboard. "Everything shipshape and
Bristol fashion, Sir; the lugger is moored off Gravesend, and we
shall be aboard her before dawn."

Sir Lewis Stucley followed the other two; the passengers settled
themselves aft, and at a word from Hart, the painter was slipped,
and the rowers thrust off.

The wherry edged out into the stream, the dark gap widening between her side and the jetty, and at another order, the rowers brought her round, her bows downstream, and settled down to a long steady pull. They were making what time they could now, for the tide would be turning in not much over an hour, and after that they would be pulling against it all the way to Gravesend. It would have been better if they could have taken the tide at the turn, and had it with them the whole way, but that would have meant broad daylight at one or other end of the journey, and they quite understood that their passenger, leaving as they had been told for foreign parts after a quarrel with the Spanish Ambassador, might find it inconvenient to do so except in the dark.

In the stern of the wherry, between his kinsman and his old Captain, Ralegh sat, unmoving and aloof, wrapped in his own peculiar solitude as in the folds of his cloak. The other two glanced at him from time to time, but he seemed unaware of their existence, his whole attention given to the river itself. London River, flowing to the sea; and who should say when, if ever, he should come up London River again on a making tide? The faint mist was growing luminous under the rising moon, and out of the glimmering gauzy swathes of it swam the tall ships at anchor in the Pool; here a poop lantern, there the dark thrust of a bowsprit looming overhead as the wherry slid by. In one vessel, a dog barked, aboard another, a fiddler was playing, and the tune followed them a long way across the water: "Time to go—time to go."

They were clear of much of the shipping now, clear of the mist, too; and the rising moon cast a living fish-scale of light into every ripple of London River, as it flowed—more slowly now, for the tide was near its turning—to the sea.

Once or twice, as the shipping of the upper reaches fell astern, Stucley glanced behind him, unwillingly, almost furtively, as though expecting to see something. Presently he looked back yet again, and a faint escape of breath and a tensing of his figure caught at Ralegh's attention, so that for the first time he also turned and looked back. A long way astern, but clearly visible on the moonlit water, another boat was travelling down river.

Well, there was nothing unusual about that. Ralegh watched the boat intently for a few moments, then turned face-forward again without a word. But Captain King, who had also seen the following boat, spoke under his breath to Hart, and the rowers quickened their stroke. The wherry thrust forward at an increased rate, but already it was slack water, and soon the tide would be against them. And Captain King, looking back again after a while, said uneasily: "They are overhauling us steadily. I do not like this, Sir Walter."

Stucley glanced over his shoulder. "Yon boat? Why, man, the Thames is not our private waterway."

"None the less," Ralegh spoke for the first time. "I should be the easier in my mind if it were clear of other users in our wake."

"Hey day! This is not like you!" his kinsman told him, laughing a little, but with an edge to his laughter. "We shall get but a short way in this venture if you turn faint-heart already!"

Ralegh turned on him with a flash of disdain. "I do not think that I am one who can be accused of that, Lewis. I am running for my life; is it then so wonderful that I mislike unknown runners on my heels?"

"Nay now, I did not think to call your courage in question. I meant merely that there is no need for any of us to feel alarm. This boat comes in our wake surely by the merest chance that has nothing to do with us. It is maybe some soul bound for a jovial night at Greenwich, or a sea captain going to join his ship in Limehurst Reach—a thousand different people bound on a thousand different errands. Think now, how should the Spanish faction have winded our trail?"

There was something in his low, hurried whispering, in the piling up of unnecessary detail, which failed to carry conviction, and Ralegh turned and looked at him very straightly in the moonlight. "Aye, Cousin Lewis, I am wondering that," he said slowly. "There is but one way, that I can think of."

A long, tingling pause followed his words; and then Stucley said in a tone almost of horror, "Walter, no! You cannot mean that! Good God! We were boys together!" He reached out as though on a sudden impulse, and laid his arm across the other's shoulders in a rough, oddly boyish gesture, and kissed him.

Ralegh did not return the kiss, but after a moment's further pause, he said: "Forgive me, Lewis. A hunted man is apt to snap at shadows."

"That boat is overhauling us hand over fist," King put in urgently. "She's a fast rowing barge. If her business is with us, we have not a chance, with the tide turning."

Again Hart spoke to the rowers, and again the men quickened their stroke; but at the state of the tide, the wherry was no match for the barge behind. After a short while Stucley said hurriedly: "If by some appalling mischance this should be the hunt on our trail, our best chance will be for you to claim that you are already under my arrest, in that way we may well persuade them to leave us alone. Do you hand over to me quickly all that you have in your pockets; that will lend colour to the claim." He hesitated. "Unless——"

"Unless?"

"Unless you still mistrust me."

"That is ungenerous," Ralegh said, "when I have already asked forgiveness that I mistrusted you at all." He began to turn out his pockets. He had still a boy's attitude to pockets; among loose money and lengths of cord and scraps of paper, he produced his tobacco box and silver bowled pipe, a small and very ugly idol of gold and copper, a naval officer's whistle, a jaccynth seal; another seal with, fastened to it, the piece of rose-quartz that he had brought home from Guiana because it was kin to his quartz mask—that tiny, terrible quartz mask which had gone home to its own country, and now lay with Little Watt in his grave under the ruins of San Thome; charts of the Orinoco delta; a map of Guiana. Strange personal luggage for a man to carry with him into exile, but typical of this particular man. He handed the things over silently, the Guiana map last of all. The moon on the yellowing paper showed the fine network of lines that meant rivers and mountain ranges, showed even some of the names printed so carefully by Lawrence Kemys, five and twenty years ago. "Manoa, that the Spaniards call El Dorado," he read. It was the landscape of a dream.

He handed it to Stucley, who stowed it with the rest, in his pockets.

Past the lights of Deptford and the shipping of the Royal Dock-yard they went, with still the unknown barge behind them. They were coming down to Greenwich now, and the following barge was closing steadily in their wake; very near now, and somehow there had ceased to be any doubt on board the wherry as to its business. It was Ralegh himself who ordered Hart to bring her in to the Greenwich shore; Ralegh with his actor's instinct for the right gesture at the right moment, disdaining to be run down like a panting hare by a greyhound, terrified and without dignity. He had his one last card to play, but he would play it decently, and if he lost, lose in decent and seemly fashion.

"We might still have a chance, Sir," Captain King protested.

"You judged otherwise, a while back, when the distance between us and them was half as great again as it is now. We have as much chance of winning across to France in a sieve as we have of shaking off a fast rowing barge in this wherry, with the tide against us," Ralegh said; and then to Hart: "Bring her alongside the lower Palace Steps."

They were threading their way among the shipping that lay below the clustering towers of Greenwich Palace, slipping in and out of the moonlight, through water that was now sheeted silver, now black as obsidian in the shadow of stern castle or jutting prow.

Looking back again, Captain King uttered a harsh exclamation. "They have turned in after us!"

"Aye," Ralegh said, not troubling to look round.

Stucley sat completely silent.

The wherry bumped lightly against the water steps. Ralegh rose in the stern, and setting a hand on Hart's upheld wrist, stepped ashore. The stair gleamed sugar-white in the moonlight, between dark masses of shrubs; and mingled with the cold river smells, the faint summer night warmth of honeysuckle breathed upon the air, speaking of quiet hedgerows and sleeping gardens, the very essence of peace and happy things. Ralegh mounted the stair with King and Stucley beside him, and turned at the top to look down.

The wherry had drawn to one side, the men resting on their oars, awaiting further orders; and the barge was almost at the steps, the plash of the oars swelling clear and urgent in the stillness. They could see her darkly etched against the moon-silvered water, until she slid into the shadow of the bank. She came alongside with a flourish, her rowers backing water with the precision of a trained crew, and several figures sprang ashore.

Ralegh watched them mount the few shallow steps, standing serenely and in perfect command of the situation, to receive them at the top. The leader's face was clear in the moonlight, under the narrow curled brim of a fashionable tall hat. "Ah, Sir William St. John," Ralegh greeted him levelly. "Your business is with me, I imagine?"

Sir William bowed, sweeping off his hat. "I deeply regret that it is so, Sir Walter."

Ralegh regarded him with a faint, bitter twist to his mouth. "Of course. How much was it that I paid you two years ago, for your help in obtaining my freedom? No matter, it cannot have lasted a man of taste and fashion very long—yet I doubt if the King pays very much better."

"Sir Walter, I am but doing my duty——"

Ralegh cut him short. "Sir William, your duty is not needed at this time; I have already submitted to the arrest of my kinsman, Sir Lewis Stucley, who stands beside me."

St. John turned his head quickly. "Is that true, Sir Lewis?"

Stucley made a small, uneasy movement with his shoulders. "Why no—not as yet," he said after a moment. "It is a matter easily remedied, however." He turned to the man beside him, raising his voice. "Sir Walter Ralegh, I arrest you in the King's name."

For the space of a dozen heart-beats the scene seemed frozen into brittle stillness. Ralegh had swung round on his kinsman with a look before which the other gave back a hasty step; King, with a furious exclamation, had whipped a hand to his sword hilt, only to find his arms caught and twisted behind him by two of the men who had come up with St. John; other men were closing in on the group. Yet the illusion of complete and frozen stillness persisted. Ralegh splintered it with a harsh outgoing breath. "Yes, we were boys together, were we not, my coz? I used to think you were a fool, but it seems I did you an injustice. You're no fool, Lewis, and you're a superb actor; you should be at the Globe. I was the fool, to trust you in this or any other matter; but as for Captain King ——" his eyes went to the seaman's face and remained there for a moment, meeting his startled look with an unmistakable command. "As for Captain King——" his compelling gaze whipped to Stucley, "As for Captain King—— No, I think no man could brand me fool for trusting one of my own Captains. How much did his loyalty cost you, Lewis?"

The faintest shrug of his cousin's shoulders told him that Stucley was prepared to let the lie pass. What, after all, was Captain King to him?

But Captain King himself was of a different mind. "Thank you.

Sir Walter." He almost choked on the words. "But I am by way
of being particular as to the service I take. I have been your man
for twenty years and more, and I'd as lief not change to serve Sir
Lewis and his kind now," and drawing his guards with him, he
moved a deliberate step away from Stucley, as from the vicinity of
a bad smell.

Ralegh looked at him with a suspicion of a smile. "So be it,
then. I've done my best to save your stubborn neck for you,
William, but I confess I shall be glad of your continued company."

"Sir Walter," Stucley thrust in hurriedly. "There has been
enough delay. I regret—I must needs trouble you for your sword."

Ralegh slipped it free and offered it to him without a word, laid
ceremoniously across his forearm. The other took it with a less
perfect ceremony, and handed it to one of the waiting men.

"Yours also, Captain King." William King, his arms being
released, also yielded up his sword.

"And now that these formalities have been safely accomplished,"
Ralegh said, "do we return to the Tower tonight?"

"A lodgment for the night has been made ready for you here at
Greenwich," St. John told him.

"So? Gentlemen, I am a trifle confused; in whose custody?"

"In mine. Sir Lewis, I believe, returns immediately in the barge
in which we came. That is so, Sir Lewis?"

Stucley nodded, already edging towards the steps. His father,
who had been a great rogue, would have carried off the situation
with a flourish; but Lewis, being only a small one, could not; he
was abashed and ill at ease in the accusing presence of the man he
had betrayed, and would clearly be only too thankful to be on his
way back to London.

"Before you go," Ralegh said, "is it too great a thing to ask, that
you return to me my pipe and tobacco box?"

Stucley felt with a kind of unwilling haste in his pockets, and
produced the required articles. "The rest of your gear will doubtless
be returned to you in due course."

"Oh, doubtless." Ralegh took them from him, and as he did so,
the moonlight caught the Queen's ring on his hand, striking a
spark of bluish fire from the single diamond.

Stucley saw it, and for a moment greed and shame were oddly

mingled in his face. "I was forgetting," he said, the hurried uneasiness growing in his manner. "That ring: I regret that I must for the present relieve you of it also."

"Queen Elizabeth gave me this ring," Ralegh said, his voice suddenly harsh. "By what right do you relieve me of it?"

Stucley gathered up a rather tattered effrontery, but could not prevent a slight stutter. "By—by the King's orders. It is not fitting that a traitor to his most gracious Majesty should wear the gift of the Queen who named him her successor. Should you be acquitted, it will be returned to you with all else."

"Acquitted? Acquitted of what, in God's name?" Ralegh demanded, and then, as the other remained silent, he drew off the Queen's ring that he had treasured through so many years, and dropped it into the hand held out to receive it.

Even Sir William St. John wore a faint look of distaste, as Stucley pocketed it with the rest.

"God den to you. A most pleasant journey back to London, now that your work is done." Ralegh seemed to be holding his kinsman's eyes with his own, so that the other, trying to turn away, checked and could not break clear. "Doubtless you have deserved well of the King," he said levelly; and the men watching remembered afterwards, how quiet, almost gentle, his face looked in the moonlight. "But, Sir Lewis, these actions will not turn out to your credit."

Stucley turned, muttering something, and went down the steps to the waiting barge. As he did so, a rough voice called out to him from the wherry, where Hart and the boatmen who had seen his kiss bestowed on Ralegh, had been witnesses to the whole scene played out at the head of the river stair close above them. "Goodnight to you, *Sir Judas Stucley*."

It was the name that was to cling to him through the remainder of his life.

Very early next morning Ralegh went back to the Tower that he had left two years before; back up river, to be stranded at last on the steps of Traitor's Gate.

It was not much past high water, and the lower steps were awash as he stepped from the boat, and stood an instant looking up the worn flight—worn by the feet of so many, men and women, innocent and guilty, who had never walked down them again, nor out through the Byward Tower, save to their graves. The great mass of St. Thomas's Tower was dark above him, the gate-arch black as ancient sin. The gates were opening now, and he glimpsed the blue undress uniform of the Yeoman warders inside. Then as King and St. John landed beside him, he turned for a last look at the morning. It was a grey morning, but with a gleam of silver-gilt in it that seemed to promise sunshine later. A string of swans had come down river from Westminster as they sometimes did, to glide brotherly among the tall ships that lay at anchor off the Tower Wharf. Swans and shipping and wheeling gulls, and the swift grey river.

He turned again to the stair, to find himself face to face with the new Lieutenant of the Tower, who had come down in person to meet him; that same Sir Allen Apsley, who had been with him at Cadiz and Fayal; the young Gentleman Adventurer who had apologetically ordered away the jolly boat for Lady Ralegh on the day that Ralegh forgot her.

He greeted his old comrade-in-arms with quick warmth. "Why, Apsley, this is good in you, to come down to welcome me yourself."

His hand was caught and wrung, but it was a moment before Sir Allen Apsley could answer him. "I would to God, Sir Walter, that I might welcome you by another gate and in other circumstances."

"Why, the circumstances might be happier, I admit, but as to the gate——" He glanced up at the grim entrance. " 'A loyal heart may enter under Traitor's Bridge' saith the proverb, and has before now, and will again, I doubt not. The Queen—*my* Queen—came this way once; and I should not be ashamed to follow in her footsteps." He put out a hand to draw forward his Captain. "Here is another for our reunion; William King. I think the last time we three met together was at Cadiz. That was a great day, eh, Apsley?"

"A great day," said Sir Allen, as he wrung his second prisoner's hand. "A great day, and we shall not see——" he broke off abruptly, but the end of the sentence was clear to all of them. "We shall not see its like again." That was what he had nearly said, but it was not wise to say such things in public.

He stood back, with a gesture of invitation to them to enter. And so, with the Lieutenant of the Tower beside him, and Captain King close behind him, with Sir William St. John, whose presence no one had so far troubled to notice, bringing up the rear, Ralegh mounted the steps and passed under the dark archway into Water Lane; and heard the clang and rattle of Traitor's Gate closing behind him.

At about the same time, Bess was standing in the parlour of the house in Broad Street, gazing in fixed horror at a stout merchant with law officers at his back, who was informing her that her husband had been taken in the act of escaping, that he was back in the Tower by now, and that henceforth she was a prisoner in her own house, in his, Master Wollaston's, custody.

She took the news quietly; too quietly for Master Wollaston, who would have preferred tears, faints, anything but this white stillness which had the odd effect of making him uncomfortably aware that though he was one of the richest men in the City, he was not quite a gentleman.

But poor Bess had no idea that she was giving offence. She neither wept nor fainted because she had no desire to do either. "I think I knew," she was saying. "I think I knew."

CHAPTER 24

THE TIDE RUNNING TO THE SEA

King James was having an acutely embarrassing time. His dear brother of Spain had by now indicated that while he held James to his promise, and Don Gualto Raule must assuredly die, he had no desire to see to the matter himself, but was content to leave the unpopular task to his dear brother of England. Harassed by the constant bullying of Count Gondomar, and perfectly aware that he was powerless to execute Ralegh without some sort of pretext, the sorely tried man bade, or rather begged, his lawyers to fashion a case for him; a case of some sort, that would at least look all right on the surface.

The Commissioners whom he appointed duly set to work to concoct the required case out of Ralegh's Guiana expedition. They had no easy task, and though they left no stone unturned—setting spies on Ralegh to report his every word, opening his letters to his wife, and tampering constantly with the *Destiny*'s crew in an effort to persuade them by bribes and threats, to give damning evidence against him—they were forced at last to report to the King that there was no possibility of putting Ralegh on trial on any charge arising out of the Guiana expedition. The only thing they could suggest was that since, under the Winchester sentence of fifteen years before, Ralegh was already legally a dead man, his Majesty should simply withdraw his merciful reprieve, and allow the sentence to be carried out. And Lord Chancellor Bacon handed up to the harassed Sovereign proposals for Ralegh's public examination before a tribunal of judges and Privy Councillors, as a means by which his crimes might be made known to the country, and James justified in the withdrawal of his mercy.

But James, remembering Winchester, was unsure of the power of even a packed Court to produce the effect he needed, at a public hearing, and therefore decided to have the examination held behind closed doors, with any results that seemed helpful made public afterwards.

Meanwhile, as late summer turned to autumn, and the last roses withered in the gardens of Ely Palace, Bess was still a prisoner in her own house, all her frantic appeals for leave to see her husband refused. She was allowed no friend near her, not even Nicholas, who had come up from Beddington leaving the harvest to fend for itself, and remained in London ever since; certainly not Captain King, who had been released from the Tower against his will, as a creature of too little importance to be worth troubling about. She was allowed no part in the efforts that George Carew and the rest of Ralegh's friends were still making to save him. They were loyal friends—even when best hated by the world at large, Ralegh had always had the knack of making loyal friends—and now they were striving heart and soul to stir the King's pity or strengthen his mind; but they knew, all of them, that they fought for a lost cause. The Queen, now lying mortally ill at Hampton Court, was writing letter after letter to her husband, pleading for Ralegh's life because Henry had loved him, even humbling herself at last to write to Buckingham. "If I have any power or credit with you, I pray you let me have a trial of it at this time, in dealing sincerely and earnestly with the King, that Sir Walter Ralegh's life may not be called in question."

And Ralegh himself, in his room in the Tower, watching the

last leaves that he was to see on the trees of this world turn gold and russet in the Lieutenant's garden, and go whirling down the autumn wind, heard of all these doings for and against him remotely, as the rumour of the sea in a shell: and was grateful for the love of his friends without wasting the faintest hope on the result of their efforts. Cut off even from Bess, surrounded by spies, and suffering constantly recurring bouts of old fever, he prepared himself, as he had done fifteen years ago, to make such an exit as would linger in men's minds long after the last of those who witnessed it had followed him.

On October 22nd, he was brought before the Commissioners for his examination in the Council Chamber of the Lieutenant's Lodging. The long panelled room seemed over-full of lawyers—a breed he had never liked; he saw their shuttered faces and smooth hands against the darkness of their gowns, and liked them no better. To his tired mind, they seemed of very little import—of far deeper significance that through the window of the Council Chamber he could see the grey river and the wheeling gulls.

The light tones of Francis Bacon's voice recalled him to the matter in hand, and finding that the Lord Chancellor had opened the proceedings, he withdrew his gaze from the river to give them the courtesy of his attention.

The proceedings which followed had little likeness to any examination that could be so called, seeming to consist simply of a string of charges, all the old charges, over and over again, while he himself was denied any sort of hearing. That of course was only natural. The Commissioners were not interested in his guilt or innocence; they were there simply to find him guilty for the King's convenience. Wearily, he withdrew the greater part of his attention from them again.

The tide was running out, swiftly and more swiftly, hurrying to the sea. Beyond the masts of the shipping at the Wharf he could see a tall merchantman lying warped out into mid-stream. Soon she would drop down river and away. His tired mind followed gull-wise in her wake, down to the seas that he would not sail again.

The tide of Ralegh's life was running out very fast now, very near to the sea. Six days after his examination he was roused out of his bed early in the morning, to go before the Justices of the King's Bench to hear his sentence. He was blue and shivering with the old fever as his guards hurried him in the foggy dawn, back through the ways by which he had come, to the Traitor's Gate.

Fog clung low over the water, hiding familiar landmarks as the barge pulled up river, so that even London Bridge, as they lay waiting for the fall of water to lessen between the piers, was veiled in the drifting dun-coloured murk, the tall houses upon it lost in vapour as Ralegh looked up at them. They shot the bridge at last, swinging dangerously through the dark turmoil of water between the piers, and came in the same drifting murk, to Westminster.

The fog was everywhere; even in the hollow vastness of Westminster Hall, when Ralegh was brought into it, faintly dulling the outline of the great West window, and smearing the flames of the candles that had been lit for lack of daylight. Even, it seemed, in the throat of Sir Henry Yelverton the Attorney General, when he rose to speak, so that he must clear it loudly.

"My Lords"—Yelverton looked round him at his brothers of the King's Bench assembled in full panoply of Scarlet and Miniver. He had a fine voice, but the fog had certainly got into it; he cleared his throat and began again. "My Lords, Sir Walter Ralegh, the prisoner at the bar, was, fifteen years since, convicted of High Treason committed against the person of His Majesty and the State of the Kingdom, and then received the judgment of death, to be hanged, drawn and quartered. His Majesty of his abundant grace, hath been pleased to show mercy upon him until now, that Justice calls upon him for execution." The fine voice swelled and deepened. "He hath been a star, at which the world hath gazed; but stars may fall; nay, they must fall, when they trouble the sphere wherein they abide. It is therefore His Majesty's pleasure now to call for execution of the former judgment, and I now require order for the same."

The Attorney General gathered his scarlet robes about him, bowed to the Lord Chief Justice, and sat down.

In his place, the Clerk of the Crown rose to read the indictment, the old indictment; and as he listened, Ralegh seemed to hear again the frantic beating of a peacock butterfly against a sunlit window in the Great Hall of Winchester Castle. The record of the old conviction and judgment followed, and then the old question in a slightly changed form. "Sir Walter Ralegh, hold up your hand. Have you anything to say why execution be not awarded against you?"

Ralegh raised his hand, bringing himself back by a conscious effort from Winchester to Westminster, gathering himself for one last fight. He was warmly conscious of Sir Allen Apsley standing close beside him, not as the Lieutenant of the Tower, who had brought here his prisoner, but as a friend, powerless to help him in any way, but still a friend. From the smooth faces and scarlet robes, he singled out those of the Lord Chief Justice, Sir Henry Mountague.

"My Lord, all that I can say is this; that the judgment I received to die so long since—I hope it cannot now be strained to take away my life; for that since it was His Majesty's pleasure to grant me a commission to proceed on a voyage beyond the seas, wherein I had power, as Marshal, over the life and death of others, so, under favour, I believe I am discharged of that judgment."

The Lord Chief Justice set down the nosegay of herbs and autumn gillyflowers with which he had been playing, and leaned forward. "Sir Walter, this of which you now speak, touching your voyage, is not to the purpose. Neither can your commission in any way help you; by that you are not pardoned, for by words of a special nature, in case of treason, you must be pardoned, and not by implication. There was no word tending to pardon in your commission, and therefore you must say something else to the purpose; otherwise we must proceed to give execution."

Ralegh made a quiet gesture of acceptance. "If your opinion be so, My Lord, I am satisfied, and so put myself on the mercy of the King."

There was a moment's pause, full of the hollow murmuration of activity from other parts of the Great Hall; and then again the voice of the Lord Chief Justice. "Sir Walter, you had honourable trial and were justly committed. Ever since judgment was pronounced against you, you were a dead man in the eyes of the law, but the King had mercy on you. Now, your new offences have stirred up His Majesty's justice. I know that you have been valiant and wise, and doubt not that you retain both these virtues; and now you shall have occasion to use them. I would give you counsel, but I know you can apply unto yourself far better than I can give you." The Lord Chief Justice picked up his nosegay, sniffed it, and laid it softly and deliberately down again, evidently deciding on a little counsel after all. "Fear not death too much, nor fear not death too little; not too much, lest you fail in your hopes; not too little, lest you die presumptuously. So I make an end, with my prayer to God that he may have mercy on your soul." He looked round him at the red robed figures of his brethren; at the Attorney General, not again at Ralegh. "Execution is granted."

There was little more to come. Ralegh was told the hour and place of his execution, and handed over to the custody of the waiting Sheriffs of Middlesex, whom he kept waiting a short time longer, while he took his leave of Sir Allen Apsley.

"Goodbye, Apsley; God keep you, and reward you for your gentle usage of me in these past weeks. Remember me kindly, since I shall not see you again."

"May God keep you, Sir," the other returned, wringing his hand. He would have said more, but the words would not come; and as Ralegh turned to leave the Court between his guards, the Lieutenant of the Tower was unashamedly weeping.

Outside in Palace Yard, the fog wreathed about the ancient buttresses; a chill, clean fog, smelling of the river, and as he crossed it with his guard, Ralegh all but collided with Sir Hugh Beason, an old acquaintance, who checked at sight of him with a startled exclamation. "Ralegh! Why man, it was to hear news of you that I came this way. What verdict?"

"Was the verdict ever in question?" Ralegh asked gently.

The other's round pink face puckered distressfully. "Sorry," he said. "Very sorry, you know—not much of a one for words —— " He thrust out a hand as pink as his face, and Ralegh gripped it.

"Thank you, Beason. Come you tomorrow, and see me on my journey."

"I wish there was more that I could do. At what time and place?"

"Here in Palace Yard, eight o'clock; but you had best come early to be sure of a good place." Ralegh had already begun to move on, but he looked back with a sudden quirk of laughter. "I myself am in the happy position of being sure of one."

He went on with the Sheriffs of Middlesex, to the cell in the old gatehouse, where he was to spend his last night.

It was drawing on to evening before the news was brought to Bess, by Master Campion, who had succeeded Master Wollaston as her gaoler some weeks previously. She had been walking all day, to and fro, to and fro, distractedly, in the parlour of the little house in Broad Street, while Carew, who had been allowed to join her at last, stood by the window, sometimes watching her, sometimes staring blindly out into the fog.

But she was still enough now, listening to what Master Campion had to say, and staring at his eyebrows. How little and shrivelled he was, compared with Master Wollaston, and how grotesquely over-large for him were those eyebrows. So large that if they grew any larger they would surely take charge of him altogether—and if that happened——

She pulled herself up sharply, aware that she was wavering on the brink of hysteria.

Master Campion was telling her that Walter was to die in the morning; at eight o'clock in the morning.

"I must go to him," she said dully. "I must go at once. Master Campion, I am to be allowed to go to him?"

Master Campion had not been a gentle gaoler, but he answered her with unexpected kindness. "My orders are that you are no longer under house arrest, Lady Ralegh, and that you are to be free to visit Sir Walter for a short while, later." He held out to her a folded note that she had not before noticed in his hand. She took and opened it. It was a dog-eared scrap of paper which Ralegh must have had in his pocket, and on it, he had written a few hasty lines.

"I am to be allowed your dear companionship but for an hour, Bess, therefore do you come to me in the hour before midnight, for I would fain see your face as near as maybe to the last that I see in this world. Bring with you my good clothes, for I would not go forth tomorrow in a threadbare doublet unworthy of the occasion. My love I send you not, for you have it, dearest Bess, now and always."

No, he would not go forth tomorrow in a doublet unworthy of the occasion. That was the Queen's Captain to the finger tips.

When Master Campion had gone downstairs again, Carew spoke for the first time. "When they sentenced father, all those years ago, it was for plotting with Spain, wasn't it, mother?"

"Yes," she said. "Yes, Carew."

"And now they are going to carry out the sentence—the same sentence—because of the things they say that he has done *against* Spain." The boy's newly broken voice jumped uncontrollably, and settled into a husky monotone. He swung back to the window, beating a clenched fist lightly against the glass with every choking word. "One day, when I am a grown man, I will make people know that; I'll make the whole world know—what those bloody murderers did to father; how King James murdered father, to pick favour with the King of Spain!"

CHAPTER 25

THE NIGHT AND THE MORNING

In his prison chamber in the old gatehouse of St. Peter's Monastery, Ralegh held better court that evening than James could do in Whitehall Palace, as, all through the hours a steady stream of friends came to bid him God speed. He greeted them with obvious gladness, making of their last gathering a joyous occasion, so much so that some of his visitors found themselves disapproving, even while they fell under his influence. Courage they understood, but this gay courage of Ralegh's was almost unseemly in a man who was to die with the morning. Had he no thought for what lay beyond tomorrow's quittance? Did he, perhaps, believe that beyond it lay nothing at all? Old rumours of his atheism, of which even the Lord Chief Justice had acquitted him returned to them, and refused to be got rid of.

Presently the Dean of Westminster, attending on him as his spiritual adviser, found himself occupying the one stool, with the man whose last hours he had come to solace sitting on the edge of the narrow plank bed and gazing down at him with obvious serenity and even a glint of amusement, which was not what he had expected. The Dean spent some little while in trying to persuade Ralegh to confess to the crimes for which he was to die, that his mind might be the more at ease. But Ralegh's mind was already at ease; more so, perhaps, than the Dean of Westminster's. "No, Dr. Townson, I will make no false confession. I am innocent of all the charges against me."

"Then God help you," said Dr. Townson, "as doubtless in His infinite mercy, He will. You take it very calmly, for an innocent man, Sir Walter."

"If I were a guilty man, maybe I should take it the less calmly," Ralegh said.

"Sir Walter, we can none of us be too sure of our worthiness to meet our Maker. Beware lest, being innocent of this, you fall into the sin of spiritual pride."

Ralegh looked him over, Dr. Robert Townson, Dean of Westminster, Chaplain to the King; noting the faint sleekness and the air of self-appreciation; and his eyes, for all their tolerance, made the cleric suddenly a little smaller in his own estimation than was usual with him. "Oh no, friend. I believe there is no need that you warn me against that particular sin," Ralegh said. "Surely you, a Christian priest—if you believe as you teach—should of all men find least cause to think it strange if a man face death with quietness. It is not spiritual pride, but faith in the Grace of God and in His mercy, at which I light my candle tonight.   . As for tomorrow—I have maybe seen more of death and in uglier forms than you, Dr. Townson. I had sooner die so, than of a raging fever."

He sat for a while, still looking down at the other man, then with a courteous gesture, got to his feet. "I beg your forgiveness; I think you come to pray with me."

So, kneeling side by side, they prayed together, while the little moaning wind which had been rising since dusk wuthered desolately between the window bars, and set the flame of the candle jumping so that the shadows leapt upon the stone walls; and from outside came the sinister sound of hammering from the Palace Yard. And presently, promising to return at dawn, the Dean of Westminster went his way, carrying with him an uneasy sense that he had been praying with a man who felt little need of his prayers, and who had himself been praying to a God who was not quite the Dean's.

Thomas Hariot was the next comer, and Ralegh greeted him joyously, and settled him on the stool. "This is a most famous forgathering!—So—now the School of Night is in being again— though a small meeting, to be sure."

"Ah, the School of Night," said the astronomer. "A long, long time since first we forgathered under that name, and we were young men in a happier world than this. I was newly back from making you your survey of Virginia, I remember. Those were hopeful days, and we had great hopes of Virginia."

"Aye, we had great hopes of Virginia," Ralegh said, trimming the candle. "Great hopes of Guiana too. Well, they have planted Jamestown. The seed of a new England in the New World, though 'twas none of my sowing."

Thomas Hariot put out a blunt hand, and laid it for an instant on the other's. "The seed was before Jamestown," he said gently. "Other men have sown it, but the seed was before the sowing."

"Thanks, Hariot." Ralegh closed his fingers for an instant over his friend's hand, and then releasing it, rose and turned to the high, barred window. "The wind has blown the fog clear away, and we have stars—Universe beyond unfolding universe of stars. . . . Those questions that we used to ponder, seeking the key to the jest of life itself in a cloud of tobacco smoke: before this time tomorrow I shall be as wise as John Dee—wiser than he was in those days, for I may know the answer to them all."

A little later the bolts rattled back, and again the door opened. Ralegh looked hastily towards it, but it was only Captain King. They greeted each other casually as they had greeted each other on a thousand other occasions, and Ralegh said unemotionally, "King, you are of all men the one I need most just now. Lady Ralegh will be here soon, and you must take her home again—afterwards. I would not that she went home from this place with no company but a strange servant's."

"I would to God that there was more than that I could do for you, Sir Walter," King said huskily.

"Poor William King; you did your best to die with me, did you not?" Ralegh said. "Man, you are of more use to me living, for you are a friend to Lady Ralegh, and she will have need of every friend she has, in the days to come."

Hariot, who had risen at the other man's coming in, began to gather himself together, saying that he must go. Ralegh saw him to the door, and when the much-tried gaoler had opened in answer to the signal knock from within, patted him on the shoulder, bidding him be sure to drink a hot posset before he went to bed, lest he take cold in the wind, and sent him on his way. Then he returned to Captain King at the window. "And now, I think, a pipe, for there is more tobacco in my box than I shall be like to smoke before dawn. Come now, smoke one in fellowship with me, William."

A few minutes later the door opened yet again, and Bess stood in the small deep-set entrance.

Hesitating there for an instant, her gaze went across the narrow space to find Ralegh smoking serenely by the high barred window, and beside him, Captain King, staring at nothing and puffing with grim determination at a pipe which had gone out. As she entered, Ralegh laid down his pipe on the high window ledge, and next instant Captain King had turned, wrung his old Admiral's hand as though he meant to wring it off the wrist, and was gone past her without a word.

The door swung to behind him, and she moved forward, and set down on the table the bundle that she had been carrying. "I have brought your good clothes, Walter."

Ralegh made no move towards her, but his gaze, which had met hers like a physical touch on the threshold, never wavered from her face, as she turned from the table and went to him. And next instant she was in his arms, caught up and bruised against him, with a fierce and agonised strength.

A few moments they clung together, wordlessly, and then abruptly his clasp slackened. He was still holding her, but with a careful lightness that had in it already something of renunciation. Before she could say a word, he began to talk quietly, of her future and the boy's. He had been making plans, he said, and she was to do this, and she was to do that; she was to keep Carew his full time at Oxford if that might be. As far as he could work it out, she would have just such and such an amount a year to live on. Nicholas had all the details and would see to everything for her.

Holding to him with the same careful, undemanding lightness, Bess listened obediently. Yes, she would do this, and she would do that.   And all the while there were so many more important things to be said, and no words to say them, and the time slipping by.

"Bess, do you remember the scent of the lime trees at Sherborne, when we would go walking under them on summer evenings?"

"I remember—I remember all too well."

Nobody but Ralegh could have thought her beautiful now. Her face was haggard and stricken, grey-white to the very lips, with eyes that seemed to strain in their sockets with a wild and aching brilliance. She looked old, older than Ralegh. But Ralegh, with his restless vitality, the strength of life within him, could no more be made old by an ageing body than shabby by a threadbare doublet, and something of that quality of the young in heart had conditioned her love for him, to her own cost, so that now, to the hopeless sorrow of the woman losing her life's companion, was added the wild grief of the girl whose love is torn from her.

Yet almost distraught as she was, she held to her self-control, determined not to mar with tears and ugly clingings this last little silver hour that must go down to death with him tomorrow, and be with her through the empty years ahead.

For a while they remained, holding to each other with that careful lightness; speaking sometimes, of happy things—Sherborne—and Little Watt. . . .

And then the sound of hammering, which had fallen silent in the last few minutes broke out again. A dreadful sound that seemed to fall on Bess's heart, making her start and flinch. "Walter, that hammering—what are they making, down there?"

He put back her hood with a quiet hand. "Look up, My Heart, not down there. See, the wind has blown the fog away, and between the clouds the sky is full of stars; the first clear skies for a sennight, and an infinity of stars. . . . Look, here stalks Orion from behind that sailing cloud, with his sword-chape ringing on the pinnacles of Westminster. God sends us a jewelled night for our Valedictory."

"They are building the scaffold," Bess said. "That is the hammering, is it not, Walter?"

"Yes." His arm tightened round her convulsively. "Would God tomorrow's axe might fall on me alone. I have lived beyond my peers, and tomorrow will return to me their company; but you may have twenty—thirty years to be alone."

"They would matter the less, if I could be sure of finding you again when they are accomplished." Bess's voice was hoarse and toneless with grief held in check.

"Sweetheart, from the outermost curves of Infinity, God led your spirit and mine to find each other. I will not believe He would have taken so great pains, if we were to meet only once between the dark and the dark."

"Oh, it is not God's mercy that I question. . . . Always you have outdistanced me, following your dream, and I have run behind, calling to you, calling and calling. How can I be sure that you will turn back for me at the last?"

"How, save by faith, may we be sure of anything that is beyond sight or touch? Yet in all my wanderings, something of myself *has* turned back to you; in all my wanderings you have been—you are —with me in my innermost sanctuary, far deeper than the need to think of you, in the same quiet place from which those dreams are sprung."

He was holding her close, compelling her belief. The first note of the Abbey clock striking midnight thrummed out into the windy darkness. "A new day, Sweetheart," Ralegh said.

"Not yet—I need not go just yet——?"

"Very soon. Any moment now, Bess."

The clock went on striking, the slow remorseless notes pulsing behind her rush of words. "Then listen—listen, Walter: in the morning I shall be in the little room that looks this way—my linen room. Think of me there, when the time comes—close to you, so close——"

The clock had finished striking.

They had time for little more, before footsteps sounded outside, and with a loud rattle, the door was unlocked. "Time's up, Sir," said the gaoler. "Five minutes extra, the lady's had, for I let her up before her time."

"Thank you," Ralegh said. "Captain King waits to take you home, Bess. Now kiss me, Sweetheart, and go."

But at this last moment, Bess's hard held-control broke under the strain upon it, and she clung to him after all, frantically, sobbing and shuddering. "Not yet—Not just yet! Only five minutes more! Walter, I can't, I can't——"

"It is but for a while."

But the prospect of some distant coming together again in a thin and alien Heaven could give poor Bess no comfort now. This world was all she had, and his living presence with her that made it sweet. "Walter, I *can't*—not yet—just a little longer! Walter, don't let them take me away—I love you—I love you so——"

His hands were on her wrists, gently but inexorably breaking her hold. "Beloved, it is no easy thing to part from you; don't make it harder. .   King, for God's sake take her!"

His hoarse voice, and the sight of his drawn face steadied her;

and with an effort that seemed to wrench at her whole being, she caught back her self-control. She ceased her broken entreaties. She allowed him to lift her hands away; stood for an instant looking into his face as though to be sure she had it by heart, and then, speaking his name once, turned and dragged herself to the door.

She had no recollection of getting home, until she was actually in the narrow candlelit hall, and Joan, with face all bloated with weeping, had come to take her cloak; and somebody was bending over her hand, saying that he was going to his lodging now; that she knew where to find him at any hour of the day or night; that he was her servant and her friend in all things.

She looked at him wildly for a moment, then saw that he was William King. "Captain King, what do you do here?"

"I have brought you home, My Lady," he said gently. "Sir Walter bade me."

She gave him both her hands then. "I beg you forgive me. My wits are all broken. I shall see you again?"

"Whensoever you need me, Lady Ralegh."

"Walter has many enemies, but very faithful friends," Bess said. "Goodnight, Captain King."

He went into the night, and as she turned from the closing door, she saw someone else waiting at the stair-foot. Carew.

"You should be in bed, Carew," she said dully.

The boy seemed not to hear, but came towards her, a little uncertainly, his eyes on her face. "There is—no news, then, Mother?"

She knew what he meant. "No, there is no news."

"There may be yet—There is still time."

"It would need all the time from now until the Judgment Day, to move the King's mercy towards your father."

She found that she was in the parlour, sitting by the hearth. The fire burned brightly, but it was cold, so cold. She held her frozen hands to the blaze, but the flames had no warmth in them. She was dimly aware of Joan hovering round her; of Carew watching her —waiting for something. His eyes were fixed on hers, wide and expectant. What was it that he waited for, she wondered.

"Mother, did—did Father speak of me at all—or send me any message?"

The question caught her like a physical blow, and looking into the boy's stricken face she was stabbed by self-accusation. They had spoken of him, yes, of his schooling and his future; but only to keep other things at bay; they had not spoken of him as they had of Watt. They had shut him out, forgotten his existence. She realised now, for the first time, that Carew had not asked to go with her, that he might see his father for the last time, and even had he been older, it would not have occurred to her to take him. It had not occurred to Ralegh to ask for him or send him any word of good-bye. "He talked of your future," she said; but how cold that sounded. And then the words she needed came to her, out of a letter written fifteen years ago. She had it still, upstairs in her almost empty jewel casket, with Watt's battered Testament with a tiny scarlet feather pressed between the pages. They had been for her and Watt, those words; she gave Watt's part in them to Carew now, as the only reparation she could make him. "He sent you his blessing; he said to me, 'The true God hold you both in His arms'."

Carew knelt beside her, without a word, beginning to chafe her cold hands between his. Then still holding them, he dropped his head on her knees and burst into a storm of tears. He was only thirteen after all.

. . . . .

Alone in his prison after Bess had gone, Ralegh trimmed one of the candles, which had begun to gutter, undid Bess's bundle, and spread out on the pallet the garments she had brought him, that the creases might have time to smooth out before morning, relit his pipe, and sat down with his Bible open on the table before him. He regretted for a passing moment those maps and charts that had gone with Lewis Stucley; and yet he had small need of them, for he knew their every line as he knew the back of his own hand; knew them as he knew Hayes Barton woods when he was a boy.

He sat for a long while puffing at his pipe, and staring at the opposite wall, or rather through it, seeing perhaps those maps of Guiana; perhaps Guiana itself, all the wide green promise of Guiana. Seeing perhaps Hayes Barton woods with the sea wind swinging through the branches, and the world shining as a small boy's world can shine.

A long road he had come since those days, and now he stood at the end of it, in the gateway of the unknown. With his passing through that gateway, in the morning, there would be none left of Elizabeth's Round Table. He was the last of them, the lonely one.

Grenville and Frobisher, Drake and Hawkins, all gone, by fever or Spanish shot; Essex and Robin Cecil; Philip Sidney long ago. His mind lingered over them and many more, men who had been his friends and his enemies, a few whom he had loved. Watt, too, and Lawrence Kemys. He had not relented towards Lawrence Kemys's memory in all these months, had not spoken of him save with bitterness; but there was no bitterness in his thoughts of his old Captain now. Well, in a few hours time he would have rejoined their company.

He did not lie down on the pallet, as the long hours wore away. He had no wish for sleep, and many things to think about; his speech from the scaffold to polish into perfection; his peace to make with his own unorthodox God.

Some time in that night, his winged muse returned to him. The pen and ink-horn which he had demanded for writing his note to Bess were still on the table, and for paper, he had the fly-leaf of his Bible.

And on the blank page he wrote almost word for word, the lines which he had set down in a mood of furious pessimism, when first the Earl of Essex had threatened to oust him from the Queen's favour.

> Even such is time which takes in trust
> Our youth, our joys, and all we have,
> And pays us but with age and dust.
> Who in the dark and silent grave
> When we have wandered all our ways
> Shuts up the story of our days.

Then, dipping his pen again into the ink-horn, he added two more lines in a different mood; lines which rang like a trumpet call.

> And from which earth and grave and dust,
> My God shall raise me up, I trust.

When the Abbey clock struck five, he proceeded to dress himself for his last appearance. Black taffeta breeches and grey silk stocks, a doublet of fawn-coloured satin, and over all, a gown of wrought black velvet. The effect was perhaps a little sombre for his taste, but they were his best clothes, and suitable for the occasion, and he donned them with infinite care, making as fastidious a toilet as ever he had made in his life; he, the Queen's Captain. Smoothed his hair and pointed his beard—he would have liked to have had his beard trimmed—and fingered for an instant his one ornament, the pearl drop that still hung in his left ear. The lack of a mirror troubled him, but he contrived as best he could without one, to make sure that he had achieved perfection.

All his life, Ralegh had had his full and more than full share of the vivid self-awareness, the conscious and cultivated grace of living that had belonged to the men of his own day more than to the men of any other. He had lived life with an air, making of the raw fabric of it something rich and shining beyond the common run. Now he prepared to make a final exit that would be worthy of the play that had gone before.

At dawn, Dr. Townson, still a little shaken out of his comfortable self-satisfaction and somewhat chilly without it, returned to compose his mind for him, but found the prisoner far more composed than he was himself. Ralegh still refused to admit any guilt. He took Communion, and when the Dean had gone, ate a hearty breakfast, and finding that there was time to spare, filled and lit his silver-bowled pipe for the last time.

Time to go, and his pipe smoked out, he put on his hat—a cap edged with bone lace under it, for an added protection against the morning chill and the fever that ached in his bones—and said to the Sheriffs of London, who stood by, "Now Gentlemen, shall we go?"

At the gatehouse entrance a man stepped forward to offer him a cup of sack. He took it with a word of thanks, and stood a few moments on the threshold, to drink it down, glancing about him at the morning as he did so. The wind was still blowing up from the river, with an edge to it that cut like a knife; the morning was bleak and cheerless under a lemon-grey sky, nothing left now of last night's stars. The narrow alleyway before the gatehouse was empty save for the men gathered about him in the arched entrance, and the garbage fretting to and fro before the autumn wind; but from the direction of Palace Yard came the murmuration of a gathering crowd. A faint quirk of satisfaction twitched Ralegh's lips as he heard it. It was Lord Mayor's Day; chosen for his execution, he was well aware, that the rival attraction of a pageant might prevent a crowd gathering to witness his departure. But it seemed that the plan had miscarried. He drained the cup in his hand, and returned it to the official.

"The sack was to your liking, Sir Walter?"

Ralegh smiled. "I will answer you as did the fellow who drank of St. Giles's bowl as he went to Tybourne; 'It is a good drink, if a man might but tarry by it'."

The plan to prevent a crowd gathering had certainly failed. Palace Yard was a seething mass of people, gentle and simple, on horseback and on foot; faces at every window, boys clinging to every ledge. A murmurous and sympathetic crowd who pressed in on Ralegh and his guards from all sides as they edged through towards the scaffold that rose like an obscene island in the midst of a sea of heads. A noble, a merchant, a ballad seller, a pickpocket, a bawdy-basket from the bankside stews, a soldier with tears trickling down his nose; a young woman with a black-eyed infant in her arms. In the forefront of the crowd, an old man with a head as bald as an egg caught Ralegh's attention, and he checked an instant to ask what he did, coming out on such a raw morning.

The other looked at him with blue seaman's eyes in a face as weathered and deeply wrinkled as his head was smooth and shining. "I come to pray for you, Sir Walter."

"That is kind of you," Ralegh said. With a flicker of grim humour he caught off his hat and the lace cap under it, and tossed the cap to the old man. "You have more need of this now, my friend, than I," and clapping on his hat again, he continued on his way.

As he limped composedly up the steps to the scaffold, the Dean was beside him again; the Sheriffs who had escorted him from the gatehouse, the Earl of Arundel and two more of the Council; a tall figure in black velvet who stood aloof from the rest, leaning on a long-handled axe.

Arundel and his fellows gathered round him, pointedly, to shake his hand before the eyes of the world, and Ralegh turned from one to another, with a brief word of greeting and farewell. Only to Arundel himself he had a little more to say. "For God's sake use your influence with the King, that he blacken not my name when I am no longer here to speak in my own defence."

"I will do all that lies in my power," Arundel promised, as they shook hands.

Ralegh cast a quick, all-embracing glance about him. "I thank God in his infinite goodness, that he has brought me into the light to die, and not suffered me to die in the dark of the Tower," he said, as though to himself, or to someone not visible to those around him. His gaze passed out over the still-swelling crowd, as though it would pierce through the tall buildings that hemmed him in, through the grey distances of the morning, and find Bess at her linen room window.

Beside him, an officer was making the proclamation for silence; and Ralegh's gaze dropped to the sea of upturned faces. What chance, after all, had a Lord Mayor's pageant, which happened every year, compared with the taking-off of the last of Elizabeth's champions, which could happen only once? But that was hardly just; doubtless the rabble below him had been drawn here partly by the lust for sensation that always drew huge crowds to the execution of a well-known figure, but he knew that they had also come to wish him God speed on his journey; and he looked down on them kindly. They were a cross-section of England, and he was glad that he was not to be hustled out, as at one time he had feared he might be, without the chance to defend himself in their eyes.

But the autumn chill that made the old wound ache intolerably seemed to have eaten into his fever-ridden bones; and he was shivering as he stood above them, and unsure of the strength of his voice. With a sudden fear that they might misconstrue these things and believe him to be afraid, he began: "Good people, I crave your indulgence if that my voice seem weak and some of you find it not easy to hear. This is the third day of my fever."

And that matter having been taken care of, he launched into the speech that had occupied him during the night. One by one, he defended himself from the charges made against him. New charge and ancient calumny, even to the oldest of them all, whose shadow had clung to him for seventeen years. "It is said that at the death of the Earl of Essex, I stood in a window over against him when he suffered, and puffed out tobacco in disdain of him. God I take to witness that I shed tears for him when he died! And as I hope to look God in the face hereafter, the Earl of Essex did not see my face when he suffered, for I was afar off in the armoury where I saw him but he saw not me. I confess indeed I was of a contrary faction, but I knew My Lord of Essex was a noble gentleman, and that it would be the worse with me when he was gone; for I got the hate of those that wished me well before, and those that set me against him afterwards set themselves against me, and were my greatest enemies. And my soul has many times been grieved that I was not nearer to him when he died; for it was told me afterward that he asked for me at his death, to have been reconciled unto me."

There was little more that he wished to say. Looking down at the hushed multitude, he took off his hat. "And now I entreat you all to join with me in prayer to the Great God of Heaven; for I have many sins for which to crave his pardon. I have been a seafaring man, a soldier and a Courtier, and in the temptations of the least of these there is enough to overthrow a good mind and a good man. Pray therefore with me, that He will forgive me, and that He will receive me into everlasting life. So I take my leave of you all, making my peace with God."

The crowd stirred as though a wind blew through their ranks, and a hoarse murmuring rose from them.

Now the scaffold was clearing. A few moments more, and there were left upon it only three dark figures; those of the Dean, the headsman and the Queen's Captain. The Queen's Captain standing in the eye of his world for the last time.

He slipped off his gown and gave it, with his hat, to an attendant on the scaffold steps, then turned to the terrible black figure beside him and asked to examine the axe. The executioner hesitated, clearly distressed, then gave it into his hands. Ralegh turned it over, looking at it, ran an experimental finger along the blade, and nodded in satisfaction. "This is a sharp and fair medicine to cure all my ills." He handed it back. "When I stretch out my hands, dispatch me."

For answer, the headsman, still holding the axe, dropped on his knees. "Forgive me, Sir. Forgive me for what I do."

Ralegh looked down at him an instant, then patted the bowed black shoulder very kindly. "Man, I forgive you freely."

He turned once more to the crowd, as the headsman, stumbling to his feet, spread his own cloak before the block for him to kneel on. "Now, friends, give me your hearty prayers, for I have a long journey to go."

The Abbey clock was striking eight as he knelt down on the kindly spread cloak, and all the clocks of London taking up the chime one from another. Bess heard it, standing at her window

with her drained face towards Westminster, and felt Carew start
and shiver in the protecting curve of her arm. But it was only the
clocks striking, nothing more, nothing more as yet. "When he goes,
I shall know it."

The Dean, who had been murmuring to Ralegh from time to
time, was bending over him, bidding him lie with his face turned
toward the East.

"What matter which way the head lie, so that the heart be
right?" Ralegh said. Then, quietly putting aside the headsman's
offer of a kerchief for his eyes, "Blindfold? Nay, man, think you I
fear the shadow of the axe when I fear not the axe itself?"

He laid his head on the block, settled himself as comfortably as
might be, and so remained for a few moments, praying, then
stretched out his hands in the pre-arranged signal. But the headsman, thoroughly unnerved, hesitated to obey. There was a long
moment of tortured silence, and then Ralegh spoke once more,
with a flash of his old imperiousness. "What dost thou fear? Strike
man, strike!"

The axe crashed down, once, twice. Ralegh's body jerked at the
first blow, not at the second.

The last of Elizabeth's Round Table had made his triumphal exit,
and Bess, at her window on the other side of London, felt him go;
and knew that he was away on his long journey.

High on the scaffold in Palace Yard, the executioner was holding
aloft Sir Walter Ralegh's severed head, showing it, according to
custom, to the motionless crowd; and a voice, topping the ragged
and furious tumult that arose as they looked upon it, cried out:
"We have not such another head to be cut off!"

On the other side of London, the wind through the dark branches
of the ilex tree made a soft sea-hushing, and the whitethroat from
the churchyard of Allhallows-by-the-Wall, who should have flown
south by now, sat singing his thin and shining under-song in its
topmost spray; and a prentice lad came whistling Greensleeves up
the alley beside the little house in Broad Street, and Bess was back
in the lime avenue at Sherborne on any of a hundred summer
evenings, with Ralegh coming whistling to join her across the grass.
She was beside the river at Richmond, and the Queen's Captain
with her. "Why have I never seen you before? . . . I have danced
with all the Queen's Ladies." She was sitting in the ditch at the foot

of Lady Sidney's garden, beside a young soldier newly back from Flanders, listening spellbound as he declared unto her a Far Country; and there was a Jenny-whitethroat singing in the damson tree, hidden by the white tide of blossom, so that it was as though the tree itself were singing.